Praise for *Rules for Thieves*

"The world building is magnificent and intricate, and it would be a shame if there isn't a sequel, even if Ott does wrap up the key plot points; Alli and this inviting setting both deserve another outing." —*BCCB*

"Alexandra Ott's funny, thrilling debut, *Rules for Thieves*, will have readers flipping pages from the very first scene." —*Shelf Awareness*

"This compelling debut fantasy novel with complex themes, lots of action, and a good cast of characters will appeal to fantasy readers across the spectrum." —*School Library Journal*

"Alli's southern European–inflected fantasy world is built carefully and tightly, complete with class structures, customs, and a patron saint–centered culture. The ending isn't squeaky clean but provides a sense of closure as Alli makes a meaningful discovery about her heritage. A smooth debut." —*Kirkus Reviews*

Also by Alexandra Ott

Rules for Thieves

The Shadow THIEVES

· A Rules for Thieves Novel ·

By Alexandra Ott

ALADDIN

New York London Toronto Sydney New Delhi

This book is a work of fiction. Any references to historical events, real people, or real places are used fictitiously. Other names, characters, places, and events are products of the author's imagination, and any resemblance to actual events or places or persons, living or dead, is entirely coincidental.

ALADDIN
An imprint of Simon & Schuster Children's Publishing Division
1230 Avenue of the Americas, New York, New York 10020
First Aladdin hardcover edition June 2018

For information about special discounts for bulk purchases, please contact Simon & Schuster Special Sales at 1-866-506-1949 or business@simonandschuster.com.
The Simon & Schuster Speakers Bureau can bring authors to your live event.
For more information or to book an event contact the Simon & Schuster Speakers Bureau at 1-866-248-3049 or visit our website at www.simonspeakers.com.
Jacket designed by Jessica Handelman
Interior designed by Greg Stadnyk
The text of this book was set in Bembo Std.
Manufactured in the United States of America 0518 FFG
2 4 6 8 10 9 7 5 3 1
Library of Congress Cataloging-in-Publication Data
Names: Ott, Alexandra, author.
Title: The shadow thieves / by Alexandra Ott.
Description: First Aladdin hardcover edition. | New York : Aladdin, 2018. |
Series: Rules for thieves ; 2 | Summary: "Alli must risk everything to save her new family from a rogue organization that is threatening the Thieves Guild's existence—and the lives of all its members"—Provided by publisher.
Identifiers: LCCN 2017040906 | ISBN 9781481472777 (hardcover) |
ISBN 9781481472791 (eBook)
Subjects: | CYAC: Orphans—Fiction. | Brothers and sisters—Fiction. | Loyalty—Fiction. | Stealing—Fiction. | Magic—Fiction. | Fantasy. | BISAC: JUVENILE FICTION / Action & Adventure / General. | JUVENILE FICTION / Social Issues / New Experience. |
JUVENILE FICTION / Girls & Women.
Classification: LCC PZ7.1.O88 Sh 2018 | DDC [Fic]—dc23
LC record available at https://lccn.loc.gov/2017040906

For my family

The Shadow Thieves

Prologue

They left the note on his pillow this time.

Beck drew a dagger with his right hand and held a candle aloft with his left. His room looked empty, but it was clear someone had been here. The coin pouch he'd left on the table was missing, and a nearby candle stub was tipped over. And, of course, there was the note, a threatening square of crisply folded brown parchment like a stain upon his pillowcase.

Beck crossed the room swiftly, knife in hand, and checked the bathroom. Empty. He peered behind the bathroom door and inside the tub, just in case, but whoever had been here was gone.

Pocketing his knife, he returned to the main room and lifted the note from his pillow with the tips of his fingers, as if it might burn him. He held up the candle, illuminating the parchment. The note was written with a thick, spidery hand:

We're waiting.

There was nothing else, except for a single black smudge in the lower corner. It could have been anything—an inkblot, an accidental smear. But they'd left an identical mark on the first note, and Beck knew what it meant.

It was a shadow.

The first note, which had been shoved underneath his bedroom door a few days ago, had been more ominous:

Tell no one.

But it was this second note that Beck found most threatening. Not shoved hastily under a door this time. They'd gotten in.

It should've been impossible. Enchantments protected every door in the Guild, preventing members from breaking into one another's rooms. In a society of thieves, doors had to be guarded.

Had a magician broken the protection spell on his door? Unlikely. The magicians were among the king's most loyal supporters, mostly because of how well he paid them. These traitors probably didn't have a magician in their ranks, and while their funding seemed to be growing, it wouldn't be enough to bribe one into breaking such a strong spell.

But then how was it possible?

Beck strode over to his dresser and rummaged through the top drawer. He withdrew the first note from its hiding place beneath a tangled pile of old socks. Laying both notes out side by side on the nearby table, he knelt and examined them. The handwriting on both was clearly the same. And the longer he stared at them, the more certain he was that he knew who had written them.

Even in a guildhall full of the world's most talented thieves, there was only one person Beck knew who could find his way into any room, past any lock.

It was the only possibility that made sense, yet it was the one he least wanted to believe.

If it really was him . . . well, there was no other alternative. Beck had to confront him.

Leaving the candle atop the dresser, he picked up the notes, stuffed them into a safe interior pocket of his coat, and strode out the door.

He walked as fast as he dared down the hall, his footsteps echoing off the gray stone floor. Luckily, he didn't have far to go—the new bedroom he'd been assigned after passing his trial was conveniently close to that of his best friend.

Beck knocked on Koby Mead's door.

"Mead? It's me," he called when there was no response.

Beck knocked again. No answer.

He turned and paced down the corridor, hardly knowing where he was going. He couldn't let this go on any longer, couldn't sit back and pretend that these thieves, these *shadows*, weren't a threat.

Beck wanted to protect Mead, if he truly was involved, but that was a stupid instinct. Mead, like any true thief, wouldn't go out of his way to protect anyone other than himself.

Beck needed to protect himself, and he needed to warn the king. Enough was enough. He had to act.

He pivoted and strolled in the other direction, ducking through narrow stone passageways until he emerged into the hall that housed the steward's office. It was still early in the evening, so Durban would likely still be at his desk—

Up ahead, a figure emerged from the shadows, blocking the hall.

Beck slowed to a stop.

"Hey, Reigler," the thief said.

"Keene," Beck replied flatly.

"Didn't expect to see you here at this hour," Keene said. His tone was casual, but his posture was not. He crossed his arms and took a step forward, positioning himself squarely in the middle of the hall. There was no getting past him.

"Thought I'd grab an early dinner tonight," Beck said, willing his voice to stay steady. He nodded toward the end of the passageway, where the final door opened into the dining hall.

"You might want to rethink that," Keene said, lowering his voice. "I hear they're serving up something *special* later tonight."

Just like the notes, Keene's words were vague, yet the threat was unmistakable. Whatever it was the Shadows were planning, it couldn't possibly be good.

And they weren't going to let Beck get in their way.

If Alli were here, she'd do something reckless—lie her way past Keene, or even charge past him, demanding to see the steward, refusing to take no for an answer. For the thousandth time since his trial, Beck wished she were here.

But she wasn't, and Beck didn't have her bravado or her talent for improvising. It was probably best to play it cool, to let this go for now. He'd find a way to see Durban later. Keene couldn't lurk in this hallway forever, after all. And maybe Beck could track down Mead in the meantime, get some more information out of him. . . .

"In that case," Beck said, "I think I'll grab something to eat later."

"Wise choice," Keene said, but he didn't move.

Reluctantly Beck turned to leave.

"Oh, and Reigler?" Keene called after him. "You should think about the choice you have to make. And choose quickly."

His meaning was the same as the note in Beck's pocket:

We're waiting.

Trying not to shudder, Beck hurried away. He didn't look back, but he could feel Keene watching him all the way to the end of the hall.

He made a few more turns at random, putting distance between himself and Keene. As soon as he was sure no one was watching, he doubled back, choosing an alternate route to Durban's office.

No matter how many times Keene threatened him, he had to tell. The king was in danger.

The Shadows had made a mistake in sending Beck these taunting messages and making their threats clear. They had let him know that they were serious, that the danger they posed was real. Instead of giving in to their demands like they thought he would, Beck was going to expose them, before things got worse.

Durban would take this seriously, of course—Durban took everything seriously. The steward would make sure that Beck's warning reached the king. Beck just had to hope that Keene and his shadowy friends had gone to lurk elsewhere.

The hall outside Durban's office was now empty. Beck rapped sharply on the door but got no response. He reached for the handle, to see if it was locked—

A scream pierced the air.

Beck whirled around. Commotion sounded from the direction of the dining hall, where most of the Guild was probably gathering for dinner right now.

Something special, Keene had said.

Beck ran.

He shoved open the door at the end of the passage and found the dining hall in chaos. Thieves were running in all directions, some rushing into the room and some scrambling to leave it. Shouts echoed through the cavernous space, chairs and tables crashed to the floor, steel weapons flashed in the torchlight. Something strange was happening at the far end of the room, but Beck couldn't see it through the crowd.

Someone grabbed Beck's arm from behind, and he reached instinctively for a knife.

"Don't just stand there!" said a very familiar voice.

Beck didn't let go of his knife, but he did let Mead tug him across the hall and through another door, where they entered a dark passageway. Mead finally let go of Beck's arm but continued to lead the way through the halls, checking over his shoulder every few seconds to make sure Beck was following.

"What's happening back there?" Beck asked, nearly tripping in his haste to keep up with Mead's long strides.

"It's Durban," Mead said, not slowing down.

"Durban?"

"Didn't you see? They just hung his body in the dining hall."

Beck froze.

Durban. The king's steward. One of the most powerful people in the entire Guild.

Dead.

No, not just dead.

Murdered.

Beck was too dazed to pay attention to where they were going and was surprised to find himself in front of Mead's bedroom door for the second time that evening. Mead unlocked it and unceremoniously shoved Beck inside.

As Mead made his way through the room, lighting scattered candles, Beck tried to unscramble the dozens of questions in his head.

"Did you know?" he asked finally.

"You'll have to be more specific." Mead's tone was light,

but he wasn't being as flippant as usual. He sounded tired.

"Did you know the Shadows were going to kill Durban?"

If Mead was surprised by the question, he didn't show it. He dropped onto the sofa, his fingers tapping a jittery rhythm against his knees. "Not for sure, no."

"But you suspected."

"I guessed." Mead shrugged. "Knew they'd have to eventually, if they were going to win. Can't get rid of the king without getting rid of his steward. The display, though . . . I have to admit, I didn't know they were so creative."

"They just announced themselves to the entire Guild," Beck said, feeling numb. Here he'd been about to expose the Shadows himself, to tell Durban of their existence, and the Shadows had beaten him to the punch.

"So it would seem," Mead said.

"Why?"

"Why do you think? The Shadow Guild is no longer in the shadows. They're done hiding."

"They've declared war," Beck agreed, though he still couldn't quite believe it. He'd known they were dangerous, but he hadn't expected it to escalate so fast. They were already in the middle of a battle he'd only just become aware of.

"It'll help with their recruitment, I expect," Mead said casually. "Must've been hard to recruit members while also trying to pretend your organization doesn't exist."

Beck narrowed his eyes. "You'd know, wouldn't you?"

Mead sighed. "Look, I don't—"

"You wrote these." Beck drew the two notes from his pocket and waved them at Mead. "This is your handwriting. You're the one who broke into my room."

Mead studied Beck's face, clearly deciding whether or not to lie. "I would hardly call it breaking in. I used a key."

"Olleen?" Beck guessed. She was the only person he'd entrusted with a spare key to his room.

"No. Just borrowed a little spell from Jarvin and duplicated yours when you weren't looking."

"Is that who got you into this? Treya and Jarvin?" Beck had never particularly liked Mead's sister or her husband; he wouldn't have put it past either of them to be Shadows.

"Essentially. They joined a while back and then told Keene to recruit me."

Beck gritted his teeth. "And why did you let him?"

Mead leaned back into the sofa cushions. His pose was casual, but there was a challenge in his expression. "Things are changing. Surely you can see that."

"I did notice that the steward had been murdered, come to think of it."

"It's not that I particularly agree with them," Mead said, maintaining his casual air. "In fact, I think they're ruining the good thing Kerick's got going here. But just because I don't like them doesn't mean I can't face the truth. This is what you have to understand, Reigler: They might win."

"Not if we stop them."

Mead just shook his head sadly, as if he were explaining

something to a toddler. "You have two options. You can pick a side and hope that your side wins, because you'll be dead if they don't. Or you can choose both."

Beck fought to keep his voice level. "When one of those sides is set on killing the other, no, you *cannot* choose both."

"Of course you can. It's not like I'm the Shadows leader or anything. I'm just playing nice, running the occasional errand for them, pretending to be sympathetic to their cause. And I'm doing the same thing for the king."

"Oh really, you're just running errands? Is that what you were doing with *these*?" Beck took a step closer, waving the notes in Mead's face. "You wrote these threats and left them for me, and you call that *playing nice*?"

For the first time, Mead looked a little less calm. "I was trying to help you."

"*Help* me?"

"I didn't want the Shadows to target you for recruitment at all. It's not my fault Keene chose you, or that you refused. I overheard him and another Shadow discussing how they were going to kill you, since you might talk. So I stepped in. I offered to leave the notes. I said that you'd come to your senses once you understood what was at stake. They're getting desperate to recruit people and didn't particularly want to go to the trouble of having to kill you, so they agreed to try it my way. I knew you'd get here eventually."

For a second, Beck struggled to inhale. He'd known, of course, that there was danger in refusing Keene's offer to join the Shadows. He just hadn't realized quite how much danger he'd been in.

"You were wrong," Beck said finally. "I'm not joining the Shadows, no matter how many stupid little notes you leave in my room."

"You don't have a choice anymore. You know too much. Either you join them or they're going to go back to their original plan and kill you, do you understand?"

"I won't do it. And I'm not going to *pretend* to join them either. What you're doing is just as likely to get you killed, if someone finds out you're playing both sides."

"Who's going to find out?"

Beck's hand shook, and he clenched it into a fist, crumpling the notes. "How could you betray Kerick like this?"

"Loyalty is a luxury we can't always afford. It's just how things work. You don't have to like it. You just have to be smart, and survive."

Beck shoved the crumpled notes back into his pocket. "It isn't too late to stop them."

Mead threw his hands into the air in frustration. "Weren't you paying attention tonight? That was the *steward* they strung up! And he's not the only one they're after."

"What do you mean? Kerick?"

"Not just Kerick." Mead paused.

"Just tell me."

Mead reached into his pocket and withdrew a tattered parchment. "This is the list."

Beck took it. A series of names were scrawled in Mead's handwriting, with Kerick's on top. And just below Kerick was—

That couldn't be right.

Beck read it again, then looked at Mead. "Is this—?"

"I think so," Mead said, nodding.

"And the people on this list . . .?"

"Are their targets. Yes." Mead took the parchment back and tucked it carefully into his pocket.

Beck didn't know how or why that name had ended up there, but it didn't matter. He had to warn them.

No, he had to do more than that. He had to stop the Shadows.

"It isn't too late," he repeated, finding that the more he said the words, the more he believed them. "They won't win. Not if I have anything to say about it."

Before Mead could respond, Beck turned on his heel and strode out the door.

He ran down the halls, hardly caring who saw him. The time for caution was long past. It was time to start thinking like Alli. What he needed was courage, and daring, and a healthy dose of recklessness.

There was a chance that the king wasn't in his office, what with the crisis erupting in the dining hall. But Kerick was never hasty in an emergency. He'd send someone else out first, to examine the situation. He probably wouldn't emerge from his office until tomorrow, when the dust had settled and he'd had time to consider his response. Which meant there was a very good chance that Beck could find him.

As Beck dove deeper into the dark halls of the Guild, the magic protecting the king's inner sanctum should have stopped him from entering. Without the steward or one of the magicians to lift the spells, he shouldn't have been able to pass through them. But he kept walking, and nothing happened.

Maybe the spells were able to sense his purpose, his loyalty, and let him through. Maybe they'd been disabled because of the emergency. Maybe their magic had died with the steward. Whatever the reason, there was nothing keeping Beck from his goal.

He reached his destination in record time. Pulling the notes—his single scrap of concrete evidence—from his pocket, he pounded on the king's door.

Chapter One

The sunlight glinting off the silver barbed wire makes my eyes water. I always forget how bright it is outside. Prison is nothing but gray.

"This way," the warden says impatiently. She clutches my release papers in her left hand. I blink to clear my eyes and follow her across the courtyard toward the gate.

My heart flutters in my chest. This is it. I've been waiting one hundred and eighty days, and now I only have to wait for them to open the gate. Freedom is on the other side.

It's taking way too long for the gate to move. Maybe the magician is napping on the job or something. They claim that there's one up in the tower who's enchanted the gate and has to lift the spell before anyone can pass. I have no way of knowing if that's true, but it could be. This place is supposed to be the most secure juvenile facility in all of Ruhia. It turns out that once you've broken out of prison the first time they try to lock you up, they don't take any chances the second time around.

Luckily, I'm the only one being released today, but the wait is still agonizing. The warden shows my papers to the guard, and I stare down at the chalky gravel of the courtyard. I'm going to see real grass in a second. Real grass and real trees and . . . my brother. My real, actual brother.

Finally, in one long, excruciating motion, the gate swings open.

Will he really be there? They told me that he'd agreed to pick me up. Surely he wouldn't back out now. Unless this has all been some kind of horrible joke. A mistake, like everything else.

And even if he is here . . . what will he think of me?

The warden strides through the gate and peers down the drive. "Are you Ronan Rosco?" she asks.

He's here.

My feet shuffle forward on their own, leading me across the threshold of my new life.

I've waited one hundred and eighty days for this, but I'm not ready.

I stop beside the warden, just on the other side of the gate. The long drive up to the prison is lined with browning grass and stark, barren trees. It was early summer when I went in, but now it's Vyra's Month, and winter is already settling in for a long stay. This will be my first Ruhian winter, my first experience with heavy snows and freezing temperatures and weak sunlight. I can't say I'm looking forward to it.

A few feet down the gray gravel drive sits a carriage. A cheap rent-by-the-hour one, painted a shockingly bright orange and pulled by a skinny brown horse. The driver looks half-asleep on the front seat, his elbows resting on his knees.

And walking up the drive toward us is my brother.

Ronan is tall, tall enough that I have to crane my neck to look at him. I remember him being about five years older than me, and I don't think I was too far off the mark—he looks eighteen or nineteen. Like me, he has shaggy dark hair that resists all efforts to comb it. Unlike me, he seems to have made an effort to tame it anyway, having tied the loose bits back at the nape of his neck. He's wearing a real, actual suit, with a tie and everything.

But if he's trying to make a good impression on the warden, she doesn't care. She barely glances at him as she riffles through my papers. Having finally arrived at the correct one, she reads a statement in a flat monotone: "As a representative of the glorious state of Ruhia, I now release this ward—Alli Rosco, age twelve, originally of Azeland—to you, Mr. Ronan A. Rosco, hereby establishing you as her legal guardian until she comes of age. In accordance with the law of the glorious state of Ruhia, her guardian must ensure her attendance at all forthcoming probationary meetings and/or hearings until such a time when her probation ends. Failure to comply will result in penalties for both ward and guardian. Do you understand these terms?"

"Er, yes," Ronan stammers.

"Right then." The warden shuffles a few more papers and holds one out to Ronan. "Sign here."

He signs his name with the pen she offers, and then it's done. Just like that, I'm free to leave.

"Best of luck to you," the warden says briskly as she turns back to the gate, but I'm not sure if she's talking to me or to Ronan.

My brother smiles at me. He has a kind face, with soft eyes, and he looks even kinder when he smiles. "Ready to go, Alli?"

No, I think I'll just hang out at the prison a bit longer. The sarcastic response rises up automatically, but I bite it back. "Yeah," I say instead.

He leads the way back to the carriage, each footstep raising a puff of gravelly dust that clouds his shiny black shoes. His suit isn't anything super fancy, like the nobles wear, but it's still a suit. He really *is* a lawyer's apprentice.

I glance down at my feet. They let me change out of the prison-issue jumpsuit, but the only thing I had to change into is what I was wearing when they booked me: a baggy, moth-eaten sweater, and pants that are too small for me, the cuffs hanging too far above my ankles. These clothes are prison-issue too, something they gave me to wear during my meeting with the judge after I got out of the Healing Springs. Probably donated by some charity, just like the stuff we used to wear at the orphanage. It never would've bothered me much before, but they seem shabby now. Do lawyers' apprentices always wear nice clothes? I'm not sure how much money they make or what kinds of houses they live in.

Why didn't I think about any of this before? I've been so busy worrying about what Ronan would be like, I forgot to worry about the rest of it.

Ronan yanks the carriage door open. The whole thing groans as we climb in, and I wouldn't be surprised if it's held together by only glue and prayer. But still, it was nice of him to bring a carriage at all, instead of just walking.

"Nice" is a word that I'm beginning to associate with my brother, even though this is the first time I've seen him in person since I was three. I mean, there really isn't any other word for a guy who apparently agreed to take in his estranged sister after she managed to get herself thrown into juvenile prison before she turned thirteen. I can only imagine how that conversation went over on his end. *So, hi. I know you haven't seen me in a decade, but I'm your long-lost sister. Hurray! Oh, and also, I'm homeless and in jail on multiple charges. Think I can come live with you when I get out in a few months?*

Yeah, way to make a good first impression.

It's only made worse by the fact that Ronan had, apparently, been leading a very successful life until I came along. The list of facts I know about my brother is short, but it includes a few key details.

Number one: His name is Ronan A. Rosco.

Number two: He's a lawyer's apprentice currently living in Ruhia.

Number three: He must be a good apprentice, because the judge handling my case thought well enough of him to recommend I be released to live with him once my sentence was up.

Number four: He owns a real suit.

From these facts, I can conclude that things have been going well for him. At least until his long-lost sister was dumped in his lap.

The carriage lurches, almost throwing us against the far wall. Ronan winces. "Sorry about the bumpy ride. I had to save a few weeks' allowance for this."

I don't think he means it to be cruel, but I cringe. Only the first of many expenses I'm going to cost him.

He glances out the window, fidgeting with his tie. His fingers are long and ink-stained, his nails neatly trimmed. A ray of sunlight cuts across his cheekbone and nose, throwing half his face into brightness and the other half into shadow. On the surface, he looks a lot like me—messy dark hair and tan skin and brown eyes. But lots of other people have those features too. There is a deeper resemblance between us, but only if you look for it: His face is fuller than mine, but he still has hints of sharper angles in the same places I do—chin, nose, cheekbones. His eyebrows are as shaggy as his hair, giving a more serious tone to his playful, bright eyes. He looks like my brother only in the smallest of ways. Fitting, I guess.

I should probably say something now, but I don't know what. We sit mostly in silence as the carriage clatters its way down Ruhia's streets. Judging by the way Ronan keeps cutting glances at me and then looking away, I don't think he knows what to say either. We've missed so much of each other's lives that we could never run out of things to talk about, but the gulf is too wide. We don't know where to begin.

Plus, I don't exactly have a great track record when it comes to saying the right things. I've sworn to myself that I'll be on my best behavior, that I won't smart off, that I won't lose my temper. But I don't know how to go about doing that, precisely, and right now everything I want to ask seems too perilous.

Well, I guess we can start small. "What's the *A* stand for?" I ask.

"Hmm?"

"In your name. Ronan A. Rosco."

"Oh." He smiles again. "I have no idea. I made it up."

"Really?"

"Really. I don't know my middle name. Don't know if I have one. But I needed something that sounded official."

"For lawyering?"

"Right." He grins wider, the corners of his mouth twitching, and it looks so much like that *other* grin that it makes my heart stutter. The way his lips always used to quirk up at the corners . . .

Get out of my head, Beck.

"So, I probably don't have a middle name either," I say.

His smile fades. "I don't know. I'm sorry."

I shake my head. "Not your fault."

We go back to staring out the windows.

The city of Ruhia looks so much different from the last time I saw it. Before, in the late spring, the trees were full, the flowers blooming, the streets crowded with pedestrians taking advantage of the mild weather. Now it's the start of winter, and the trees are already bare, the grass brown. Fewer people walk the streets, and those who do wear thick coats, scarves, and hats.

Carriages now clog the roads, most pulled by ordinary horses like ours. But I catch glimpses of thilastri guiding the fancier carriages and crane my neck to get a better look. I hardly ever saw thilastri back home in Azeland, but they're much more common here. They tower over the horses in the streets, their golden beaks and bright blue feathers standing out against the landscape of grays and browns.

Our carriage finally stops, and the driver thuds twice on the wall behind my head. We're here.

Ronan climbs out first and helps me down. As he pays the driver, I glance around. The street is cobbled and quiet, neat brick buildings lining it in rows. So different from Azeland, where everything is a haphazard cluster of different sizes and materials and people. There, the building's materials would tell you how wealthy its owners were. Ruhian architecture makes it impossible to figure out what kind of neighborhood this is. While this street certainly doesn't belong to the nobility, I can't determine much else about it.

"This way," Ronan says, leading me down a sidewalk and toward a tall redbrick building. I memorize the number—the only way to distinguish it from its neighbors—as Ronan unlocks the front door and leads me inside. We enter the mostly empty front room of the apartment complex, and then climb three flights of stairs before arriving on Ronan's floor.

The hallway is narrow and dim, but everything seems nice enough. There are only a few apartments per floor, and Ronan leads me to the second door on the right. 4B, according to the bronze plate.

"It's pretty small," he says, sounding apologetic as he unlocks the door. "And I'm no good at decorating."

I almost laugh. Like I care about decorations.

Still, I have to admit he's right. The room we've entered is pretty bare, just a battered sofa, an armchair, and a rug in front of a fireplace. A low, partial wall that runs only half the length of the room divides it from a small kitchen with faded white cabinets and a single paned window. A dark hallway leads to the right. Lots of books and papers are stacked around the room.

And that's about it. But it's clean, it's warm, it's safe. I've lived in worse.

Ronan looks embarrassed, fidgeting with his tie again. He tosses his keys onto the table in the kitchen and grabs a matchbox off the fireplace mantel. "It gets a bit drafty in the winter," he says in that same apologetic tone. "But the building supplies firewood, so we don't have to worry about that."

"That's nice," I say.

Now that I've heard him speak more, the traces of Azeland in his accent are obvious. The past few months in prison, all I ever heard were Ruhian voices, and I didn't realize until now how much I missed hearing other people who speak like me. It's a small thing, but it makes Ronan feel more like my brother.

He strikes a match, tosses it into the grate, and watches the flames catch. "Bathroom's down the hall on the left. My room is at the end of the hall; yours is on the right."

"Mine?" I say, certain I've misheard.

"Yeah, your room. It's down the hall on the right."

My own room. *Thank you, Saint Ailara.* I've never had my own room before.

Except for that one time. In that one place. With that one boy I will not think about.

"So," Ronan says, straightening up from the fire, "how about dinner?"

Dinner. With real, actual, nonprison food.

This day is rapidly improving.

We head into the kitchen, and Ronan lifts the lid on the small white ice chest. "I didn't know what you'd like," he says quickly, "so I haven't really been shopping yet, and there isn't very much . . ."

Ronan's idea of "very much" differs greatly from mine. He's able to produce a loaf of bread, some sliced ham, a bit of cheese, two bowls of fresh berries—the weird Ruhian kind that manage to grow in frigid winter—and two glass bottles of milk. Practically a feast.

He then makes the questionable decision of trusting me with a knife, letting me slice the bread for our sandwiches. I've just cut four slices when he fidgets with his tie again. "So, Alli," he says, inky fingers tugging at his collar, "would it be all right with you if a friend of mine joined us for dinner tonight? She'll be getting off work in a few minutes, and she occasionally drops by . . ."

"Um, sure." He wants his friends to meet his delinquent sister? Might as well just announce it to the whole neighborhood.

I clear my throat. "Does she know . . . ?" I'm really not sure where to go with the rest of that sentence.

"I told her about you coming to live with me," he says carefully. Which is nice-guy code for *I told her you just got out of prison.*

"Okay," I say, because that's what he wants me to say. "So, six slices of bread, then?"

"Right." He smiles. He's a major smiler, my brother.

The knock comes at the door a few minutes later as Ronan is sweeping stacks of paper off the kitchen table to make more room. "Come on in, Mar," he calls.

The front door swings open, and a young woman strides into the living room. She looks about Ronan's age, probably in her late teens. Her skin is a rich, warm brown, and her dark hair is pulled back into a thick braid. She's dressed casually, in pants and a simple red blouse.

She's also very pretty.

Friend. Yeah, right.

"Hey, Ronan," she says, stepping into the kitchen. But she's looking at me. "You must be Alli."

I nod, and she offers me a handshake, smiling. "I'm Mari. I live next door to you, in 4A."

Two things I like about her instantly: One, she uses the same tone of voice with me as she does with Ronan, not that condescending one some people use to talk to children. And two, she said "to you," not "to Ronan." As if this is my house as much as his.

I try to remember Sister Perla's etiquette lessons. "Nice to meet you," I say.

"You're just in time for sandwiches," Ronan tells her, setting the last plate on the table.

"Sandwiches, huh? Did you forget to go shopping again?" she teases.

"I didn't *forget* . . ."

"Uh-huh." She drops into the chair at the end of the

table, and Ronan settles beside her. I sit in the remaining chair opposite Mari, with Ronan between us.

Ronan rushes through a grace, and then we dig in to the meal. It's all I can do not to shove it into my mouth as fast I can. I haven't had food like this in months. But I'm trying to make a good impression and remember my table manners. Not that I had any to begin with.

"So, Alli," Mari says, "Ronan tells me you're new to Ruhia?"

"Right," I say cautiously. "I'm from Azeland."

She smiles. "Well, our winter's going to be a big change for you, isn't it? But I've always thought it's Azeland that really has it rough. I don't know how you can brave those hot summers."

"You've been to Azeland?"

"Once, on a family trip in the summer. Beautiful city."

You must not've seen much of it. I quickly take a sip of milk to prevent that thought from coming out of my mouth. I'm not going to let myself get into trouble like I did before. That was Old Alli. New Alli is going to make this work. If boring, polite small talk with Ronan's girlfriend is what I have to do to live with my brother, then I'll do it.

"So, Alli," Ronan says, in the same cautious way he said it before, "I know you don't, er, have much with you, so I was thinking maybe you'd like to go shopping for some things tomorrow? I have to be at work, but you could go with Mari . . ."

Is he trying to pawn me off? Or trying to be considerate?

Mari leans toward me conspiratorially. "He knows absolutely nothing about clothing. Or decorating."

"Hey, I've furnished this whole apartment," Ronan says, pretending to be annoyed.

Mari winks at me. "My point exactly."

"Okay," I say. I can't quite muster up the enthusiasm for a shopping trip, but I guess I do need some clothes other than these. I smell like mothballs.

Ronan takes a sip from his water glass. "Have you given any thought to where you might like to apprentice?"

"Apprentice?" I repeat.

"You're turning thirteen next month, right?"

Of course. I've been stupid. All this time, when we talked about my coming to live with him, we never discussed how long I would stay. No wonder he's been so kind, so willing to take me in. Because it's only temporary. Just for a month, until I turn thirteen and am old enough to live on my own or be shipped off to someone as an apprentice. He never planned for me to live here permanently.

And part of me is a little bit relieved. Being on my own is what I know how to do. And as much as I wanted this to work out, as much as I still want to be connected to my brother, I've always known this would happen. I'm the sister he doesn't want, and the sooner he can go back to his perfect life without me, the better.

I was never going to get a real home.

But despite how many times I've told myself that this might happen, the reality of it is like being punched in the gut. The conversation moves along without me for a few minutes as I stare at my plate, at the dishware and the table and the floor that no longer belong to me, that never really did.

I'm a thief again, trying to take things that aren't mine.

"Alli?" Ronan says. It's probably not the first time he's called my name just now. Both he and Mari are staring.

"Hmm?"

"Mari can pick you up about ten tomorrow morning. Is that all right?"

"Yes, fine." As if I have anywhere else to be.

Mari goes on for a couple of minutes about some of the shops we can visit, and I attempt to nod and smile in all the right places. The whole time she's speaking, Ronan's eyes are glued to her, like a moth drawn to a flame. She's a little more subtle, but her eyes keep darting over to him, too. Yep, definitely his girlfriend.

When the topic of our shopping trip has been thoroughly exhausted, she asks Ronan about some case he's working on at the office. He mentions paperwork but is vague about the details. "Anyway, how was your day?" he asks her.

"Oh, you know. The usual." Her gaze drops to her empty plate.

Ronan shifts in his chair, setting down his glass. "Oh. Good."

I know an attempt to hide something when I see it. "Where do you work?" I ask.

She darts a panicked glance at Ronan, who clears his throat and says, "We first met at work, actually. I only moved into this building after Mari told me there was a room for rent here."

"So you're a lawyer too?" I ask her.

"Not exactly." The two of them share a helpless glance, and then Mari looks at me. "I'm a protector."

For the second time in as many minutes, I feel like all the air has been thrust from my lungs. This time, the words pop out of my mouth before I can stop them. "You're kidding."

"I just finished my training a few months ago," Mari says quietly. "Youngest in my class."

I glare at Ronan. "You didn't tell me?" He has to know what this means to me. I'm not sure how much about my actual case he's been told, but working in a law office and knowing the judge, I don't doubt he's had access to my records. And even though I lied to the judge and left out some rather important details, Ronan still has to know what they did to me. How it was protectors who nearly killed me with a curse, who arrested me and threw me in prison, who got me into this whole awful mess. And he's *dating* one. Just casually bringing her over for dinner.

The heat of my anger floods my veins. This is bad, bad, bad. I swore I wouldn't get angry, I'll lose everything if I get angry, I'll say something I don't want to say—

It's too late. I'm shaking, and blood is pounding in my temples. I've got to get out of here.

I lurch to my feet, my chair banging against the wall. "May I be excused?" It's all I can do to force the words out.

I don't hear if anyone answers. I run, past the protector at my brother's dinner table and down the dark hallway, into the bedroom that belongs to no one.

Chapter Two

Sunlight wakes me, which is how I remember I'm not in prison anymore.

It streams through the tiny window above Ronan's spare bed, which is tucked into the corner of the room. There's also a wooden trunk near the door and a single white chair that belongs with the rest of the dining set but doesn't fit in the kitchen. Nothing else.

Ronan didn't bother me last night after I fled the Disastrous Dinner. Either he's trying to give me space or he doesn't care about my feelings. I'm too tired to figure out which.

I have no idea what time it is, but judging by all the light, I've probably overslept. At least there's one good thing about only owning one set of clothing: It doesn't take long to get ready in the morning.

I crack open the bedroom door and peek out. The door to Ronan's room is closed, and the hallway is dark. I don't hear anyone in the kitchen or living room. Probably safe to emerge from hiding.

A small piece of paper lies in the center of the kitchen table, almost blending in with the white paint. The note is written with neat, careful handwriting:

Alli,

I have to leave early for work, but you can heat up the bowl of oatmeal on the stove, or there's fruit in the icebox. Mari will be by to pick you up at 10.

Please give her a chance.

—R

Yeah, I'll give her a chance, all right. I shove the note aside and watch it flutter to the floor.

So far, the only redeeming quality of living here is the food. Once I figure out how to work the stove—another questionable decision of Ronan's, giving me access to fire—the oatmeal is delicious. I'm contemplating whether or not to finish off the last bowl of fruit when a key scrapes the lock of the front door.

Oh great. The *protector* has a key, and I don't.

"Hey, Alli." Mari smiles at me as if nothing happened last night.

I don't say anything.

"Ready to go?"

I fold my arms across my chest. "I don't think so." Old Alli, the defiant girl from the orphanage, has risen up inside me, and this time I don't feel like stopping her.

But Mari surprises me. She folds her arms in imitation, staring me down. "And why's that?"

"I don't want to go." I almost add, *And you can't make me,* but that would only seem more childish. If they're going to stop treating me like a child the second I turn thirteen, then they might as well stop now.

"Alli." Mari leans against the side of the partial wall that separates the kitchen from the living room. "Look, I get it. You don't know me, I don't know you. But Ronan really wants this to work out, and I do too. Can't you at least give it a try, for his sake?"

Ronan wants it to work out, does he? Could've fooled me.

But I have to admit, there's a little spark of hope rising in my chest again. *I* wanted this to work. I still want this to work.

But how in Saint Ailara's name does he expect me to get along with a protector?

Time to find out if she means what she says.

"How much did he tell you about me?" I ask.

Mari lets her arms drop but keeps her fingers interlaced, one thumb tapping a beat against the other. "He told me you just got out of the juvenile center."

"Did he tell you why?"

Her thumb taps faster. "He told me you fell in with the wrong crowd, got into some trouble. Petty theft, I think he said."

Figures. He doesn't want his precious protector girlfriend to know what a delinquent his sister really is. "Well, then he's a liar. I was in there for theft, but it sure wasn't petty."

She doesn't blink, or look shocked, or any of the other things I expected. She seems undaunted by this information. "Oh?"

"And that's not all. They tried to arrest me before, and I escaped from the holding cell. Then I broke into the Atherton mansion."

I pause, watching her for even the slightest flicker of surprise, but her face is a mask now. So I keep going. "And because I broke into the Atherton mansion, somebody died."

Mari doesn't move. "I see."

"I just want you to know that you and I can never be friends."

"Because of what you did in the past?"

"No." I take a deep breath. "Because no matter what my brother might tell you, I'm not a good person. I'm not innocent. I did things that can't be undone."

Mari waits silently for me to continue. I try to put my thoughts in order, to figure out how to explain something so obvious and yet so hard to describe. "You're supposed to catch people like me. So no matter what I say or do to try and redeem myself, there's always going to be a part of you that's watching me. Waiting for me to slip up, to be the person that I've always been. Waiting to stop me. I'll always be trying to prove to you that I'm different, and you'll always see the part of me that isn't. So you can either be a protector or you can be my friend, but you can't be both."

She waits, unflinching, until I'm finished. Then she straightens, taking a step forward. "All right. Now it's my turn. I don't care what you did in the past. You're important to Ronan, and that means you're important to me. And you're right, I'm going to be watching you. I don't want to see you throw away your life, or risk anyone else's. And if it comes down to it, yes, I will stop you. But you know what? That's exactly what friends do. They look out for each other. I'm here to be whatever you need me to be, to help you however I can."

I try to swallow away the lump in my throat. "Sending me away from Ronan will not be helping me."

"No, it won't. So let's make sure it doesn't come to that."

I take a breath. "How?"

She pulls something from her pocket and dangles it in the air, smiling. A brown leather wallet. Ronan's.

"How about we start with shopping?"

Shopping is only half as bad as I thought it would be, which means it's still pretty awful.

But at least Mari doesn't try to force me into any clothes I don't like. She lets me take the lead in picking stuff out, and she makes the occasional suggestion when I get overwhelmed by the number of things on the shelves. Still, she's very firm about the need for what she calls "winter clothing," which is what I call "extremely big overcoats designed to withstand an ice age." In Azeland, we could get away with light coats and boots during the coldest days, and I'm not used to being bundled into a thousand layers of heavy fur-lined cloth. But Mari insists.

"You'll need it in another month or so," she says, while I glare at her from beneath a wide fluffy hood that cuts off my peripheral vision.

Another month or so. Right. Because that's when they're going to cast me out on my own, and there won't be anyone to make sure I have a warm coat.

I sigh. "Can I take it off now?"

"Wait," she says, rushing toward another shelf. "Maybe you need a scarf."

The memory hits me out of nowhere. Me, standing in a room a bit like this, posing in a dress, while women bustled around me, taking measurements and adding accessories. . . . Picking out a disguise to wear for my Thieves Guild trial, before everything went wrong.

I squeeze my eyes shut, forcing the image away. I don't want to think about that. I don't want to think about him.

"Aha!" Mari returns in triumph, bearing a thick woolen scarf that she drapes across my shoulders. At least there aren't any ugly patterns on it. "That's it; it's perfect."

"Does that mean I can go now?"

"Oh, you'll need to pick out at least one more coat. For when this one's drying out and you need another."

I sigh. "I hate winter."

Mari grins. "For someone born in Zioni's Month, you really ought to have her blessing."

I roll my eyes. "So everyone keeps telling me." I don't add that I don't know when I was born, since my mother apparently never bothered to provide anyone with that information. The Sisters at the orphanage just picked the same date that I arrived at the orphanage.

Hmm. Maybe Ronan knows the real date? Or at least remembers which season it was in?

The only other upside to suddenly being in my brother's life, in addition to the food: Finally I can ask someone questions about that part of my life and get real answers. I don't know how much he remembers, but surely it's more than I do.

Funny. It never mattered as much to me before. Where I came from, who my family is. What my life was like, and could have been like. Knowing my brother. It's like I didn't even realize how important it was to me until I had a chance at having it. And now I don't want to let it go.

But I don't have a choice. Ronan made it perfectly clear. I'm only here for a month, and then I have to move on.

Mari seems to have picked up on my mood and takes pity on me. "I suppose we could always come back for the second coat another time, if you're ready to go."

I picture myself a month from now, huddling in a frigid

workshop somewhere while a snowstorm howls against the windows. Completely alone.

"No," I say, "I changed my mind. Better make it two."

Finally, once Mari has run out of things to make me try on, we head back to the apartment, weighed down by many purchases. I now own what must be the world's largest collection of thick knitted sweaters, heavy fur-lined coats, and puffy winter hats. Mari seems to think that these items are insufficient, and is already planning for another shopping trip. I make noncommittal sounds and just let her talk.

Our final purchase is a big wooden wardrobe to store all of this stuff in, which Mari buys from a carpenter's shop down the street. The shop employs a magician who helpfully enchants the wardrobe to move on its own so we don't have to carry it. I'm pretty sure this service costs extra and is the kind of thing I never would've wasted money on, but Mari hardly bats an eye. She follows the magician's instructions, using the magic words to coax the wardrobe up the stairs and into the apartment.

It's late afternoon, and Ronan isn't back from work yet. Mari helps me store the shiny new clothes away in the shiny new wardrobe in my new (temporary) bedroom, by which I mean she does all the work of hanging and folding stuff while I hold out the shopping bags and try not to sulk.

My less-than-enthusiastic attitude doesn't seem to have deterred her in the slightest. We move into the living room, where she gets a fire going, straightens a few teetering piles of books, and then proceeds to the kitchen. "Believe it or not, Ronan's actually the better cook, between the two of us," she says, sounding apologetic, "but I'm sure I can whip something up. How do you feel about chicken soup?"

"Strongly in favor," I say, with more passion than I've had for anything else all day.

"Excellent." She rummages through one of the cabinets, searching for something. She must come over here a whole lot more than just "occasionally," like Ronan claimed. She knows where to look for everything.

"Bad news," she reports after a minute. "There aren't any clean bowls. How about I wash and you dry?"

Reluctantly I join her in the kitchen. This was always one of my least favorite parts of living with a family, when I was adopted before: the chores. It's not like I'm not used to having hard chores, since I spent most of my life in the orphanage and all. But I thought the whole point of being adopted was not having to do this kind of thing anymore?

Still, beats dish duty in prison, I guess. I grab a towel and join Mari at the sink.

By the time Ronan gets home a while later, the bowls are clean and the soup is steaming. "Smells delicious in here," he says, hanging up his coat and entering the kitchen.

Mari ladles soup into a bowl. "How'd it go today?"

"The Parson case is still a nightmare. The whole office is drowning in the paperwork." He takes the bowl from Mari, sets it on the table, and looks at me. "How was your day?"

"Um, fine," I say. "We shopped."

"We picked out two new coats, some boots, these really cute hats . . ." Mari cheerfully rattles off the list, passing me a second bowl of soup.

She and Ronan keep up the casual, friendly conversation as we eat, pretending like nothing at all happened the last time we sat down to dinner. I'm not sure whether to be relieved or annoyed that my outburst has had so few consequences. It's like it never happened.

Mari finishes her soup quickly. "Hate to eat and run," she says, placing the empty dish in the sink, "but I've got a shift."

She gives Ronan a mushy look, and his face gets all soft and sappy as they say good-bye. Gross.

"See you later, Alli," she says, like we're now best friends or something.

"Bye," I mumble, taking a hasty gulp of soup.

After the door closes behind her, the apartment is filled with silence.

Ronan has suddenly become very interested in his mostly empty bowl. He flips his spoon upside down, then turns it right-side up again.

One major way in which my brother and I are not similar: He doesn't like to talk very much.

I'm going to have to be the one to break the ice, so I take a breath and plunge in. "Do you . . . do you remember when my real birthday is?"

He looks up. "I'm sorry. I don't know. We . . ." He stops.

Twirls his spoon. Tries again. "I don't know how much you remember about . . . about when we lived with our mother. But I don't think we ever really celebrated birthdays. I remember going out for ice cream for mine a couple of times, but that's about it."

I take a second to turn this information over in my head, letting it settle. "I don't really remember anything, from before," I say, hoping he'll take the hint to elaborate.

He does. "I don't remember much, myself. We lived in this little house in south Azeland, by a park. It was painted all these bright colors on the outside—yellow, with green shutters and a red front door. We lived on the second floor, I think, and shared the kitchen with the downstairs neighbors. It had these twisty wooden stairs going to the second floor, and I remember when you were born, our mother kept worrying about those stairs—she kept saying you were going to fall and hit your head. You were so adventurous. You learned to crawl really fast, and you were always wandering all over the place, and she just knew you were going to tumble down the stairs one day."

This sounds nothing at all like anything I've been imagining—my mother, the one who abandoned me, worrying about me as a baby?—but I don't dare interrupt.

"So I got together with some of the downstairs neighbor kids, and we stole some random objects from around the house and fashioned this little barricade to block off the stairs. It was this silly, flimsy little thing, made up of pillows and pots and I don't know what else—like the kind of thing a couple of eight-year-olds would put together, obviously—but we were so proud of it, so sure it would work. We propped it all up on the landing and then set you down in front of it, already congratulating ourselves."

He pauses, grinning down into his soup bowl at the memory. "You sat there for a second, taking a good long look at this obstacle in your way. Then you gave the pile this tiny little tap. And the whole thing collapsed."

He laughs, so I do too. This much, at least, sounds like me. The troublemaker, causing problems.

But as nice as it is to finally have any information at all about my past, baby Alli stories aren't really what I'm most interested in at the moment. Ronan seems to sense this; he falls silent, staring into his soup again.

I don't think he's going to say it without prodding, so I finally ask out loud the question I've spent a decade trying not to think about. "So, what happened? To our mother? To us?"

Ronan tucks a loose strand of hair behind his ear and takes his time responding. "A lot of things happened, I think. Money had always been . . . tight. Though I didn't realize how bad things were at the time, it was only with hindsight—well, anyway. I think she may have worked two or three jobs at a time. I babysat you all day. But then something must have changed—maybe she lost her job, maybe the debts piled up, I don't know. One night we packed up quickly and left the yellow house. We moved in with a neighbor family that had a bunch of kids, and slept on the floor in their living room.

I don't know how long that lasted. I don't know when she decided . . . to do what she did."

None of this is exactly surprising to me. Poverty was always an easy guess. But I don't know how I feel about having it confirmed. That maybe my mother wanted me after all, but had to give me up.

It was easier to hate her when I didn't know for sure.

"The next thing I remember," Ronan says, fidgeting with his spoon, "is a man coming to the door and asking for me. He had a little apothecary shop not far from where we lived. She'd made an arrangement for me to be his apprentice. He fed and housed me in exchange for my work."

"Weren't you too young to be an apprentice?" I ask. Unless my estimate of his age was *way* off. It was the reason I'd always been sure that she chose him over me—I thought he was too young to be on his own. You have to be thirteen to get a job or apprenticeship.

"Not back then," he says. "Ruhia's had its labor laws for decades now, but Azeland adopted them only recently, maybe six or seven years ago. I was only nine, but there was no law against it at the time."

Well, that would've been useful information. Why didn't the Sisters ever teach us this kind of thing in history class?

It's the simplest part of his story, but it's turned everything I thought I knew upside down. Maybe she didn't choose him over me at all. We were both sent away. But he was able to get a job, while three-year-old me had no other option but the orphanage.

All this time, I've hated her, and maybe I was wrong.

Ronan continues speaking, oblivious to my inner turmoil. "I didn't know." He leans forward, as if this is the point he wants to emphasize. Now that he's started his story, he's warming up to it, the words pouring out faster. "I didn't know what was happening. Either she didn't tell me the truth or I didn't understand it. I thought we'd be neighbors, that she'd come to visit, that I could come to visit both of you. When I left for the apprenticeship, I didn't know that I was saying good-bye to both of you for good."

"But you were."

He nods. "She never came to visit me. As soon as I had a weekend off, I went back to the neighbor's, but both of you were gone and they didn't know where you went. I tried the yellow house, but you weren't there either. I wrote her dozens of letters, but I couldn't send them without an address. I had no idea how to find her. Or you."

"Did you ever find out?" I say, sitting up straighter. "Is it possible that she's still out there somewhere?"

He pauses for too long before shaking his head, and I know what he's going to say before he says it. "I'm sorry, Alli. She's gone."

"Are you sure?"

Another nod. "A few years later, a courier showed up at the apothecary's door with a message addressed to me.

It was an official notification from the city, informing me that my mother was dead. They didn't say where or how she died."

Well. That's still way more notification than I ever got.

"I asked about you. I tracked down the official who sent the message and asked for more information. But all he would tell me was that he didn't know anything about you. He said she lived alone. I didn't know . . . I didn't know if you were dead too."

Suddenly Ronan's decision to take in his long-lost imprisoned sister makes a whole lot more sense. Finding out you have a delinquent sister is probably better than believing you have a dead one.

Ronan might be a vague memory from my past, but I'm a ghost from his.

An annoying lump is forming in my throat, so I swallow it and try to move the conversation to less emotional ground. "So how'd you end up in Ruhia? What happened to the apothecary?"

"He moved here, and brought me with him," Ronan explains, looking grateful for the change of subject. "He was always kind to me, and I appreciated it. But the truth was, I didn't want to be an apothecary's apprentice. Sweeping floors and brewing herbal remedies didn't really interest me."

"Really? Didn't you get to learn, like, magic potions and stuff?"

He laughs. "Not really. We did sell some potions in the shop, but we bought them off of local magicians. We didn't get to brew anything like that ourselves."

"Oh."

"I was much more interested in learning other subjects. I'd always been fascinated by books. I taught myself to read, with a bit of help, and spent my nights studying by candlelight, trying to learn more about the world."

"What did you study?"

"Letters and spelling, penmanship, geography, history, mathematics, basically anything I could get my hands on."

Another way in which we're nothing alike. I can't imagine why anyone would want to study voluntarily. Especially stuff that's so boring.

"By the time I was fourteen," he continues, "the apothecary insisted I should apprentice somewhere else, where I could read and study all the time. He spoke to one of his clients, who happened to be a lawyer. How he managed to convince him to take me on is a mystery to me, given my lack of credentials, but at any rate, next thing I knew I had an apprenticeship at the law firm Avinoch and Co."

It's just as I suspected. Ronan's leading a ridiculously successful life, all things considered. And now I come along, the wayward orphaned sister with the tragic past who took a terrible turn into a life of crime right before he met me. The sister who isn't wanted by anyone but has nowhere else to go. Except for prison, of course.

"So that's it, really," he says, smiling a little sheepishly. "So . . . what about you?"

Now it's my turn to suddenly find my empty bowl of soup fascinating. "You've read my case file," I mumble.

"Yes," he admits. "But I want to hear it from you."

I give him an abbreviated version of my time in the orphanage, deliberately skipping the parts where I was adopted and ran away; I don't know if that's in my Ruhian file or not, and I really don't want him to know how much trouble I caused with other families. Let him think this is my first chance at a new life, not my third.

I also leave out everything having to do with the Guild, carefully giving him the same story I gave the judge after my arrest. How I ran away from the orphanage and was cursed and desperate, how I came to Ruhia with a boy named "Berkeley," how we were being paid to steal Lady Atherton's necklace, how it all went horribly wrong. How Lady Atherton died, and how her daughter almost did too. I give a lot of emphasis to how much I regret everything that happened, and how I'm done with thieving now for good.

It's mostly the truth, even if it is a slightly selective version.

Ronan listens carefully, rubbing circles into the tabletop with his index finger. He doesn't speak until I'm done.

"So anyway," I finish, "then the judge contacted you, and you know the rest."

He nods slowly, considering.

I reach for my glass and take a big gulp of water, because all that talking hurt my throat but also to have something to do while waiting for him to speak.

"It wasn't your fault, you know," he says. "What happened to Lady Atherton. You couldn't have known what would happen."

That wasn't the response I was expecting, but since I had nothing to do in prison except think about this issue, I already know what I want to say. "I should have, though. Maybe I couldn't have known *exactly* how it would all play out, but I knew that people might get hurt. I knew and I didn't care. Not until after."

He considers this. "So if someone had told you beforehand that she would die, would you really have done it anyway? Would you have said that you didn't care?"

I have to think about that one for a minute. "Well, no. But I probably would've looked for a reason not to believe them so I could do it anyway. I would've still risked it."

"Exactly," he says. "You didn't really think anyone would get hurt. You were taking a risk and hoping it would work out for the best. That's not the same thing as knowing—absolutely, one-hundred-percent knowing—that someone would die as a result."

I lean back in my chair. "Are you lawyering me right now?"

He laughs. "Maybe a little. Sorry."

I sigh. "What kind of lawyer are you anyway? Like, do you put people in prison or keep them out?"

"Neither, really. Avinoch's handles business law. Mostly drawing up contracts for business arrangements, that sort of thing."

"So you don't get to go to trials or anything? What fun is that?"

He laughs again. "We get to go to court sometimes, when there's a dispute over a contract."

"Sounds boring."

"It's maybe a little boring," he concedes.

"You should consider being a defense attorney instead. You'd be good at it." I'm only half joking.

He smiles. "But why handle exciting murder cases when I can fill out paperwork and argue about liability clauses instead?"

Actual sarcasm. Now I know for sure we're related. I grin back at him. "Well, I can't argue with that."

He pushes his chair back from the table and stands. "I'd better get started on the dishes. I need to get to work on drafting the super exciting contracts for a new subcorporation."

I rise from my chair and pick up my plate. "Guess I'd better help. Wouldn't want you to miss something so thrilling."

My brother and I stand side by side in the kitchen, cleaning the dishes and joking about his job, and maybe, possibly, it's starting to feel like I belong here.

Chapter Three

The next week is a mild improvement. Having my own clothes and a few more pieces of furniture makes the bedroom feel a little more mine, even if it's only temporary. Ronan pretty much leaves me to myself, thank God. He works long hours, so he's usually gone before I wake up, and I don't even see him until the evening. Most of the time Mari is off protectoring or whatever, but she does come over for dinner two more times. She and I don't fight again, but we tiptoe around each other, as if both of us are afraid to upset the delicate balance we've achieved. Mostly she just visits so she and Ronan can make gross mushy faces at each other over the table.

The lack of supervision means I have an abundance of free time and a million ways to spend it. But I'm still sticking to my pledge of keeping out of trouble. Even if Ronan plans to send me off to an apprenticeship, maybe I can convince him to let me stay a little longer, if I prove

I can behave myself. While he's working, I take over the meal preparation and shopping, haggling for the best prices in the marketplace (and not stealing anything, thank you very much). I explore the neighborhood around Ronan's apartment a bit, roaming the streets and taking roundabout routes to the market just to see what's there, but I don't get into any trouble. It's pretty quiet in this part of town, really. There's a park on the corner, an old lady upstairs who walks her dog every day at noon, and lots of houses. Not much trouble to be found, even for me.

Ronan and I start to develop a bit of a routine. He leaves some coins and a shopping list for me in the mornings. I run to the marketplace in the afternoon, pick everything up, and then swing by Ronan's law office to meet him on his way home from work.

It's only a few blocks from the market to Avinoch and Co., but the air is bitterly cold today, and I wrap my scarf tighter around my neck. I haven't yet braved one of the furry overcoats Mari bought me, but I don't think I'll be able to hold out much longer. Winter is definitely making an appearance.

The cobbled streets are crowded now as people rush home from their jobs or dash into shops to pick something up before they close. But it's a pleasant kind of bustle, polite and uniform, not at all like the chaos of an Azelandian marketplace. Suddenly I miss my old city so much, it startles the breath right out of me. I never expected to miss it. Azeland never felt like home. Ruhia is clearly meant to, with all of its snug little shops and cozy brick-lined streets, but all of that just emphasizes what I'm lacking. I don't feel at home. I just feel cold.

I round the corner and run the last couple of steps to the law office. For a building that looks so much like its neighbors, it still manages to be imposing—long stone steps lead up to the entranceway, which is flanked by twin statues of Saint Julina, the patron of justice. The lettering on the door reads AVINOCH AND CO.

I must be running late today. Ronan is already waiting for me, just inside the door. He walks briskly down the steps, his heavy overcoat flapping open, his dark hair ruffled as usual. "Hey," he says, smiling. "How was the market?"

"Busy." I glance up at the office door. "You know, when you own this place, it'll say Rosco and Co. Ha! Co and co, get it?"

I expect Ronan to laugh like he usually does at my jokes, but he stops smiling.

"No, wait, you should make it *Ros and Co*!"

He takes one of the grocery sacks from my hands without responding.

"Ros and Co," I repeat meekly. I must've said something wrong, but I'm not sure what. "That's brilliant, you should definitely use that."

Ronan looks down at the groceries. "Let's head home." He starts walking in the direction of the apartment.

I don't know what to do, but I feel the need to do *something.* So I keep talking. "If you start using Ros and Co for your company name, does that mean I get some sort of commission? For coming up with the idea?"

Ronan dodges a couple of pedestrians and keeps walking.

I leap forward, trying to keep up with his brisk pace. "Just a teeny, tiny commission," I say. "How about eighty-five percent?"

He stops walking. "I'm not going to own the company, Alli."

I freeze. "But you're Avinoch's apprentice, right? I thought you were going to be a lawyer."

"I am going to be a lawyer, if I'm lucky. But Avinoch will pass the company on to his son, and my apprenticeship is ending soon. Hopefully I'll be kept on as an associate when the time comes. But that might not happen."

"Why not?"

He exhales slowly, his breath a cloud of white in the chilly air. "Nobody picks an Azelandian orphan to be their law associate."

My breath joins his in the air. "Oh."

Ronan starts walking again, more slowly this time.

"He could still pick you," I say quietly.

"He won't."

"Then what will happen? When your apprenticeship is up?"

"I might get hired by another office."

He probably thinks this answer is reassuring, but I'm not fooled. I didn't miss the "might." "But you might not?"

He nods. "I might not."

"Oh."

Ronan's smile slowly slides its way back onto his face. "Your sudden interest in my job wouldn't have anything to do with your own apprenticeship, now, would it?"

This is a favorite topic of Ronan's. He seems to think I need to develop an interest in some kind of career path. Probably so that he can ship me off as soon as possible. "Do I *really* need an apprenticeship?" I say. "I mean, look at what a great shopping assistant I am. You could totally hire me to do this forever."

Ronan rummages through the grocery sack, checking what I bought. "Candy again?"

"I have no idea what you're talking about. Professional shopping assistants never buy candy they're not supposed to buy."

Ronan draws the bar of white chocolate from the bag and playfully swats at my head with it.

"Oh, *that*."

"Yes, that."

I skip over a crack in the sidewalk. "Okay, but you'll thank me when you get to eat some of that chocolate. I mean, I'm sure there will be plenty left over for you."

"Oh, I'm sure."

Sarcasm again. The one thing that makes me feel 100 percent certain we're related. I beam at him. "I'll just eat, like, the entire bar, and then you can have the crumbs in the wrapper at the end."

The wind has picked up, sending another chill through me, but Ronan's smile makes everything seem warmer. "It's all yours."

"I'm going to remember you said that."

We've reached the apartment building. Ronan leads the way up the stairs and unlocks the door.

We rush into the warm apartment and are instantly assailed with scents of cooking—meat and broccoli, probably a stew. Mari stands in the kitchen. She promised to cook today; I almost forgot. "How's it going?" she calls.

Ronan sets the grocery sack on the kitchen table and strips off his gloves. "Alli was just trying to distract me from talking about where she might like to apprentice."

"Oh? Did you have any ideas yet?" she asks.

I slowly unwind my scarf, which has been attempting to strangle me for the last five minutes. "Nothing in particular," I say. I glance around for a distraction. "So what's for dinner?"

"Beef stew," Mari says. "Hope you like it."

"I'm sure I will," I say.

Mari raises her eyebrows. "Did you murder someone today?"

"Whatever gave you that idea?"

"The flattery," she says dryly.

"I have no idea what you're talking about."

"Did you two discuss tutoring?" she asks, glancing at Ronan.

I freeze. "What tutoring?"

Ronan and Mari are looking at each other in that annoying way adults do, where they're clearly communicating something about me. And that something is never good.

Ronan hangs his coat up on the peg in front of the fireplace. He runs a hand through his hair, ruffling it even more. "Let's sit down," he says to me.

"Probably a good idea," I mutter. I have a feeling this conversation isn't going to go well.

I sit on the sofa and start unlacing my boots, casting glances at him out of the corner of my eye. He moves a stack of papers from his armchair and sinks onto the cushion.

"I was thinking," he says slowly, "that to prepare you for an apprenticeship, you should start being tutored."

He must be joking. Only rich kids can afford tutoring, and Ronan clearly isn't rich. Besides, while the Sisters tried to teach us some basic subjects at the orphanage, I wasn't exactly the best student. Or the best behaved. A tutor wouldn't know what to do with me.

"Master Avinoch, the lawyer I'm apprenticed to, generously provides a tutor for the children of all his employees. When he heard that you were coming to stay with me, he offered to let you join the class. It's not exactly nobility-level tutoring, but it will help prepare you for an apprenticeship."

"Um," I say. "I don't think that's a great idea."

"Why not?"

"I—I tend to get in trouble a lot when it comes to tutoring."

"What kind of trouble?"

"All of the kinds."

Ronan clearly doesn't get it. "I'm sure you'll do fine. It's nothing to be nervous about."

"That's not the problem." I carefully slide my right boot off, not daring to look at him.

Ronan rubs his eyes. I look back at my remaining boot. "I don't get it, Alli," he says as I give my laces a sharp tug. "What's wrong?"

"No, you don't get it," I say. It comes out harsher than I meant, and Ronan's head jerks back in surprise.

Still, he keeps his tone even. "Why don't you want to talk about this?" His calm is kind of infuriating.

My voice rises. "Because I don't."

"Alli. I know you can handle tutoring. You're such a smart kid. There's so much you could do, if you'd take an interest in your future."

Right. The future I'd better prepare for, because I'll be on my own. I spin around to face him. "How do you know?" My voice rises again, louder and higher. "How do you know what I'm like?"

A thud sounds in the kitchen. Mari, listening in, has dropped something.

Ronan is taken aback, his eyes widening. "I know you're not a bad kid, Alli. I just want to know why—"

The alarm bells ring in my brain, but they're too late. The anger is already here. "How do you know that? You think you know me just because you've read my stupid file?"

"Alli—"

"I know what you think. You think I'm just some pitiful little orphan girl who never had a chance, and if you're just nice enough, maybe I'll magically become a good person. You want to know the truth? I am a bad kid. I'm so bad that I was adopted twice before, and both times they hated me so much, they let me run away and never took me back. Did they tell you *that* in your precious file?"

I don't wait to hear what he says. I push away from the sofa and stomp out of the room.

Except I'm still wearing only one boot, so it's a bit undignified.

Oh well. I slam the bedroom door harder to make up for it.

In the safety of my bedroom—no, Ronan's second bedroom, which I am borrowing—I fling off the offending boot and sink to the floor, my back pressed against the door.

The hum of voices starts almost immediately. Low at first, then louder, and louder still. They're arguing.

Great. Now I've ruined his relationship, as well as everything else. I'm completely destroying his life.

I look around the room, which is now filled with all the things Mari and I bought. God, why did I ever think it was a good idea to buy all this stuff? All the clothes and the shoes and the stupid coats? He's only an apprentice, one who might be about to lose his job. And now I've given him an even bigger financial burden. No wonder he wants to get rid of me as soon as possible.

Somehow I ruined this before it ever even began.

I turn onto my side, pressing my ear against the crack in the door, but I can't make out what they're saying. Probably debating how to get rid of me.

I stand and walk over to the wardrobe, its expensive oak doors taunting, and start pulling clothes out. Most of this stuff hasn't been worn yet. I can sell it and get some of the money back. Pay him most of what I owe. Then at least I won't be leaving him in debt when he sends me away.

Somewhere a door slams. Mari leaving, probably. After a minute, footsteps thud in the hall. I hold my breath, willing him not to open the door. Not to tell me what I already know. Not yet.

The footsteps move on, past my room and into his. The door clicks shut.

I spend about an hour folding the clothing back into the shopping bags they came in, making it look like they never even came out. Then I line the bags up neatly in the bottom of the wardrobe, so they'll stay folded and won't get wrinkly.

By the end of this process, my stomach is rumbling. The smell of the stew we never ate drifts down the hall and into my room, beckoning me.

Well, if no one else is going to eat it . . .

I crack my door open and peek down the hall. Ronan's door is still closed. The apartment is silent.

I tiptoe into the kitchen, where the table is still set for three. The empty dishes glare accusingly at me. Another perfect little family dinner, ruined.

I snatch up my bowl, glaring right back at it, and spoon in a healthy serving of stew from the pot on the stove. I have no idea whether Mari was finished with her recipe or not, but it tastes just fine to me. More broccoli than I'd like, but I can't complain. I've had way, way worse. Especially in that place I don't think about, with the boy I definitely don't think about.

Not wanting to linger in here, I eat the stew so fast that it scalds my tongue. Ronan might have the same idea I did and emerge any minute. And what would I say to him then? *Sorry I'm a terrible person, but please don't send me away?*

I scrape the bowl clean and set it in the sink. I'd wash it, but Ronan would hear the water. Better just to get out of the kitchen quick—

Something bangs on the front door, and I jump. Probably Mari. I should run back to my room—

But Mari has a key. She wouldn't—

Knock. Quieter this time. Hesitant.

I tiptoe across the living room, holding my breath as if whoever's out there could hear me. Should I open it? Maybe it's a thief or something. . . . The thought almost makes me laugh. I've had more than enough experience dealing with thieves.

It's probably just a friend of Ronan's, or someone from his office. Or maybe Mari forgot her key and came back to apologize about the fight. Either way, I don't really want to open the door. I don't want to talk to anyone.

But my curiosity has gotten the better of me. I could crack it open, just for a second, find out who it is, tell them Ronan's not here . . .

I lift the latch. Take a deep breath. Pull the door open.

And gasp.

It *is* a thief.

Beck Reigler is standing on my brother's doorstep.

Chapter Four

"Oh my God," I say.

Beck stares at me, his eyes wide, as if he's seeing a ghost. In fairness, I *was* dying the last time he saw me. But he should know that I didn't die, because he's the one who saved my life.

He's taller than before, I think. His hair has grown out again, curling down around the top of his neck. But his eyes are just as warm as they've ever been.

It's really him.

"Hey," he says quietly.

I try to collect my scrambling thoughts. "What are you doing here?"

"I—" He pauses. "I need to talk to you."

"You need. To talk. To me," I repeat slowly, as if the words will make more sense. "All this time, all these *months*, I don't hear a single thing from you, but now all of a sudden you come all this way and show up on my doorstep because you need to *talk* to me?"

"Well, I couldn't exactly contact you before, or the protectors would've caught me. Besides, this is . . . this is important."

I glance behind me, making sure Ronan hasn't heard anything. Lucky his room is in the back— Oh God. Mari. She's next door.

I turn back to Beck. "You can't be here!"

His eyes fall to the floor. "I'm sorry. I didn't want to bother you. I know you're with your brother and everything now. But I need your help, and I didn't know where else to go—"

"Shh," I say. "It's not safe to talk out here." I point in the direction of Mari's door and mouth the word "protector."

Beck curses and glances around the hall. "Come with me. I have a place we can talk."

I hesitate. I don't know how to feel about him being here. I don't know what to think.

"Alli," he whispers. "I think your brother is in danger."

The wild swirl of thoughts in my head slams to a stop. "What?"

He glances at Mari's door again. "Come with me and I can explain."

I look back at the dark apartment, where Ronan still hasn't emerged from his room. What if he comes out and notices I'm gone?

"Please," Beck whispers. "I have to warn you."

I might not know how to feel about Beck right now, but I

do know that he wouldn't lie about danger if there wasn't any. "All right," I say finally. "Just give me one second."

I dash back into the living room and run toward the fireplace. Ronan's coat is still hanging there, and I dig around in his pockets until I find his keys. Wouldn't want to get locked out. Then I throw the coat over my shoulders, since my own is still in my room and I don't want to take the time to grab it. My spare boots are by the fire, so I throw those on too.

A creak echoes down the hallway, and I freeze. If Ronan walks in right now, he'll see me holding his keys, the front door standing open, with a thief on the doorstep. But it isn't Ronan. There's nothing but silence. I tiptoe back across the room as fast as I dare, step outside, and lock the door behind me.

Silently we sneak past Mari's apartment, then dash down the stairs and out of the building. Beck leads the way across the street. "Where are we going?" I whisper.

"You'll see," Beck says, which isn't an answer at all.

It's a cloudless night, the moon and stars providing a little illumination in addition to the streetlamps on the corners, but long stretches of the road are still shadowed. I stumble through the dark, rushing to keep up with Beck, who's running like we have a dozen protectors chasing us. "What's the rush?" I say as he rounds the corner and speeds up again.

"We need to get out of the open," he says, glancing over his shoulder at the darkened street behind us. "They could be watching."

"Um, okay, that doesn't sound ominous at all." But Beck doesn't elaborate, just keeps running up the street.

We pass the park on the corner and head a block north, where Beck stops in front of a long row of identical brick houses. I don't exactly see a decent thief hideout anywhere, but Beck is scanning the tops of the trees behind the houses like he's trying to find something.

"What are we looking for?" I whisper.

Beck points. "That."

I follow his gaze and spot it: a long pale object that rises out of the woods on a distant hill, so tiny that I never noticed it before. It's thin and white, almost like . . . "Is that a steeple?"

"Yep."

"What's a church doing in the middle of the woods?"

"You'll see."

"Stop saying that."

Beck slips quietly between two houses, heading for the hill.

"There's no path to get up there," I protest.

Beck fakes a gasp. "Oh, the horror."

"Shut up." As we trudge up the hill, I add, "You know, that's a weird thing about Ruhia. You have all these little sidewalks everywhere. Azeland mostly doesn't bother with them."

"It's not weird. It's called organization."

I roll my eyes, even though he can't see me in the dark. "Being that organized is weird."

"Spoken like a true Azelander."

"What's that supposed to mean?"

"Have you *seen* your city? I mean, given the way your streets twist around all the time, I'd think no one in the whole town knows what a straight line is. And none of your buildings match."

We've reached the denser swath of the woods, and I have to shove aside a tree limb before I can answer. "Buildings aren't supposed to match. Different buildings are for different purposes, so why would they all look the same?"

Beck just shakes his head hopelessly at me. "And here I was hoping you'd have turned into a true Ruhian by now."

"Don't be ridiculous. I mean, haven't you noticed how cold it gets here? It's not even midwinter yet and I have to wear all these stupid scarves and things. How do Ruhians stand this every year?"

Beck's not even wearing a coat. And he's been outside for who knows how long. I open my mouth to tease him about his ridiculous Ruhian tolerance for cold, but I stop. I don't actually know what's going on or if Beck had to flee the Guild in a hurry. Maybe his lack of a coat isn't by choice. And here I am complaining about wearing warm clothes.

Brown leaves and twigs crunch under our feet as we hike deeper into the woods. The trees look a little lonely, all bare and wispy. The farther uphill we go, the denser the trees and underbrush get, until we have to start pushing branches out of the way and avoiding the thickest bushes.

A bird flies overhead, rustling the branches. It's eerily quiet in here, like the entire city surrounding us has disappeared. There's nothing but dead leaves and bare trees and prickly brush, all of it casting strange shadows in the near-dark.

Now that we're almost to the top of the slope, the steeple isn't visible anymore, what with the darkness and all the trees blocking the view. But as long as we keep moving in the same direction, we should be walking right to it. It seems like there should be a path or something, if there really is a church up here. Maybe a path used to exist, but if so, it's been completely overgrown, like the forest just swallowed it up. The thought makes me shiver.

"It's kind of creepy up here," Beck says, echoing my thoughts.

Finally, after we've been scratched and tripped by a million branches, the trees start to thin again, and we stumble into a clearing. There, a few feet away, is the church.

It's smaller than I expected. More of a chapel, really, with a tiny arched doorway in the front and the single steeple in the back. Unlike most of the buildings in Ruhia, it seems to be made of some kind of white stone instead of brick, but the color is fading and patchy, much of the stone chipped away in places. The dead winter grass grows up high around it, the woods reclaiming the chapel for its own.

"Is it totally abandoned?" I whisper.

"Seems to be." Beck leads the way across the clearing. "I

checked it out earlier today, and it doesn't look like anyone's been here in ages."

He seems to be right about that. But I approach tentatively, not sure what we're going to find inside. We might not be the only ones who know about this chapel's existence. It's these kinds of places—the ones that the rest of the world forgot about—that make the perfect hideouts. Beck taught me that.

And anyone who might need this kind of hideout is definitely up to no good. Like us, for instance.

The ground is littered with leaves, and we crunch loudly through them as we make our way closer to the chapel. Announcing our arrival to anyone lurking inside, no doubt. I wait to see if anyone or anything will react to the sound, but nothing happens. We shuffle closer.

Passing under the arch, we walk up the three stone steps and reach the door. It's been intricately carved with some kind of pattern, but it's so weathered and dirty that I can't really make out the design. Small stained-glass windows frame either side, but I can't see through them, and there's no other way to look in.

Beck pushes on the door, which creaks in protest, but after a few good shoves, it gives. Inside, the chapel is pitch-black.

"Hang on," Beck whispers. "I left a lantern by the door." He steps across the threshold and fumbles with something in the dark.

"How'd you even find this place?" I say. "Is it a Guild hideout?" Guild members have hideouts scattered all over, so it wouldn't surprise me if they had one mere minutes from Ronan's apartment. Even if the thought does creep me out.

"No," Beck says. "We wouldn't be safe in a Guild hideout."

"What's *that* supposed to mean?" His cryptic hints are getting both alarming and annoying.

"I spent the day searching your neighborhood for a decent hideout that the Guild wouldn't know about," he continues, ignoring my question. "I saw the steeple from the street and decided to check it out."

Something rustles, and a spark of fire bursts into life. It takes a second for my eyes to adjust—and my heart to stop racing, what with the sudden appearance of fire and all—but now I can see a lot better. Beck lifts the lantern by the handle, the flickering ball of flames dancing within it. Flames that are emitting *green* sparks.

Contrary to what most people seem to believe, I don't routinely go around setting things on fire. But even with my lack of knowledge about how flames work, I do know that they're not normally green.

I sigh. "What did you just do?"

"Enchanted matches," he explains. "They light more easily, that's all. The green's just a weird side effect."

"Guild perk?" I ask quietly.

The flickering lantern provides enough light for me to

see his face, so I can tell he at least looks a little ashamed. "Yeah, something like that."

He holds the lantern up and ushers me across the threshold, giving me a real look at the chapel for the first time. I don't know what I expected, but I guess I shouldn't be surprised by this room. It looks like . . . well, like a church. There's a little raised altar in the back, and two neat columns of pews lead from it to the doorway, forming an aisle down the center. A few runes are carved into the walls as well as appearing on the stained-glass windows, but otherwise it's fairly free of decoration. In true Ruhian style, they even built a little fireplace, tucked into a recessed corner beside the altar. You'd never see *that* in Azeland. Otherwise it's exactly like any other chapel I've ever been in.

Yet at the same time, it's nothing like that at all. Because this chapel looks like it was abandoned and left to rot for a million years. What must be several inches of dust coat the floor, as well as every other surface. The wooden pews are gray with it and cracking in places. It's eerie, and yet . . . strangely beautiful.

I step farther into the room, my footsteps echoing against the dirty stone, and Beck follows. The air is cold and stale and thick with dust, making it hard to breathe. The ceiling curves above our heads, its arches a deep blue that's speckled with white in places where the paint has faded or chipped away. A small loft is tucked above the doorway, just wide enough for another row of pews. Probably for a choir or something.

Beck walks down the aisle, gazing around with a critical eye. "It's not exactly the most secure hideout ever," he says, almost as if he's apologizing about it. "No way to keep other intruders out." He gestures toward the door. I'm tempted to roll my eyes at him again. This isn't the Thieves Guild, for God's sake. He can't expect a magical lock on every door.

A little white statue of a saint—whoever the chapel is dedicated to, I'm sure—is perched on a ledge at the back of the altar. I step closer, curious.

It's Saint Harona.

I back quickly away. Saint Harona, the patron of families and children, also known as my least favorite saint. The one who never seemed to acknowledge my prayers at all . . . until recently, I suppose. Still, I avoid the statue area altogether. The way she's staring and smiling is creeping me out.

The flickering green light of Beck's lantern dances across the pew beside me. Lying there is a little blue booklet—probably a hymnal. Which is kind of stunning. It's so expensive to print hymnbooks that only high churches usually have them—and if they do, they don't just leave them lying around to collect dust.

What happened here? Did everyone in the world forget about this place? Did everyone die off in a plague or something so suddenly that they didn't have time to collect their books? Was there something so terrible about it that they just decided to leave the chapel behind, hymns and all?

I shiver again, walking quickly back up the aisle.

"I don't like that the steeple is visible from the street either," Beck says, continuing his list of the chapel's shortcomings. "But it should work. It's secluded, it's dry, and I don't think anybody in the Guild knows it's here. It'll be fine."

"Fine for *what*? What are we doing here, Beck?"

He looks me right in the eyes. "I came to warn you. I think someone wants to kill your brother."

Chapter Five

I gape at Beck, refusing to believe what he just said.

"Maybe we should sit down for this." He moves to sit on the altar step, and I plop down across from him on a pew, raising a poof of dust into the air that stings my eyes. He turns the lantern's handle around and around, sending shadows dancing wildly across his face. He doesn't look at me.

"Explain," I say when I can find my voice.

"I'm trying to figure out how," he says quietly.

The silence stretches, forcing me to remember the last time I saw him. Climbing out the window of the Atherton mansion, the stolen necklace clenched in his fist. On his way to the carriage that would take him to the Guild. The carriage that was supposed to take me, too. The carriage that was supposed to save me.

Is he remembering that night too? Does he regret it?

I should probably resent him for everything that's happened.

For leaving me there, for leaving a girl to die, for not going to prison like I did. But everything is all jumbled up. Beck left me behind . . . and then used his Guild money to save my life. I had to go to prison, but that was my choice. And at the end of it all I managed to find my brother, which wouldn't have happened if Beck hadn't brought me to the Guild in the first place. I don't know how to even begin sorting this out. Which is why I've tried to avoid thinking about him at all, up until tonight.

But now he's in front of me, and I have to decide whether or not to be happy he's here.

Which is impossible to do when I'm simultaneously freaking out about Ronan being in some kind of danger. "Just tell me whatever it is you have to tell me already."

"Okay. I just . . . I'm just trying to figure out how to begin."

"You know what I always say. Begin at the beginning."

If he recognizes the reference to one of our previous conversations, he doesn't show it. "It's not that simple."

I lean back against the pew, its coldness seeping into my spine. "How did you even find me?"

"Your brother's name and address were in your file. At the courthouse."

"How'd you read my file?"

His lips quirk up at the corners, a movement so familiar, my heart does this little extra thump in response. "I stole it, Alli."

"Oh. Right."

Finally he turns to look at me. Greenish-orange light flickers against his cheek. "I didn't actually know which courthouse your records would be in, so I searched all of them. Only took five tries before I found the right one, luckily."

"Lucky," I repeat. "Wait—how'd you even know about my brother?"

"I didn't. I just figured that wherever you were sent, somebody would've made a record of it somewhere. I searched a bunch of files until I found your name. And then it said you'd been released to your brother, and it listed his name and address. After that, you weren't hard to find."

"Oh."

He pauses. Although he's looking in my direction, he can't quite meet my eyes. "Did you . . . did you know you had a brother?"

"Yeah. I mean, I didn't know where he was, or anything about him. I was only three when I went to the orphanage, so for a while I didn't even remember his name."

He pauses, looking down at the lantern in his hands. "What's he like? Do you like him?"

"I guess so. I mean, he's nice. He's been *really* nice to me so far, actually. But I don't think he really wants me to be here. And I kind of messed everything up already."

"Really?"

"Yeah. Turns out I'm not so great at this whole normal-life thing."

Beck laughs. "You knew that already, Allicat. You ran away from how many adoptive families before you left the orphanage?"

"Ha-ha. Thanks for reminding me." But I smile. It's nice to have someone to talk to about the whole Ronan thing. Someone who already knows me and everything I've been through.

I'd never admit it to him out loud, but I missed Beck.

"So how did *you* find him?" he asks. "Your brother, I mean."

"Well . . ." I pause. "Turns out the judge knew him. He saw my last name and asked if we were related, and then I remembered . . ."

It doesn't take Beck long to pick up on the crucial information in that story. "How did the judge know him?"

I take a breath, not knowing what Beck's reaction will be. "He works at the courthouse sometimes. He's apprenticed to a lawyer."

Beck's eyes widen. "Are you kidding me?"

"He can't know that I talked to you, or that you're in the city at all. He might . . ."

"He'll turn me in?"

I hesitate. "I think he would. I never told anyone about the Guild, or who you really were—"

"Yeah, I know. I saw what you told the judge in your file. Nice cover story."

"Yeah, well, they still know you were with me, and they

know what you look like, because the Athertons told them. If my brother sees you, he'll know who you are. And he . . ."

"Is a lawyer," Beck finishes. "So he'd uphold the law. Turn me in."

"He'd try to do the right thing," I say. "And even if he didn't . . ." I have to get this over with. I say it in a rush, the words jumbling together. "Hisgirlfriend'saprotector."

"What?"

"His girlfriend. She lives in the apartment next door to us. And she's a protector."

"Well," Beck says slowly. "That complicates things."

"Complicates *what*? What did you mean about someone wanting to kill him?"

He hesitates. "I'm not sure I know where to begin."

I groan. "You said that already."

He ignores me. "Something bad is happening in the Guild."

"Way to be specific."

He sighs. "Do you want to hear this or not?"

"Sorry. Go on."

"At first it was just . . . whispers. Rumors. I didn't believe them. But some people were saying . . . Well, some people have been complaining about Kerick—you remember, the king of the Guild?—for a long time. Questioning his leadership. It all goes back to when he first took the throne. Kerick had a sister who also wanted to rule, and some people supported her instead of him. His sister left the Guild eventually, and everyone accepted Kerick as king, but some of her supporters weren't happy about it. And it didn't help that Kerick's pretty young for a king—some of the older Guild members have always been reluctant to accept him.

"Only now it's become something else. People have been criticizing the king more and more, and doing it more in the open. And then rumors started going around that there's this new group within the Guild—conspirators who want to remove the king. People are calling them the Shadow Guild."

"That doesn't sound pleasant. But what does any of this Guild stuff have to do with Ronan?"

"I'm getting there. Okay, so at first I didn't think much of these rumors, like I said. But then I was assigned to work a heist, with this guy called Keene. I didn't know him very well, but he always seemed pretty shady to me."

I can't help but laugh. "Really, Beck, a shady Guild member? Who would've thought?"

"You know what I mean. There was something about him I didn't trust. But I never really knew the guy, so when I was partnered with him, I didn't object. At first everything went well—we did the heist, stole the money, and got out fine. But then, when we were supposed to meet up with the carriage that would take us back to the Guild, Keene led us in a different direction. He had the money, so I didn't have much choice but to follow him.

"We went to this abandoned warehouse, and there were a couple of other Guild members there, guys I didn't know. And that's when Keene told me he's one of the Shadows. These guys have been skimming money off the top for months, funding their movement instead of handing it all over to the Guild. And all in an attempt to stage a coup and overthrow the king."

"And by 'overthrow' they mean 'assassinate'?"

"Yes."

I shiver. For a second, it feels almost like a game—Beck whispering scary stories in the dark. But his scary stories are real.

"Wait a minute," I say. "They just *told* you all of this? They admitted it?"

He nods. "They were trying to recruit me. That's how they've been increasing their numbers—speaking to people in small groups, getting them on their side. I don't even know how many Guild members are part of this by now."

"But why did they approach you? Was it coincidence, because you were paired with Keene? Or did they think you'd be a good recruit or something?"

Beck exhales slowly. "I think they thought I'd be open to what they were saying, because I have friends who are part of it too."

The chills race up my spine and across my neck. "Which friends?"

He still can't meet my eyes. "Like I said, I don't know everyone who's in it."

"But who *do* you know?"

"Mead."

I gasp. "You're kidding." Koby Mead is a lot of things, but a shady cloak-and-dagger conspirator isn't one of them.

"I confronted him about it, and we had a fight. Mead doesn't really care about who leads the Guild, but he's trying to play both sides. Get in good with the Shadows just in case they're actually successful."

"Okay, that sounds like Mead," I admit. He's not the type to back only one horse in any given race. And he certainly wouldn't let pesky things like morals get in the way. "So, okay, the Shadows tried to recruit you because you're friends with Mead. No offense, Beck, but I'm missing the part where this involves me or my brother."

Beck sighs. "Patience. I'm getting there. Okay, so, the Shadows approach me about joining them, and you can probably guess what I said."

"Um, no?" I say. But for the smallest of seconds, I'm not actually sure. Beck has lived in the Guild for too long. He's the boy who saved my life, but he's also the boy who left me behind—and left an innocent girl to die.

"Of course," he says, and I exhale. "For one thing, Kerick has been nothing but kind to me. When my mom got sick, he was always understanding, and when she died, he didn't kick me out like most people would've. I mean—you've met him. You know what he's like."

I nod. When Beck brought me to the Guild, the king was willing to let me, the stray orphan picked up off the streets, earn a place in the Guild. And he also tried to warn me away, because he knew what the cost would be. As far as terrifying and mysterious leaders of legendary bands of thieves go, Kerick doesn't seem so bad.

"And secondly," Beck continues, "even if they do have legitimate grievances, I don't like their methods. Skimming money off, recruiting people in secret, plotting murder . . ."

"That does sound questionable."

"So, basically, I told them I wasn't interested in joining. And they didn't take it well."

"No . . . ," I say slowly. I'm starting to see where he's going with this. "I don't suppose they would."

Beck pauses. He sets the lantern down between us, its flames casting only half of him in light. "They murdered Durban."

"Murdered?" I repeat, as if it's a foreign word. I know Guild life is dangerous, but I always thought the threats were external—something that happened on a job. I've never heard of Guild members killing one another. And especially not *Durban*, the king's icy and terrifying right-hand man. My head spins. "But isn't that risky? I mean, that's like announcing to the entire Guild that they're real."

"Exactly," he says. "Everyone knows they exist now, but not who they are or how to stop them."

"Except you," I say. "You know who they are. Some of them, anyway."

There's a sinking feeling in my chest, like I've swallowed a lead weight. This story can't end well.

"Yeah," he says, "except me. They're not giving me a choice anymore, Alli. My time is up."

"Meaning . . ."

"Meaning either I join them now, or I end up like Durban."

"So you're telling me you're joining the Shadows?"

"Not exactly." He smiles grimly. "I couldn't bring myself to join them. So I went to the king and told him everything I knew."

"Saints, Beck, that could've gotten you killed."

He shakes his head. "I was careful. No one knows I did it. And the king and I came up with a plan."

"Why do I get the feeling I'm not going to like this plan?"

"He already knew a lot about the Shadows, of course," Beck continues.

"Hard not to know, considering they murdered his steward."

"Right. But he needs more information in order to stop them. He needs to find out more about their members, how they operate, how they're recruiting people. Most importantly, he needs to know who their leaders are."

I have a feeling I know where this is going, but I really wish I didn't.

"To get that kind of information, he needs somebody on the inside. Someone he can trust."

I close my eyes. "Please tell me you did not agree to do what I think you agreed to do."

His voice is quiet but no less determined than it always is when he has a plan. "I'm going to infiltrate the Shadows and spy on them for the king."

I open my eyes. "That is the worst possible idea I've ever heard. And I've heard a *lot* of bad ideas from you, Beck."

He sighs. "Listen—"

"No, you listen. You're talking about joining a secret group of criminals that's even more dangerous than the secret group of criminals you're already in, one that has orchestrated a public murder and God knows what else, in order to spy on them and try to get information about them to the king of the Thieves Guild, who is their sworn enemy, and you think you're going to do all of this without getting caught by anyone. Do you even hear yourself?"

"It's the only way," he says. "The king needs someone on the inside that he can trust. He chose me."

I draw my knees up to my chest. "Yeah, about that. Doesn't it seem a little strange to you? I mean, no offense or anything, but you're not exactly one of the Guild's most experienced members. If this is so important and the Shadows are so dangerous, why would the king entrust a thirteen-year-old who only just passed his trial three months ago?"

"That's exactly why he chose me," Beck insists. "If the king chose one of his most experienced members, the Shadows would know instantly that they were a spy. I'm already being recruited by the Shadows. They came to me first, not the other way around. They have no reason to suspect me. But the king knows how loyal I am to him, and I proved it when I went to him in the first place. He trusts me, but the Shadows don't know that."

He makes a reasonable point, but something about the whole thing still seems suspicious. Unless . . .

Unless the king realizes how incredibly risky this assignment is, and he chose Beck for it because he didn't want to send someone more valuable. Didn't want his best assets to end up dead.

"So," Beck continues, "after planning this with the king, I went to the Shadows and told them I'd changed my mind and I wanted to join. They told me there will be a meeting here in Ruhia for new recruits, sometime soon. I'm supposed to wait for further instructions. The problem is, if the Shadows' headquarters is here in Ruhia—and the king and I both suspect it is—then I need to stay here in the city, where I can be closer to them. The guildhall was too risky anyway. I don't want the Shadows to figure out what I'm doing, obviously, but I also don't want loyal Guild members to think I'm really a Shadow."

"Which is why you're hiding out in an abandoned chapel that hopefully no one else knows about."

"Exactly."

"But what's the long-term plan here? Hide out forever?"

"No. This whole Shadow thing is going to end, one way or another. I just have to lay low for a while, just until I have enough info for the king to take them down."

"And if they win? If they take control of the Guild and find out you betrayed them, you can never go back."

"I know." He looks down at the dimming fire in the lantern. "If that happens, I'll just figure something out."

My eyes widen. This is completely unlike him. Beck always has a plan, always strategizes until he comes up with something. His plans are usually ridiculous, but he always has them. If the Shadows win . . . either they'll kill him or they'll force him to run from the only place he's ever called home.

"Now," Beck says, "about your brother."

"Finally you get to the point."

"Mead told me that the Shadows have other targets besides the king. Other people that they want to go after. He showed me a list of names. Kerick was first, of course. But the second name on the list is Ronan A. Rosco."

All the air whooshes out of my lungs like I've been punched in the chest. "That's not possible."

"I know what I saw. I recognized his name right away, since I'd looked up your file before."

"Wait. You found my file *before* seeing his name on the list? Then why were you looking at my file to begin with?"

Beck drops his gaze. "I . . . I just wanted to make sure that your curse got cured and you were okay."

"You went to all that effort to find my file just to check up on me?"

Beck looks very intently at the floor, and I get a funny

feeling in my chest. The topic of Ronan's impending doom suddenly seems like a safer conversation than this, so I steer us back to it. "You're sure it was his name?"

Beck nods.

It has to be some kind of mistake. Or maybe it's a different person. But "Rosco" isn't as common a name here in Ruhia as it is in Azeland, and "Ronan" is even more unusual. And that middle initial, the one I asked him about . . . There's no way that's a coincidence.

"But Ronan's not involved in the Guild or thieving or anything," I say. "He's just a lawyer's apprentice. Why would the Shadows be after him?"

"I don't know. And I don't know who put his name on that list. But clearly the Shadows are serious about going after their targets. Durban won't be the last, if they have their way. That's why I came to warn you."

My head is spinning. "I have to tell him he's in danger. I have to . . ." No. I can't do that. Because if I tell Ronan all of this, he'll tell Mari. And both of them will want to know where I got this information. I don't want to give Beck away. Mari and her protector friends would go after him just as soon as they'd go after the Shadows. "I can't tell him."

"You won't have to. If I can infiltrate the Shadows, I can stop them before they go after any more of their targets. I just need your help."

"I . . . I don't know if I can. I'm not a Guild member. And I don't steal anymore."

"I know. I didn't want to drag you into this mess. But I don't know where else to go. I have no way of knowing who's a Shadow and who isn't, so I don't know who to trust. You're the only person I know outside of the Guild. The only one who can help me."

This admission makes my heart seize up for a second. Sometimes he seems so normal, it's easy to forget that he's never had a life outside of the Guild, never known anything or anyone else.

But it defines him. I knew it when I watched him disappear out that window, and I can never forget it again.

I don't know what to say. I still don't know exactly where we stand after everything that's happened, but if I'm being honest, I just want us to be like we were before.

It's been a long time since I had a real friend.

"How can I help?" I ask finally.

Beck leans back a little, looking relieved. "I haven't exactly worked out all the details yet. But do you think you could meet me here again?"

"Possibly," I say. "My brother is usually at work all day. But we need a way to communicate. I won't know if you need anything, or if something happens and you need to move locations . . ."

"Good point. Let's see . . ." He pauses for a moment, tapping his fingers against his knee. Green lantern light plays across his face.

"Okay, how about this?" he says finally. "That park a

block from here. Near the gate, there's a tree with a knothole in its trunk. We can stash notes there."

"Yeah, that works."

"And maybe we should have some kind of system for when you come up here. Like, knock three times so I know it's you."

"You're going to know it's me anyway," I say. "Nobody else is going to knock first."

"Good point."

This is absurd. There are so many ways this could go wrong. What if Ronan or Mari find out I'm helping him? What if the Shadows find him—and, by extension, me and Ronan? I shouldn't be doing this. I shouldn't even be thinking about doing this. Getting involved with the Guild again—getting involved with *Beck* again—is only going to get me into trouble.

But it's Beck. Who saved my life when he didn't have to, more than once. And if he's right about Ronan being in trouble, then I have to do something. At the very least, I have to find out why my brother's name is on that list, and if it really means what Beck thinks it means.

"Okay," I say. "Let's do it. How about I meet you here tomorrow after my brother goes to work?" I can meet Ronan at the law office afterward like normal. He'll never have to know anything's changed.

"Okay," Beck says.

It feels like hours have passed since we sat down. When

I finally stand, my legs are stiff. "Well, I guess I'd better get back before he notices I'm gone."

We stand awkwardly, staring at each other. The lantern's fire is dying, providing only a few sputtering flames.

"So. I guess I'll see you tomorrow," I say.

"See you tomorrow." A smile twitches the corners of his mouth. "Thanks, Allicat."

I'm suddenly finding it difficult to swallow. "Yeah, whatever."

I turn around and take a few steps away from him. And stop. There's one more thing I need to say.

I turn around again. "Hey, Beck?"

"Yeah?"

"Thanks. For sending Mead. For the money, I mean. You didn't have to . . ."

The lantern goes dark, and I can't see his face anymore. "Yeah," he says, "I kind of did."

"Well, thanks."

"You're welcome. And thank you for taking the fall for me. I saw the transcripts of your interview with the judge. I know you didn't rat me out and kept the Guild a secret."

"Yeah, well, I kind of had to, didn't I?"

I still can't see his face, but I imagine he's smiling.

"I'm glad we got that off our chests," I say. "Now let's never talk about this ever again."

"Whatever you say, Allicat."

Chapter Six

After walking back from the chapel, I tiptoe blindly back into the apartment building, trying not to wake anyone up. With my luck, they'll think I'm a burglar and call Mari to arrest me.

There are so many ways that all of this could go wrong that I'm beginning to lose track of them. But what else can I do? It's not like I can tell Ronan about Beck. Even if we could convince Ronan not to turn Beck in, he'd probably tell Mari, and then she'd do it. I could try to make something up, tell him a friend needs help . . . but he'd be too suspicious. He knows I don't have any friends in this city who aren't thieves.

I stumble across the fourth-floor landing in the dark and freeze, listening to the thud echo off the walls. The noise fades until I don't hear anything except for my own heart-beat. I creep over to the stairwell door and slip through it.

Ronan and Mari are standing in the hallway. Both of

their apartment doors are open, lights streaming into the hall.

Oops.

They look stunned to see me. Mari is clearly frozen in the middle of saying something, her mouth hanging slightly open. They stare at me without speaking.

"Er, hi?" I say.

"Alli." The relief in Ronan's voice surprises me. "Where have you been?"

"I, um, went for a walk. I needed to clear my head."

"You went alone?" Mari says. "At night?" She sounds concerned, but she might be faking it. It's her job to sound concerned.

"I didn't go far," I say. Not technically a lie. "Just wandered around a bit."

"You just disappeared," Ronan says. "I thought . . ."

It takes me a second, but then I get it. He thought I'd run away.

Given my track record, I guess that's only fair. But then he went running to Mari the protector to . . . what? Report me missing? Send every protector in the city after me? So they could send me to another orphanage, another prison?

Mari and Ronan exchange glances. They seem to be arguing about something. Again. Whatever it is, Ronan wins this time. Mari presses her lips together, changing her mind about whatever she was going to say. "Well, if you're all right," she says, "I'll head back to bed, then."

"Sorry," I say unconvincingly.

Mari says good night and disappears into her apartment, and Ronan gestures to ours, where the front door hangs open. "I don't suppose you have my key?" he says.

"Oh, right. I didn't want to get locked out," I say. Also not a lie.

We head inside, and I return the key to him. He makes a production of latching the front door behind us, like he's trying to decide what to say. Or trying to draw this moment out because he doesn't want to say it.

"Well," I say, faking a loud yawn, "I'll be going to bed."

"Wait." He turns around, slipping the key into his pocket. "We need to talk."

"Sorry I disappeared on you. Really. Didn't mean to. Won't do it again." I take a giant step backward in the direction of my bedroom. "Good talk."

"Alli." He has a really remarkable way of putting a lot of emotion into my name. A minute ago, he said it in an "oh thank God" kind of way. Now it's more like a "you're in so much trouble, young lady" way. He's going to make a great lawyer, with that kind of skill.

He sits down in his armchair, settling in for the long haul. I don't think I'm getting out of this one.

Shoulders slumping, I shuffle to the sofa and take a seat, close enough to the edge that I can bolt if necessary.

Ronan rubs one hand over his eyes. He looks tired. "I'm not mad at you," he says.

"Oh." So much has happened since our fight, I almost forgot that I'm in trouble.

"I'm just trying to understand," he says. "I know you've been through a lot, and I know I'm not doing enough to make it easier for you. The truth is . . . the truth is, I don't know how to do this. I don't know how to be an older brother, and I definitely don't know how to be a parent. I'm still figuring it all out."

For a moment, I'm stunned into silence. *He's* figuring it out? *He* doesn't know how to do this? I thought it was just me. It *is* just me.

It takes me another minute to work up the nerve to admit it out loud. "You're not the problem," I say quietly. "I am."

His eyes widen, and he shakes his head. "No, you aren't. I meant what I said before. You might have a talent for getting into trouble"—he smiles—"but you're a good kid. I know."

"How?" Earlier tonight I shouted it at him. Now the question is a whisper.

"I can tell that you're trying."

"But not succeeding," I say.

"You might be a little more successful if you didn't go *looking* for trouble."

An image of Beck in the chapel flashes in my head. "I think trouble finds me."

This time his smile is sad. "You want to tell me why you're so opposed to tutoring?"

I pause. "I just know that it won't go very well."

"Why not?"

The question surprises me. Adults usually just object instead of asking. "I'm not exactly a great student. Never have been. And I didn't . . . I just didn't want things to go badly."

"I see," Ronan says slowly. "And that's it?" He's turned the full force of his lawyerly skepticism on me.

"Am I on trial here?"

"No." He waits.

"I just didn't want you to be disappointed in me, is all."

"Oh, Alli. I'm not going to be disappointed."

"You mean you aren't already?"

He looks taken aback for a second. I can practically see him riffling through my file in his brain, putting it together. "You think I'm disappointed in you because of what happened at the Athertons'?"

No wonder Avin-what's-his-name wanted Ronan for an apprentice. He's scary good at this. "Why wouldn't you be?"

"You made some mistakes. But you also saved a girl's life that night."

I shrug uncomfortably. "'Saved' is putting it generously."

"I don't think so."

"Only if 'saved' means 'almost accidentally got her killed out of sheer stupidity but then miraculously didn't,' then yeah."

"That's not how I heard it."

"Well, you heard wrong. And I don't want to talk about it again."

"Okay." He senses the edge creeping into my voice and literally backs off, leaning farther into his chair. "But you know we're going to have to talk about preparing you for an apprenticeship eventually."

"Believe it or not, the thought had crossed my mind." Because he mentions it constantly. For someone who acts so forgiving, he sure is eager to get rid of me.

"Okay," he says, ignoring my sarcasm. "I'll spare you the lecture. We'll revisit the tutoring issue another time. But, Alli?"

"Yes?"

"I don't want you wandering around alone at night. And when you do need to *go for a walk*"—the way he says it makes it clear he knows perfectly well that's not what I was doing—"I need you to at least let me know, okay?"

"Gotcha."

"All right. Lecture over."

I spring to my feet. "I'm going to bed then. Night."

"Good night."

I race to my room. Once the door is closed, I lean against it and exhale slowly. I have to admit, that went better than I expected. I can't remember the last time an adult was so . . . understanding. So willing to listen, instead of lecture.

So willing to see the best in me.

Despite his faults—his protector girlfriend being number one—Ronan is probably the best thing that has ever happened to me. I'd be stupid to mess this up, to throw away this chance. He's the only family I have, the one person who has any interest whatsoever in my life. The only person whose life *I* have any interest in. So I need to make this work for as long as I possibly can, to give us a shot at having something resembling a real sibling relationship.

This is my one chance at family, and I'm not going to let anything get in the way of it.

Especially not the Shadow Guild. I'll help Beck stop them, if that's what it takes.

But I don't know how to do both—how to be the good kid Ronan sees and the runaway whose help Beck needs. How to truly be reformed while also keeping secrets, while being a liar.

How to be both Ronan's sister and a thief.

As soon as Ronan leaves for work the next day, I rush through breakfast, preparing to meet Beck at the chapel again. I stuff some extra bread and a canteen of water into my bag, because I'm not sure if Beck actually has anything to eat. A guilty little knot forms in my stomach. Is it stealing from Ronan to give his food to Beck? Ronan wouldn't care if I were the one eating it, so does it matter? I'm not sure, so I decide to stop thinking about it.

It's way easier to walk through the woods in the daylight, but the trudge up the hill is still slow going. I'm breathing hard and covered in leaves and twigs by the time I reach the chapel.

Inside, it's slightly less creepy now, with bright sunbeams

streaming in through the stained glass. Beck lounges on a pew, wearing the same clothes he was in last night. His eyes are closed, but I'm sure he knows I'm here. I walk over and sit down in the pew across the aisle from him.

"Bring any food?" he asks without opening his eyes.

"Hello to you too."

He looks up, grinning. "So that's a yes, then?"

I tap my bag with two fingers. "You know, I'm not sure you really deserve this."

"Who, me?" he says innocently, like a puppy asking for a treat.

I sigh and toss him the bag.

"Maybe I could bring you some more stuff later," I say. "You know, blankets and candles and"—I glance at the filth below our feet—"maybe a dust rag or two . . ."

Beck laughs. "Honestly, it's fine. I'd settle for the food." He pries out the bread and eagerly tears off a chunk.

As Beck eats, meticulously catching every crumb, I perch on the back of the pew beside him, making circles in the dust with my boots.

"So . . . ," he says hesitantly. "Everything still going okay with your brother?"

"Pretty much. He almost caught me last night, coming back, but I made up a story and he mostly bought it."

Beck nods, still chewing. "Did you get in trouble?"

"Not really. He's not very strict, I guess. I don't know. How strict are guardians supposed to be normally?"

Beck laughs. "You're asking the wrong person."

"True. I guess he is strict, by Guild standards."

"Yeah, but you probably shouldn't judge by Guild standards."

"Probably not." I pause. "So aside from the whole Shadows thing, how's everything in the Guild been? Since you passed your trial?"

Beck swallows. "It's kind of hard to think about anything but the Shadows. But it was okay, I guess."

"Just okay?"

He hesitates again. Whatever it was he wanted to say, he seems to change his mind. "It was great, really, being a full member. Everything I thought it would be."

There's something hidden in his voice that he's not telling me, so I smile to try and lighten the mood. "I mean, I know it had to be terrible without me there, of course."

"Of course. We could hardly bring ourselves to carry on."

"You didn't win any more ice sledding races without me, did you?"

"Oh, definitely not. You know we were all completely hopeless at ice sledding until you graced us with your presence."

"Obviously," I say. "You needed me to show you how to *really* race."

"And nearly got killed doing it," Beck says, almost fondly. "I still can't believe you pulled that stunt on your first race."

"Only race," I correct without thinking.

That kills the mood quick.

Beck takes a long, slow sip of water before speaking again. "I think the whole sledding team missed you. Mead and Dryn were already fighting about who was going to recruit you first."

I look at the wooden pew beneath my feet, smudging the dust circle I've made with my boot. "Yeah, well, too bad that didn't work out."

Beck sits up straighter, as if he's gathering courage for whatever it is he wants to say. "Maybe it still could."

"What?"

"There might be a way you could come back to the Guild."

My heart speeds up, as if to keep pace with my racing thoughts. "What are you talking about? I failed my trial."

"I know. And normally that would be it, you couldn't come back. But I think maybe the king might be willing to make an exception, if you help me out. The Shadows are kind of a big deal. Anyone who helps the king take them down will gain his favor."

I sigh. "You have some kind of plan in mind, don't you?"

He sets down the water canteen and leans back, looking up at me. "There's a part of this whole Shadows thing that I haven't told you yet."

"Oh great, there's *more*?"

Beck drums his fingers against his knees. "Have you ever heard of the King's Coin?"

"Um, no."

"Okay, so, you know how rulers normally have a crown, right? To symbolize their rule or whatever."

"Yeah, so?"

"So the king of the Guild doesn't have a literal crown. But there's this silver coin that, according to legend, has been passed down through generations of Guild kings. It symbolizes the transfer of their power, just like a crown would."

"Okay . . ."

"But it's even more than that. There are all of these stories and legends about the coin being magical, about how it bestows some kind of power on the king. Nobody knows for sure how much of that is true, but enough people believe it that it helps the king maintain his authority in the Guild. Nobody wants to go against him, because nobody is quite sure what kind of power he might have. If anyone does successfully kill a current king, they have to take the coin in order to officially take control within the Guild."

"Okay, but it's still just a coin, right? I mean, how hard can it be to take it? It's easier to steal a coin than a crown."

"Well, yeah, that's kind of the problem. See, kings have to hide or guard the coin carefully, to make sure that no one steals it. Anyone who does could challenge their right to rule."

"But that doesn't make sense. If someone stole, say, the king of Ruhia's crown, that wouldn't automatically make them king."

"Right, but that's where the Guild works differently than a monarchy. This is a guild of *thieves*. Stealing is associated with power. To steal the King's Coin is to steal his power—symbolically, at least, and maybe even literally, if the coin really is magic. Some people even say that the coin *chooses* the king, that it can only be claimed by those who are worthy of it."

"So, if I were to steal the coin from Kerick, the Guild would just let me be king?"

"It wouldn't be quite that simple. Kerick would just try to kill you and take the coin back, and some would remain loyal to him and likely help. But it would give you a claim to the throne, for sure. And—here's the important part—you can't really have a claim to the throne *without* it."

He runs a hand through his hair, making it stick up all over the place. "You remember how I told you before that Kerick had a sister? One who helped him overthrow the previous king?"

"Yeah."

"Well, there's this legend," he says. "I don't know how much truth is in it. I was really young when all this happened, so I don't remember it myself. But they say that Kerick and his sister figured that neither of them could face the king alone—possibly because of the coin's magical power—but together they took him down. After the two of them killed the previous king, it was Kerick who took the coin from him."

"Let me guess. Kerick suddenly decides he doesn't want to share power with his sister?"

"Right. The story goes that Kerick and his sister fought each other, and she tried to get the coin from him. You remember that scar Kerick has on his hand?"

Now that he mentions it, I do remember. When I met Kerick, there was a long, angry gash on the back of his hand.

"According to the version of the story that I heard, his sister gave him that scar. He was holding the coin in his palm, and she sliced the back of his hand with a knife to try to force him to drop it."

"But it didn't work?"

"It didn't work. Kerick kept the coin. Now, this is where the story gets important. Like I said before, some Guild members were loyal to one of the siblings over the other. Some wanted Kerick to be king. Some wanted his sister. But it was decided: Kerick had the King's Coin, so Kerick would be king. Even her loyal supporters agreed. No matter who they preferred, enough people recognized the legitimacy of the coin. She left the Guild and was never seen again.

"When people in the Guild talk about the importance of the coin, this is what they mean. If there's a dispute over Guild leadership, it's possession of the coin that will decide things."

I'm starting to get where he's going with this. "So if I were, say, the leader of the Shadows and I wanted to kill Kerick and make myself king, I'd also have to figure out how to get this coin from him?"

"Exactly. Now, here's the problem: The Shadows already have it."

"What?"

"When I spoke with the king, he didn't just ask me to spy on the Shadows. He also asked me to find the coin. It's missing, and he thinks the Shadows have stolen it. That's why they're doing all of this now, why they suddenly started recruiting people and everything. All they have to do is get rid of Kerick and his most loyal followers, and the rest of the Guild will have to accept their leader as the new king. Now that they have the coin, the Shadows have a real claim to the throne. And Kerick's claim is weakened."

"Wait, so how can Kerick still be king at all? If he doesn't have the coin?"

"That's the only good news. No one in the Guild knows it's missing yet. I'm the only person Kerick told. He thinks the Shadows stole it in secret, and they're hiding it until they're ready to make their big move. We have to steal it back before that happens."

I sit up. "What do you mean *we*?"

"This is the part where I thought you could help me. Searching for the coin is way less dangerous than infiltrating the Shadows, but it's probably even more important. If you help me find it and both of us bring it back to the Guild, the king will probably reward you. And he already knows there were, er, complications during your trial. The only reason you failed was that you stayed behind to help someone. He might be willing to make an exception and let you back into the Guild."

His words hit me like a blast of cold air, unexpected and painful. I have to let all of this settle in my mind for a second. "You really think that would work?"

"Yes."

My stomach churns. I am not supposed to want this. I thought I'd already made my decision. I said no to the Guild, said no to stealing and being a thief. I said I'd never go back. Being in the Guild would mean getting more innocent people killed or hurt, like the Athertons, and I already decided the price isn't worth it. Besides, I have Ronan now. I have a real, actual chance at living a normal life with my brother.

But.

Ronan is already planning to get rid of me, to send me off to some apprenticeship somewhere. And things aren't exactly going smoothly regardless. This could give me an alternative—a place to go if I need to.

But do I even want that? I don't really want to be a Guild member anymore . . . Right?

Okay, maybe the idea of ice sledding again sounds fun. And there would be advantages to living in the guildhall. No more sneaking around at home, no more lying to my brother and keeping secrets from him, no more pressure to be Ronan Rosco's good little sister. Plus, I could see everyone I met in the Guild before—Mead and Peakes and Dryn and Flint and . . .

And Beck.

Most importantly of all, I could be with Beck.

But becoming a thief again and hurting people, getting people killed—it isn't worth it. I already decided. I made up my mind. I can't go back. Besides, I could never tell Ronan where I'd gone. I'd probably never see him again.

Would he care? Or would he be glad to have me out of his life? One less nuisance to worry about?

No. I look down at my hands. I force myself to see them, to remember Ariannorah Atherton's blood pooling all over them, while her mother lay dead on the floor. I did that. We did that. The Guild did that. I can't ever let myself forget.

But there is another option. If the king would be willing to reward me for finding the coin . . . Maybe joining the Guild isn't the only favor I could ask for. What if I just ask for money instead? The Guild has plenty of gold. If the king agrees to give me some money, maybe I can give it to Ronan. Then it won't matter if he loses his apprenticeship. Maybe I could convince him to let me stay. Maybe it will be enough.

And if not, I can always take the money and go live on my own.

"You don't have to decide right now," Beck says quietly. He's watching my reaction carefully. "But if you help me find the coin, it could be an option later."

I can't quite look at him. He might be upset if I tell him I'd rather live with Ronan than join the Guild, and I can't bring myself to say it. I should keep this whole plan to myself for now. "Let's say, theoretically, that I might be thinking about it," I say. "What would we have to do to find this coin?"

"The king gave me an address, here in Ruhia. He said he thinks the coin might be there, but he can't check himself, in case it's being guarded. Which means I can't check it out either, in case the Shadows notice me poking around. But you can. It's just a vendor's cart in a marketplace. All you have to do is look for the coin."

"Well, that doesn't sound *so* bad. . . ."

Beck grins. "I knew you could do it."

"Maybe," I say quickly. "I don't want to be too involved in thieving and stuff. I've been down this road before, you may recall."

"Right, sure."

"Stop smiling."

His grin widens. "Meet me here tomorrow after you've checked it out?"

"I suppose . . ."

"Great." His spirits apparently restored, Beck reaches for his food again and tears off another hunk of bread.

"Why does the king think this coin is in some marketplace, anyway?"

"He didn't really say." Beck frowns. "Something about how the vendor might be involved." He gives me directions to the market and a description of the cart I'm supposed to look for.

I glance up at the windows, trying to guess the time, but I can't see the sky well enough through the stained glass. I'm probably running way late by now. I have to get my usual shopping done and meet Ronan at his office like normal or he'll get suspicious.

Beck catches me looking outside. "It's okay if you have to go."

"I kinda do," I say reluctantly. It's so shadowy and depressing in here, and the idea of leaving Beck alone is giving me a weird feeling in the pit of my stomach. I have to remind myself that this is *Beck*. He grew up in the caves of the Thieves Guild. He knows his way around hideouts. He's used to being on his own. And he knows how to take care of himself.

He just looks so . . . alone.

"It's fine," he says again. He makes a big show of leaning back into the pew like it's super comfortable, even though it creaks ominously when he shifts his weight.

"Okay then," I say, hopping down from the back of my own pew. "If you're sure . . ."

He waves me away, taking another bite of bread. "See you tomorrow."

"See you."

I walk back down the aisle. At the door, I hesitate. The feeling in my stomach won't go away.

And I can't help thinking about what happened before. About how, until last night, the last time we saw each other was when Beck walked away from me, out a window, into freedom. And he didn't look back.

Now I'm the one walking away, and I understand why

he didn't look. Because if I do, I won't be able to keep walking.

So I keep my eyes fixed straight ahead, even as I pull the door closed. But I can feel both Beck and the statue of Saint Harona staring at me as I leave them behind in shadow and dust.

Chapter Seven

Ronan doesn't seem to notice that anything's wrong. When I meet him at his law office after leaving Beck in the chapel and running my errands, he only asks how today's shopping went, to which I shrug noncommittally, and then I change the subject. Mari doesn't come over for dinner, but I'm not sure whether it's because she's working late or because she and Ronan are still fighting about me. I can't work up the nerve to ask him.

Ronan is quiet at dinner, seeming lost in thought. He sifts through a mountain of paperwork beside his plate while he eats (a habit that Mari tries to talk him out of, but he always does it when she's not around).

I'm beginning to suspect that Ronan is working harder than is normal for an apprentice. He's definitely worried about losing his job, even if he won't really say so. How much longer does he have before his apprenticeship ends? What happens to him if Avinoch's doesn't offer him a permanent position?

I know what will happen to me, of course. Ronan will send me packing.

As I pile my dinner dishes into the sink, he looks up suddenly, checking his watch. "Oops," he says, almost to himself. "We're late."

"Late for what?" He didn't say anything about having plans tonight.

"I meant to tell you earlier," Ronan says, stuffing his papers into a messy pile and rising from the table. "It's Wintersnight."

I'm still not getting why this is significant.

"There's a festival," Ronan says, seeing my blank look. "One of the biggest parades comes through this part of the city, just down the street from here. We should watch it."

"Um, okay," I say, still not really getting it. We have a Wintersnight festival in Azeland, of course. It's to celebrate the coming of winter and all that. At the orphanage, we used to peek out the gate to watch the parade pass by—people in blue-and-white costumes dancing and singing and stuff. It was never one of the more interesting parades, though. And both Ruhia and Azeland have *lots* of saints' day festivals, so I don't get why this particular one matters.

Ronan smiles. "You'll see," he says. "Wintersnight in Ruhia is . . . different from what we're used to in Azeland."

It's a silly thing to notice, but I like the way he says "we." Like Ronan and I have some kind of shared experience, being from Azeland, even though we didn't actually experience any of it together. Somehow we're united in being outsiders.

Ronan crosses to the fireplace, grabs both of our coats, and holds out mine. "We can still get a good spot if we hurry," he says.

I'm not totally sure I want to brave the cold for some silly festival. But I don't want to refuse Ronan either. I guess it might be nice to spend an evening doing something with my brother. Reluctantly I take my coat from him and button it up.

We make it downstairs and out of the building in record time and hurry through the darkened streets. We're hardly the only ones. Everywhere I look, people are out, bundled in coats, all making their way in roughly the same direction. There are lots of young kids, running and laughing and shouting. Several people are waving Ruhian banners and flags.

So Ronan wasn't wrong. There's *something* going on.

A block from the apartment, the people congregate all along one street, lining it on both sides. Ronan reaches for my hand and holds on to me as we make our way through the crowd. I can see several parents doing the same for their kids as we pass, and something warm and heavy fills my chest.

We reach a spot at the front of the crowd. While everyone assembles on the sidewalk, several protectors walk down the street, clearing people out of the way. The flash of their red uniforms still makes my heart seize up for a second. I try to force it to calm down. I don't have to be afraid; I'm allowed to be here. Just an ordinary citizen now, watching a parade with my brother. I don't have anything to hide.

Except for the thief I'm hiding in an abandoned chapel up the street, that is.

I'm so distracted by the protectors—and the pounding of my own heart—that I miss whatever it is Ronan asks me, and he has to repeat the question. "Do you want one?"

I look where he's pointing. A vendor is making his way down our side of the street, pushing a little cart full of steaming cups of something. I don't answer, because I don't know what it is, but Ronan doesn't wait for my response; he tosses the seller a few jamars and grabs two cups from the cart as it passes.

"Spiced apple cider," Ronan says, pressing one of the cups into my hands. "A Wintersnight tradition. Careful, it's hot."

I take a tentative sip, and my mouth is flooded with warm sugar and cinnamon and nutmeg. It's so delicious that I take too big a second sip, nearly scalding my tongue.

"How long have you been coming to this?" I ask when my mouth has sufficiently recovered. "This is amazing!"

Ronan smiles. "The apothecary showed me when we first moved to Ruhia. He used to take all of his apprentices to Wintersnight. He said it was the best of the city's festivals all year."

I take another, more careful sip of cider. "Did you like him? The apothecary?"

"Very much. He was . . . he was the only family I had for a long time. Until now, of course." He gives my shoulder an affectionate nudge.

I'm saved from having to figure out how to respond to that by the rumbling of drumbeats echoing up the street. I'm familiar with the rhythm—it's something I've heard in Azelandian parades—but being so close to the drums, as opposed to listening through the orphanage's garden gate, makes everything so much louder and more intense. The beat pulses in my bones.

The drummers make their way up the street, clad in matching blue uniforms. They're followed by two figures in dark cloaks whose hands are raised. Above them, glowing spheres of magical blue light dance in the air, flickering in time to the drumbeat and illuminating the incoming parade below.

Ronan nudges my arm again and leans close to my ear to be heard over the noise. "This is where it really gets good."

A few feet behind the magicians trots a small white horse, its mane decked in festive blue and silver ribbons. A young girl with raven-black hair and a sparkly blue gown sits astride it. From what I remember of the Sisters' lessons at the orphanage, this must be a young Saint Zioni.

I can't say that I paid much attention to any of the Sisters' history lessons, but since Zioni is supposedly my patron, I did give slightly more consideration to her story. Zioni was a young Ruhian girl whose little sister was lost in a snowstorm.

No one dared brave the blizzard to look for the missing girl, but Zioni charged into the woods on her horse, determined to find her sister. Everyone thought that both Zioni and her sister would surely be killed—but when sunrise came and the snow had stopped, Zioni emerged from the woods, carrying her sister, both of them alive and unharmed. When asked how she had survived, Zioni said that she'd prayed for protection from the cold, and God had kept them warm. This was the first miracle attributed to her and the reason she later became the patron saint of winter.

I always thought this was kind of a boring origin story, but there's something fascinating about watching it play out in front of us now. The crowd is quiet, almost hushed, as pretend-Zioni draws her horse to a stop. The magical blue spheres dance overheard, illuminating the scene as the two magicians creep forward, waving their hands. Suddenly a blast of magical snowflakes flies into the air, swirling around pretend-Zioni and her horse.

The horse looks unimpressed with this display, but pretend-Zioni sticks to the script. She throws her head back, looking up to heaven, and begins to sing. The words are super old-fashioned and boring, like something out of a hymnbook, but her voice is pretty. The crowd watches silently, enchanted by the performance.

The girl stops singing, and silence hangs in the air. Then, just as suddenly, every magical snowflake surrounding her stops moving. They hover in place, shimmering and still.

Zioni's prayerful song has frozen the storm in its tracks.

Pretend-Zioni nudges her horse forward, and as it moves, the snowflakes in the air literally spin out of the way, surrounding but never touching her. She lets out a cry, so suddenly that I almost jump, and leaps down from the horse. Out of nowhere—or, rather, out from behind one of the magicians who was shielding her—a second girl appears, lying in the middle of the street on a blanket of white. This smaller girl wears a long white dress, and white ribbons are strung through her hair. Zioni's sister, who is supposedly almost frozen in a snowbank.

But as pretend-Zioni approaches, the girl stirs to life. Zioni begins to sing again as she lifts her supposed sister into her arms, snowflakes still suspended in the air around her, and carries the girl down the street. I crane my neck to follow their progress as they walk farther and farther away from where Ronan and I are standing.

"Is that it?" I whisper to him. The magical snowflakes were kind of cool, sure, but I still don't get what was worth rushing out here for.

Ronan laughs. "Just wait."

As if on cue, the snowflakes hanging in the air suddenly whirl and multiply, moving faster and faster, bursting into a spinning storm. From the epicenter, a single figure emerges. A flute player, wearing a shimmering costume, performs the same melody Zioni sang a moment ago. From up the street, the next batch of performers emerges—a group of kids in glittery snowflake costumes, dancing to the music.

The song picks up tempo, going from soft and entreating to swift and celebratory. The swirl of snow bursts apart with a flash of blue light, and a flurry of silver and white confetti rains down as the crowd cheers. The drumbeats start up again, adding to the song, and more and more snowflake dancers fill the street.

Ronan taps my shoulder and points, as excited as the little kids surrounding us, as the snowflake dancers disappear up the street and another swirl of magic ushers in the next performer. A massive pair of thilastri, their blue feathers adorned in silver sparkles, comes into view. They're pulling a huge tiered sleigh that's festooned with ribbons and streamers and glitter. On top of the sleigh rests a throne made of ice, and sitting upon it is the grown-up version of Zioni, a woman with the same dark hair and an even more magnificent blue ball gown.

The crowd roars and cheers and gasps as adult pretend-Zioni smiles and waves. The drumbeats crescendo, the tempo quickens again, and Zioni raises her hands above her head.

A streak of blue light soars into the air, rises above our heads, and explodes. Fireworks burst above us in a cascade of light.

Old Alli is tempted to point out all the silly things about this performance. Like, why exactly is adult Zioni sitting on an ice throne? She isn't a queen. Also, I highly doubt that young Zioni went into the woods wearing an ornate sparkly ball gown during a blizzard.

But New Alli has to admit that this is, maybe, a little bit fun.

Ronan grins at me, plucking a piece of white confetti from his eyelash. "What do you think? Better than Wintersnight in Azeland?"

"Possibly," I say, smiling back at him. "Although, the apple cider is clearly the best part."

Ronan laughs. "I think I got too much confetti in mine," he says, looking woefully into his cup.

"You mean you didn't already drink it all before the confetti part? For shame."

"You're right. I should've finished."

"I can see I'm going to have to teach you how to properly appreciate your beverages."

He nods, still smiling. "I'm lost without your guidance."

The crowd gradually disperses as the performers vanish, and vendors make their way through the confetti-strewn street, offering people more cider and candy and little pennants with the Ruhian flag on them.

Ronan quickly discards our old cider cups and purchases two more. I shouldn't let him spend this much money, but I don't feel quite guilty enough to refuse it. The drink keeps me warm as we trudge back in the direction of the apartment, waving glitter and confetti and magical snowflakes out of the air.

"Do you like it here better than Azeland?" I ask Ronan as we reach our building.

He pauses, giving my question way more consideration

than it probably deserves. "There are some things that I like better about Ruhia, and some things that I miss about Azeland."

"Like what?"

"Ruhia is much older, and I like how rich its history is. There are cathedrals here that have stood for centuries, for instance. And I love some of its traditions—like Wintersnight—that Azeland doesn't have. But I miss how vibrant and energetic Azeland feels, how bright and busy its marketplaces are, how it always feels like something exciting is about to happen there."

"I miss the colors," I say. The marketplaces, the buildings . . . everything in Azeland is brighter.

He nods. "Me too."

"And the warmth, obviously. That's like the number one selling point."

"What about the lack of snow?" Ronan teases.

"That too."

We reach the apartment, and Ronan ushers me inside. I set down my empty cider cup and unbutton my coat. "Everything here is very . . . traditional," Ronan says. "There are families that have been doing the same thing in the same way for generations. Take my law office—it's always been Avinoch and Co., with new generations of Avinochs inheriting it. It makes it harder, for . . ."

"For people like us," I finish for him.

He smiles wryly. "Right. I've been very lucky to have

Avinoch take me on, but I don't know what the future will hold. It's hard to make a name for yourself here."

"Have you ever thought about going back to Azeland?"

"I considered it once. But I think it would be just as hard for me there, since I no longer know anyone in the city. It would be starting from scratch."

"Oh." I'm glad he's telling me this, but it also scares me. No wonder he wants to send me away when I turn thirteen. The last thing he needs is a troublemaking little sister to look after.

But I *do* want to stay with my brother. I wasn't sure before; I hardly dared to hope that it might work out. But it's getting harder to deny that I like Ronan, and I like spending time with him. I might have a few complaints, but let's face it: Living with my brother is the best thing that's ever happened to me.

Helping Beck is risky, in the short term. It's going to get me into trouble, and might even jeopardize things with Ronan if he finds out what I'm doing. But if Beck is right about what that list means, if Ronan's name really is on it . . .

Ronan smiles ruefully as he shakes a fleck of glitter off his shirt and takes another sip of cider. He's so calm, so carefree. Which he wouldn't be at all if he knew about the list. Should I tell him? Warn him somehow?

But I have no idea how that conversation would work. *Hey, so, by the way, I think there are some dangerous thieves who want to kill you for no apparent reason, and I know this because another thief told me. . . .* There's no way I can say that. I can't tell him where I got the information, or explain about the Guild and the Shadows.

Besides, I don't even really know anything yet. Maybe the list doesn't mean what we think it means. Maybe there are two different Ronan A. Roscos. Maybe he isn't in danger at all.

Something in my gut tells me that isn't true, but I don't want to make a big deal out of this until I have more evidence, until I know who put his name on that list and why. There's no point in freaking Ronan out and potentially getting Beck arrested when I don't know anything for sure.

Beck and I will figure this out, somehow, and stop the Shadows if that's what it takes. I'll make sure Ronan is safe.

I don't know the truth yet, but I'll find it.

Chapter Eight

The next morning, I speed through breakfast as quickly as possible. Ronan, who must've stayed up all night judging by his bleary eyes, looks a little taken aback. "Big plans for today?" he asks. I don't think I'm imaging the note of suspicion in his voice.

"Not really." I shove another spoonful of oatmeal into my mouth.

"Why the rush?"

"No reason."

He rubs his eyes tiredly. "Well, don't choke on your food."

"Okay." But I eat faster. I've got to search for the coin in the marketplace today and spend time in the chapel with Beck before meeting Ronan at his office, and I want to get started right away.

I practically have to drag him out of the building, but finally Ronan leaves for work. A few minutes later, I'm bundled up in my coat and heading out the door. The second I step out onto the sidewalk, I'm met with a blast of ice-cold wind. I shove my hands into my pockets, wishing I'd worn the gloves Mari bought me.

I follow the main streets, which are still bustling at this hour as people make their way to work and apprenticeships and tutoring and whatever else it is that normal people do. The big marketplace is only a few blocks south.

I make it to my destination without incident. Marketplaces in Ruhia are much more structured than those in Azeland. There aren't any shiny tents dyed with bright colors, no mobs of people clamoring for deals, no tangle of stalls and wares and bodies. Instead vendors have little wooden carts that are all lined up in rows, and people proceed from one cart to another in an orderly fashion. It's *boring.*

And, as a quiet little voice in my head points out, it makes it much harder to steal here, without the chaos to hide you. But I quickly tell the little voice to shut up. I'm not here to steal. Not today, not ever again.

I do have to admit that the Ruhian system makes it much easier to locate what you're looking for. I spot the right vendor immediately—a silk peddler's cart painted dark red and gray, with a banner on the front declaring BEST SILK IN THE CITY. Just like how Beck described it. It's a small cart, not much room to hide the King's Coin or anything else on it. Okay, this should be easy. Just go over and take a look around. . . .

As I approach the cart, the vendor standing behind it

brightens. He's a young man, maybe Ronan's age, with tidy brown hair and a large crooked nose. "Good afternoon," he says cheerfully. "How can I help you today?"

"Er, hi," I say. "Could you . . ." I need to distract him somehow, get him away from the cart.

"Are you looking for anything in particular?" He gestures toward the array of brightly colored silks and fabrics.

"Um, no. I actually just need directions," I say, stalling for time. "I got a little turned around a few blocks back."

"No problem," he says, seeming not at all disappointed that I'm not a paying customer. "Where are you trying to go?"

"Um . . . Avinoch and Co.," I blurt, because it's the first thing that pops into my head. "The law office."

His expression changes for a second, but then he smiles. "Ah, yes, I know the one. It's about three blocks west, then two more south. If you see Grammercy Gardens, you've gone too far. Look for Thistle Street and you can't miss it."

"Thanks," I say slowly, still stalling. How can I get him away from his cart?

He frowns, looking concerned. "Are you sure you should be wandering about by yourself? Is there anyone who can accompany you to Avinoch's?"

"I'm thirteen," I say indignantly, because it's *almost* true. "And anyway, my brother works there. I'm going to meet him."

That funny expression passes over his face again, so quickly that I may have imagined it. "All right, then," he says with another big smile. "Have a nice day."

I still need to get him away from his cart. And I need to get information about him somehow. Well, nothing like the direct approach. "Excuse me. What's your name?"

His eyebrows wrinkle in confusion, but he's still polite. "Garil Gannon."

The name doesn't mean anything to me, but I file it away to tell Beck later. "Right, well, thanks for the directions, Mr. Gannon." At the last second, an idea pops into my head. "Actually, would you mind helping me with something?"

"Of course, of course," he says.

"A friend of mine is actually here in the marketplace with me," I say. "She's just up the street. I was hoping to buy a birthday gift without her noticing, so I wandered up here, but then I got a little lost. . . . Anyway, would you mind keeping her distracted for me, just for a minute, while I pick out a gift?" If he stops to think about it for a second, he'll realize this story doesn't make any sense. I offer a quick prayer to Saint Ailara.

"Of course," he says. "Happy to help. But, er . . ." He glances down at his cart.

"I'll watch your cart for you," I say quickly. "I'll just be over there, at the"—I turn around and glance at the cart across the street—"perfume place."

"Well, all right, as long as you keep an eye out. There are thieves in this market, you know."

I try not to laugh. "So I've heard."

"Who am I looking for?"

"Um, a girl about my age, with blond hair and, um, green eyes, wearing a pink jacket," I say, making up the details at random. I point in the direction I came from. "Two blocks that way. She was buying some, um, bread, last I saw her."

"All right. I'll go look."

"Keep her from coming this way, just for a couple of minutes," I say.

As soon as the man disappears around the corner, I rush behind his cart. I don't have time for stealth, so I just start shoving fabrics out of the way. He'll know I ransacked it, but I can't worry about that right now.

The top two shelves of the cart are covered in nothing but bolts of fabric. The cart itself is smoothly carved wood, with no nooks or crannies that might be hiding a coin. Short of carving holes in the shelves to see if they're hollow, I don't think the coin is there.

The final shelf is the one hidden from customers' view, walled in on three sides. There are a few personal possessions here—a pair of eyeglasses, a wallet, a jug of water. There's nothing else, except—

A coin pouch.

Small and red with a drawstring top, and absolutely brimming with coins.

I don't have time to dump them all out and hunt through them to see if they're anything other than ordinary jamars. The vendor could be back at any second, once he fails to find someone fitting the random description I gave him.

But there's nowhere else on the cart that the coin could be hidden.

I'll have to take the whole pouch.

My heart pounds. I remember this rush, the spike of adrenaline that comes with the risk, the feeling that comes with a good theft—

My stomach twists. I don't even know who this guy is or why the king suspects him. Maybe he's innocent, and I'm stealing his entire week's earnings. Maybe his entire *month's* earnings.

But I'm all out of options.

I take a deep breath. If the King's Coin is in here, then this pouch could be the ticket to stopping the Shadows and keeping Ronan safe. I just have to steal this last thing, and then I can finally stop being a thief.

I just need to steal one more time.

I shove the coin pouch into my bag and run.

My heart pounds harder as I head in the opposite direction from where the silk vendor went, but the market doubles back on itself, and eventually I circle all the way around and end up in almost the same spot where I began.

By the time I finally make my way to the chapel, the wind has turned biting and my feet ache. But finally, at long last, the steeple comes into view in the distance.

This, of course, is when it starts snowing.

I shiver, pulling my coat tightly closed and wishing for like the hundredth time today that I'd worn some gloves.

The dead grass and leaves crackle under my feet as I make my way up the hillside, watching little flakes of white snow drift down from the cloudy gray sky.

I shove my way through the trees and emerge into the clearing, panting from the exertion. I shuffle forward quickly, glad that I finally get to see Beck—

Something is wrong.

The door is open.

It's just a crack, really. Just a little crack of light where the door isn't *quite* closed tightly. I didn't leave it like that, but of course Beck has been in and out since then. But why would he leave the door cracked open? He wouldn't be so careless as to do it accidentally. This is Beck, after all. But why would he do it on purpose? It's letting the cold in.

Unless Beck didn't do it at all.

Unless someone else has been inside the chapel.

A shiver that has nothing to do with the cold races up my spine. I don't know what to do. Someone might be in there right now. I might be walking into some kind of trap. But I can't just leave, either. Beck might be in trouble.

I take a deep breath, summon all my courage, and walk forward.

The whole way up the steps, I check for signs. Signs that something is wrong, or that something happened, or that Beck left me a note or a warning, anything. But everything looks fine, except for that glowing crack in the door. It seems wider now that I step closer, a *lot* wider. There's no way it's an accident, no way Beck hasn't noticed.

I reach for the door and shove it all the way open.

Snowflakes blow in through the opening, twirling down to rest on the floor and the pews. Sitting sideways in one of those pews is Beck, his eyes wide, looking at me.

And standing in front of him, in the center of the aisle, is Rosalia Peakes.

Chapter Nine

The last time I saw Rosalia, I threw a large object at her head. Two large objects, actually. So it's no surprise that she scowls as soon as she sees me.

"No need to break the door down, Rosco," she says dryly.

"Someone left it open. I thought Beck was being attacked!" I look suspiciously at Rosalia. "*Is* he being attacked?"

"It's fine, Alli," Beck says, sounding weary. "I asked Rosalia to meet me here."

"And why would you do a stupid thing like that?"

Rosalia's scowl deepens. Aside from the fact that she constantly looks like she's swallowed something sour, she's pretty, with long waves of brown hair and delicate features. She's only a few years older than Beck and me, but the way she carries herself, all regal and poised, makes her seem more grown-up. She's dressed down from when I last saw her in the Guild, though, replacing her fancy gowns with plain street clothes and a heavy coat. She can't have been inside the chapel for very long, as snowflakes still cling to her hair.

"For your information," she says icily, "I'm here to help Beck."

"No, that's what *I'm* doing." I take a few steps forward, trying to get a better look at Beck without getting too close to Rosalia. She held a knife to my throat once, and I'm not particularly eager to repeat that experience. Although, she could probably kill me from across the room just as easily. She might look delicate, but she's a Guild thief through and through.

Beck seems distracted, gazing off into space. His legs dangle off the side of the pew, his shoes scuffing patterns into the dust coating the floor. He looks even worse than the last time I saw him. Dark circles have deepened under his eyes, and he's hunched in on himself for warmth, his arms drawn across his chest. A piece of debris, possibly ceiling plaster or a bit of gravel, is stuck in a tuft of his messy hair.

"Did you find the coin?" Beck asks eagerly.

Rosalia's eyes widen. "You sent *her* after the King's Coin?"

I ignore her. "I found the cart and grabbed a coin bag off it. Haven't had time to go through it."

I take out the drawstring pouch and dump its contents onto the nearest pew. The rattle of coins echoes through the room.

Beck crouches beside me, and we quickly sort through them. An ordinary jamar, and another, and another . . .

Rosalia looms over us, but she doesn't deign to actually

bend over and help. "Do you even know what the King's Coin looks like?"

"We know what regular jamars look like," I mutter.

Beck tosses the last of the coins down with a sigh. "It's not here."

"It couldn't have been anywhere else on that guy's cart. I checked."

Beck leans back on his heels, looking disappointed. "That's okay. It was a long shot anyway. The king said he didn't know for sure if that guy was involved in the Shadows."

"So we're no better off than when we started," Rosalia says. Someone needs to tell her that I'm supposed to be the negative one around here.

"At least I tried something helpful," I say pointedly.

"No, you tried something and it failed to be helpful."

As usual, Rosalia's pretty much right. And as usual, I hate her for it. If only I had another heavy object handy to throw at her head. "I'm sorry, what exactly has *your* contribution been?"

Rosalia doesn't respond, and Beck doesn't defend me. I glare at him. "I'm so glad I bothered trying to help you. Apparently you don't care, because thank goodness *Rosalia* is here to save you. What happened to, 'Oh, I need you, Alli. You're the only one I can trust!' Remember that speech?"

Beck starts to speak, but I steamroll over him, letting my anger fill me up and push the words out. "I *stole* for you today, Beck."

A shadow falls over his face, and now he looks properly

ashamed of himself. He knows that I don't want to steal anymore.

But Rosalia doesn't know, and she's looking at me like I'm a piece of trash stuck to the bottom of her shiny black boots. "So what?" she asks, casting a glance at Beck.

I glare at her. "*Some* people don't just go around stealing things from other people. Or normal people don't, anyway. Saints, I am so tired of you thieving, rotten Guild members!" I spin away from them and pace across the tiny aisle.

Rosalia casts a second, sharper glance at Beck. "She's not going to agree."

Beck shrugs. "We haven't told her yet."

I stop pacing. "Told me what?"

Rosalia crosses her arms. "Believe it or not, Rosco, I'm not here to bring Beck piles of ordinary coins, since you seem to have that so well taken care of."

"Then why *are* you here?"

She smiles. It's possibly the only genuine smile I've ever seen from her, and it's a sharp and terrifying thing, like the edge of a knife. "I'm here," she says, "to help take down the Shadow Guild."

I look at Beck. "Do we actually want her help?"

He hesitates. "Let's start from the beginning."

"Oh God. It's never good when you say that." I sit down on the edge of the pew across from him, draping my feet over the edge just like his so that I can look him straight in the eyes. "Start talking."

"There are places in the city where Guild members leave messages for one another. It's how we communicate with the guildhall during assignments and how those who live in the guildhall communicate with those who don't. I've been checking some of these spots, just because . . . well, I need to know what's going on up there. Anyway, Rosalia left me a coded message, saying she knew I was working for the king to infiltrate the Shadows and that she wants to help."

I give him an incredulous look, raising my eyebrows as high as they will go. "And you believed her?"

Rosalia levels her steely gaze at me. "Just because you don't like me doesn't mean I'm a Shadow."

"It doesn't mean you're *not* one."

Beck closes his eyes and rubs his temple. "Can you two work this out later?"

But I've just realized something and give Rosalia another suspicious glance. "Why would you want to help, anyway? What's in it for you?" I might not know her well, but I know this isn't like her. Even if the Shadows threatened her the way they did Beck, she'd just disappear into the night. Or possibly slit someone's throat. Seeking Beck out and offering to help him isn't her way. It isn't the *Guild* way.

She hesitates, like she's debating whether or not to tell me something. "The Shadows have stolen a lot of people," she says finally.

It takes me a second to put it together, but then it clicks.

There's one person who I know Rosalia cares about. "Your brother," I say quietly. "Did they hurt him?"

Her mouth twists. "They recruited him."

For a second I almost don't believe her. I remember her brother, Peakes—a smiling, cheerful kid about my age, one who was teased by the others in the group but who was always good-natured about it. We ate dinner with him in the Guild and raced against him on sleds in the ice caves. Of all Beck's friends there, Peakes is the one who seemed the least . . . thieflike. How could he possibly be a Shadow?

But I look at Rosalia's face, and I know it must be true. Somewhere, behind her scowl, she looks upset. And angry.

"I don't know where he is," she says. "He left the guildhall, to help *them.* They got to him somehow. And I don't doubt they'll kill him once he outlives whatever usefulness they think he has. Maybe they already have. But dead or alive, I'm going to find him."

I remember the coldness of her knife against my throat, and I believe her.

Beck's story makes sense now. He knew about Peakes, and that's why he trusted Rosalia when she sent him that message. That's why he told her to meet him here. He knew she'd want revenge.

"So what's the plan?" I say. This is Beck, after all, so of course there's already a plan. "And more importantly, how does it involve me?"

"It's not just about Peakes," Beck says quietly. "There's

your brother, and every other name on that list, and every other thief they've targeted. The Shadows have to be stopped. They're ripping the Guild apart from the inside."

"Why are they doing all of this anyway? I mean, what's the point?"

"Power," Rosalia says. "Whoever the leader of the Shadows is, they want the power that the king holds. And they're using Kerick's unpopularity as an excuse. Many of the thieves they're recruiting probably don't care about Kerick one way or the other; they see this as an opportunity to gain a more powerful position within the Guild. Others might hold a grudge against Kerick, or against some of the thieves who are loyal to him, like Durban."

Beck grimaces. "We've got to find a way to take them down, once and for all. But to do that, we need more information to pass on to the king."

"What kind of information?"

"We still don't know who their leader is," Rosalia says. "Beck and I can identify some of their members, but too many of them are still a mystery. We need to find out who's leading them, and how they're recruiting people like Peakes. We need to know what they're planning to do next. And we need to know how to stop them."

"Not to mention we have to find out where the coin is," Beck adds. "And figure out who put your brother's name on that list."

"So, basically, we know nothing and we need to know everything. Great."

Rosalia lets out a sigh, as if to demonstrate just how much suffering my presence is causing her. "The problem isn't so much the lack of information as the lack of a way to gather it. I've already made myself an enemy of the Shadows. I was . . . vocal about my opposition, when Durban was killed. Members of the Shadows would kill me sooner than they'd trust me, and we can't even be sure who is and isn't a member."

"Okay, but I'm not really seeing the problem," I say. "Beck can still pretend to let the Shadows recruit him and spy on them like he was already planning to do. What difference does it make if you can't help?"

Beck taps his toe against the edge of the pew. "When I was checking for messages from the Guild today, I also checked for messages from the Shadows. They sent me information about their next meeting date and location. But here's the catch—they're testing me by asking me to recruit someone else to bring to the meeting."

"In other words," Rosalia says, "he can't show up to the meeting by himself. But I can't go with him, because they'd know I was a spy."

I really don't like where this is going. "Oh?" I say, my voice coming out a little higher pitched than I'd planned.

Rosalia pins me with a steady gaze. "You're going with Beck to infiltrate the Shadows."

Chapter Ten

I look back and forth between Beck and Rosalia, waiting for one of them to say, *Ha-ha, just kidding!* But no one does.

"Maybe you haven't heard," I say finally, "but I'm not actually a Guild member. So how can I pretend to be a Shadow Guild member if I'm not even in the regular, reasonable-amount-of-shadows Guild?"

"We thought about that," Beck says. "But the thing is, most people in the Guild don't even know who you are."

"Uh, yeah, that's my point. They don't know that I'm a Guild member, because I'm not one."

"But," Beck says, leaning forward, "they also don't know you're *not* a Guild member." Some of the light has returned to his eyes, and they're shining with excitement in a way that's painfully familiar. Beck loves a good plan. Or, rather, a bad plan that's most likely going to fail. "Not very many people know that you didn't pass your trial, because not very many people even know you had a trial at all. Some of the people you met in the Guild asked me about it when . . . when I got back. But otherwise, nobody knows. You can tell the Shadows you recently passed your trial, and they won't know any different."

"Right, so I can just walk up to some thieves and say, 'Hey, guys, I'm in the Guild too! Trust me with all your most dangerous secrets!'"

Rosalia glares daggers at me. "*Obviously* not."

I open my mouth to say something rude to her, but Beck cuts me off. "They'll believe you're a Guild member," he says, "because you'll have one of these."

He reaches into his pocket and withdraws a small object. It's a golden pendant shaped like a coiled snake, with a massive emerald set into the center. Even in the dim light of the chapel, it sparkles. It's a key to the entrance of the guildhall in the ice caves of Arat, as well as other Guild hideouts. And, now that I think about it, Beck told me once that it's how Guild members recognize each other. The pendants are enchanted, so that they can't be seen by just anyone, and they can't be stolen.

"Rosalia will let you borrow her pendant for the meeting," Beck says. From the look on Rosalia's face, I'm guessing she didn't agree to this beforehand, but she doesn't argue.

"It still seems risky," I say stubbornly. "They might guess that someone gave me the pendant."

"It's definitely risky," Beck says. He gives me a serious

look. "This is very dangerous, Alli. We're not going to pretend it isn't."

Rosalia nods in agreement. "It will be very, very bad if you get caught. Do you understand?"

I gulp. When two thieves tell you something's dangerous, that's when you know you're probably going to die. These Shadow people . . . they're not just thieves, and they're not just killers. They're thieves who are successfully killing *other thieves.*

But if Ronan really is in danger, then the risk is worth it.

Besides, the last thing I'm going to do is admit to Beck and Rosalia that I'm scared. "Oh, please. I laugh in the face of danger."

"Yes, that's what concerns me," Rosalia mutters.

I roll my eyes at her. "Okay, I get it. Getting caught is bad. So how do we make sure we don't get caught? I mean, for one thing, you've already told me that both Mead and Peakes are Shadows. And both of them know who I am. They'll know I didn't pass my trial, won't they?"

Beck nods. "That's true. And it's definitely a risk. But we're counting on the fact that neither of them is likely to expose you."

"And why is that?"

"My brother," Rosalia says, "may have gotten in over his head with the Shadows, but I don't think he'd intentionally endanger you."

I'm not so sure about that. I wouldn't have thought Peakes was Shadow Guild material either, but clearly none of us know him as well as we thought we did. Before I can argue, Beck jumps in. "Both Peakes and Mead think of you as a friend. Or as a friend of mine, at the very least."

"Yeah, I've seen how Mead treats his friends," I say.

Beck frowns. "What do you mean?"

Oh. Right. I never told him about the time Mead almost got me blown up by a spell. It was an attempt to warn me, and he probably thought he was doing me a favor. But there had to have been easier, less-likely-to-kill-me ways to warn me.

I have more pressing concerns than recounting that story at the moment, so I ignore Beck's question and ask one of my own. "When exactly is this meeting?"

Rosalia grimaces. "Tomorrow evening."

"And you're *sure* they won't suspect me?"

"As we told you before," Rosalia says, "they don't know you. They don't have any reason to distrust you."

"They don't have any reason to trust me either."

"True," Beck says. "But it seems like they're getting a bit reckless. Not only by displaying bodies in the dining hall, but also by trying to recruit people like me. Anyone who asked around would've figured out I'm loyal to the king, but they seem to be desperate enough to give it a shot anyway. You've got an even better chance of fooling them than me. You have a clean slate, and they have no reason to question you. They might be just desperate or reckless enough to accept you."

"*Might* be," I say. "There seems to be a lot of guessing in this plan of yours, Beck."

"Like I said, it's dangerous. You know I wouldn't ask you to do this if there were a better alternative. But something has to be done. Someone has to stop them."

"And you think that someone should be us."

"I think that someone *has* to be us."

I'm not sure I agree, and I'm very sure that I don't care as much as they do about what happens in the Guild. If the Guild tears itself apart fighting over leadership, that's not my problem. I should just walk away from all of this and let the thieves sort it out.

Except that they might kill Ronan, and I can't just sit back and do nothing if he's really in danger. I don't care if the Shadows target other Guild members, but I can't let them win as long as my brother's name is number two on their hit list.

Besides, walking away and letting people fend for themselves is exactly what Beck did at the end of our trial. What the Guild trains people to do. What I swore I wouldn't do. New Alli isn't supposed to be selfish.

I sigh. "Okay. Let's say for just a moment that I agree to this ridiculous plan of yours. What exactly do I have to do? I go to this meeting with you, pledge myself to the Shadows or whatever . . . and then what?"

"You'll need to play along with whatever they tell you to do," Rosalia says. "They'll likely test you at first, give you some simple tasks. Maybe ask you to recruit other members. You'll need to complete these tasks without protest, or at least make it seem as though you've completed them. You'll look for the coin, if you can. In the meantime, you'll be gathering information. Try to learn the names of everyone you meet. Find out what they're doing and what they're planning. Earn their trust, and then learn their secrets."

"Right," I say, "I'm sure that will be *super* simple. So after I've gathered all of these secrets, what do I do next?"

"Nothing," Rosalia says. "Beck will take that information to the king, and I'll take it to my own Guild connections to help bring the Shadow Guild down."

By "bring the Shadow Guild down," does she mean kill them? I'm not sure I want to know the answer, so I don't ask. "In other words, you want me to be your spy. And steal the coin back. And that's it."

"Right," Beck says. "It's simple enough."

It isn't, actually. It isn't simple at all. But they're not asking me to steal anything other than the coin. They're not asking me to hurt anyone. And although I swore I'd never be a thief again, I didn't technically say anything about *pretending* to be a thief in order to take down bad thieves and save my brother. . . .

But thinking about Ronan makes my gut twist with guilt. I could get arrested or killed doing this, and I can't even tell him why I'm doing it. With every decision I make, it's like I'm getting further and further away from him, even when all I'm trying to do is get closer. But I don't know how to stop. I don't want to keep any more secrets from him, but this is so much bigger than me. When I swore off thieving,

I also swore off being selfish—doing things solely for my own personal gain. And isn't this the opposite of that? Isn't protecting Ronan and helping Beck (and, unfortunately, also helping Rosalia) the opposite of being selfish?

Ronan might not see it that way. But maybe Ronan never has to find out.

"All right," I say, "teach me how to be your spy." I push off the pew and leap to my feet. But I leap a little too energetically, and I stumble over a few spilled coins on the floor. My feet slide out from under me, my arms flailing for balance and accidentally whacking Beck. I hit the ground in a poof of dust.

Rosalia looks down at me, arms crossed, eyes narrowed. "We have a *lot* of work to do."

I scowl. "Who made you the boss of everyone?"

"Someone has to be. And neither of you are qualified."

"Excuse you," Beck says, pretending to be offended. He rubs his jaw where my flailing arm hit him. "I'm the one the king chose to do this, you know."

"And you'd be a total failure without us," I say.

"Would not!"

"Would so," Rosalia and I say at the same time.

I glare at her. "Stop stealing my lines!"

"What makes it *your* line?"

"I'm the clever one here. Clearly I thought of it first."

Rosalia closes her eyes and pinches the bridge of her nose, pretending to be in pain. "Do something with her," she says to Beck.

"Believe me, I've tried."

"He has," I say. "Too bad he's just no match for my stunning wit."

"'Wit' isn't the word for it," Rosalia says, but I think she's trying to hide a smile.

For a second, it's like I'm in the Guild all over again, laughing and joking with Beck and his friends. It was always so easy, fitting in with them. Feeling like one of them.

It's not like Ronan hasn't tried to get along with me, and it's not like I don't want to live with him. But there's always this pressure to be New Alli, to not let him down. I don't have to care about that with Beck and Rosalia. I don't have to constantly hold my temper or watch my mouth. I can let Old Alli run free.

Unfortunately, my good mood doesn't last long. Rosalia seems determined to annoy me.

"It's filthy in here," she says, striding around the chapel like she owns the place and surveying it with a scornful expression.

"How dare an abandoned chapel in the woods not be up to your standards," I mutter.

She ignores me and quickly takes control of this operation. Before Beck or I can form a single word of protest, she's cleaned and rearranged half the chapel.

"It makes the most sense to sleep in the loft," she explains, dragging Beck's blankets up the ladder. "You'll have a better vantage point if anyone enters. You'll see them before they see you. Besides, it's a little warmer."

"But if someone comes in, he'll be trapped up there," I say. "They'll be between him and the door."

She waves my comment away. "That will happen regardless, since there's only one exit. But from up here, he'll have the advantage. He could even throw a knife at someone from above."

While I have no doubt that Rosalia is excellent at throwing knives, I've never seen Beck exhibit this skill. But before I can ask, Rosalia has already climbed back down and moved on to her next point of contention. "You *cannot* eat off these pews. They're filthy."

"I haven't—" Beck starts to object, but she's already brandishing a cleaning cloth—one that *I* brought, I might add—and attacking the nearest pew with a rather terrifying efficiency.

"Are you just going to sit back and let her do all this?" I mutter to Beck.

He grins, watching her work. "I'm thinking about it, yeah."

As if she heard him, Rosalia's head snaps up, and she points at us. "You two. Make yourselves useful. Clean out that fireplace and make plenty of space in front of it."

"Wait," I say, "shouldn't he sleep closer to the fire?"

Rosalia shakes her head. "Only if necessary. There's a lot of dry wood in here. It might not be safe to keep the fire burning at night. It could spread while he's asleep."

"What's he going to burn?" I ask. "Wood from the forest?"

"He could," Rosalia says, bustling past me and attacking a cobweb with her cloth, "but that should be a last resort. He'll end up freezing to death collecting firewood. But I see plenty of wood to burn in here, don't you?" She gestures toward a particularly crumbled pew that's sagging in the middle where the boards have split.

I cast a glance at Beck, eyebrows raised. I wouldn't exactly call myself devout, but defacing the chapel seems like asking for trouble. And Harona is a saint I really don't want to be offending right now. "These are too big," I point out. "They'll never fit inside that fireplace. Unless you've got an ax lying around somewhere?" Now that I think about it, I wouldn't put it past Rosalia to be hiding an ax. I'm sure she'd be proficient with it.

"We'll figure out the wood later," Beck says. "Let's see if the fireplace is even usable first."

"Won't someone see the smoke from the chimney?"

"It's a risk," Rosalia says. "But given how isolated this spot is, it's a small one. Just make sure to use only dry wood to reduce smoke, Beck."

I expect the fireplace to be disgusting, but it turns out to not be so awful. There's a layer of dust and grime and ash in there, but once we sweep it all out, it doesn't look half bad. There don't seem to be any leaks over here, so there's no moisture or mold to worry about.

"I think this thing might actually work," Beck says, and I nod in agreement.

We stand up, surveying the results of our labor. "Rosalia, what do you think?" Beck asks.

She turns around, takes one glance at us, and bursts out laughing.

Beck and I look at each other. Dirt is streaked across the left side of his face, his clothes are now darkened with ash, and his hands are stained with soot. I look down at myself, only to find that I'm just as dirty. "Oh great," I say.

Beck starts laughing too, which only makes Rosalia laugh harder. She puts one hand to her mouth to stifle it, but her laughs just come out as squeaks. It's possibly the most undignified thing I've ever seen her do.

"It's not *funny*," I say, glaring at both of them. "I have to go home like this, you know."

That sobers Beck up instantly. "Sorry. I forgot. Will your brother be mad?"

Of course he forgot. He doesn't really understand that I have this whole other life now. Not because he doesn't care about me or anything, but because a normal life is such a foreign concept to him that he can't really imagine it. It's like trying to explain snow to someone who lives in a desert.

I sigh. "I guess it doesn't matter at this point."

Rosalia has stopped laughing too, and she's giving me a look that's almost curious. But whatever she wants to know, she doesn't ask.

I glance up at the sunlight receding through the windows. "I probably should be going," I say reluctantly. I didn't meet Ronan on his way home from work, and he's probably wondering where I am. Plus, I don't want to wander through the woods in the dark.

"We're almost finished here anyway," Rosalia says. "We'll need to gather some wood and get a fire going. It's supposed to keep snowing tonight, and besides, we need to keep those bottles of water by the fire so they don't freeze. But otherwise we should be good to go for now."

I nod. "Will you be staying here too?" I ask her.

"I'm not ready to give up the guildhall just yet," she says, looking grim. "The Shadows consider me an enemy, and they'll come after me eventually. But until then, I need to make arrangements and ensure that my family is safe."

I'd nearly forgotten about that. But Rosalia and her brother aren't the only Peakes family members. I don't even know how many of them there are.

"All right," I say. "I'll meet you guys here tomorrow evening, then?"

"Come around six," Beck says. "The meeting is at seven, and we'll need time to discuss the plan and then walk across the city and find the meeting place."

That will be difficult. We usually eat dinner then. I'll have to figure something out. "Okay," I say. "See you then."

Rosalia nods in acknowledgment, which is as much of a good-bye as I'm going to get from her. But Beck grins at me. "Later, Allicat."

I smile back, but mine is grim. Tomorrow we infiltrate the Shadows.

Chapter Eleven

The snow is falling harder by the time I leave the chapel, and out on the streets my feet slip and slide over the damp pavement. My coat doesn't have a hood, so I keep my head bowed and move as quickly as possible.

Outside the apartment building, I hesitate. I don't have a key. But when I try the handle of the outer door, it's unlocked. After climbing the stairs and making my way to Ronan's apartment, I find the door cracked slightly open.

He's waiting for me.

That's the first sign that I'm in trouble.

Ronan sits on the sofa, a heavy law book in his lap. More books surround him, piled in the armchair and on the table and on the floor. I walk in, and he looks up.

The fireplace crackles loudly. Neither of us speaks.

Ronan opens his mouth, but my appearance seems to have startled whatever he was going to say right out of him.

Beneath the layer of recently fallen snow, I'm still covered in ash. "Have you been climbing up a chimney?" he blurts.

I should come up with an explanation for the dirt, but I'm too tired from everything that's happened today to think one up. I close my eyes. "Just get it over with."

"Excuse me?" He sounds more confused than angry.

"The lecture. I know you're mad at me because I'm late and didn't meet you at the office. So just start lecturing and let's get this over with."

Silence.

I crack open one eye. Ronan has a strange look on his face. It isn't anger, like I was expecting. It's . . . sadness?

"I was really worried, Alli," he says quietly.

"Oh."

Ronan closes the book in his lap, holding the spine in his left hand. "I had no idea where you were or if you were okay."

"I—I didn't think it would be a big deal. It's not like it's a rule that I have to meet you there every day."

"But you didn't tell me that you wouldn't. I waited outside the office for an hour."

I exhale. A couple of half-melted snowflakes fall from my shoulders to the floor.

Ronan rubs the bridge of his nose with his right hand, looking exhausted. Finally, he looks up at me. "What were you *thinking*, Alli? What were you doing? Where were you today?"

I bounce on the balls of my feet. "Nothing. Nowhere."

Ronan sighs. "Wrong answer. Try again."

"I . . . wandered around," I say. "I went to the marketplace. I went in some shops. I walked through a park. You know, around."

Ronan drops the book in his hand onto the stack on the floor in front of him. The thud makes me jump. "You want to tell me what really happened?"

"I just did."

"Alli." It's the sternest his voice has ever sounded. And the most exasperated. "You still haven't told me why you've been crawling around the inside of a fireplace."

It's abundantly clear why my brother is studying to be a lawyer. He's really good at this whole interrogation thing. "I was . . ." I falter, looking for an explanation he will believe that won't give away the truth. I can't let him know about Beck, but maybe a partial truth would work. "I was meeting someone," I blurt.

"Meeting someone?"

"I got a message from a . . . friend. He's in town and wanted to see me. I skipped going to your office today so that I could meet him."

Ronan tries not to react, but his eyes widen in alarm. "It's that boy from before, isn't it? The one who broke into the Atherton mansion with you."

I hesitate, but he already knows it's true. "Yes."

"Alli—"

"It's not what you think, okay? We didn't do anything

bad. We didn't steal anything. He just wanted to talk. He wanted to know if I'm doing okay."

"Alli. The protectors are still looking for him. You should've come to me."

"Why, so you can tell your protector girlfriend to arrest him?" The words fly out of my mouth before I can think about them, and Ronan recoils. "I didn't want him to be arrested," I add quickly. "At least not . . . not before I had the chance to talk to him again. I hadn't seen or spoken to him since the summer. And I . . . I don't know anybody else here. I just wanted to talk to a friend."

For several agonizing seconds, Ronan doesn't answer. "I know you want to protect your friend," he says quietly. "But you're still on probation, do you understand? If you're involved in anything else—if you're even *suspected* of being involved in anything else—they'll send you back to the detention center. Just like they will if you get caught with him at all. You know that he's wanted by the protectors; you have a legal obligation to turn him in."

"I don't care," I say, more loudly than I intended. "I don't care about probation or obligation or any of that other lawyer-speak you just said. All I did was talk to my friend."

"No," Ronan says, rubbing the bridge of his nose again. "What you did was run around the city without telling me where you were and associate with a wanted criminal. I think I understand why you did it. But it was wrong, and you know that."

I'm not sure what he wants me to say, so I don't say anything.

He exhales and looks down at the books on the floor. "Mari was out looking for you tonight," he says to the stack. "She searched half the city in the cold, looking. If you hadn't turned up, she was going to call a whole team of protectors to search."

"To arrest me?"

He looks up. "No. To bring you home. Because I was worried about you. Because *both* of us were worried about you."

I open my mouth. Close it.

I don't think anybody has ever worried about me like that. Ever. I don't know what to say.

Ronan leans forward and stands up. "It's been a long day," he says. "We're both tired. Let's continue this discussion tomorrow. There's a bowl of stew for you on the stove. Get cleaned up, and I'll heat it for you."

"Thank you," I say, edging toward the hallway. I can't believe I'm getting off this easy. For now, anyway.

"And, Alli?"

I stop. "Yes?"

"You shouldn't talk to that boy anymore, understand?"

I nod.

I understand, but I don't promise.

The next morning, I don't feel any better about lying to my brother.

I sigh and roll over onto my back, staring up at the ceiling. It's chilly in here, and I don't want to get out from under the blanket. Maybe I can just lie here forever. Maybe then I'll never have to "continue the discussion" with Ronan and hear him tell me how he's going to kick me out. Maybe then I'll never have to see him look disappointed in me again.

It's somehow worse that he didn't yell at me last night. In fact, he hardly said anything more after I ate dinner, just sent me off to my room and went back to his books. But I don't feel relieved. I feel . . . anticipation. Like there's a weight hanging over my head, ready to crush me, and I'm just waiting for it to drop.

I close my eyes. Yes, I'm definitely staying in this bed forever. Forget about my brother and his disappointment, forget about his way-too-perceptive protector girlfriend, forget about Beck and Rosalia and . . .

Beck. Rosalia. The Shadows.

My eyes fly open.

Today's the day. The day I'm supposed to go to the Shadows meeting. It isn't until this evening, but I've got to figure out a way to get to the chapel by six. Which is a problem, because Ronan will be home by then, and we'll be eating dinner. Mari might be here too.

I could just run out on them again, but there's no way I'm doing that. Not after yesterday. If Ronan isn't planning to kick me out right now, he definitely will if I just disappear all evening. But what else is there? What can I pretend to be doing?

There's only one solution: I'll have to pretend to be sick. That'll get me out of dinner and give me an excuse to stay in my room all night. It'll be hard convincing Ronan that I'm not faking it, but I've had more than enough experience faking illnesses at the orphanage. It will have to do.

I spring from my bed, ignoring the chilly air, and throw on some clothes. I work out the details of my idea as I attempt to brush my unruly hair into submission. I'll need a damp washcloth, to make my skin feel clammy, and maybe I can make it look like I'm sweating. . . .

A loud thud sounds outside my door, like someone's dropped something in another room.

But that doesn't make sense. I overslept. Ronan should've left for work hours ago.

My heart thuds erratically. Could it be . . . could it be the Shadows? Or someone from the Guild? Has a thief broken into our apartment?

Could they be here for Ronan? What if I led them here, what if they're lying in wait, what if they already killed Ronan in his sleep, what if—?

I take a deep breath and let my Guild training kick in. I tiptoe toward the door, my bare feet hardly making a sound. I crack the door open and scan the hallway.

To my right, Ronan's bedroom is dark. So is the bathroom. To my left, a light streams from either the kitchen or the living room. It's a light that's too yellow-y and flickering to be sunlight. Someone's lit a lantern or a candle in there.

I slip out the door and creep down the hall, my feet whisper-soft against the floor. A strong smell wafts in from the kitchen, something familiar, like . . . pancakes?

I peer carefully around the corner. A candle sits on one of the kitchen counters, flickering. And Mari stands at the stove, holding a pan in one hand.

Here I am expecting to find thieves in the kitchen, and it's just my brother's girlfriend sent to babysit me. Who's making breakfast, apparently.

The Shadows haven't come for Ronan. Not yet.

I try to steady my breathing and act casual, walking into the kitchen.

"Good morning, Alli," Mari says cheerfully. As if she didn't spend all evening yesterday trudging through the city in the cold, looking for me. Maybe she doesn't know Ronan told me that. Or maybe we're just going to play pretend. "Would you like some pancakes?"

"Sounds great," I say, sliding into a chair at the kitchen table. "Smells great too."

Mari is usually a worse cook than Ronan—all she really makes are simple stews and soups—but her pancakes are perfect: warm and soft and delicious, served with a side of cranberries and drenched in sugary syrup. I devour them as quickly as possible, barely pausing to breathe.

I can't remember ever having homemade pancakes before.

Mari joins me at the table, watching me eat. There's an expression on her face that I can't quite read.

"So," I say when I've scraped the plate clean, "did Ronan ask you to babysit me?"

"Something like that," she says carefully, watching my reaction.

"Don't you have to work?"

"Not until this evening. I've got a night shift this time."

I nod. "And tomorrow?"

"We'll see how it goes," she says vaguely. I take this to be code for *We don't know what to do with you, but you can't be trusted alone.*

Well. This complicates my plan but doesn't destroy it. And if getting along with Mari for a few hours is all I have to do, that seems like a small price to pay.

I should just play nice. Mari will probably assume that I'm faking it to make up for yesterday, but that's fine. If she thinks I'm trying to atone for what I already did, she won't guess that I'm up to something else. I look down at the table, doing my best I'm-embarrassed-to-be-telling-you-this impression. "I was thinking about maybe doing something nice for Ronan today. You know, because of . . . yesterday. So I thought I'd make dinner or something. What's his favorite?"

"You cook?" Mari says, not bothering to hide her surprise.

"Not really. I kind of need your help." I pause, pretending to be self-conscious. "Forget it. Dumb idea."

Mari takes the bait. "It's a great idea," she says. "I think Ronan would really like that. Although we'd have to make his favorite dessert: honey melts."

"What's that?"

"It's a Ruhian specialty. Powdered sugar pastries covered in honey."

"That sounds amazing. Are they easy to make?"

"Sure. I need to go shopping anyway, so why don't we head down to the market and buy some ingredients?"

"You think so?" I ask, raising my head a little.

"Sure." She smiles.

It's easy to trick her. I might, maybe, feel a little bit guilty.

But there will be plenty of time for that later. Right now I've got to play nice with Mari all day, then pretend to be sick at dinnertime so that I can sneak out of the apartment, all before meeting Beck and Rosalia at the chapel.

With any luck, my brother and his girlfriend aren't the only people I'll be fooling tonight.

Mari takes me to the market to buy ingredients for dinner, and we spend most of the day in the kitchen. It's nice, actually, just hanging out with her. She's kind of cool, when she isn't being all strict and protector-y. And she tells me things about Ronan that he won't tell me himself, like how he's the youngest apprentice at Avinoch's to pass his first exam, and how he's doing all this studying to keep up with apprentices who have been there twice as long as he has. Or like how honey melt pastries are his favorite, and how he always takes three lumps of sugar in his tea.

It's weird, learning all of these things about my own brother from somebody else. Somebody who knows him better than I do, because she's had time with him that I haven't. But it's also kind of nice, to learn these things about him. And to have her share them, as if I'm somehow an important person in his life who needs to know all of this.

By the time dinner is ready, I don't even have to fake a stomachache. A massive ball of guilt is lodged in my gut.

I stick around long enough to greet Ronan with his surprise dinner, and he acts all grateful and everything. Mari tells him I did most of the cooking, which is an outright lie that no one believes, but Ronan thanks me anyway. I excuse myself to the bathroom, where I rub my forehead with a damp cloth. I wait a few minutes, then emerge from the bathroom and announce that I don't feel well.

Mari's eyes narrow, but Ronan leaps up and presses his palm to my forehead. "You do feel clammy," he says. "Would you like to lie down?"

"Yeah," I say, "just for a while. My stomach doesn't feel so good."

"Would you like some warm tea?" Mari asks. I can't tell if she's suspicious or not.

"No, thanks," I say, heading down the hall toward my room. "I'm just going to lie down."

I climb into bed, throw the blankets over myself, and watch the clock tick down.

The sounds of dishes clanking and distant voices drift through the walls. Eventually the front door opens and closes—that'll be Mari leaving for her night shift. Another minute passes. Ronan is moving around in the kitchen. A minute later, the door creaks open as he peeks in to check on me. I pretend to be asleep, and he retreats. His footsteps tap slowly down the hall, and his bedroom door thuds closed.

I spring out of bed. I have ten minutes left to get to the chapel.

While lying in bed, I decided to write a note for Ronan, just in case he realizes I'm missing. I don't want to worry him again, or get into any more trouble. I scrounge up a scrap of paper and scribble quickly:

> Ronan,
>
> Just went out to get some fresh air. Not running away. Don't worry. Don't look for me.
>
> —A

I bunch my pillows underneath the blanket so that if he glances in from the doorway, it will look like I'm still in bed. But I put the note on top of one of the pillows, just in case he pulls the blankets back and discovers the truth.

I throw on my coat and a thick woolen scarf. I pick up my clunky snow boots but don't put them on yet; they'll be too loud in the hallway. Carefully I open my door and slip out. Only a single lantern burns in the kitchen, and the living room is shrouded in shadows. I step cautiously, not wanting to trip over a stray book on the floor. Finally I reach the front door, ease it open, and leave the apartment behind.

Outside, the wind is bitter. Most of the snow from yesterday didn't stick, but the pavement is still wet and slippery. I shove on my boots, wrap the scarf all the way up to my nose, and set out.

A few minutes later, the chapel looms before me. This time around, Beck and Rosalia were courteous enough not to give me a heart attack and left the doors closed. Still, I approach the building cautiously. I don't want any more surprises.

Inside, a small fire now burns in the hearth. Most of the debris from the center aisle has been cleared away, pushed to the edges of the room. Rosalia sits on the step leading up to the altar, facing the door. She wears a heavy blue traveling cloak that's pooled gracefully around her. With her straight-backed posture and disdainful expression, I swear she thinks she's sitting on a gilded throne instead of a dirty, crumbling step.

"You're late," she says.

Two seconds in her presence, and my temper is already flaring up. "Hey, you don't even *know* what I had to do to get here. You have *no idea*—"

"You're right, Rosco, I have no idea," she interrupts. "I just spent the last day smuggling my family out of the Thieves Guild without alerting any of the other thieves in the hope that we wouldn't be assassinated by the Shadows before we could make it out. But you're right, I'm sure the last few hours of your ordinary life have been very trying for you."

My hands ball into fists. "For your information," I say through clenched teeth, "there is nothing ordinary about trying to sneak away from my brother and the *protector* who lives next door, and meeting up with thieves from a secret organization in order to attend a meeting of an even secreter organization whose members are trying to kill everyone. But you're right, you're the only person who has any problems at all."

In one swift movement, Rosalia rises to her feet. She opens her mouth to respond, but a voice floating above our heads interrupts. "Could the two of you maybe be in the same room for one minute without trying to kill each other?"

I turn around and look up at the choir loft. Beck leans against the railing, his arms dangling over the side. It's dark up there, and his face is shadowed.

"No," I reply. "I have a very low tolerance for condescension."

I still can't see his face, but I get the distinct impression that he's rolling his eyes at me.

"We don't have time for this," Rosalia says from behind me. "Let's go."

"Wait," I say, spinning back around. "I thought you weren't coming?"

She glares. "We aren't sure if the Shadows will be watching those who enter and leave their meeting place. We don't want any of them to follow you back here and discover this chapel, so you and Beck are going to take two separate, roundabout routes to and from the meeting. I'm going to show you the way, and you can walk back on your own after. Any objections?"

"I can think of a few."

This time she ignores me. She sweeps forward, her cloak billowing behind her, and stops right in front of me. She reaches into her pocket and withdraws a glinting object. A golden pendant, studded with a massive green gemstone.

Her key to the Guild.

"You'll need this," she says quietly. "To prove you're a member."

Even though we already discussed this part of the plan, the significance isn't lost on me. Guild members don't entrust their pendants to just anyone. It's her entire life, and she's handing it over to me.

Before I can figure out how to respond, Rosalia taps her foot impatiently. "Sometime today, Rosco."

I hold out my hand, and she drops the pendant into my palm. It's heavier than I expected, and I tuck it hastily into my pocket.

Without another word, Rosalia strides past me and throws open the chapel doors.

I glare at her retreating back, then look up at Beck. "Do I have to?"

He grins, teeth flashing in the dark. "Good luck, Allicat. I'll see you there."

I sigh and trudge toward Rosalia. "You *so* owe me for this, Beck Reigler."

As I pass underneath the loft, his response floats down from overhead, barely a whisper:

"Be careful."

Chapter Twelve

Rosalia walks quickly, and I have to trot after her, barely avoiding being hit by her flapping cloak. "Why can't you wear a coat like a normal person?"

Rosalia seems to have decided that the best policy for dealing with me is to pretend she can't hear me. "Remember, you're a member of the Guild. But you don't feel that you've been treated fairly under Kerick's rule, and you support a change in leadership. Tell them Beck invited you to the meeting. If they ask for an additional endorsement, name Koby Mead."

"And if Mead tells them I'm lying?"

"If they know you're lying, run."

She says it so matter-of-factly that it takes me a second to realize she's serious. "Run where?"

"Away."

"Oh, great, that's *so* helpful, thanks." Her cloak snaps

toward me, and I dodge right, narrowly avoiding a collision with a nearby signpost.

"Keep your mouth shut as much as possible. Don't speak unless spoken to. Don't make any snide comments, if you can help it."

I leap forward, trying to get level with her again. "Who put you in charge, anyway?"

"Yes, comments like that," she says dryly.

"Yes, Queen Rosalia, I'll follow your every command." I give her a mock salute.

"And that."

I huff in exasperation. "What exactly is your problem with me?"

She stops so suddenly that I skid past her and have to whirl around. She stares me down, frozen on the sidewalk.

"I warned you," she says. "Back at the Guild, I warned you. I knew you weren't cut out for this. I knew you'd fail your trial. You're just lucky you didn't take Beck down with you, as I worried you would. And now, through an absurd twist of fate, Beck's relying on you again. And once again, you're probably going to mess it up. Only this time, you might not be so lucky."

My pulse quickens in time with my temper. I take a big step forward, closing the distance between us, and look up into her eyes. "You don't know *anything* about what happened during my trial."

Her eyes narrow. "You didn't come back," she says,

pronouncing each word with a slow, cruel carefulness, like positioning a knife before plunging it into my heart. "That's all I need to know."

I don't dare take a step back from her. I don't dare blink. I will not be the first one to back down. "What you need to know," I say, mimicking her slow, even tone, "is that Beck left a girl to die that night. And I didn't."

She doesn't blink. Doesn't even look surprised. Either Beck already told her about it, or she's even better at hiding her reactions than I expected. "And that," she says, "is exactly what I'm talking about. You might be able to pick a few pockets, but that doesn't make you a real thief. When things get tough, you don't have what it takes. You don't have the stomach for it."

I take a slow, even breath, willing myself not to punch her in the face. "You know what, Rosalia? Maybe you're right. Maybe I'm not Thieves Guild material. And right now, you should be *so* glad that I'm not. Because if I were like the rest of you, I wouldn't be out here right now, risking my own life to protect my brother and help Beck. I'd be saving my own skin instead of wandering around in the cold, listening to you lecture me about how to behave. So don't you *dare* act like you're better than me."

She blinks.

When she speaks again, her voice is a whisper. "I don't think I'm better than you. I think you're too good to be out here."

With that, she stalks past me, her cloak billowing out behind her.

A few steps later, she stops and turns around again.

"And you're not the only one who's trying to save their brother," she says.

"Sorry," I say. "I didn't mean it like that."

"Yes, you did."

"Well, okay, maybe I did. It's just that you don't seem like the most touchy-feely person. No offense."

She glares at me. "I'm not. But that doesn't mean I don't care about my family."

"Right. Sorry."

She sighs. "Look, Rosco, I think you and I both want the same thing here. We both want to stop the Shadows. When I'm hard on you, it's because I want you to do better. I need you to be successful, all right?"

This is possibly the least mean she's ever been in my presence, even though I suspect I'm still being insulted in some way. I should probably accept the peace offering. "All right," I say. Then, because I can't resist, I add, "Though, you could be nicer about it."

Rosalia smirks. "I'm never nice."

"I've noticed."

She turns and starts walking again, but more slowly this time, allowing me to walk beside her.

"I'd think you'd understand that," she says after a moment. "Since you're not so nice yourself."

"Nonsense. I'm practically angelic."

For just a teeny tiny second, she almost smiles. But when I catch her, she frowns and walks faster. "Keep up," she says briskly. "We're late."

We walk in silence the rest of the way, Rosalia striding purposefully and me trailing after her.

A few blocks north of the chapel, she stops. We're in a perfectly ordinary-looking neighborhood, lined with more Ruhian-style brick houses. "This is as far as I can go," Rosalia says. "I don't want to risk anyone seeing me with you. Just follow this street for two more blocks and go to 218 South Astian Street. Knock twice, and someone will answer. Good luck."

She turns away, barely sparing me a second glance. I take a deep breath and continue up the street.

It turns out 218 South Astian is a narrow redbrick house nearly identical to every other building on the block. It's squeezed tightly between its neighbors and stretched thin, taller than it is wide, with at least three stories and a peaked slate roof. There isn't much of a lawn, but a little decorative gate leads up to the front porch, which is laden with empty, brightly colored flowerpots. Bright flower boxes, also empty due to the season, dot the windows all the way up.

I double-check the house number. Then I check it again.

I almost wish Rosalia were still here, just so I could turn to her and say, *You've got to be kidding me.*

No, scratch that. I wish *Beck* were here, walking into this with me. I've never done any of this thieving stuff without him before. And even though our trial was basically a disaster and I've regretted it ever since, I don't regret the parts where we helped each other.

I take another deep breath, steeling myself. He's on his way here to help. He's counting on me. I can do this.

I walk quickly up to the narrow front porch, dodging the flowerpots. The door knocker is in the shape of a heart.

What kind of secret thief hideout *is* this?

I knock twice.

Five pounding heartbeats later, the door opens. Standing on the other side of the threshold is a young woman I don't recognize. She's in her twenties, with wavy fair hair that's almost as pale as Mead's. She looks profoundly ordinary.

Did Rosalia give me the wrong address? Was this all an elaborate prank? I open my mouth, about to mumble an excuse and walk away, when the woman speaks.

"Invitation?" she asks.

Okay, she's not surprised to see a stranger on her doorstep. I'm in the right place. But nobody said anything about needing an invitation. What should I say? Is there a password? Can I just talk my way in? Could I—

Oh. The pendant. The one that proves I'm in the Guild. *That's* the invitation.

I reach into my coat pocket, preparing to draw it out—

The woman's eyes narrow. "Slowly," she says.

"I'm not armed," I say honestly. Beck debated giving

me a knife to tuck away somewhere, but we figured I'll be searched anyway.

"Slowly," she repeats. I'm starting to see the Guild in her already. Something sinister lurks beneath the surface.

I withdraw the pendant inch by inch and hold it up for her inspection. She gazes at the emerald in the center, then nods curtly and steps aside. I shove the pendant back into my pocket and enter the house.

A braided throw rug covers wooden floorboards that creak under my feet. To my right, small framed paintings cover the wall. To my left, the hallway opens up into what looks like a small formal parlor, with floral couches and expensive-looking glass vases. Heavy curtains are drawn tightly across the front window.

Immediately in front of me, a narrow staircase reaches up into the darkness. The woman is already walking past it, farther down the narrow hall. "Come on," she says.

I follow her past the staircase and toward the end of the hall, where a tiny doorway opens onto a dimly lit room. A burly man dressed in black stands guard over the threshold. Several knives and other sharp steel objects dangle from his belt.

This is the Guild I remember.

"Ivo will search you," the woman says crisply, and it takes me a second to realize she's talking to me. "Leave your coat on the rack." She nods toward a slender coatrack in the corner. This seems ridiculously courteous, until I realize they just want me to take off my coat so they can search my pockets.

The woman withdraws the way we came, probably going to let more people in. I turn out my coat pockets for Ivo, holding the pendant tightly in my hand, then take the coat off and fling it onto the rack. After unwinding my scarf, I add it to the pile. I turn out my pants pockets next; then Ivo makes me take off my boots and searches those too.

Finally he grunts, which I take to mean that I passed inspection. He steps aside, and I walk into the room.

It's a small square sitting room, with windows overlooking the back of the house. Candles flicker in various corners, but the majority of the space is still full of shadows. All of the furniture has been shoved against the walls, to make more space for the room's occupants.

At least six or seven other people are strewn about. Most sit on the floor or lean against the discarded furniture. One sits sideways on top of a table that's shoved against the far wall.

Everyone is talking amongst themselves, but a few people look up when I enter. For several long, awful seconds I just stand there, not knowing what to do.

"New recruits," says a deep voice from across the room, "in a line against the wall."

After a second of squinting into the darkness, I identify the speaker. He's leaning casually against the wall by the empty fireplace, his ankles crossed. A wide-brimmed hat is pulled low over his head, obscuring his face. With his head tilted down, he doesn't seem to be looking up at what's going on in the room, but I have a feeling he's watching everything.

After another second, I find the place where he told me to sit. Two other figures are huddled against the wall closest to me, which slants underneath the stairs. I sit beside the nearest figure, the floorboards creaking under my weight. I glance at the person sitting next to me, but it's so dark that I can't make out any details.

The other thieves in the room chat quietly amongst themselves, but the new recruits beside me don't say anything. I sit in silence, praying for Beck to hurry up.

Scanning the room again, I finally spot it.

Tacked to the fireplace mantel is a massive, scroll-like sheet of parchment with words written across it in big blocky letters. Across the top, largest of all, is written: *THE KING*.

And right below it, the second name on the list: *RONAN A. ROSCO*.

My heart drops through the floor. It's real. Beck was right.

The Shadows do have a hit list, and my brother's name is on it.

I scan the rest of the names quickly, and while a few of them sound like Guild members I've heard of, none of the rest really stick out to me. Except, of course, for *THE STEWARD*, which has a big black slash mark right through it.

If I had any doubts about what the list is for, they're gone now.

These are the people the Shadows mean to kill.

Before I can properly panic, the door opens again, and Ivo escorts someone in. Beck. He shakes a drop of snow from his hair and crosses the room to sit beside me.

"Okay, Allicat?" he murmurs quietly.

"Fine," I whisper back. "You?"

He nods, his eyes scanning the room. I incline my head slightly toward the fireplace, and he pauses, clearly reading the list. "It's the same as the one Mead showed me," he whispers. "Except I think they've added more names."

I try to focus on taking deep, steadying breaths. This tiny space under the stairs isn't helping me feel any calmer. It's too small, too much like a prison cell, where I'm boxed in on all sides. I close my eyes and try to pretend I'm somewhere, anywhere, else. Someplace with lots of wide open spaces, nothing resembling a tiny jail cell at all . . .

As usual, Rosalia was right about something; we *were* running late. Beck is the last to arrive. After another minute or two passes, the woman from the front door enters, Ivo trailing after her. She picks her way across the floor until she reaches a white wicker chair that's against the wall, facing out toward the center of the room. She sits gracefully and nods at someone—everyone? Ivo stands beside her, his arms crossed.

Her arrival seems to have been some kind of signal. The

murmurs of conversation cease, and a lone figure stands up in the center of the room.

I don't recognize this guy either. He looks younger than most of the people here but still older than me, maybe seventeen or eighteen. He has short dark brown hair, a medium build, and a thin, sharp chin. As his eyes scan the room, I catch sight of a small scar across one side of his nose.

"New recruits," he says, looking in my direction. "Stand up."

Beck and I get to our feet, and the other two figures beside me do the same. I shove my hands into my pockets to hide their trembling.

Scar Nose points at me. "You. Step forward."

I walk toward him until he gestures for me to stop. We're only a foot or two apart now. Everyone in the room is watching.

"How did you find out about this meeting?" he asks.

"Beck Reigler invited me," I say, sticking to Rosalia's script and tilting my head in Beck's direction.

"Is that so?" Scar Nose turns to Beck, who nods. "Show me your pendant."

I hold it out for him. He examines it, frowning. "What's your name?"

"Alli Martell." It seems like a good idea to give a fake last name, since my own is so prominently displayed over the fireplace.

Scar Nose glances around the room. "Anyone here know Martell?"

There are murmurs of dissent.

Scar Nose smiles coldly. "Anyone besides Reigler who can vouch for you?"

"Koby Mead," I say quickly. "He knows me."

"Really?" Scar Nose turns to someone. "Get Mead for me." Behind me, someone gets up and leaves the room. A moment later, his footsteps pound up the stairs.

I gulp. I hope we were right to trust Mead.

Scar Nose smiles again. "You'd better hope he can verify your story, since no one else here seems to know you."

"I'm new," I say quickly.

He gives me a cutting glance. "I can see that. How old are you, eight? Have you even passed your trial?"

"Yes," I say defensively. "I passed at the end of last spring."

Scar Nose leans forward, his eyes boring into mine. "Then why haven't we seen you around the guildhall, Martell?"

The truth spills out of my mouth before I have time to think about it. "I was in prison."

He laughs. "You hear that, everyone? Brand-new recruit and she's somehow managed to get locked up already! You expect me to believe that?"

More words spill out of me, but this time they're lies. "It was my first job, okay? After I passed my trial, I got given this ridiculous assignment and paired up with some rookie idiot who didn't know what he was doing and got us both arrested. I spent the whole summer and fall locked up and just got out. But that's why I'm here."

His eyes narrow. "That so?"

I pause. This is the part where I have to tread very, very carefully. "I don't hold much respect for kings who send out inexperienced crews on jobs that were rigged from the start. I spent the past few months paying for other people's mistakes, and I don't think that's fair. I'm here because I heard this is the place to go to find people who have similar feelings."

A hush has fallen over the room. Scar Nose is regarding me carefully, but he isn't smiling now. "You may have heard right," he says, very quietly. "But we're not about feelings here; we're about action. You okay with that?"

I stare back at him, not daring to blink. "I spent months in lockup waiting to take action. I'm more than okay with that."

Scar Nose turns and looks over at the woman, who's still sitting in the wicker chair. She nods once. In approval, maybe? So, despite doing all the talking, this guy's not in charge. She's the one who makes the call.

I'm about to breathe a sigh of relief when footsteps sound overhead. A moment later, the door swings open, and two people squeeze past Ivo and into the room. One of them is Koby Mead.

He looks even thinner and paler than the last time I saw him, if that's possible. His light hair is ruffled and standing on end, which only accentuates his height. His pale gray eyes flicker quickly across the room, linger on Beck, and settle on me.

Whatever he says next will likely determine my fate.

"Oh, it's you," he says.

Scar Nose looks at him. "You know her?"

"'Course." Mead leans casually against the wall. "Met in the guildhall a few months back."

"When?" Scar Nose asks.

Mead tilts his head back, considering. "Late spring? Beginning of summer? Something like that."

"And did you—"

Mead sighs. "What is this, Keene, an interrogation? Come on. Did you really drag me all the way down here to vet some scrawny kid? I was *busy*."

"You were asleep," mutters the guy who came downstairs with him.

Scar Nose—Keene?—glares at Mead. "Why don't you ever—"

"Enough." The woman's voice cuts through the conversation, and both Mead and Keene stop talking. "We need to move on to other matters. Martell, take a seat. Keene, call the next recruit forward."

I move away from Keene and slide down to the floor in relief. I barely pay attention as Keene moves on to one of the other new recruits. I focus on steadying my heart rate and willing my hands to stop shaking.

The whole time, I can feel Mead's eyes on me, but it's too dark to see much of his expression. And he's not the only one—the guy in the hat is watching me too. He never looks up, and I never see his face, but I feel it.

Beck's turn is next, but it's easier than mine. Since everybody knows Beck, and Keene invited him personally, he only has to answer a couple of questions. No one seems suspicious of his answers.

Finally, after the last new person has been interrogated to Keene's satisfaction, the real meeting begins. The other members take notice now, sitting up and focusing their attention on the center of the room.

"Listen up," Keene says. "A few quick orders of business. First, for those who don't know, Jarvin broke an ankle on assignment a few days ago and will be off the street awhile. We'll need someone to cover his shifts, so until we get somebody new trained, I want McCulver and Vellan on it. Second, with the influx of new members, we need to add an extra supply run every week. Eckers, you're in charge of working that out. All clear?"

People murmur yes or nod. Keene glances at the woman in the chair. "Anything else?"

The room falls silent again as the woman speaks. "Just a reminder," she says. "This building? This is not the guildhall. You can't come and go here whenever and however you please. It's not enchanted or hidden from sight. This is my home, with actual neighbors living next door. I need *all* of you to be more careful while staying here. No loud noises. Keep the curtains closed at all times. Use the back entrance whenever possible. Never enter the house under the sight of any neighbors."

This seems like a fairly impossible checklist to me. I mean, this house is so close to its neighbors that they're practically on top of it. Which makes it even more of a concern, I suppose. But I have to wonder why they even picked this house in the first place, if it's so inconvenient. Who is this woman, and why is her house important?

Keene keeps droning on, addressing various people in the room and tossing out names I don't recognize. I try to remember all of them, but there are so *many*. And half the time I'm not sure if they're talking about someone already in the Shadows or someone they want to recruit or someone they want to get rid of. It doesn't help that half of this conversation seems to be in code. Keene keeps using words I don't recognize and phrases that make no sense, and he moves so fast that I don't have time to puzzle it out. I hope Beck's getting more from this than I am.

The one recurring theme in all of this is Kerick. Multiple times, Keene or one of the other thieves mentions some grievance they have with the king. Kerick didn't give them a fair assignment, Kerick didn't give them their fair share of the profits, Kerick gave an assignment that should have been theirs to someone else. And so on and so on, all in pretty much the same vein. I have no way of knowing if their complaints are legitimate or not.

Finally things seem to be winding down. The woman stands up, and both she and Keene make their way around the room, addressing people individually and giving them instructions. Several of the thieves start filtering out of the room, and others start up their own conversations.

Mead doesn't move from the wall behind me, and when I glance back at him, he winks. I wish I could talk to him, but there are too many people around.

After another minute the woman walks up to me. "That was an impressive speech you gave," she says, but she doesn't sound impressed. She sounds suspicious. "Will you need to stay here overnight?"

I don't know what she means, so I shake my head. "No, thanks."

"Good." She walks away, but Keene is right behind her.

"Reigler," Keene says, and Beck straightens. "You'll be completing your training with me directly."

Beck nods. His face is nearly expressionless, but I know him well enough to catch the slight frown at the corners of his mouth.

Keene turns his attention to me. "Ready for your first assignment, Martell?" he says.

"Yes."

"New recruits get trial runs only. We'll need to pair you up with someone."

Please pair me up with Beck, please pair me up with Beck . . .

He glances back at Mead. "Since you and Mead seem to know each other already, why don't you assist him with trade for now."

I'm not exactly thrilled by this suggestion, since Mead is

hardly trustworthy. Then again, I know him better than any of the other Shadows, so maybe it's the best possible outcome.

Mead seems to disagree. "That won't be necessary," he says to Keene. "I'm sure someone else needs help more." The way he's looking at Keene, eyes narrowed and sharp, they clearly don't get along.

"Oh, I think it is," Keene says, his tone threatening. "Unless there's any particular reason you don't want to work with Martell?"

My breath catches. Keene's laid some kind of trap here, though I'm not sure what. Mead knows it too. He gives Keene a very thin, very dangerous smile. "I'm sure we can work something out."

"That's what I thought." Keene smirks and looks back at me. "Do what Mead tells you to do. Do your job right, and you might just get a real assignment. Don't, and you and I will have a problem. Clear?"

"Very."

Keene shoots Mead another smirk and walks away. Beck looks regretfully at me and Mead before trailing after Keene.

Mead sighs. "Come on, *Martell*."

I follow Mead through the room, out a side door, and into a dark kitchen. We exit through the back and walk outside into a tight alley behind the house. Mead doesn't speak as he leads me through the alley, down the street, and around the corner. Only once we've walked a good three blocks away from 218 South Astian does he stop. We pull up short next to a small bench outside a bakery. The street is dark, with only a distant lantern on the corner providing any illumination.

Mead sits casually on the bench, draping one arm over the back. "So," he says. "You want to tell me just what it is you think you're doing?"

"Not really, no."

Mead sighs. "I figured Reigler would try something stupid, but I didn't know it would be *this* stupid."

"What's that supposed to mean?"

Mead stares right into my eyes. "Go. Home."

"No."

"Rosco, you're forcing me to be serious, and you know how much I hate it when I have to be serious. Get out now, while you still can."

"Haven't you been paying attention? That's my brother's name on that list!"

"I know. I'm the one who told Beck to warn you. But I thought you'd heed the warning and run, not go *looking* for the Shadows."

"What does that list mean? Why is my brother's name on it?"

"Isn't it obvious? It's a hit list. This is one of the ways they recruit people—by promising to go after anyone they've got a grudge against. Once you're officially a Shadow, you get to add a name to the list."

"Who added my brother?"

"I don't know. It's been second on the list for as long

as I've been with the Shadows." He frowns and meets my eyes. "Whoever it was, Rosco, they've got to be pretty high up in leadership for his name to be second only to the king."

I shiver. "Well, that's why I've got to help Beck spy on them. We have to stop the Shadows before they go after my brother."

Mead rolls his eyes. "Two thirteen-year-olds aren't going to take down the Shadows by themselves. Both of you are in way over your heads here. Don't be stupid. Take my advice and run."

"No," I say. "You don't get to do that. You don't get to act all superior and boss me around and act like you know what's best for me. Considering the fact that you're in league with the *Shadow Guild*"—I lower my voice and hiss the words at him—"you don't have the right to lecture me."

"'In league,'" he quotes mockingly. "I'm not 'in league' with anyone. As usual, I'm just looking out for myself. And as usual, that's a concept you seem to be incapable of understanding."

"You know, I really don't get you. I know you care about Beck—and don't even *try* to deny that—and yet you not only refuse to help him, but you sit around helping the people who are probably going to kill him."

Mead glances up the street, making sure no one's around. "There are things you don't know. You weren't in the Guild long enough to understand how it is."

"Enlighten me, then."

Mead drums his fingers along the edge of the bench. "Kerick is in trouble. He has been for a long time. You don't get to be king of the Thieves Guild without making a few enemies, especially when you're as young as he is."

"I heard what they were saying in there. All their complaints."

He nods. "It was only a matter of time before something like this happened. Even if Kerick manages to stop the Shadows, there will just be someone else to take their place. The Guild is not a democracy; its leadership doesn't change hands peacefully. Whoever holds power here at any given time isn't likely to last for long. The best thing that any of us can do—the *only* thing we can do—is be willing to swear loyalty to whoever that person is today, but also be prepared to change allegiances tomorrow. Whether it's Kerick or the Shadows or anyone else who takes control, I plan to make myself useful to them. If Beck wants to remain in the Guild, he needs to learn how to do the same. And if *you* were smart, you'd stop helping him dig his own grave and get as far away from all of this as you can."

"This is ridiculous," I say. "I thought the Guild was all about loyalty."

"Sure we are," he says, a hint of a grin creeping onto his face. "Loyalty to the Guild itself. Which means loyalty to whoever happens to hold power in the Guild at the moment."

"Which is Kerick," I point out. "Is it just me, or is plotting to overthrow him not considered loyal?"

"I'm not *actually* plotting to overthrow him," Mead says, waving one hand impatiently. "I'm just doing the occasional odd job for the people who *are* plotting to overthrow him, just in case they're successful. And in the meantime, I'm maintaining my normal life and going on assignments for Kerick, just in case *he* is successful awhile longer. Either way, I win."

"Unless someone finds out what you're doing."

"How can they find out?" He grins wider. "The Shadows are all going about their normal lives in the Guild to avoid suspicion. And if Kerick were to find out I've been with the Shadows, I can claim that I was infiltrating them to get information. Just like *you're* trying to do, I believe."

"So why are you so against it, then?" I snap. "Why don't you want me here? If you're just pretending to go along with what the Shadows want, why can't I do the same thing?"

"Because," he says dryly, "no offense, but you're not a thief. You're not a Guild member. You don't have any idea what you're doing. You're a kid who's gotten caught up in something she doesn't understand."

I throw my arms up in exasperation. "If that's how you feel, why did you vouch for me back there? Why not just tell them I failed my trial?"

"Two reasons," he says. He raises a single slender index finger. "One. If I told them you're not a Guild member, they'd want to know why Beck invited you and vouched for you. Well, as you so gracefully pointed out, I might—*might*—have a soft spot for our mutual friend, and I don't really want to draw any more Shadow attention to him, even if I think he's being monumentally stupid."

Before I can reply, he raises a second finger. "Two. I don't particularly like you, and I don't particularly care what happens to you. But I also don't have much of a desire to see you murdered by a bunch of bloodthirsty, overly ambitious thieves with very poor decorating taste. Which—and let me be very clear about this, Rosco—is exactly what will happen if they find out what you're doing."

"Aww," I say. "That's so sweet. You *do* have a heart."

He points at me irritably. "Don't make me regret my decision to help you."

I uncross my arms and give him my best fake innocent smile. "Who, me? I would never."

He grins. "Well, this has been fun and all, but it's late, and I have things to do. So how about we just skip to the part where you recognize my wisdom and decide to go home?"

"Sorry, I don't believe that's on the agenda."

He tilts his head up to the heavens. "Saints help me, what do I have to say to get rid of her?"

I smile sweetly. "Come on, Mead. You and I both know that I can be *very* stubborn. I could just stand here and chat all night."

"Oh, God, what did I ever do to deserve this suffering?"

"Get over yourself. I'm not going anywhere, so just tell me what it is we're supposed to be doing."

"*You* aren't supposed to be doing anything," he says. "*I* am supposed to be selling some of the Shadow Guild's stolen goods."

"But Keene said I'm supposed to help you."

"Keene was just trying to annoy me. Successfully, I might add."

"Well, now you're stuck with me. So when do we start selling things?"

Mead examines me for a moment. "Two nights from now, I have an . . . appointment. *If* I decide to let you stick around, you can come too, I suppose."

"Okay, so where is this appointment?"

He pauses. "The Night Market."

"The *Night Market*?" I've heard of this before, but I thought it was a fairy tale. Just like I used to think about the Guild. "Isn't that where they sell, like, spells and magic and stuff?"

Mead rolls his eyes. "And stuff. Yes."

"That's so cool!"

He sighs. "Yep, already regretting this decision."

"Does that mean I can come?"

He stands up, brushing imaginary dirt from his cloak. "If you absolutely insist on doing this ridiculous, stupid thing, then yes, you can come. Meet me here two nights from now, eight o'clock. And bring Reigler with you. Maybe he'll manage to keep you out of trouble for once."

"Okay."

"And you tell Reigler that I strongly oppose this entire plan."

"I'm sure your opinion will be noted."

He takes a few steps forward. Shadows dance across his face as he walks closer to the lantern at the end of the street. "And, Rosco? Don't say I didn't try to warn you."

Chapter Thirteen

I make my way back to the chapel using the roundabout route Rosalia showed me. It's hard not to imagine Shadows following me as I walk through the quiet streets. Once I reach the woods, every snapping twig or rustling leaf makes me jump.

The chapel is dark and empty. Rosalia must've gone back to wherever she and her family are hiding, and Beck hasn't returned from the meeting yet. I stumble through the darkness, nearly banging my foot on a pew, until I find the candle and matches that Rosalia left on the altar step. I light the candle, then get a fire going in the fireplace using the wood Beck's been salvaging from the broken pews. After a few minutes of work, the fire is blazing merrily, and the chapel is starting to look almost homey.

I stretch out on the nearest pew—which is now dust-free, thanks to Rosalia's fervent cleaning efforts—and prepare to take a nap. Surely Beck won't be too much longer.

But it's hard to sleep while thoughts of the Shadows are still swirling around in my head. Maybe Mead's right and we *are* going to get caught. Nobody seemed suspicious once Mead vouched for me, but what if there will be more tests we have to pass? What if the Shadows figure it out?

Worse, what if someone finds out my real last name? I doubt that would go over well. And what happens when they decide to go after more of the targets on their list? How soon will they come for Ronan? I'm no closer to figuring out who added his name, but I do know that the list is for real, and so is the danger.

I'm getting a sinking feeling that deciding to infiltrate the Shadows wasn't exactly the best decision, but I'm not sure what else to do. Beck's plan to find the coin and get information to the king is the only strategy we have to stop them, and I have to make sure they don't come after Ronan.

Plus, there's Beck. The Shadows will probably find out he's loyal to the king sooner or later. If they win, he'll end up on their hit list too. He'd probably have to flee the Guild.

Although, that possibility doesn't fill me with as much dread as it probably should. Beck would be devastated if he had to leave the Guild, but . . .

The thought hits me so suddenly that my eyes fly open, and I stare at the arched ceiling above. *That's* the thought that's been nagging at me, that I haven't been able to voice even to myself. I don't want to be in the Guild anymore—I already made that decision. But I don't want Beck to be in it either. Once all of this is over, I don't want him to disappear into the guildhall again. I don't want him to be swallowed up by the Guild and its darkness.

But he'd never agree to leave. Not after he worked so hard to join. Not after we got Lady Atherton killed. Not after he left Ariannorah Atherton to die. He'd never even consider anything else.

A loud creak echoes through the chapel, and I bolt upright. Beck slips through the door, accompanied by a blast of wintry air. Beside me, the candle on the altar step flickers.

"You're letting a draft in," I complain.

Beck closes the door and bounds down the aisle. "How'd it go with Mead? What did he say?"

"Hello to you too."

He ignores me. "Did you find anything? See where they might be hiding the coin?"

"Are you kidding me? Did you *see* that house? It could've been anywhere in there. We didn't even get a chance to look upstairs."

"True." He sits down on the pew across from me, his face lit by flickering candlelight. "But I think it's got to be somewhere in there, don't you? I mean, at least we've partially narrowed down the location."

"Yeah, but that doesn't help us. There were thieves crawling all over that place. No way we'd ever be able to search it. And it would take *forever.*"

"We'll just have to spend more time there," Beck says, blatantly ignoring my objections. "Go early to the next meeting so we have time to look around."

I sigh. "Is this coin really so important? It's going to be impossible to find something so small."

"I told you before. The king can't keep his claim to the throne without it."

"Did the king at least give you any useful information about this coin? Did he tell you if it's really magic or not, like the legend says?"

"Not really. He was kind of vague about the details."

"Figures," I grumble.

"So did you find out anything useful from Mead?"

"He said to tell you you're an idiot."

The corners of Beck's mouth quirk upward. "Figures."

"What did you do with Keene? Anything interesting?"

"Not much," Beck says, sounding irritated. "Mostly he just goes around threatening and intimidating people."

I shudder. "Sounds fun."

"What did you and Mead do?"

"He wants us to go with him to the Night Market. Two nights from now, eight o'clock."

Beck's eyes light up. "That's perfect. We can meet some of the fences who are selling to the Shadows. And maybe the coin's hidden there!"

I frown. "You just said the coin's probably at the house. Why would it be at the Night Market?"

"It's a market full of magical objects. If you want to hide a single magical object, it's not a bad place to consider."

"I guess . . ."

"Let's just look for it while we're there. See if we can find any clues."

"All right," I say skeptically. "Did you know any of the other thieves who were there tonight? Did you recognize that woman who was in charge?"

"I could identify a couple of other people. Mostly ones I would've suspected anyway, though. And I don't know who that woman was. I've never seen her before."

"How's that possible? You grew up in the guildhall. Don't you know, like, everyone?"

"Not all Guild members choose to live in the guildhall."

I frown again. "Well, this at least gives you something to go on, right? When you report back to the king?"

"Yeah. I can at least describe the woman to him. He'll have to know who she is, even if I don't."

I pause. The thoughts I had a few minutes ago are still ringing loudly in my head. "So do you really think the king will be all grateful to us and everything, when this is all over?"

"Of course," Beck says. "He'll be sure to offer you a place in the Guild. Don't worry."

I swallow hard. That isn't exactly what I'm worried about. But I don't think Beck will ever understand choosing to live a normal life with Ronan over life in the Guild.

The world outside of the Guild isn't something he thinks about . . . is it?

I try to make my next question sound completely casual. "What about you? Will you ask the king for anything?"

Beck shrugs as if he hasn't thought about it, though I'm sure he has. "More money, I suppose. Some better assignments, maybe. I don't want to ask for too much—I'd rather not use up all his goodwill at once."

"Right," I say. "But is there, I don't know, anything *else* you might consider?"

He turns toward me, frowning. "Like what?"

"I don't know. I mean, you could ask him for *anything*. You could, like, take a million jamars and leave the Guild and do whatever you wanted."

He laughs. "What else would I do?"

"Whatever you want," I say. "I know the Guild's always been your home and everything, but there's so much more out there, Beck. So much more that you could do."

He raises his eyebrows at me. "You want me to leave? For good?"

"I . . . I don't know. It was just a thought."

He shakes his head, like he's trying to get rid of the very idea. "I've never been anything other than a thief, Alli."

"I know."

"I couldn't leave."

"I know." But I can't let it go. "You know what you're going back to. No matter who rules the Guild, there's always going to be unnecessary death. Like Lady Atherton. That will always be the price."

Beck just smiles sadly. "Not all of us get to choose our home, Alli."

I don't know what to say to that.

Pressing the issue might just scare him away, so I try to change the subject. "Well, guess I'd better be going. It's late. Past my bedtime and all."

Beck snorts. "Like you've ever had a bedtime." He tilts his head, considering. "Wait, *do* you have a bedtime now? With your brother?"

"Technically yes? I think staying up all night would be frowned upon, although I haven't been given a specific time. Ronan's pretty lax about the rules."

Beck nods. "That's nice."

"Yeah. It's not how I expect adults to be, you know? Like, try explaining the concept of flexible bedtimes to the Sisters at the orphanage, or the wardens at the prison."

Beck flinches, and only after the words are out of my mouth do I realize we've never talked about the time I spent in prison.

More specifically, we've never talked about the time I spent in prison, and he didn't.

It's not like I'm mad at him or anything. I knew what was going to happen when I chose to stay behind with Ariannorah, and I don't regret making that choice. Besides, Beck still saved my life afterward, by giving me most of his Guild money.

Maybe I shouldn't have forgiven him for leaving, but I have.

Judging by the way Beck's staring guiltily at the floor, he doesn't know that.

"It's okay, really," I say quietly. "It wasn't that bad."

"It wasn't?" He looks up, clearly not believing me.

"It . . . Well, okay, prison wasn't exactly fun. But it was basically like living at the orphanage, only with stricter rules. Having to do chores, sharing a room with a bunch of other kids, being guarded all day . . . all stuff I'm used to. The orphanage was always its own kind of prison."

This is mostly true, although I'm leaving out the part about how tiny and dark my cell was, and how sometimes when they closed the door at night I'd have trouble breathing, convinced the walls were closing in on me, convinced I was going to die in that tiny concrete tomb. But Beck doesn't need to know about that.

He still doesn't look like he believes me, but he lets it go. "Well, at least you're with your brother now."

"Right," I say. "He's not so bad."

Beck hesitates, as if he's thinking carefully about what to say. "Did he tell you anything about what happened to your mother?"

I decide to keep it simple. "He said she died."

"I'm sorry." From anyone else, the sentiment might sound empty. It's just the thing you're supposed to say when someone tells you something sad. But it isn't hollow coming from

Beck. He knows a thing or two about dead mothers.

I shrug. "It's okay. I never really expected to see her again, so it's not like I was disappointed, you know? Getting to meet Ronan already feels like some kind of bonus."

"Yeah." He watches the candle flicker below the altar, and I try not to feel guilty about the fact that I got to live with a member of my family after all, while Beck never will again.

"Well. I guess I really should get going," I say reluctantly.

"Yeah, you'd better."

We say our good-byes, and I walk quickly out of the chapel, leaving Beck alone in the dark.

Chapter Fourteen

In the morning, it takes me a second to remember why I feel so awful.

My head aches, and my eyes do *not* want to open.

But now I remember: sneaking back into the apartment after my conversation with Beck. Tiptoeing into my bedroom, changing my clothes, and slipping into bed, only to watch the hints of sunrise peek through my window. I haven't been asleep very long, and it's already morning.

Late in the morning, in fact. Ronan let me sleep in again.

Oh, right. He and Mari still think I'm sick.

A twinge of guilt churns in my stomach, but I ignore it. The deception was necessary. And anyway, I needed the sleep.

I rub my eyes and force myself to get up, following the sounds of Ronan's and Mari's voices into the kitchen.

They're both seated at the table, surrounded by the remains of breakfast.

"Hey," Ronan says, "are you feeling better?"

"A little," I say, yawning. "What's for breakfast?"

They both laugh. "Your appetite wasn't gone for long," Mari teases.

Both she and Ronan are looking awfully happy about something. They're grinning. In fact, they look positively *joyous.*

"What's wrong?" I say, staring between the two of them. My brain is finally waking up, and the alarm bells are starting to go off. Now that I think about it, why are they both here? It's late. Shouldn't they be at work?

"Nothing's wrong," Ronan says, but something's still off.

"Why aren't you at work?"

Ronan and Mari exchange secretive smiles. "Why don't you look out the window?" Ronan suggests.

Now I'm really confused. Why would I—

I glance out the kitchen window, and my eyes widen.

I look at Ronan, then at Mari, then back out the window. They're both grinning again.

"It's white," I say. "The outside is *white.*"

I take a few steps forward. Cold air leaks through the window. It's all frosted up, but I can still see bits and pieces of the street—or what used to be the street. Because I can no longer tell where the street is. The entire ground is absolutely covered in white, glittering snow.

I've seen snow before, of course. In Azeland, we'd get an occasional snowfall that blew down from the mountains during the winter, and I've already seen some here in Ruhia. But I never knew it could be like this. It's piled up so high that the doors and windows across the street are blocked. I can't tell the difference between street and lawn and sidewalk. Rooftops are covered. Windowsills are covered. Lampposts and benches and street signs, all covered. And the *trees.* I can only see a few of them out the window, but they're so bowed over with snow, it looks like the limbs are going to break. Overnight the city has completely transformed.

"Did I sleep through a *blizzard*?" I ask.

"First big snowstorm of the season," Ronan says cheerfully.

"You mean this is going to happen more than once?" I rub at the spot where my breath has misted up the window, trying to see more.

"Of course," Mari says. "We'll have several more snowstorms throughout the winter. Bigger ones too."

I glance back at them. They're still smiling. "And we're . . . happy about this?" I know I'm not the biggest fan of winter and everything, but I can't figure out why an overnight blizzard would have the two of them acting like giddy five-year-olds sharing a secret.

"I don't have to work today," Ronan explains. "The law office is closed during heavy snows."

"And I don't have to work either," Mari says. "We send out fewer protectors during storms, since fewer people are out on the streets."

Well, that's a piece of information that's very good to

know. "Okay, so, what are you so excited about?"

"Since we're both home for once, we thought we could do something special," Ronan says. "If you're feeling up to it, of course."

"Okay," I say hesitantly. I have no idea what this means. "Can I eat first?"

Ronan laughs. "Of course. Here, Mari made you some soup."

"And Ronan made hot chocolate, if your stomach's up for it," Mari adds.

The little twinge of guilt in my gut gets bigger and more insistent. I've never had anybody make me soup when I was sick before. Or hot chocolate. It's the kind of thing I didn't even know I wanted because I didn't know what I was missing.

And now I've found two people willing to do that for me, and I'm lying to them and ruining everything.

I force myself to smile so they'll stop looking at me. The guilt might be visible on my face. "That sounds great." I sit and ladle a heaping bowl of warm chicken soup. I slurp the whole thing down while Mari and Ronan chat idly. Then I pour a mug of hot chocolate and take a tentative sip.

Oh my God. This is the best thing I have ever tasted. It even puts the spiced apple cider at Wintersnight to shame. This is like actual heaven in my mouth. It's warm, sweet, sugary, chocolatey perfection. I gulp it down so fast, it burns my tongue, but I don't care.

"Mmmmm," I sigh, closing my eyes. I want to live in this moment forever. I want to drink hot chocolate forever. Why have I ever wasted time with any other beverage? What have I been doing with my life when I could have been drinking hot chocolate?

Ronan sees my expression and laughs. "It's good, then?"

"Not good," I say, shaking my head. "'Good' is an inadequate word." I could go on for hours about just how inadequate, but I'm too busy gulping more hot chocolate.

Ronan starts to laugh, but then a weird expression passes over his face. "You've had hot chocolate before, right?"

"Nope. Never had it." Never going to stop drinking it now. I lick a stray dribble of chocolate from the rim of the mug before it can escape.

I look up and catch Ronan and Mari exchanging glances again, only this time they're not smiling. I know that look. It's the *what a poor pitiful orphan* look. Adults are very fond of it. I hate it.

"I mean, I think I had it before," I amend hastily. "It's just been a long time."

Ronan nods, but clearly they don't believe me.

Reluctantly I set down the mug. "So, about this special surprise thing we're doing . . . ?"

"Right," Ronan says eagerly, pushing away from the table. "We'd better get going. Mari, you want to help Alli get dressed?"

"I don't need help getting dressed. I'm not five," I say. All the joy of the hot chocolate has gone as quickly as it came, and now I'm just irritated. How dare they pity and baby me? I'm not some helpless infant. I thought Ronan got that, but maybe not.

"No, I mean to help you get ready to go outside in this weather," Ronan says. "If you're not prepared for cold like this, it'll be . . . unpleasant."

"Wait, we're going outside? In this? Why would we do that?"

Mari winks. "You'll see."

"Would now be a bad time to mention that I hate winter? And snow? And all things cold?"

"Well," Mari says, smirking a little, "then this should be fun."

I pick up my mug of chocolate and cradle it. It might be the last bit of true warmth or happiness I experience today.

Ronan disappears into his room, and Mari coaxes me into mine to begin the preparations. She digs around in my wardrobe, looking for some of the stuff she bought me that I never wore. She produces something she calls "long underwear," which is exactly what it sounds like, and makes me put on two pairs. Next go a long-sleeved sweater and heavy pants, which I put on without complaint. "Am I ready now?" I ask, scanning the room for my coat.

Mari laughs, and I know I'm doomed.

She withdraws the massive fur overcoat from where I shoved it in the back of the wardrobe, stuffs me into it, and zips it all the way up. Then she finds three pairs of woolly socks, two pairs of thick mittens, a long scarf, a hat, and my biggest pair of boots. By the time she's finished, I'm a puffy, overstuffed bundle of wool with only my eyes and nose poking out.

"Is this *really* necessary?" My voice is muffled by the scarf.

Mari just laughs again. "Come on. Let's see if your brother's ready."

This has to be some kind of elaborate revenge plot she concocted to make me look ridiculous. "I don't think I can walk. Or lower my arms. Or see," I say.

She sighs. "Who knew Azelanders were such babies?"

She's only teasing, but I take the bait anyway. "Excuse you," I huff. "We are *not*. I bet you Ruhians couldn't last a single second in a real Azeland summer. You don't even know what real sunlight is."

"I bet you won't last five minutes in the snow!" she shoots back, heading for the door. She's only kidding around, but now I *have* to do it. I just can't ignore a bet.

"Sure I can. I'll prove it," I say with a sigh.

"Are we ready?" Ronan asks, appearing in the doorway behind Mari. Like me, he's bundled up in a thick overcoat, snow boots, gloves, a scarf, and a massive knitted hat. And even though I look just as ridiculous as he does, I can't help it—I giggle.

"What are you laughing at?" Ronan says, but he grins and winks at me.

We wait in the hallway outside the apartment while Mari dashes next door to put her coat on. She returns moments later suitably dressed for a blizzard, but unlike me and Ronan, she somehow still manages to make the coat-scarf-hat combo look nice. Pretty, even. I have to admit that I can see why my brother likes her, even if she did stuff me into this stupid outfit.

Mari passes Ronan a large black bag and carries a second one over her shoulder, but she refuses to tell me what's inside. "You'll see" is all I get out of either of them when I ask questions, so I sigh and allow myself to be led into the blinding, freezing nightmare that the outside has become.

I knew it would be cold, of course. But I didn't know it would feel like this. Every time I turn into the wind, my face feels like it's being stabbed with frozen, pointy icicles. I quickly pull my scarf tighter around my mouth.

There's even more snow than I originally thought. Now that we're level with it, I can tell it's several feet deep, and some of the drifts are piled as tall as I am. Luckily, it looks like someone's already shoveled a path from the door of the apartment building to the street, so we're able to trudge forward.

There are a few other people around, but the streets that would usually be bustling at this time of day are quiet and mostly empty. We pass a man shoveling snow off his porch, a woman trying to walk a dog that keeps rolling around in the snow, and a couple of kids who run and tumble through the drifts. The sunlight is so bright against the white snow that I keep having to blink and close my eyes. My nose is already runny.

"Okay, I've seen enough now. Time to go back and drink hot chocolate," I say.

"Azelanders," Mari says, rolling her eyes.

"It's been five minutes. I win. Let's go celebrate my victory. Inside."

"I see one!" Ronan calls from up ahead, pointing down the street.

"One what?" No one responds, but a second later my question is answered anyway.

A horse trots around the corner, tiny bells on its bridle jingling. It's pulling a large wooden sleigh behind it. The sleigh's runners glide across the surface of the snow, its red paint gleaming in the sun. A man sits in the front, his gloved hands holding the horse's reins.

It looks like something out of a fairy tale. The kind of thing we'd see in drawings in some of the books at the orphanage. I remember laughing with some of the orphanage kids, saying that it couldn't possibly be real.

But the horse and sleigh gliding down the street toward us are very real.

Well, only the sleigh is gliding. The snow is a bit high even for the horse, and it's kind of plodding along through the powder. Ronan waves to the driver, who turns the horse toward us and pulls the sleigh to a stop.

"Five jamars per passenger," the driver says, which sounds awfully overpriced to me, but I guess on a day like today he can charge whatever he wants. This is probably the only form of transportation available anywhere in the city right now, except for the nobles who can afford thilastri.

Ronan withdraws the coins from somewhere in his oversize coat, and the three of us climb aboard the sleigh behind the driver's seat. The wooden bench is padded, but the cushions are a bit damp. I kick a few clumps of snow off the bottoms of my boots, watching it fall to the wooden floor of the sleigh. Ronan squeezes onto the bench beside me, the sleeve of his coat brushing against mine.

"Where to?" the driver asks.

"Saint Ilaina's Park," Ronan says, which doesn't give me a clue about anything. A lot of parks are probably named after the patron of nature.

The driver tips his hat and taps the reins, and the sleigh lurches forward.

It's definitely not the most dramatic or terrifying ride I've ever had—that award goes to the flying carriage pulled by a thilastri that soared hundreds of feet into the air and perched on precarious mountain cliffs while taking me to the Guild—but it's not exactly the smoothest either. The sleigh bumps and skids much more than someone with a stomach full of chicken soup and hot chocolate would prefer. The driver takes a wide turn, and the sleigh slides a little too far out, nearly hitting an innocent lamppost, before righting itself again and lurching forward. I grip the nearest railing with one heavily gloved hand.

Mari is completely undisturbed by the sleigh's movements. She leans back, one arm draped over the side railing, admiring the view of the snow-covered city around us. But Ronan keeps both arms inside the sleigh and looks at me with sympathy. "The rides take a while to get used to," he shouts at me over the wind. "But you do get used to it."

"Yeah, Ronan nearly passed out during his first one," Mari jokes.

"How would you know? You weren't even there," he protests.

"I have a good imagination."

They exchange romantic smiles that are a little bit cute but mostly gross, and I have to look away.

As we turn down the street, the white point of the chapel's steeple gleams in the sunlight. Oh God, I didn't even think about Beck until now. How's he handling all this snow? Is he warm enough? Does he have enough firewood? Is he trapped inside? Does he have food and water?

I wish I could check on him, but the snow makes that impossible. There's no way I'd make it up the hill and through the woods in this mess, even if I could get away from Mari and Ronan. Maybe Rosalia will be able to check on him. I hope.

I try to push the thought of Beck freezing to death out of my mind. He's tough. He's survived worse than a little snowstorm. He'll be fine. Probably.

As we travel deeper into the city, the snow grows deeper too. The horse has to move more slowly, his hooves plodding into the thick powder. We could probably walk faster than this on an ordinary, snowless day. We pass another sleigh filled with passengers at a cross street, but otherwise the city is deserted, the doors and windows on buildings we pass shut tightly. The wind is brittle and sharp as it buffets my face, and I shiver.

"You know, we really should have brought some of that hot chocolate along with us," I say.

"Good point." Mari looks at Ronan. "Why didn't we think of that?"

"Hey, I'm the one who *made* the hot chocolate. I can't be responsible for packing it too."

I shake my head at him. "Honestly, what good is making it if we can't drink it?"

"Another excellent point," Mari says with a grin.

I shudder against a gust of wind. Without seeming to think twice about it, Ronan reaches over and wraps his arm around me. I freeze, and not from the cold. This has never happened to me before. What do I do?

After hesitating for a second, I let myself lean in closer to him. This feels sort of . . . nice. Also weird, because we're both wrapped in massive furry coats and our poof creates a literal barrier between us. But the warmth of his arm against my back starts to seep through my coat, and it's okay, I guess.

"You know what else this sleigh ride needs? Heated seats," Mari says.

"Mm." I nod in agreement. "Also a built-in fireplace. And walls and a ceiling and an actual floor."

"So, a house," Ronan says.

"Exactly. Indoors. With no snow. Or cold. Or wind. Or—"

Mari just shakes her head at me. "Azelanders."

"Would you stop saying that? Hating cold and snow is a perfectly reasonable position. Also practical. Because, you know, it can kill you."

Mari laughs. "Really? I'd never heard that before."

"Hey. Sarcasm is *my* bit. I have that area of humor covered, thanks."

Mari just grins mischievously. "I learn from the best."

Ronan laughs, giving my shoulder an affectionate squeeze.

The sleigh lurches to an abrupt halt, nearly throwing us forward into the driver's seat. "Your destination," the driver says gruffly.

Mari leaps out of the sleigh, yanking her black bag with her. "Let's go!" she says.

Ronan grins and jumps out after her, landing in a puff of white powder. He turns and offers a hand to me, but I brush past him. If they can climb out by themselves, I don't need any—

My right boot slips on a slick spot, and my foot flies out from under me. Ronan swoops down and catches my flailing arm, keeping me from falling. "Careful," he says. "It's slick."

"Oh really? I hadn't noticed," I grumble, regaining my

footing. Ronan releases my arm but reaches for my hand instead, and together we follow Mari.

Saint Ilaina's Park is way, way bigger than most of the ones I've seen in Ruhia so far. On the far side, across from the entrance, it's bordered by a series of small hills. Ahead and to the left is a frozen pond, stretching out farther than the eye can see. To our right is what looks like a series of tree-lined gardens (though it's hard to tell, because any plants that might be there are buried in snow).

"Now will someone tell me what we're doing here?" I ask, but I already have an idea. Several kids dart by us, and families are everywhere—laughing, running, shouting, playing. This must be what Ruhians do to pass the time after a blizzard.

"We're here to have fun," Ronan says, confirming my guess. "In Azeland there's not much snow to work with, but here you can do everything. Build snowmen, make snow angels, go sledding . . ."

The word "sledding" brings back the memories again: a sled careening down an ice-covered tunnel, me flying through the air, racing thieves through the ice caves outside the Guild—

It makes me think of Beck, which brings my guilt lurching back. I can only imagine how awful it must be for him right now—

"You forgot the most important thing," Mari says to Ronan, jolting me from my thoughts. She reaches into her bag and pulls out . . . an ice skate.

I've never seen an actual ice skate in person before. In Azeland, the ice is usually so thin that skating is dangerous, and it's not like there are many bodies of water in the middle of the city anyway. Even if there were, I never would've seen them, having been in the orphanage for most of my time there. The skate looks pretty much like I pictured—a little boot with a blade strapped to the bottom. But the blade is thinner than I would've expected. Much, much thinner.

"You're actually going to walk around on that death trap?" I ask.

They both laugh. "No," Mari says, "we all are." And then she pulls another skate out of the bag. One that looks like it's my size.

"Oh no," I say, backing away. "No, no, no, no, no."

"Come on," Mari says, "it's fun."

"Azelander, remember?" I say, pointing to myself. "We don't skate."

"Ah, but you're a Ruhian now," Mari says, "and *we* do."

I imagine myself attaching tiny little blades of metal onto my feet and attempting to glide forward on them. I imagine myself falling on my face and breaking it. "No, no, no, no, no."

"I didn't get it at first either," Ronan says, reaching into his bag for his own skates. "But it's fun."

"He's actually still terrible," Mari says cheerfully, producing a second me-size skate from her bag of death. "Don't worry. You won't look any more ridiculous than he does."

"Aw thanks," Ronan replies dryly, but he doesn't seem embarrassed.

"Oh, come on," Mari says. "We're wasting daylight!" She takes off toward the pond, and Ronan gestures for me to follow her. I groan and trudge through the snow.

"I'm already a fur-covered puffball," I say irritably. "Now you want me to strap little metal blades to my feet and try to balance on them. How much more hardship can I possibly be asked to endure?"

Mari rolls her eyes at me. I wish she'd stop imitating all of my signature moves. "You'll manage."

We sit on a bench at the edge of the pond and exchange our snow boots for ice skates. Mine aren't a perfect fit, but they're pretty close. Where did Mari get these? Have she and Ronan been planning this little excursion this whole time, and just waiting for it to snow?

It gives me a weird feeling in my chest, thinking about Ronan and Mari making plans for me. Planning to do fun things, like going to the park and ice-skating together.

Almost like a real family.

I push those thoughts aside and focus on lacing up my skates. I do it as slowly as possible, to delay my impending humiliation. Also because I have to take my mittens off to do it, and my fingers are stiff with cold.

Once we're all laced up, Ronan stands and offers me his hands. This time I don't refuse his help. I grip him tightly as I rise from the bench, already wobbling on my skates. "It gets easier on the ice," Ronan says, tugging me forward, but I don't believe him.

Mari takes the few steps down to the pond as gracefully as a swan. Once her blades hit the ice, she glides forward, then does a smooth little spin to face Ronan and me. We're locked arm in arm, moving one cautious, wobbly step at a time toward the edge of the pond. To her credit, Mari doesn't laugh at us. She looks amused, though, and I can't say I blame her.

At the edge of the pond, Ronan steps onto the ice first. He takes a few shaky steps, looking less like a swan and more like a clown. *Now* I see why Mari wanted to do this. Watching Ronan flail around is hilarious.

But Mari isn't watching him; she's holding out a hand to me. "Come on, Alli," she says. "Show him how it's done."

The only thing I'm going to be showing anyone is how to fall down. I take a single step forward, my right blade landing on the ice—

And skidding wildly out from under me, just like on the patch of ice earlier. This time it's Mari who catches me, bracing my arms before I hit the ground. Both of my skates are on the ice now, wobbling uncontrollably, and I flail my left arm, trying to balance, as Mari keeps a strong hold on my right. Despite her best efforts, I almost pull her down too.

"Just relax," Mari says. "Try to keep your legs steady."

"I can't balance on these things!"

"Try to keep your eyes focused on a single point. That will help with your balance."

I glare at a button on her coat. "This is stupid." But it does seem to help a little.

"You're doing great!" Ronan calls, wobbling past us.

"Bend your knees a little more," Mari says, tightening her grip on my hands as I try to adjust. "There you go!"

"I can't believe you actually do this for fun." Although it does look fun, the way Mari does it.

"Okay, I'm going to let go for a second," she says. "See if you can balance on your own."

She drops my hands and backs away.

Instantly I lose my focus on the button on her coat, and I can't stop wobbling. I fling my arms out for balance, but I overcorrect and topple backward, feet flying out from under me.

I'll say one thing for all of this padded winter clothing: It really helps cushion a fall.

"Are you okay?" Mari asks, gliding toward me.

"No. I'm dead. I've broken everything and now I'm dead."

Mari rolls her eyes again. "You're fine." She helps me to my feet, and we start the whole process all over again.

After falling down for the five thousandth time, I give up. I let myself tumble into the snowy edge of the pond, my head landing in the powder. I groan.

"Surely you're not done yet," Ronan teases, skating shakily in my direction. He's probably fallen down a hundred times but is still more successful at staying upright than me.

"Just leave me here to die," I moan.

Ronan stops beside me, flinging his arms out wide to find his balance. Mari laughs at both of us as she skates by, loops around, and does a perfect figure eight.

That's the last straw. I pull myself farther up the bank and gather some of the snow in my hands. Before Mari or Ronan realize what's happening, I lob the snowball right at her. It smacks into her arm, and the surprise is just enough to mess up her balance. Her skates fly out from under her for the first time all day.

She sits for a moment, completely stunned, and then her face breaks into an evil grin. "Oh, you're going to pay for that."

Oops. I scramble farther up the snowbank, but it's nearly impossible to move in this outfit and skates. Mari has already regained her feet and is now racing toward me, reaching for her own snowball.

Frantically I scoop up another handful of snow, pack it as best I can, and toss it in her direction. It goes wide, and she throws one right at my chest. It bursts against my coat.

"Direct hit!" Mari yells, throwing her arms up in triumph.

My next snowball knocks the hat off her head.

Behind me, Ronan bursts out laughing. Mari's eyes narrow, and we exchange conspiratorial glances. We bend down almost in unison, scooping up more snowballs. I give her the signal. "One!" I count.

Too late, Ronan realizes what's happening. He tries to get to his feet, but he's too shaky on his skates. "Two!" Mari yells.

On three, we both hurl snow right at him.

Ronan goes down in a flurry of powder, laughing all the while. Mari and I run toward him, still flinging snow in his direction. (Well, Mari runs. I stumble.)

Ronan tosses a halfhearted snowball at me, but it bounces uselessly off my leg. I aim another at his chest. It hits directly over his heart—

And something hits me in the back, sending me tumbling into the snow beside Ronan.

"Cheat!" I shout at Mari. "My back was turned!"

Ronan and I both lunge for her, and she falls into the snow beside me, laughing. On my other side, Ronan lies back, smiling up at the sky. A snowflake is stuck to his cheek, and the whole front of his coat is dusted with powder.

Mari lies down too, shaking snow from her gloves. I sit between them, catching my breath. I've practically stopped noticing the cold—I'm too warm from exertion and energy.

Ronan turns toward me, giving me one of his infamous smiles. "Mari might be the expert on ice-skating," he says, "but I am a champion snow angel maker."

"Is that so?" I raise my eyebrows, though he probably can't see them under the brim of my woolly hat. "Well, I'm afraid you're about to lose your championship, because I am the *queen* of snow angels."

"Oh?" Ronan says, his arms already carving wings through the snow.

"The snow in Azeland is never thick enough to do anything *but* make snow angels," I say. At the orphanage, sometimes the Sisters would let us play out in the garden when it snowed, but there usually wasn't enough on the ground to make snowmen, and fighting with each other was strictly prohibited, even in snowball fights. The Sisters were big fans of snow angels, though, so we'd cover the garden with them. Everyone picked out a spot, made their angel, and then stood back to judge their handiwork. Dozens of little imprints on the ground, all a little separate from the others, all a little alone.

Now, as I pump my limbs back and forth through the snow, my arm keeps brushing against Ronan on one side, my skate nearly colliding with Mari on the other. I should get up so that I'll have more room, but I don't.

Ronan stands first, stepping carefully around the shape he left in the snow, and offers me a hand up, then Mari. We stand together and look down at three angels, their edges overlapping, side by side by side.

I get a funny kind of lump in my throat and have to turn away quickly.

Or I try to turn away, but I completely forget that I'm still wearing stupid ice skates instead of boots. The blade on my left foot refuses to find purchase in the snow, and I crash into Ronan. We both go down, landing at the foot of his snow angel.

"Sabotage!" Ronan cries, pretending to be indignant. "Intentional destruction of my angel!"

Mari laughs, but I don't. "It's fine," I say. "We all know yours was the best anyway."

Ronan looks right at me, and something in his eyes makes me think he has a funny lump in his throat too. "Of course it was," he says playfully, but he sits up, pats me on the shoulder, and helps me to my feet.

"Okay, I think it's past time to get these death contraptions off my feet," I say, gesturing dramatically to my skates.

Mari sighs. "Fair enough." We trudge back over to the bench where we left our boots. Actually, Mari trudges; Ronan and I stumble after her, clinging to each other for balance.

I try to lace my boots back up, but my hands are so numb, I have to leave them undone. This doesn't escape Ronan's notice. "I say we head back home for the rest of that hot chocolate. What do you say?"

"Finally!" I cheer, but it's only an act. This was actually . . . fun? Sort of? Minus the whole falling on my face a thousand times part. And the cold part.

We all agree that Mari is the fastest when navigating this frozen wasteland, so Ronan and I appoint her to go find us another sleigh to take home while we wait.

Ronan idly brushes a clump of snow from the top of my hat. "What do you say, Alli? Is the snow maybe slightly more fun than you thought?"

"Definitely not," I say, but he knows I'm lying.

"So you didn't have any fun at all? Not even a teeny tiny little bit?"

"Nope. No fun was had here."

"Not even when you hit me with a snowball?"

"*Many* snowballs, Ronan. There were *many* snowballs."

He laughs. "And wasn't at least one of those many snowballs just a little bit of fun?"

"You know, I think you're right. I need to hit you with another one right now. *That* would be fun."

He laughs again. "Well, I for one had a lot of fun. I think we should drag you out here every time there's a blizzard."

My heart does an excited little leap in my chest. Is he really planning to let me live with him all winter, even though my birthday is only a few weeks away?

I try to imagine it—me, Ronan, and Mari, spending the whole winter together, eating warm soup and drinking hot chocolate and making our own traditions, like snowball fights and festivals and ice-skating in the park. It sounds like a fairy tale, something I would have dreamed up in the orphanage back when I still believed there might be a family out there waiting for me.

But it doesn't feel so far-fetched anymore. It feels real. Maybe it *could* be real. This is what my life should've been—having snowball fights in the park with my brother. We can't make up for the time we've already lost, but maybe we can have a future. As long as I don't mess it up.

As long as we stop the Shadows.

I swallow past that annoying lump in my throat. "You and Mari can go without me. I plan to stay indoors like a civilized human being."

"No way," Ronan says, giving my shoulder a playful nudge. "It wouldn't be as much fun without you."

I look down, trying to figure out what I'm supposed to say to that.

I'm saved from having to respond as someone whistles behind us. Ronan and I turn around. Mari waves from the park entrance, standing next to a sleigh.

We walk together out of the park, leaving three angels in the snow behind us.

Chapter Fifteen

Sneaking out is harder this time.

The day after Ronan and Mari took me ice-skating, the snow is still piled several feet high outside the apartment. Ronan is off from work again, and we spend most of the day curled in front of the fire, sipping hot chocolate and finishing Mari's chicken soup. Ronan spends a lot of time studying his gigantic books and filling out paperwork, but we play some games too. He tries to teach me how to play chess, and I beat him soundly at a dozen rounds of cards.

It would be a perfect day, if not for the fact that I have to sneak out. I'm supposed to meet up with Mead to go to the Night Market.

Ronan isn't planning on leaving anytime soon, and he's using his newfound free time to keep an annoyingly close watch over me. I doubt playing sick will work twice in a row. I can't get him out of the apartment, but I don't know how to sneak past him either. Even if I could, there's the problem of my clothing. I'll have to bundle up in a heavy coat and everything to go outside, and it's not like he'll fail to notice that.

Luckily, Mead and I aren't supposed to meet until late in the evening, which means I *might* be able to sneak away after Ronan goes to sleep.

After dinner, I ask him for some of his herbal tea, not because I want any but because I know it makes him sleepy. Sure enough, by nine he's already getting droopy. He yawns over one of his big books but doesn't move from his armchair.

I can't suggest going to bed, or he'll know something's up. I never go to sleep early. I resist the urge to keep checking the clock.

Finally, *finally* Ronan finishes his tea and closes his book. "It's late, Alli," he says.

"Five more minutes?" I ask innocently.

"Come on. I might have to be at work early in the morning."

I sigh dramatically but don't put up too much of a fight in case he changes his mind. I pretend to retreat to my room; then I count backward from one hundred. By the time I emerge again, Ronan is in his bedroom with the door shut and the lights off.

I run to my wardrobe, fling out my heavy winter clothes, and dress quickly. I'm already running late.

Which is a problem, I realize, because of all the snow. There's no way I can trudge through that mess fast. Meaning

I'm even later than I thought. And Mead won't wait for me if I don't turn up.

Which leaves me with only one option. An option that I really, really hate.

You're doing this for Beck, I remind myself. *And Ronan will never have to know.*

I sneak into the living room and dig through Ronan's stacks of books until I find the spare coin pouch he keeps tucked away. I'd guess there are maybe twenty jamars in there. More than enough to rent a sleigh.

It's not stealing. It's borrowing, just like the clothes. I'll pay him back later, after we stop the Shadows.

I creep quietly to the front door. Unfortunately, Ronan still hasn't given me the apartment key. (It's like he doesn't trust me or something. Can't imagine why.) I have to take a risk and leave the door unlocked so that I can get in when I come back. Hopefully there won't be any thieves strolling by at this particular moment who decide to try the door. But as far as I know, I'm this building's only resident thief, and I will be otherwise occupied tonight.

With absolutely no time to spare, I leave the building and venture out into the night.

"You're late," Mead says.

He's lounging on the same bench where I last saw him, almost as if he hasn't moved an inch the entire time. The only difference is that he's now wearing a much thicker coat, and the bottoms of his boots are caked with snow.

"Do you have any idea how hard it was to walk here through all this muck?" I say, pointing at the ground.

"You didn't walk here." He gestures lazily in the direction of the sleigh that dropped me off, which is just disappearing around the corner.

"I walked *some* of the way here," I amend. "It took forever to find a sleigh at this hour, and then the first one wanted to charge fifteen jamars to take me this far. It's outrageous. I had to find a cheaper sleigh."

Mead sighs. "You're supposed to haggle with the drivers, Rosco. They'll always go lower than they say they will."

I frown. "I took a sleigh with my brother the other day, and he didn't do that."

Mead snorts dismissively. "The fancy straightlaced lawyer? Yeah, I'm sure he didn't."

"What's that supposed to mean?"

"Rich people never have any common sense."

"Ronan's not rich. He's an *apprentice*, for Ailara's sake."

Mead yawns as if my protestations are boring him. "Sure, an apprentice to one of the wealthiest lawyers in Ruhia."

"How do you know that?"

Mead gives me a sly smile. "I thoroughly investigate the backgrounds of all my associates. Which now, unfortunately, includes you."

"Seriously? You work with the *Shadows* and you're busy investigating *me*?"

"Okay, fine, maybe I didn't actually waste my time investigating you. Reigler told me which firm your brother works for, and I've heard of them. Everyone has."

"Oh."

Mead stands in one swift movement, brushing the snow from his coat. "Well, now that you've graced us all with your presence, we can get going."

"Wait, what about Beck?"

"He's going to meet us there. Sent me a message earlier, said he had to finish up something with Keene first. Luckily, I've already arranged our transportation."

He whistles sharply, and a large shadow moves forward, detaching itself from the building in front of us. I step back instinctively, but a second later I figure out what I'm seeing.

"It's about time," a deep voice rumbles. It's the sound of a rockslide. A familiar, recognizable rockslide.

"Jiavar!" I say.

The thilastri turns toward me. In the darkness, her bright blue feathers are a shadowy gray. She picks delicately through the snow, her claws leaving deep imprints. "Rosco," she says, nodding her massive, beaked head at me. "It's been a while."

The last time I saw Jiavar was in the middle of my trial to join the Guild with Beck, when we broke into the Atherton mansion. She pulled the carriage that flew Beck away to the Guild . . . and left me behind.

It was my choice. My decision to stay behind, to save a life instead of completing the trial. But Jiavar was never exactly my biggest fan, and I doubt she complained when Beck climbed into her carriage without me that night.

Of all the thilastri in the Guild, Mead had to pick this one.

"Won't this be suspicious?" I ask him. "Wandering around the city at night on a thilastri?"

"This is Ruhia, not Azeland. Lots of people here travel by thilastri, especially during heavy snows like this. Nobody will think twice. Anyway, it's fast, and we're late. Let's go."

I look from Jiavar to Mead and back again. "Er," I say. Before, Beck and I always rode in carriages that were pulled by thilastri. We never actually rode *on* a thilastri. But there's no carriage in sight. Because, of course, a carriage's delicate wheels could never plow through all this snow. Still, shouldn't she be pulling a sleigh or something?

Apparently not. Mead starts to walk toward her, then stops when he sees the look on my face. "Oh saints, don't tell me you've never been on a thilastri before."

I point to myself. "Azelander, remember?"

He sighs. "Come on, I'll give you a lift."

"I don't like the sound of this," I mutter, but I take a step closer.

"On three," Mead says, closing the distance between us. "One, two—"

On three, he hoists me up into the air and practically throws me onto Jiavar's back. I clutch desperately at a handful of her feathers for balance.

"Ow," Jiavar rumbles. "Watch it up there."

"Sorry," I say, releasing my grip. I give the rumpled feathers a gentle pat. Jiavar huffs.

I manage to steady myself, my feet dangling just above her massive wing joints. Mead slides smoothly up behind me. "Let's go," he says.

With no more warning than that, Jiavar bounds forward and leaps into the air.

Something between a shriek and a scream comes out of my mouth, and the wind tears it away, along with my breath. I grip Jiavar's feathers as tightly as possible, desperate to hang on. Everything lurches around me, the wind whipping in my face, and I squeeze my eyes shut. I might be about to faint or fall off or puke or something equally embarrassing.

Behind me, Mead laughs. "Having fun, Rosco?"

I can't even answer him. I'm too busy praying to every saint I know. Is there a patron of not falling to your death?

Something soft whacks me in the face, and I open my eyes. A gust of bone-cold wind buffets the end of my scarf into my face. I could tuck it under my coat, but I'm afraid to release my death grip on Jiavar's feathers. I squeeze my eyes shut again.

"You know," Mead says conversationally, his voice low in my ear, "I always thought you were pretty fearless, what with your death-defying stunt at the ice-sledding race and all. Guess I was wrong about you."

"I'm not afraid," I mutter through chattering teeth. "Just c-cold."

"What's that? I can't hear you."

"I'm not afraid!" I yell. I crack my eyes open a tiny bit, focusing on the tufts of feathers on Jiavar's head.

Jiavar's deep voice rumbles, and I can feel its vibrations beneath my hands, like the way cats feel when they purr. "Oh really?" she says, and I'm totally not imagining the amusement in her voice. "In that case, why don't we have some fun?"

I open my mouth to respond, only to feel my stomach drop out from under me as Jiavar swoops into a steep dive.

This time I definitely scream.

We keep dropping, plummeting through the air, falling, falling—

I keep my eyes closed as I'm blasted with freezing air, but Jiavar's wings beat so powerfully that I can hear them. Two beats, three beats, four . . .

I open my eyes again. We're climbing steadily back up into the air. I can't see much of the city below us except for the swaths of light, which are much, much farther away than would really be preferable. The buildings are like little pinpricks, their glow just visible beneath the gray clouds surrounding us.

Mead is laughing, and Jiavar lets out a little rumble that might be a thilastri giggle.

"That wasn't funny," I pant, trying to catch my breath.

"Oh, it was very funny," Mead says. He's gasping for breath too, but only because he's laughing so hard. "Wouldn't you agree, Jia?"

"Don't you dare say anything, Jiavar!" I say loudly.

I can't see her face, but I can imagine her look of amusement. "It was maybe a little funny," she rumbles.

"You know what? I was going to apologize for probably pulling out your feathers, but now I'm not going to. You deserved it."

"Er, Rosco," Mead interjects, "it might not be the *smartest* decision to antagonize the thilastri while you're currently still airborne."

Jiavar nods. "We could go for another drop if you'd like."

"Okay, okay, point taken," I say hastily. "Let's just get to this Night Market place already! I thought we were running late?"

It might be my imagination, but I'm pretty sure Jiavar sighs in disappointment at not getting to torment me further as she glides to the right with another big beat of her wings.

"Can we find another mode of transportation home?" I ask.

Mead pokes me in the back. "You'll be lucky if you even survive long enough to go home."

"Oh, shut up with the doom and gloom already. You forget I walked into the Thieves Guild once. This is nothing."

He gives me another poke, right between my shoulder blades. "Yeah, like you were in the Guild long enough to learn anything. Don't be stupid."

"You're stupid. And stop poking me!"

"Oh, nice comeback, Rosco. Very smart."

"I—"

"Children!" Jiavar interrupts. "I will turn around and take you both home if you don't stop squabbling. Hush and get ready to land."

"Was she always this bossy?" I ask Mead. "I don't remember her being this bossy. . . ." My voice trails off as her words run through my head again. "Wait, what do you mean *get ready to land*? What should I—"

For the third time tonight, a high-pitched and undignified sound comes out of my mouth and I grip Jiavar's feathers for dear life. She swoops down, spiraling toward distant spots of light, and my stomach completely vacates my body again. I regret every decision I have ever made that has led me to this moment. If I survive this, I am never flying anywhere ever again. Not in carriages, not on thilastri, nothing. I am gluing my feet to the ground.

I keep my eyes closed for the remainder of the long, long descent, not daring to move until Jiavar shudders and thuds to the earth. She runs forward a few steps, tucking her wings into her sides. "We're here," she announces unnecessarily, tossing her head.

I collapse forward, burying my face in Jiavar's feathers. I'm not totally certain whether all of my body parts have remained attached. My limbs have turned to jelly.

Mead slides casually from Jiavar's back, and his boots thump lightly into the snow. "Honestly, Rosco, I had no idea you were afraid of heights," he says.

"I wasn't until now," I grumble, refusing to move.

Jiavar sighs. "Get off before I throw you off."

I suddenly find the will to move. I sit up and stumble off Jiavar's back, releasing my grip on her only at the last possible second.

She gives her feathers a little flutter. "Do I have a bald spot back there now? I think you tore them all out."

"Oh, don't be so dramatic," I say. Mead raises his eyebrows at me, and I'm pretty sure Jiavar would be doing the same if she had eyebrows to raise. I ignore them. "Let's get this over with."

Mead mutters something to Jiavar involving the word "street," and she turns and clomps through the snow, disappearing around the corner behind us. "All right, Rosco. This way," he says.

I look around, trying to figure out where we are. We've clearly landed in the outskirts of the city—the street is mostly empty, and the buildings are sparse. And Mount Arat seems closer and bigger, I think, though it's hard to tell in the dark. Maybe we've gone west?

The snow hasn't been cleared from the streets at all here, and it's so thick that every step is a struggle. I let Mead lead the way and try to follow in his wake, having him clear the path for me, but I can barely keep up with his long strides.

"How much farther?" I say as we pass another building. There are no more structures of any kind in sight ahead of us, just a dark street stretching out into emptiness. There's only one lantern illuminating this entire street, and it's somewhere behind us.

"See that post there?" Mead says. He points to a dark smudge off to the side of the road just ahead of us, peeking up out of the snow.

"Um, maybe?"

"That's the end of the city limits," Mead says. "Congratulations. You've now left both the city and nation of Ruhia. This is as far west as it goes. We're nearly in the foothills."

"So, if we're not in Ruhia anymore, then where are we?"

"Exactly," Mead says, nodding. "We're nowhere. Like the Guild, the Night Market operates on land that doesn't belong to any city, to any country. There aren't any protectors out here; as far as they're concerned, there aren't any people out here to protect. Not their jurisdiction, not their problem. We still move the location around a lot, just in case anyone gets any ideas, but it always operates in the middle of nowhere."

"So how much farther till we get to nowhere, exactly?"

Mead turns around suddenly, facing me. "I need you to understand something," he says, using that tone he has for the rare occasions when he wants to be serious. The tone that makes me pay attention. "There are no laws at the Night Market, Rosco. No rules of any kind. The Guild is very influential here, but even we have limited authority. Even if I wanted to, there's not much I can do to protect you. Like the Guild, it's every person for themselves. So be very careful.

Don't cross anyone. Don't touch anything. And please, for the love of all the saints, *don't open your mouth*."

"I—"

He holds up a hand. "Don't. Speak."

I sigh.

He waits for a moment, then nods. "Better. Okay, now just stick close to me, and you might get through this."

"But you haven't told me what we're *doing*," I say, and Mead throws his hands up in exasperation. "I mean, what is it we're doing for the Shadows right now?"

"We're selling, obviously."

"Selling?"

"The Shadows are taking their stolen goods—goods from Guild thefts that should've been handed over to the Guild—and selling them here. This is how they're funding their little operation. This is how they're getting the gold to bribe other members into joining them, and it's how they get the currency that gives them their power."

"But if the Shadows are selling, who's buying?"

Mead smiles a little. "You'll see. Oh, and one more thing. There may very well be Guild members who aren't Shadows here as well, since the Guild uses the Night Market to sell their goods too, of course. So it's very important that no one recognize us, and it's even more important that we don't mention the Shadows at all. We can't risk a Guild member overhearing, or figuring out who we are."

"What happens if they do?"

Mead shrugs. "Like I said, there are no laws here. A particularly loyal Guild member might decide that something like, say, a knife in the back is fair punishment for traitors."

I gulp. "Well, then, let's maybe try to avoid that." I pull my scarf higher over my face and tuck my hair up under my hat. It's not much of a disguise, but not many Guild members know me by sight anyway. Mead raises his coat hood over his head, casting his face in complete shadow.

"All right," Mead says with false cheer, "time to go into the Night Market."

Chapter Sixteen

Up ahead, I see the lights.

Unlike the fiery yellow of Ruhia's lanterns or the green of Beck's enchanted matches, the spots of light glow blue, shimmering like dark beacons in the night. Dozens of little bursts of color dot the landscape.

"What are those?" I ask Mead.

"Magic," he says. "Lots of magicians set up shop at the Night Market, to sell enchantments and objects that are . . . less than legal."

"But why are they blue?"

"How should I know? I look like a magician to you?"

I look at his long, hooded cloak and dark clothing. "Um, yes."

"What did I say about not talking?"

I glare. "We're not even in the market yet!"

"Well, let's extend that rule to the entire trip, shall we?"

"I'm not sure if you're aware of this, but I am not a big fan of rules," I say.

"Believe it or not, I've noticed." He sighs. "Just stick to the plan."

"Also not a big fan of plans," I say brightly.

"God help me, how did you and Reigler ever work together?"

"Not very well, as I recall."

Mead is silent for a second. "He managed to pull off one of the most difficult trials I've ever heard of for someone his age, and came back to the Guild with a necklace snatched right out of a heavily guarded noble estate. Sounds somewhat successful to me."

I laugh. "I suspect that Beck's version of events may have left out a few key details. There was the time he got captured, for example. And the time we were locked in a prison cell. And the time a protector nearly caught us in a shop. And several near-death experiences. And—"

"Point taken," Mead interrupts. "But—"

Whatever he's about to say is cut off by a high-pitched whistle in the distance. Mead whistles back, in three short notes. I look around for the source of the sound, but all I can see in the darkness is snow and shadow.

A woman appears right in front of us.

She *literally* appears. I blink, and she's still there. One second nothing, the next second there.

She wears a dark, heavy cloak with a hood that obscures

her face, just like Mead. Her hair is in long braids that hang past her shoulders. She cups a glowing blue prism of light in her hand.

"Not all may come," she intones. "Not all may go."

"Not all will prosper," Mead says in a bored tone. "But no rules must they follow."

The light in her hand glows brighter, making me blink and look down at the snow. "Welcome to the Night Market," she says.

Mead gives a curt nod and walks past her. I scramble after him. A few steps later, I turn and look back, but the woman is gone.

"What was *that*?" I whisper.

"The Guard," Mead says. "One of the magicians who help organize the market. Her enchantments keep people out. Wouldn't want anyone stumbling into this place accidentally. Now, what did I say about no talking?"

I'm barely listening. Ahead of us, a street has appeared out of nowhere, just like the woman did. It's a long, winding path made of cobbles, completely cleared of any snow. Streetlights dot it here and there, their lanterns filled with that strange, shimmery blue glow. And all the way down the street, on both sides, are the vendors.

They're using a combination of Ruhian-style carts and Azeland-style tents, a jumble of signs and wares and people and structures. It resembles the chaos of my home marketplaces in Azeland more than the neat orderliness of Ruhia, but with one major difference: the colors. Every tent and cart and stall is white, as if someone had seized one of Azeland's markets and leached it of all color and pattern.

"Why's everything white?" I whisper as Mead strides forward. "I would've thought the *Night* Market would be, like, black or something."

Mead sighs. "You can see white more easily in the dark, Rosco."

"Oh."

"Now shut *up*."

"Who put you in charge?" I mutter.

We've reached the first few vendors. To my right is a long stall with a flat surface displaying what looks like a selection of pastries. A banner hangs down from the top, proclaiming THE SWEETEST DELIGHTS. As we pass, I'm overwhelmed with scents of cinnamon and fresh bread and something that smells *amazing*.

I take a step in that direction, inhaling deeply, but Mead tugs sharply on my sleeve. "Don't even think about it," he says.

"I just want to *look*," I protest. "It smells so—"

"It's magic," he says. "Those sweets contain all kinds of enchantments. And the smells entice you to eat them."

"What kinds of enchantments?" For a second I think I might want to risk it. There's a massive breaded pastry slathered in chocolate that looks like it might be stuffed with cream . . .

"Bad ones." Mead tugs my sleeve harder.

"How do you know they're all bad?"

"Otherwise they wouldn't have to be sold here, now, would they? Plenty of magic shops in Ruhia sell things like these to the rich, with all kinds of pleasant little spells. But the nasty curses, the ones illegal in Ruhia? Those come here."

The word "curse" gets my attention. No way I want to go down *that* road again, even if that chocolate pastry does look delicious. I sigh and turn away.

"Getting into trouble already?" asks a familiar voice. Approaching us from a nearby tent is Beck. His face is mostly obscured by a dark, hooded cloak like Mead's, one that I most definitely didn't bring him. He must've gotten it from Rosalia.

"Always," Mead replies, giving Beck a cordial nod. "Ready to go?"

"Sure," Beck says. I want to ask him if he's had a chance to look around for the coin yet, but I don't dare say anything in front of Mead. I don't know how much Mead knows about the coin, and I wouldn't trust him with that information for a second.

We head up the path, pushing past clusters of cloaked and hooded figures. The blue light from above casts cold, flickering shadows onto everyone. Unlike regular marketplaces, where people shout and laugh and chat, this one is eerily quiet. Most people walk alone, keeping their heads down, going about their business. Vendors call out to passersby, and an occasional shopper will chat with a seller, but otherwise most conversations happen in whispers. The whole market is hushed, like the sound of an inhaled breath.

Mead doesn't have to remind me to be quiet anymore. I don't dare say a word.

We come to a fork in the path and continue left, winding deeper and deeper into the heart of the market. We pass so many strange sights and smells that I hardly know where to look, but Mead's quick pace doesn't allow much time for sightseeing.

Beck was right about one thing: If you wanted to hide a magical object, this would be the ideal place to do it. The coin could be *anywhere* here. It wouldn't even stand out among all the other strange sights. I don't know how we're supposed to find it.

We pass a large canvas tent, its whiteness almost blinding in the dark. A single sign out front, illuminated by a low blue lantern, declares: ALL THIEVES WILL BE TURNED TO STONE.

Mead leans closer to me. "I forgot to warn you," he whispers. "Most vendors here protect their wares against theft with magic. So don't get any ideas."

Despite the hush surrounding me, I'm tempted to laugh. "Are you serious? *You're* warning *me* about stealing?"

He just gives me one of his lazy, mischievous smiles. "Wouldn't want you picking up any bad habits from me."

We pass a cart that seems to be made entirely of sharp steel knives, a juggler tossing glass balls of white flame outside an open tent, and a man sitting beside a stall bedecked in white roses that are arranged to spell out FORTUNE-TELLING: OMENS ONLY.

A woman passes me carrying what looks like a large bird in a cage. A stall to my left seems to be selling nothing but ticking clocks. A vendor shouts to me as we pass: "Potions, potions, get yer potions!" Another stall seems to be a perfectly normal herbalist, until I realize they have a whole rack filled with jars containing what look suspiciously like eyeballs.

"Here," Mead says, gesturing toward a nearby cart. "I need to stop here for a second."

This cart is unadorned, with no sign to explain its purpose. Its shelves are covered in ordinary-looking objects: a comb, a scrap of cloth, a key, a locket, an empty porcelain bowl. It's probably the most boring cart we've seen so far, and I'm a little disappointed.

"Do you know what this place is?" I whisper to Beck.

He frowns, examining the cart. "No idea."

"Buying or selling?" the man behind the cart asks.

"Selling," Mead says. He reaches into his cloak and pulls out . . . a book?

Wordlessly the man takes it. He examines the cover, runs a finger down the leather spine, cracks it open, and inspects the pages. "Genuine?" he asks gruffly.

"One hundred percent."

"Source?"

Mead's response is so low, I can't hear what he says.

The man frowns. "I'll give you two hundred for it."

Mead smiles in a way that seems benign but definitely isn't. "I won't take less than five hundred. In solid gold."

The man just shakes his head. "You won't find a better buyer."

"Then I won't sell. Five hundred."

"Two fifty."

"Four fifty."

"Three."

I get the feeling that they could go on like this awhile, so I stop paying attention. I gaze across the street, and a stall catches my eye. Propped upon it are three large glass cases, lit with that eerie blue light, and inside are rows upon rows of glittering jewels.

I tug at Beck's sleeve, nodding in the direction of the stall. He follows my gaze, and his eyes widen.

Mead doesn't notice as we cross the street and take a closer look. I inhale sharply. These gems look as real as any I've ever seen, and there are *dozens* of them. Red and blue and green and yellow and orange and white; amethysts and rubies and emeralds and sapphires and diamonds. I've never seen so much wealth at once in all my life.

It makes sense, I suppose. Ruhia was founded as a mining town after they discovered rare gems in the mountains. Of course a black market for jewels would exist, and of course this is where you'd expect to find it. But the sight of them all laid out at once like this is stunning. I bet the queen of Ruhia doesn't have this many jewels in her whole crown. Even Beck looks a little awed, and he's seen more of this kind of thing than me.

But I can't stop and gape for long. Two sellers stand behind the stall, gazing sharply at us. One of them has a row of knives in his belt, and I don't doubt he's eager to use them. Beck backs away, inching toward the next display, and I follow.

We bypass a tent that smells heavily of perfume; the sign declares it to be the SHOP OF SCENTED ENCHANTMENTS. Below that, a smaller sign promises, BEWITCH, ENSNARE, BEGUILE.

I'm pretty sure that's a tent I *don't* want to go into.

"Have you had a chance to look for the coin?" I whisper to Beck.

"Not really. The thing with Keene ran pretty late, so I haven't been here much longer than you."

"Where do we even begin?" I ask, making a wide gesture with my arm to indicate the many wonders surrounding us.

Beck frowns and doesn't answer. We keep walking, looking for the next stall.

"Maybe I should take one side of the street, and you can take the other?" Beck suggests. "We can see more that way. Keep an eye out for anything that seems like it has to do with the Shadow Guild."

That could be anything, but I don't argue. It's not like I have any better ideas.

Beck crosses the street, and I keep walking, peering ahead at the next attraction. Maybe there's something else fantastical here, something magical, something—

There's nothing but a mirror.

It's a *large* mirror, sure, but otherwise it's perfectly ordinary. No fancy frame, no elaborate markings, nothing. Just a big square of reflective glass, standing by itself at the side of the road.

Well, not completely by itself. A single wooden sign hangs by a cord from the corner of the mirror. In elegant script, it reads: MIRROR OF WISHES.

I look into the mirror, but there's nothing special about the reflection staring back at me. In the dark, I'm just a vague shape, with a scarf covering half my face and my coat covering the rest. Flickers of blue lantern light dance in the background, but otherwise there's nothing to see.

"You have to make a wish, girl," drawls a voice from behind me. I turn. A young woman sits on the ground nearby, her legs crossed beneath her. She's wrapped in a cloak but wears no hood, leaving her face uncovered. Her hair is the color of sawdust, and her eyes are strikingly green.

"What do you mean?" I ask. "Does this mirror grant wishes?"

She laughs. "It does better than that. It tells you how to achieve them yourself."

I scowl. "How is that better?"

"Because," she says, smiling, "then you can see what your wish will cost before you attempt to attain it."

I consider this for a moment. "I don't get it."

She just keeps smiling. "Magic never comes without a

cost. Decisions never come without consequences. Suppose you have a magic mirror that will *grant* wishes. Suppose you wish to be, say, the queen of your own country. And then, poof, you snap your fingers and the mirror grants your wish. You're the queen. You have what you wanted. There's just one problem—in order to give you the land to rule over, there first had to be a great war. And during the war, your entire family was killed. So you make your wish, you close your eyes, poof, you're the queen, but also everyone you love is dead. You see? Consequences. That is what comes of magic that grants wishes."

"So if this mirror doesn't grant wishes, what does it do?"

"As I said, it's much better." Her smile is starting to look strange, somehow, like it's contorting itself into something else. "If you declare your wish while looking into that mirror, it will show you not your current reflection but instead your reflection as it will be, should your wish come true."

"Wait. So if I just wished I were the queen, for example, then it would just show me a picture of myself being queen? How is that helpful?"

She shakes her head. "No. It shows you the reflections of *all that will be* should your wish come to pass. The woman who wanted to be queen would see images of everything it would take to get there. She would see herself fighting in the battle. She would see the war tearing her home apart. She would see herself holding her dead family members in her arms. She would see herself burying them. And so on and so on and so on, all the consequences, all the reflections, until at last she would see an image of herself coronated as queen, with her wish fulfilled, but with her beloved family members nowhere to be seen. Then she would know the cost of her wish. She would recognize its foolishness, its impossibility, its consequences. And then, of course, she would pick a new wish."

I mull this over for a minute. "So if I make a wish into this mirror, it will show me what will happen when I get what I want?"

"It will show you what must happen, and what you must do. Yes."

Now that she's explained it, it actually sounds pretty great. It doesn't grant your wishes; it just helps you sort out the good wishes from the bad ones. That *does* seem useful.

What I could I wish for? What do I want?

Two names echo simultaneously in my head. *Ronan. Beck.*

Could this mirror tell me what I have to do to protect them both from the Shadows?

The woman gazes at me, her smile looking innocent again. "You may learn how to achieve any desire of your heart, with only a wish. I offer this, a single wish, to all passersby who desire it."

Okay, now this definitely sounds too good to be true. "For free?" I ask.

Still with the smile. She never stops smiling. "Is anything ever truly free?"

So, that's a no, then. I remember Mead's warning from

before, at the pastry stall—if it were all good, it probably wouldn't be here. "Then what does it cost?"

She nods in the direction of the mirror. "Look within and find out."

"No, that's the cost of actually getting the wish. I want to know the cost of *looking*."

She just smiles.

I turn back to the mirror again. Blue lights dance across its perfectly ordinary surface.

If I get only one wish, what do I wish for? My brother, or Beck?

"Rosco!" Mead's voice shatters my thoughts. He sounds more urgent than I think I've ever heard him.

I turn around just as he grabs my arm and yanks me away from the mirror. "What were you thinking?" he says, too loudly.

"I was . . ."

"What did you do? Did you make a wish?"

"No, I was just—"

I might be imagining it, what with the darkness and his hood and all, but I think he looks relieved. He glares down at the woman, who's still sitting at the side of the street and smiling. Creepily.

"We won't be needing your services today, thanks," Mead says sharply. He tugs me away, keeping a firm grip on my arm until we pass three stalls and turn at a bend in the road, leaving the mirror out of sight.

"Didn't I tell you?" he snaps, letting go of my arm. "Didn't I tell you not to do anything stupid?"

"I didn't *do* anything. I just asked her what the mirror does."

Mead sighs, and I can't tell if he's more angry or exasperated. "I told you. Nothing here is safe."

"That's ridiculous. That book you were pawning off looked perfectly safe. And she told me what the mirror does. What's so bad about it?"

"Rosco . . ." He trails off. "Look, I don't have time for this right now. I wasted ten minutes looking for you, and we've got more transactions to make before we can get out of here. Come on. Where's Reigler?"

I point in the direction that Beck went, and Mead scowls and darts across the street.

I hurry after him, dodging several hooded figures. "This place makes you nervous, doesn't it?" I say. It's a strange thought—I never would've suspected that Mead gets nervous about anything—but it's so obvious: the way he keeps checking over his shoulder, his constant warnings, his hurried pace.

"Of course it doesn't," he says, not the least bit convincing.

I open my mouth to tease him, but he cuts me off, darting forward and seizing a small cloaked figure by the elbow. It's Beck, who was lurking outside a tent.

"Don't let her out of your sight again," Mead says to him.

Beck's eyes widen. "What did you do?" he asks me.

"I didn't *do* anything. He's overreacting."

Mead tugs Beck in my direction. "Both of you, keep an eye on each other and don't go wandering off."

I scowl. We can hardly tell him *why* we're wandering off, of course, but it's very tempting. If only I could tell him we're trying to save the entire Guild and take down the Shadows.

Mead storms up the path. Beck glances at me, shrugs, and follows him.

"Find anything?" I whisper, hurrying after him.

"No luck. You?"

"Nothing." I glance at Mead, who's a few steps ahead of us. "This place makes him nervous, doesn't it?"

Beck laughs. "Don't tell him I told you this, but Mead's always been a little afraid of magic."

"Seriously?" I didn't think Mead was afraid of much of anything.

"He made the mistake of pickpocketing one of the Guild's magicians once. The magician put a spell on him. Every time someone said his name, he'd have to start singing Ruhia's national anthem."

I laugh, trying to picture it. "How long did that last?"

"Oh, it took about a week or so for the spell to wear off. Bray and Flint had way too much fun with it."

"I'll bet."

"I'm pretty sure Bray sent that magician flowers."

I grin. "And you didn't take advantage of it at all, of course."

"Of course not. I'm too pure and innocent."

I burst out laughing. Ahead of us, Mead turns around and calls, "I can hear you, you liar."

"Who, me?" Beck says. "I would never."

Mead snorts. "Right, you're so virtuous and wholesome that you paid Rosalia fifty jamars to follow me around shouting my name all day."

"Oh, I didn't have to pay her. She volunteered."

I hide my laughter behind my hand as Mead glares at both of us before turning around. "I can't believe you didn't tell me this story sooner," I say to Beck.

"I've got *lots* of good Mead stories," Beck says.

"Don't make me come back there," Mead calls over his shoulder, which sends us into a fit of laughter again.

For a moment, I'm reminded of being back in the Guild, of joking just like this with Beck and Mead and all their friends. This was the thing that drew me to the Guild in the first place, the thing that makes me want to help Beck and Rosalia save it. Not because of the Guild itself, but because of the people in it.

"Are we almost there?" Beck asks Mead, interrupting my train of thought.

"Here," Mead responds, stopping in front of a large tent. A hand-lettered sign hanging from the top says TREASURY in fine print. "Our final stop." Without waiting to see if we're coming, he lifts the flap over his head and ducks inside. With a sigh, I follow him, Beck by my side.

The interior of the tent is dimly lit, with candles and

lanterns resting on various surfaces. Unlike the blue lanterns outside, these burn with ordinary fire. The space is crowded with wooden tables, benches, and chairs of various sizes and styles, different pieces all thrown together chaotically. The air in here is musky and smells of smoke and something metallic I can't quite place.

Mead leads us through the maze of furniture, our feet padding softly against the plush, darkly patterned rugs on the floor. More rugs and cloths are draped across random pieces of furniture, and on top of them are seemingly endless assortments of objects. We pass a bench covered in glass jars full of liquid, a table bearing ornate golden bowls and crystal drinking glasses, some kind of fancy statue propped up on a chair, an empty blue vase so large that it's nearly as tall as I am, a little rounded table holding a set of brass scales and a tray of colored marbles . . .

There's too much to take in all at once, and Mead is moving so quickly, I don't have time to examine anything more closely. I have no idea what all these objects are doing here, or what they have in common . . . except I do. All of these things look expensive, like something you'd see in a noble's house or in a display window of Ruhia's fanciest shops. Items like this wouldn't be placed in ordinary marketplaces, where they might be stolen.

They *are* stolen.

The realization takes my breath away. Everything I'm seeing, this maze of furniture and objects, all of it must be stolen goods. This is what happens to things the Guild steals.

The coin could be here. The coin could be anywhere. The Shadows don't want to sell it, of course, but they could easily be hiding it here. No one would ever be able to find it in a space like this. Including Beck and me.

I look at him, my eyes wide, and he looks away.

This is hopeless.

Still, I keep my eyes peeled as Mead and I reach the back, where a long counter runs the length of the tent. A salesman stands behind it, framed by glass display cases whose contents glitter in the dim lantern light. "How can I help you?" he asks.

For the first time since we arrived in the Night Market, Mead lowers his hood. "Hello, Tarren."

The man beams. "Well, if it isn't Mr. Mead, come to darken my doorstep again!" He glances curiously at me and Beck.

"Darken, yes, but also improve," Mead says. "You know you'd be lost without me."

Tarren laughs. "But I suspect we'd be much less aggravated."

"Aggravated? You wound me." Mead smiles. "How's business?"

Tarren's expression tightens. "Selling as well as ever," he says, "but it seems the king is being more . . . cautious as of late. The Guild has had fewer and fewer treasures to bring me these past few months . . . except, of course, for our mutual friends."

The Shadows. That must be who the "mutual friends"

are. I'd bet a hundred jamars—if I had that many—that this man has been double-crossing the Guild, knowingly buying from Shadow members on the side. The heat of my anger rises under my skin, but I have to keep it under control. After all, I'm technically here *with* the Shadows. I have to pretend not to care, even if I want to scream at this man. The Guild must provide most of the goods for his little illegal tent here, and this is how he repays them? By working with the Shadows?

Mead just nods. "Speaking of which, I have something I thought you might be interested in."

Tarren's smile returns. "Not official Guild business, I take it?"

"Not quite."

Tarren glances again at me and Beck. "And those two?"

"Some of our mutual friends," Mead says. Tarren nods, taking Mead at his word, and gestures us forward.

Mead pulls a small pouch from his pocket and withdraws a tiny golden object. Could it be—?

I step closer as Mead hands the item to Tarren, and my heart sinks in disappointment. It's not a coin. It looks like some kind of elaborate hairpin, the kind that noble ladies wear to balls. It's decorated with jewels and undoubtedly valuable, but it's not the coin.

Tarren inspects it very carefully, turning it this way and that. "Authentic?" he asks.

"Don't insult me," Mead says, though he doesn't sound insulted. "One hundred percent Astian gold, my friend."

"And the emeralds?"

"Genuine. Check for yourself."

Tarren places the hairpin on the counter and raises a small round eyepiece. It must have some kind of magnifier in it. He peers down at the hairpin, continuing his inspection.

It looks like this could take a while, so I glance around at the nearby items. Surely, if the coin were here, Tarren would want to keep it on this end of the tent, by the counter. But he couldn't just display something like that in plain sight. It would be tucked away somewhere, where only he could access it.

I look more closely at the display cases positioned on either side of Tarren. They're hard to see in this light, but the one on the left definitely contains some kind of crown on an upper shelf. It's not silver, not gold, so probably not a royal crown, and nothing to do with the Guild as far as I know. On the shelf below it is an engraved wooden box and a blue cushion propped up to display bright red jewels. There are a few other objects in the back that I can't make out, but all are too large to be the coin.

The display case on the right is similar: jewels, strange items, but nothing resembling a coin here either. The only other place that would make sense to hide the coin would be behind the counter, but there's no way I can just look around back there with Tarren watching. It's a long shot anyway—it's unlikely that the Shadows would entrust something as important as the coin to Tarren's care. This whole trip was probably for nothing.

Tarren and Mead finish their transaction and agree on a price, but Tarren doesn't hand over any money. Mead doesn't seem concerned, though. He simply pulls his hood over his head, gestures to me and Beck, and walks back through the maze of furniture to the exit.

"Why didn't he pay you?" I ask Mead as we step outside into the crisp, cold air of the market.

"It's too risky to hand over that much money here. The vendors might be able to protect their wares and coin with magic, but I can't. There's nothing to stop someone from stealing the money off me right now. Well, except I would never let that happen, of course. But better not to tempt anyone."

"So, what, he hands the money over to the Shadows somewhere else?"

"Exactly. But don't ask me where—the higher-ups in the Shadows handle that. I just run the errands."

I don't think that's quite true. Clearly Mead is entrusted to carry these highly valuable items and not run off with them—which seems like a questionable decision to me—plus he gets to negotiate with the vendors and determine the price. He might not be a leader of the Shadow Guild, but he's hardly just running errands.

"So that's it, then? That's all you can tell us about the Sha—"

Mead grabs my arm and pulls me to the side so suddenly that I stumble, nearly falling down. He tugs me off the path and into the darkness between two stalls, Beck following at our heels.

I yank my arm out of Mead's grasp. "What are you—?"

"Shh!" He pulls his hood further over his face as Beck slips into the darkness of the shadows behind him. Mead nods slightly toward the path, where two figures walk past us.

It's Kierr. A boy I met in the Guild. And next to him is . . . Dryn. The girl who trained me before my trial. Two of Beck and Mead's friends.

"Why are we hiding from Kierr and Dryn?" I whisper to Mead.

"I haven't been assigned to come to the Night Market recently," Mead murmurs. "I can't have word getting back to the king that I was here when I shouldn't be. He'll know what that means. Besides, I wouldn't particularly want them to recognize you or Beck. You're not supposed to be here either."

"Hey, I'm not a Guild member. I can come to illegal markets on my own time if I want."

Mead snorts. "You live with a *lawyer* and a *protector*, Rosco. You're basically a spy for the enemy now."

"Technically the protector doesn't live with me. Also, 'the enemy'? Really? You're one to talk—"

"Keep your voice down!" Mead whispers.

But it's too late.

Kierr's head has turned in our direction. He peers into the shadows. Dryn stops. "What is it?" she asks him.

"Mead?" Kierr calls, looking confused.

I try to speak as quietly as possible, barely moving my lips. "What do we do now?"

Mead exhales. "Run."

He and Beck take off, darting behind the nearest stall, and I follow. We cut past a tent, racing around a curve. I'm a faster runner than both of them, and I take the lead, heading back toward the main path. If we can get far enough ahead and get lost in the crowd—

Someone shouts behind us, but I don't stop to look. I keep running, nearly plowing into the shadowy, cloaked figures in the path, ignoring their protests and the yells of the nearby vendors. I nearly run over a man carrying a large basket of what looks like black-skinned fruits, and they tumble out onto the street. The man shouts curses at us as we flee up the path.

I don't slow until we come to a place where the path forks. "Right! Go right!" Mead shouts from just behind me.

I take the right-hand turn, but before I get much farther, Beck shouts, "Over here!"

We duck into another massive white tent and drop the flaps closed behind us, panting. "Should be okay in here for a bit," Beck says, bending over and placing his hands on his knees. "They'll think they've lost us in the crowd."

"Do you think they really recognized us?" I ask.

"Hard to say," Mead replies. "If I'm lucky, Kierr will think he was mistaken about who he saw. Not sure if he caught a good glimpse of me." He murmurs a quick prayer to Saint Ailara.

I raise my eyebrows. "I never knew you were religious."

"Only when the mood strikes me."

"So, only when you're in trouble, then."

"Naturally."

I glance around at the interior of the tent. It's dark and shadowy, with some kind of heavy purple smoke hanging in the air. A couple of cloaked figures are distracting the vendor at the back of the space. I can't tell what's being sold, but I'm not entirely sure I want to know.

Beck peeks outside the tent. "Looks like the coast is clear."

We step outside. The street is bustling, but I don't see anyone I recognize. "Think we lost them?" I ask.

"Maybe," Mead says, "but let's go before—"

Kierr and Dryn are coming around the corner, heading straight toward us.

Mead hangs his head back, looking up at the sky, and curses. "Thanks for nothing, Ailara."

We run down the path, through the market, and out into the darkness of the frigid night.

Chapter Seventeen

Outside the Night Market, Beck leaves to find the thilastri that brought him here, while Mead and I find Jiavar. She flies the two of us back to the meeting point, and though the ride is just as harrowing as before, I barely notice this time around, since I'm having trouble staying awake.

Jiavar offers to fly me all the way home, but I don't really want anyone in the Guild (Shadow or otherwise) besides Beck to know where Ronan lives. Plus I'd prefer a bumping, jolting sleigh ride over a terrifying, plummeting thilastri any day. Unfortunately, it turns out there aren't many sleighs operating at this time of night, so I end up trudging home through the snow, shivering in the cold.

I sneak back into the apartment, which is still dark. There's one problem I didn't anticipate—my boots are caked with snow, so I can't just throw them back into my wardrobe. I end up running hot water in the kitchen and rinsing the boots off, attacking the particularly stubborn clumps of ice with kitchen utensils until they fall into the sink. Then I dry the now-clean boots off with towels and put them back where they belong in my wardrobe before climbing, finally, into bed.

Not nearly enough hours pass before Mari wakes me, dawn filtering through the frosted window. "Rise and shine!" she says brightly.

Ugh. Of *course* she's a morning person. Cheerfulness at this hour of the day ought to be outlawed.

"Uhhh," I moan, throwing a blanket over my head.

Mari gives me a gentle poke. "I hear Ronan's making hot chocolate."

I perk up. "Did someone say chocolate?"

"Better get it while it's hot!"

I toss the blanket aside, blinking in the sudden light. "You should really lead with that next time."

"Noted," she says, smiling. Despite her cheerfulness, she looks tired—dark circles rest under her eyes. She must have an early shift at work today, to be up and visiting us already.

I sit up slowly, yawning. "Better get up before Ronan drinks it all, I guess."

I rush into the kitchen, where Ronan is indeed pouring hot chocolate into colorful chipped mugs. "Just in time," he says. "How was your night? Sleep okay?"

"Just great," I lie. "But it's way too early in the morning right now, so I'm going to need an *extra*-big mug."

"One extra-big mug coming up."

Ronan, Mari, and I eat breakfast together; then they both finish getting ready for work. As soon as they leave, I go into my room and bundle up in my coat again. It's times like these that I really start to miss Azeland. I never had to complete this hour-long bundling process just to go outside. This is going to get *really* annoying by the end of winter.

Now properly attired, I exit the apartment. I made sure to leave a note in case Mari or Ronan comes over to check on me or something, though, of course, it doesn't say where I'm going.

I decide to check our secret messaging place in the park first, just in case Beck left me a note last night after returning from the Night Market. But the tree trunk is empty, so I leave the park and head for the hill.

Trudging through the woods is much harder in the snow. Tree branches hang lower, their limbs weighed down with ice, and I'm constantly tripped up by the bushes and undergrowth now buried under the snow. Beck and Rosalia must be covering their tracks somehow when they come up here; I don't see a single footprint. The whole hilltop is an unbroken blanket of snow, disturbed only by the glimmering crystalline trees.

At long last, I reach the chapel. It's clear that someone has been shoveling snowdrifts away from the front doors, but they've done it very carefully, piling the snow in natural-looking mounds along the walls so that it looks like the wind just made drifts. If I didn't know they were here, I never would suspect.

I push open the chapel doors and step inside. The center of the room is empty, but a fire burns in the grate. "Beck?" I call.

"Hey," he says from somewhere above me. I turn around. He climbs down from the choir loft, brushing messy hair from his eyes. "How's it going, Allicat?"

"Fine," I say, ignoring the weird little flip my stomach does when he calls me that. "No one noticed that I snuck out last night. You get back all right?"

"Yep."

"What was it you were doing with Keene before we met up? You never told me how that went."

"Not bad." He moves over to the fire and retrieves a bowl of oatmeal that was warming in front of it. "They didn't have me doing anything important. Mostly I just stood lookout outside a building while these guys went in to steal stuff. I tried to get some info out of them, but they wouldn't budge. The Night Market was more productive."

"I wouldn't exactly call that productive. We didn't find the coin. Or even narrow down where it might be."

"But we learned who's fencing for the Shadows. That's info I can take to the king. I can't believe the Treasury turned." Beck raises the bowl to his lips and slurps some of the oatmeal out.

"Ew," I say, wrinkling my nose. "Remind me to bring you a spoon later."

He ignores me. "Did you see anything when we separated? Anyplace they might be hiding the coin?"

"Are you kidding? I saw a *million* places they could be hiding the coin."

"Hmm." Beck frowns, tapping one finger against the rim of his bowl.

"But honestly, I'm not sure it's at the Night Market anyway. I mean, it doesn't make sense. Why wouldn't the Shadows keep it? Like, wouldn't the leader of the Shadows have the coin on them at all times, instead of entrusting it to anyone else?"

Beck nods. "Good point."

"But that's just it," I say, pacing in front of the fire. "We don't even know who the leader of the Shadows *is.* It could be that woman who was at the house, but we don't know for sure. All this spying, and we've got nothing. We're no better off than when we started."

"Actually, that's not quite true." Beck grins. "I did get *one* useful piece of information out of Keene. Apparently they're having a really big meeting soon, one so important and secretive that everyone's buzzing about it. They're saying the leader of the Shadows is going to speak at this meeting. I'm not sure if new recruits are supposed to show, but I figure we should talk our way in. We definitely need to be there. To see who the leader is."

"Right," I say. "So when you say 'soon,' how soon are we talking?"

"Tomorrow."

I sigh. "Didn't we just *have* a Shadows meeting? Why now?"

"Don't ask me. I didn't plan it." Beck takes another slurp of oatmeal.

"If you were the one running this operation, everything would be so much more efficient. No time wasted with lots of meetings, no complicated recruitment processes, just simple, straightforward plans."

He lowers the oatmeal bowl. "Was that actually a compliment?"

"Of course not. Note that I didn't say they'd be *good* plans. They would be reckless, dangerous plans bound to go wrong every step of the way. But there would be plans. Outlines. Maps. Lots of maps."

"What's wrong with maps?"

"And lists and charts and schedules and—"

"And if *you* were the one running the Shadows," he interrupts, "there'd be no plans at all. You'd just point people in a general direction and say, 'Go here. Steal this. Figure it out.'"

"Hey, improvising is *much* better than relying on some stupid plan that's useless the minute something goes wrong. Besides, I'll have you know that I'm very good at coming up with strategies. How do you think I've been sneaking away from my brother to do all this Shadows stuff?"

Beck snorts. "I think you've been totally making it up as you go along and hoping you don't get caught."

That might be a little more accurate than I'd care to

admit, so I ignore it. "And *speaking* of sneaking away from my brother, I'm guessing this meeting is going to be at night again? So I don't know how I'm going to get away this time. It's not like I can play sick again or keep giving Ronan tea without raising suspicion."

Beck's eyebrows rise, but he doesn't even ask. "Actually, it isn't at night this time. It's at noon."

"Well, that's a relief, at least. My brother will be at work, so I won't have to sneak out. Ronan isn't exactly thrilled when I disappear."

"Really? What happened?"

I sigh. "Nothing. We just had a fight last time I came home late without telling him where I was. It's weird having adults care about where you are and stuff."

Something sad flicks across Beck's face for a second. "Doesn't sound that bad to me."

"Yeah, well, you'd hate it."

He shrugs. "If you say so."

He's pretending not to care, but he obviously does, and it annoys me. He's acting like *I'm* the spoiled rich kid all of a sudden, complaining about having a curfew. Which, admittedly, is exactly what I'm doing. But he wasn't there. He doesn't know hard it is for me, trying to be the good little sister that Ronan wants. It's not like I found my family and everything is suddenly perfect and happy. No matter how hard I try, I'm mostly still Old Alli, the same girl who broke into the Atherton mansion with Beck all those months ago. Better suited to being a thief than being a lawyer's sister.

But I don't know how to explain this in a way that he'd understand. The words are all tangled up in my mouth. "Whatever," I say instead. "It doesn't matter."

The front doors creak loudly, and both Beck and I jump. Rosalia walks in, dusting snow from her coat. Her cheeks are flushed red, but otherwise I could never tell she just hiked through the woods in several feet of snow. Her hair is still perfectly braided, not a strand out of place.

"Rosco. You left tracks. You could've led anyone right to us," she says by way of acknowledging my presence. She strides down the aisle until she reaches us, then stops to warm her gloved hands in front of the fire. "I have news," she says, looking at Beck.

"Where have you been?" I ask.

She continues looking at Beck as if I haven't spoken. "The new steward just issued a batch of assignments, and several people have been called to a meeting with the king himself tomorrow. You and me included."

Beck frowns. "Are you sure?"

Rosalia glares. "Of course I'm sure. I asked a couple of friends to keep me informed. They've been sneaking my family messages from within the Guild. Apparently everyone thinks the king is planning something big. It's been a while since he called this many people to a meeting all at once."

"It must be about the Shadows," Beck says.

"Exactly."

Beck leans back against the side of the nearest pew, frowning. "Are you planning to go?"

She turns away from the fire, crossing her arms in front of her chest. "I think I will. I don't want the king to think my family has deserted—he'll send people after us, and it will be harder to hide. I'll just have to be prepared for any Shadows I might encounter."

"Prepared?" I ask.

Rosalia looks at me for the first time, and something fierce glimmers in her eyes. She doesn't elaborate, but she doesn't have to. I remember the way she held a knife to my throat. She means *that* kind of prepared.

"Are you going?" I ask Beck, even though I already know what his answer will be.

"Of course," he says, just like I knew he would. "I'm sure the king wants information about what we've been doing."

"Which is a problem, because we don't have any," I point out. "We're no closer to finding the coin than we were when we started, we still don't know who the leader of the Shadows is or how to find them—"

"Did you see my brother?" Rosalia interrupts. She's trying not to look worried, but I'm getting better at seeing through her cool exterior. She's *very* worried.

"He wasn't at the meeting," I say. "And I didn't see him at the Night Market, either. Did you find out anything, Beck?"

"No," he says. "I tried to ask Keene, but he wasn't very helpful."

I sigh. "So we have zero information about anything."

Beck straightens up abruptly, sending a poof of dust flying into the air. "But we will," he says. "There's that meeting tomorrow, remember?" He turns to Rosalia. "When do we have to be back at the Guild?"

"Tomorrow at two," she says.

"It'll be tight, but we can make it. Could you have someone arrange for a thilastri to meet us?"

She purses her lips, considering. "I'll see what I can do."

Beck nods. "It's settled, then. Alli and I will go to the Shadows meeting tomorrow and learn everything we can, and maybe we can even look around the hideout for where they've hidden the coin. Afterward, I'll meet you, Rosalia, and we'll fly to the Guild to meet the king, and I can tell him everything we've found out. And give him the coin, if we find it."

Something tells me none of this will be that simple. "And if we don't find it? Or figure anything else out?"

"We already know more than you think," he says. "We know where their hideout is. We know who some of their members are. We know more about how they operate. And we know of at least a few vendors at the Night Market who are fencing for the Shadows. I'm sure the king will want to know about all of that."

"It's still not much to go on without knowing who the leader is."

"Well, then we'd better make sure to find out tomorrow." Beck has that familiar determined look on his face, the one that means he'll stop at nothing to get what he wants. It's the look that I used to find admirable, until I realized just how far he's willing to go. Now it makes me nervous.

Rosalia sniffs. "None of that will mean anything without the coin. The king *must* have it to preserve the legitimacy of his claim to power."

"Not to mention whatever magic powers it grants him, right?" I say.

"There's little evidence it does anything of the sort. It's a symbol of power, not a magic token," says Rosalia.

"If it's only a symbol, then why does the king need it back so badly?" I argue.

Rosalia gives me a very serious stare. "Don't be so quick to underestimate symbols. They have a power all their own."

I open my mouth to argue some more, but Beck raises a hand. "Regardless," he says pointedly, "I think we can all agree that the coin is important, and finding it should be our top priority."

I cross my arms over my chest. "She doesn't *know* it isn't magic," I grumble. "And anyway, the coin isn't my top priority. Finding out who put my brother's name on that list is."

"But if we find the coin, then the Shadows will be defeated, and it won't matter who put his name there," Beck says.

Rosalia frowns. "Rosco, are you sure your brother isn't involved with the Guild somehow? Or involved in something criminal? It doesn't make sense that his name would be there for no reason."

"Don't be ridiculous. Ronan is, like, the most boring person on the planet. He spends all day at his law office or studying his books. He doesn't even have the time to be involved in anything." But even as I say it, I get this weird twisty feeling in my chest. I haven't lived with Ronan for very long. How well do I really know him? Could he be hiding something that I don't know about?

"Could just be because he's a lawyer," Beck says. "Maybe he helped put one of the Shadows in prison once, or one of their friends."

Rosalia nods, as if that makes sense. But it doesn't, because Ronan told me he only handles business law. He doesn't put thieves in prison. But I don't say that out loud. I feel like I need to defend Ronan from their suspicion, even if I'm starting to feel suspicious myself.

"Or it could be because of his girlfriend," I say instead. "Maybe she arrested one of the Shadows once or something."

"But then why wouldn't her name be on the list instead of his?" Beck asks.

Rosalia shakes her head. "Could be a revenge thing. They want to threaten the protector by going after her boyfriend. That could be it."

That does make more sense, and I feel a little bit better.

Maybe it's not about Ronan after all. Maybe he hasn't done anything wrong.

"But really," Rosalia continues, "it doesn't matter. Beck's right. If we find the coin and stop the Shadows, then you won't have to worry about the list at all. Finding the coin should be our focus."

"So," Beck says, "what can we do at the meeting tomorrow to make sure we get a chance to look for it?"

"I don't know. They kept us under pretty careful watch last time. We weren't exactly allowed to go exploring."

"Right, but there will be more people at this meeting, I think. That means more distractions to take advantage of."

"Or more people to potentially catch us," I say.

Beck starts pacing in front of the fireplace, his footsteps echoing against the stone floor. He's in full planning mode now, and nothing will snap him out of it. "Maybe we should get there a bit early? They'll still be getting things set up, lots of people will still be arriving, plenty of movement back and forth . . . maybe no one would question us if they saw us walking around."

"Or *maybe* they'd decide to stab us with sharp pointy objects."

Rosalia stares thoughtfully into the fire. "Perhaps if you claimed to be looking for Mead?" she suggests. "He'd likely cover for you if asked."

Beck runs a hand through his hair, mussing it up even more. "Good idea."

"Terrible idea," I say. "How do we know for sure he'd go along with it? None of us knows what Mead will actually do at any given time. His first priority is always saving his own skin."

"Yes, but what's his second priority?" Rosalia says, a hint of something wry in her voice. I'd say it was amusement, if Rosalia were capable of being amused.

"Does he have one?" I say.

Rosalia gives me a meaningful glance and tilts her head, very slightly, in Beck's direction.

Rosalia knows what I know—that if there's anyone Mead seems to care about other than himself, it's Beck.

"So you think he'd lie for *us*," I say to her, putting emphasis on "us" so she'll know I really just mean Beck.

She nods. "Unless it directly contradicts his first priority of helping himself, I don't see why not."

"It's the only plan we've got," Beck says, still pacing. I don't think he's noticed the exchange between Rosalia and me—he's too busy turning things over in his head, putting the pieces into place.

"Just because it's the only plan we've got doesn't make it a good plan," I say, because someone ought to point it out.

Rosalia sighs. "Do you ever contribute anything useful? Or are you only good for whining and complaining while everyone else comes up with ideas?"

"Oh, come on," I say. "You did not just accuse *me* of being too negative."

She arches her eyebrows. "What's that supposed to mean?"

"You're, like, the *queen* of negativity."

Rosalia starts to respond, but Beck interrupts. "Neither of you is being particularly helpful at the moment."

"She started it," I mutter.

Beck sighs. "All right, look. Why don't you come over here as soon as you can get away from your brother? Then we'll head over to the Shadow meeting early, have extra time to search for the coin. If anyone asks, we'll say we're looking for Mead. Whether we find the coin or not, we'll stick around for the meeting, see what we can find out about who the leader is. Then I'll meet up with Rosalia and report back to the king."

"Oh, so I'm going to do all of the actual work, but Rosalia will get to report back to the king and take credit for it? That seems fair."

Beck closes his eyes. "We will be sure to mention your contributions."

"Make sure you do," I say. Rosalia rolls her eyes, so I keep going just to annoy her. "When this is all over, I'll expect nothing less than a parade in my honor. A festival. An annual Guild holiday. With confetti. And cake. And dozens of minstrels singing ballads about my heroics."

Beck laughs. "And what exactly would the lyrics of these ballads be?"

"Oh, you know. Something about how I single-handedly defeated the evil Shadows because I'm so smart and brave and talented and—"

"And modest," Beck says.

"And clever and courageous and—"

"Now you're just saying synonyms," Rosalia points out.

"And heroic and daring and brilliant and . . ." I pause, trying to think of more good adjectives.

"Bold," Beck suggests, grinning.

Much to my surprise, Rosalia grins too. "Intrepid," she supplies. "Audacious. Spirited. Witty."

Huh. Will wonders never cease.

"And *endlessly* annoying," she continues, ending the little feel-good moment as soon as she started it. "Not to mention obnoxious, lazy, arrogant, temperamental, insufferable, overconfident, reckless, unendurable, tiresome—"

"Now *you're* just saying synonyms."

"And unbearably sarcastic," she finishes.

There's a split second of silence; then Beck bursts out laughing.

"Well, on that note," I say, glaring at him, "I'll be going now. I can see that my contributions are completely underappreciated."

Beck tries to say something, but he can't stop laughing.

I make a big show of spinning on my heel and storming down the aisle toward the front door.

"I forgot 'overly dramatic,'" Rosalia says, which sends Beck into a fit of laughter again.

"You'll see," I call over my shoulder. "After we find that stupid coin, you'll owe me forever. Just you wait!" I stomp outside into the snow, closing the door on the sound of their laughter.

Okay, maybe it was a little funny. But I will never in a million years admit that to Rosalia, even if she tortures me with her big scary knife. I do have *some* dignity.

I make it a point to grab a large branch and use it to wipe out my own footprints, walking backward through the trees and trying to erase any signs of my presence. Wouldn't want to give Rosalia anything else to complain about.

There's just one problem: doing this is *so* slow. I can only take a few steps before I have to stop and scrape the branch through the snow, and it doesn't do a very good job of obliterating my tracks. Then I have to glance over my shoulder to make sure I'm not about to crash into a tree, take a few more steps, and then repeat the process all over again.

After only a minute or two my hands get cold and numb, making it harder to grip the branch. Also, dragging the branch through thick snow makes the muscles in my arms burn, and my back aches from bending over. I keep stumbling over tree roots hidden under the snow, and the low-hanging branches laden with sharp icicles keep thwacking me. I'm tempted to give up before I'm even halfway down the hill, but Rosalia's accusations about my whining and laziness keep a fire burning in my veins. I'll tidy up every inch of snow in the whole entire woods just to spite her.

Well, okay, not every inch. I'm not getting any younger here.

By the time I reach the bottom of the hill, my arms ache so badly, I can barely lift my stick, but my footprints are mostly gone. I fling the branch to the ground in triumph. Take *that*, Rosalia Peakes.

I'll show her tomorrow, too. I'll find the coin and meet the leader of the Shadows and make the king so indebted to me that he really will offer me a ton of money, and Rosalia will eat her words. Plus, I'll have so much gold, I might just hire a minstrel to compose that song about me. And then I'll have him follow Rosalia around all day and sing it loudly in her ear. Everywhere she goes, the minstrel will pop out of the shadows to proclaim my greatness, and then I'll be the one laughing.

I'll just do this one last thing, find one little coin and take the Shadows down, and then I'll be done with thieving for good.

But something in my gut tells me it won't be that simple. Despite Beck's best efforts, nothing about my life ever really goes as planned.

Chapter Eighteen

The house at 218 South Astian looks almost exactly like I remember it. Cheerful window trim, bright flowerpots, a decorative little gate. Snow blankets the lawn now, though, and jagged icicles dangle from the vacant, frost-covered flower boxes under the windows. There's also a bright winter wreath now on the front door. It's still hard to believe that *this* is where the Shadows operate from.

Beck and I didn't chat much on the way here. I met him in the chapel early this morning just like we planned, but he's acting distracted, gazing off into space and not really paying attention to me. Maybe he's just worried about what will happen today, whether we can find the coin or what will happen when he meets the king later. But it feels weird not to have him lecturing me about the plan like he normally does. I never thought I'd say this, but I almost miss it.

"Ready?" I ask him as we open the gate and walk toward the house.

He nods.

I step up to the porch, clench the heart-shaped door knocker, and rap it twice.

The young woman, the one who seems to own the house, glares down at us when she finally opens the door. "You're early. The meeting's not for another hour."

"I know," I say. "I was hoping to have a chance to talk with Koby Mead before the meeting starts. About my assignments? He's the one who's been training me, since I'm a new recruit and all."

The woman studies me for a moment before turning her gaze to Beck. "And you?" she asks.

"Hitched a ride here with her," he says casually.

The woman peers past us, toward the street. "Don't see a ride anywhere." Her voice is calm, but her suspicion is clear.

"We didn't want to have the driver drop us off in front of the house, obviously," I say. "We left the carriage a few blocks back." The snow on the street has finally melted enough today that there are horse-drawn carriages back in the streets instead of sleighs, so it's a likely enough lie.

The woman steps back from the doorway, ushering us inside. "Use the back door from the alley next time," she says. "I don't want the neighbors to see you."

"We will," Beck says quickly.

"Let Ivo take your coats," she says, which is clearly code for

Let the big scary guard guy search you for weapons. "Then you can head upstairs. Mead was on the third floor, last time I saw him."

"Thank you," Beck says. She makes an irritated sound and walks away, disappearing into the main living area at the end of the hallway. Beck and I take off our coats, gloves, hats, scarves, and boots, then get the grunt of approval from Ivo. In silent agreement, we put everything back on again, in case we have to leave in a hurry. Then we head up the creaky narrow staircase to the second floor.

The stairs end in a tiny round hallway, with doors branching off on all sides. A circular blue-and-red throw rug covers the center of the wooden floor. More framed paintings dot the walls, though they're so dusty I can barely make out the images. A single candle sits on a table opposite the stairs, casting the space in a warm orange glow.

"Which door?" I ask Beck.

He frowns. "I guess we try them all? See if we can find a clue about where the coin might be?"

"This is a terrible plan."

"Shh," Beck hisses. "Your voice echoes in here."

"Sorry."

"Just try a room, I guess."

I heave open the nearest door. It's a tiny, cramped bedroom, decorated similarly to the rest of the house—quaint wooden furniture, bright colors, portraits on the walls, floral wallpaper. A quilt is tucked onto the neatly made bed. But there's no one here.

"Do you think . . . ?" I ask.

"Doesn't look like this room is used much. Too much dust. And it's at the front of the house, where more people are likely to stumble in. Not the most logical hiding place for the coin."

"All right." We try the next door, which leads to a tiny bathroom. I open the single cupboard and flip through it, but there's nothing except a few bars of scented soap and a pile of towels. Beck runs his hands over the walls, feeling for something—hidden compartments? Hollow spaces?

I clamber over the toilet and pull back the cheerful yellow bath curtain. Nothing. No place to hide a coin anywhere.

"Check for loose tiles," Beck whispers to me. "They could slide out."

I check, but none of the tiles are loose. Meanwhile Beck inspects the toilet tank, but he comes up empty too.

"Okay, I'm thinking it's not here," I say.

We tiptoe out of the bathroom and open the next door. It's another bedroom, except it looks even more unused than the last. Cobwebs choke the corners, and there's a fine layer of undisturbed dust on every piece of furniture.

I glance at Beck, and he shakes his head. "Doesn't seem likely they'd keep it here either. It'd be in the bedroom that the leader or the woman is using, probably, somewhere they could keep an eye on it."

"But what if it *is* in here, and we're missing it?"

"We don't have time to thoroughly check every room.

Let's check the most likely ones first, and then we can always come back in here if we don't find anything."

We move on.

The last door off the circular landing leads to a much larger space. A few armchairs are tucked in a corner beside a row of bookcases. Another staircase, this one rounded and spiraling, is in the far corner, leading up to the third floor. There are more doors off this room, but further investigation reveals only closets stuffed full of spare furniture and boxes.

"The coin could be *anywhere* in here," I say, looking around at the mountains of boxes in despair.

"I still don't think it's likely," Beck says. "Look at how easy it is for us to just walk in here and poke around. They wouldn't keep the coin where any Shadow member could just stumble onto it."

"But if that's true, how are we ever going to find it? We're basically just wandering around hoping to stumble onto it."

Beck doesn't say anything, but his expression is worried. "Let's keep looking."

After checking the bookcases to make sure they don't lead to secret passages or anything—disappointingly, they don't—we head up to the third floor.

These rooms seem to be much more in use than the ones downstairs. There's a bathroom almost identical to the first one, but it's more of a mess—someone's dirty towel crumpled on the floor, the sink still wet, soap scum in the tub. No sign of a hidden compartment anywhere, though.

Voices drift over to us, coming from behind one of the other doors. We tiptoe past it, trying not to alert anyone to our presence, and try a third door. It's locked.

I step out of the way while Beck withdraws a set of lock-picks and goes to work. After a couple of minutes, he turns the lock and jiggles the knob free, and we go in.

Unlike the other rooms, this one looks lived in, and I can tell right away that it belongs to *her*, the woman whose house this is. The sheets are rumpled and twisted on the bed, the nearby dresser drawers are half-open with clothes spilling out everywhere, and the gauzy white curtains over the window are flung wide.

Beck and I look at each other. *This* room could be a possibility.

We step inside, closing the door quietly, and get to work. I tackle the dresser first. It's topped with a mirror, a hair-brush, and bottles of perfume. A teal seashell-shaped bowl holds a tangle of jewelry. I dump it out and paw through it, but there's no coin anywhere. Next I go through the drawers, dumping clothing onto the floor, searching for any hidden little compartments or coin pouches or *anything.* All I find are heaps of clothing and bare wooden drawers.

I turn away from the dresser. Beck has already torn apart the bed and is now crawling around on the ground, checking the floorboards. I head over to the nearby nightstand and ransack it. More jewelry, candle stubs and a box of matches, a comb, loose papers, a stubby quill pen . . . and a little pouch of gleaming coins.

"Beck!" I whisper loudly. He rushes over and looks at the bag in my hand.

"Empty it," he whispers. "We have to check every coin."

I dump the coins into an unceremonious heap, wincing at the noise they make. Beck starts sorting through them, examining each one before casting it aside, and I copy him. An ordinary jamar. And another, and another, and another . . .

There are enough jamars here to buy food for a whole month, but none of these coins look unique or special in any way. Nothing screams *Powerful and possibly magical thief coin belonging to the king of the Guild.* There isn't even any foreign currency.

Beck slumps back on his heels, disappointed. "It isn't here. It isn't *anywhere.*"

"We don't know that," I say. "There's still that other room to check, where people are talking. And we didn't look in those other rooms very thoroughly. It's got to be here somewhere." But even as I say it, I'm not convinced it's the truth. The coin might not be anywhere in the house.

But my words are all it takes for Beck to snap out of it, his usual fierce determination overtaking him. "All right," he says, "we need a new plan."

"How did I know you were going to say that?"

"I think you should go down to the meeting alone. You can see who the leader is and get as much information as you can. I'll stay up here and keep looking. I'll be able to search every room once everyone goes downstairs."

This seems reasonable, but I hate the idea of having to go down to the meeting by myself. "Are you sure? You don't need to see who the leader is?"

"You can tell me," Beck says, giving me a little smile. "We'll meet up outside after the meeting's over."

"Okay." I stand up and look around at the mess we've made. "What about this? Do we need to clean up?"

Beck frowns, considering. "It will take too long, and it'd probably still be obvious that someone's been in here. Let's just leave it. It's a house full of thieves, after all. Anyone could've picked the lock and come in here looking for valuables. They won't know it was us, and they won't know we were looking for the coin."

"They will if we don't pick these up," I say, pointing to the jamars scattered across the floorboards. "A real thief wouldn't just leave those behind."

"Good point." We gather up the scattered coins and slip them back inside the coin pouch, which Beck tucks into his pocket.

"Better take some of that jewelry, too," he says, heading over to the dresser.

I frown. This feels way too much like real thievery, taking things we don't strictly need. But Beck's right about the jewelry looking suspicious if we leave it behind. Anyway, I try to remind myself that it belongs to a Shadow thief, the one who's actively undermining the Guild and its king, putting Beck's life in danger, and planning to kill my brother. I refuse to feel bad for her.

But my stomach doesn't listen, twisting with guilt anyway.

Beck finishes pocketing the jewelry and slips back out into the hallway. "I'll wait in the bathroom for everyone to leave," he says. "You should head down to the meeting now. It'll probably start soon. Find out everything you can."

"Okay," I say. "See you when it's over."

"See you. And, Alli?"

"Yeah?"

"Be careful."

I grin. "Aren't I always?"

Downstairs, people have started assembling in the living room. Like before, the furniture has been pushed against the walls, and most people are sitting on the floor. But unlike before, there are a lot of people here this time. Beck must've been right about what a big meeting this is. I'm early, and the room is already almost full.

I return to the space along the wall where the new recruits sat last time, mostly hidden by the stairs overhead. It's a little chilling, looking out over the room from here—it is packed with people, and all of them are thieves and Shadows. Or pretending to be Shadows, in my case.

There are a few familiar faces in the crowd. Keene stands by the fireplace, right in front of the list, talking with some goonish-looking guys who are laughing at whatever he's saying. That guy who was at the first meeting, leaning against the wall and keeping his hat low so I couldn't see his face, is here again, and he's doing the exact same thing. All I can see of him is the hat. I don't spot anyone else I recognize, though.

More and more people troop in through the back door, while a few pass Ivo to enter from the front. The stairs overhead shake as several people thud down—the voices Beck and I heard from the third-floor room, most likely. A few seconds later, a small pack of people enters. Among them is Mead, instantly recognizable as he towers over everyone else, and a few of the others look familiar. . . .

Peakes. One of them is Peakes, Rosalia's little brother.

He looks gaunt and tired, with deep lines under his eyes, and I'd forgotten just how young he is. He was always the baby of the group we hung out with at the Guild, the one who got teased the most, the only one who hadn't had his trial yet. And as much as I loathe sharing any sentiment whatsoever with Rosalia, I can understand why she's worried about him. Seeing Peakes in this room is like seeing a scared puppy in a pack of wolves.

Mead looks around, and his pale eyes land on me. He gives me a single nod in acknowledgment before moving on, joining some of the other guys by the kitchen. He keeps scanning the room, though, when he thinks no one's looking. Probably wondering where Beck is.

After a few more minutes, the woman who lives here

comes in, flanked by Ivo, and the conversations die down as she settles into the same white wicker chair she used before. Something about the way she sits in it, with her back straight and her skirts draping elegantly around her, makes her look regal somehow, like a queen on a throne.

I expect Keene to step forward and start the meeting just like he did last time, so I almost miss it when the woman starts speaking first. An immediate hush falls over the room.

"I called you all here today," she says, her gaze moving from one face to the next in the crowd, "to discuss the moment that we have all been waiting for. The downfall of the king."

Several jeers and hoots rise up as an excited ripple passes through the room. The woman allows it for a moment before raising her hand. Silence falls almost instantly, and she continues. "Thanks to all of your contributions, our plans have been set into motion. The time has come to bring those plans to fruition. But we cannot celebrate yet. There is still work to be done. This plan requires all of us working in tandem, for the final and most important assignment of all."

The room is so hushed that I can hear the crackle of the fireplace and the creaks of the floorboards shifting.

"Most of you are still keeping up appearances within the Guild, as we have asked you to do. Many of you may have received a summons to a meeting with the king this very day."

Must be the same meeting Beck and Rosalia are going to. But if some of these people will be there . . . how can Beck tell the king anything about the Shadows with them right there in the room? It won't be safe. And how can the king not know that these people are traitors?

"We have reason to believe that this meeting regards an attempted burglary at the Night Market."

Another murmur ripples through the crowd.

"The king is attempting one of the biggest heists in the Guild's history, and will assemble many of its members tonight to organize and plan it. But do not be fooled. The timing of this theft is no coincidence. The king has learned that certain market vendors have been aiding us, and he is attempting to disrupt their influence. He hopes to buy your loyalty, to quell the protests and dissent with mere gold. He hopes to distract you with the promise of riches, all while putting down any who dare to oppose him and letting his corruption and betrayal go unnoticed and unchallenged."

I have no idea what she's talking about now. Did all those little grievances the Shadows complained about really amount to "corruption and betrayal"? But the other people in the crowd seem to be following along—there are nods, whispers, murmurs of assent.

"So I have called you here to ask you this: Will you fall for the king's ploys and allow your loyalty to be bought? Or will you join us in using the king's own heist to take him down?"

The room explodes in cheers and shouts. I can't make out individual words over the clamor, but most people look excited, even fervent. I catch Mead's gaze across the room. He's applauding, lazily, but there's something on his face that doesn't quite look like agreement. If I didn't know better, I'd say it was concern.

The woman lets the cheering continue for a moment before holding up her hand again. Silence falls as everyone waits to hear what she'll say next.

"To that end, I think it's time to introduce you to the master thief of the Shadow Guild, the man who helped bring my vision to life. We have kept his role within the Shadows a secret so as to protect him from rumors within the Guild, but now that it is time to put our plan into action, you must all know his true identity."

A figure steps forward. The man with the hat tipped low over his face reaches the center of the room, stops, and lifts the hat from his head.

Gasps rise up across the room, and one of them is mine.

I know him.

It takes me a second to remember his name, but then I do: Garil Gannon.

The man from the silk cart in the marketplace that I searched for the coin.

The one who gave me directions to Ronan's law office, who knew right away where it was.

Maybe he just knew it because Avinoch's is a prominent law office, like Mead told me before. Or maybe he's the one who put Ronan's name on that list.

And he probably knows that I ransacked his cart and stole his coin pouch.

I slink back into my corner, willing him not to see me. He might recognize me from our conversation and suspect that I searched his cart. I can't even think what might happen if—

"Good afternoon," he says, smiling. Like the woman, he casts his gaze from one face in the crowd to the next, but where it made her seem calculating and guarded, on him it's practically charming. There's something so innocent and disarming about that smile, the same something that fooled me back in the marketplace. I never suspected he was anything other than a silk seller, even when I was searching his cart for the coin, and even when he gave me perfect directions to Ronan's office. I never believed he was dangerous.

But right now, standing in a crowd of thieves and winning their trust with a single smile, he may be one of the most dangerous people I've ever met.

"Thank you for the introduction, Leta," he says to the woman, snapping me out of the spiral of my thoughts. *Leta.* It's the first time the woman has been given a name. I'll have to tell Beck.

And I'll have to tell Beck that the king was right to suspect the silk vendor, because apparently he's the ringleader of the Shadows.

"I know most of you already, I believe," he continues, nodding to different faces in the crowd. "I have been watching many of you for months, and I have been quite pleased with your work on behalf of our organization. Together we can bring an end to Kerick's tyranny once and for all. And we will do it at the very heist that he hopes will bring him glory."

He smiles again, and they're falling for it, they're all falling for it—the faces in the crowd look nothing but charmed.

"I believe I now have an accurate idea of your strengths and weaknesses individually, and I will be assigning each of you a task for tonight's events. Some of you I will ask to meet me later, so that we may discuss your role in more detail."

He turns to Keene and starts rattling off instructions. There are so many names and words I don't recognize that I can barely follow, but Keene is nodding, looking determined. Gannon mentions entrances, positioning, something about a north-side wall . . .

Then Gannon starts talking to other people, making his way around the room and addressing them in turn. Most people receive simple instructions—be at a certain place at a certain time, or follow so-and-so's lead. After he finishes speaking with each person, they leave the room.

The crowd's nearly cleared out by the time Gannon turns his gaze to where I and a few other new people are sitting. Oh, Saint Ailara, don't let him recognize me . . .

"Ah, the new recruits," he says, giving me a grin as slick as ice. "Each of you has been previously assigned to someone who's been showing you the ropes, I believe?"

We nod.

"Very good. Each of you will report to that person for further instructions on how you can assist them."

We nod again, and he turns away, clearly dismissing us. The other two beside me walk toward the back door, and I scramble to my feet, intending to head to the front to find Beck. But Gannon turns, and his gaze latches onto me. My stomach drops through the floor.

He knows. He *knows*.

"Miss Rosco," he says quietly, "stay a moment."

I'm frozen. I try not to glare at him, not wanting to make this any worse, but I can't seem to resist the impulse.

Gannon steps closer, directly in front of me. He towers over my head and has to bend lower to look into my eyes.

"I recognized you right away in the marketplace," he says, his voice barely above a whisper. "As soon as you mentioned having a brother who worked at Avinoch's, I could see the resemblance. You can imagine my surprise at finding Ronan Rosco's baby sister again at our last meeting, as a member of the Guild. And I'm sure you can imagine how much more surprised I was to learn, afterward, that you aren't a Guild member at all."

A shudder runs up and down my spine, and I clench my teeth, willing myself not to let him see my fear.

"Captured during your trial. Imprisoned for several months. Reunited with your long-lost brother, the lawyer's apprentice at Avinoch and Co. And yet here you are, among the Guild members, as if you're one of them."

"I can explain," I say quickly.

"Oh, I'm sure you can. No doubt you've concocted an elaborate lie. But I think you'll find I'm not easily lied to."

He turns away from me abruptly and looks toward the door, where Ivo is watching dispassionately. "Bring him in," Gannon says. Ivo straightens and shoulders through the door toward the front hallway.

Before I can figure out what's happening, Gannon turns back to me. "I know all about your little scheme, you see. You and Beck Reigler, spying on our meetings, hunting through the house, trying to discover our secrets, reporting back to the king. What did you think—that you could somehow save your brother from me and my Shadows?"

A thousand thoughts are churning through my head, and I don't know what to do. I want to punch him. I want to fight. I want to run. My feet move before my mind catches up—

Gannon slams his hand against the wall between me and the door, barring my escape. "Don't think you'll be getting very far, Miss Rosco. I know your brother, Ronan, quite well, you see. Such a smart, well-mannered young man. It would be a pity if anything *unfortunate* were to happen to him."

Ice slides down my spine, even as the heat of my anger surges through my blood. My fists clench. "Don't you dare," I say, looking him straight in the eyes. "He has nothing to do with this. Don't you *dare*—"

"Not to mention," Gannon continues as if I haven't spoken, "I can think of someone else you might care about." He looks toward the door again. "Ivo!"

The door swings open, and Ivo walks in, dragging a struggling figure behind him.

Beck.

He fights against Ivo's hold, pulling away, but his hands are bound behind his back, and Ivo's grip is too strong.

I don't know what to do. I can't overpower Ivo by myself, not to mention Gannon. I scan the room, looking for help, a way out, someone who might—

Mead is still in the room. He stands in front of the fireplace, watching everything, completely unmoved. His face is a blank mask.

And instantly I know what happened.

"How could you?" I lunge forward before I can think. "How could you—"

Gannon grabs my coat and tugs me backward, away from Mead, as if I'm a disobedient dog on a leash.

"The Guild was on to me," Mead says, his voice infuriatingly calm. "They recognized me that night at the market, you know. Dryn and Kierr. They put two and two together and reported me to the king. Gannon managed to get me out safely before they had a chance to capture me. I would have been killed."

"I always look out for my Shadows," Gannon says, smug. "But I still had to be convinced, you see, that Mr. Mead here really was one of ours. There had been some . . . questions about his loyalty here as well. But Mead was quite eager to prove his worth. When I told him of my suspicions about you and your connection to his friend Mr. Reigler, he was all too willing to share what he knew of your plans."

So Gannon let us come here today, knowing we'd be trapped.

How long did it take Mead to spill his guts to Gannon? How much convincing did he need? Did his friendship with Beck mean so little that he tossed it aside when it suited him? Or did Gannon coerce him?

Mead looks at me with those familiar colorless eyes, and I don't know the truth about anything anymore.

Gannon spins me around to face him again before releasing his hold on my coat. "So you see, Miss Rosco, I'm afraid your little game has come to an end now. But not to worry—I'm sure you'll be reunited with your brother very soon."

Beck hangs limply from Ivo's arms, not moving. Defeated.

I have to do something, I have to—

"But until then, we can't risk letting you interfere with our plans." Gannon turns to Ivo. "Take that one to the basement. I'll handle the girl myself."

Beck looks up. Our eyes lock, and I am seeing two moments simultaneously—Beck, captured by guards last spring in the Dearborn gardens, pinned to the ground, and Beck, now, mere feet away from me. And both of them are mouthing the same word.

Run.

Chapter Nineteen

I don't think. I just move.

I spin out of Gannon's hold, stumbling backward. He lunges after me, but I grab a small chair leaning against the wall and swing it around, using it as a barrier between us. Beside me, Beck struggles in Ivo's grip, keeping him busy. I don't see the woman, Leta, anywhere, but Gannon is flanked by Keene and another thief, and Mead is still standing by the fireplace.

Gannon makes another lunge in my direction, but I swipe at him with the chair, and he's forced to dodge it. I back up on instinct, but it's the wrong move. I'm against the wall. Ivo blocks the path to the front. The only way out is through the back, but there are multiple pieces of furniture blocking the way. I'm boxed in.

"Where do you think you're going to go, little Rosco?" says Gannon, almost politely. He reaches into his pocket and withdraws a long, shiny knife. "I had hoped it wouldn't have to be this way. But don't worry; I'll be sure to pay a visit to your brother to let him know what happened to you."

I inch sideways, gripping the edges of the chair as tightly as I can, trying to dodge the furniture lining the walls. If I can just reach the back door . . . "I appreciate the thought," I say, "but I think I'd rather tell him myself."

Keene tries to move in on my left, but I shove the chair legs into his chest. It doesn't do much more than knock him off balance for a second, but I use the distraction to run to the other side of the room. The fireplace is now to my immediate left, with the back door somewhere behind me. Just a few more steps . . .

"Have it your way," Gannon responds, his smile now menacing. "After I hunt you down, I'll do the same to your brother."

I'm close, but not close enough. Even if I sprint to the door, I'll never make it out before Gannon or the other thieves grab me. I need something to distract them while I run for it—

Mead moves calmly away from the fireplace, toward the far wall. He turns, meeting my gaze, and tilts his head slowly, deliberately, in the direction of the fireplace.

What is this? More of his games? An attempt to trick me or distract me or—

He places one hand on the back of the small table nearest to him. A table similar to the one behind me. He taps his index finger against the lacy decorative cloth that covers the table, just like the one behind me. Then he tilts his head toward the fire again.

My eyes widen in a flash of understanding.

Gannon sighs. "As fun as this little chase has been, I have other things to attend. It's time to end this."

"I couldn't agree with you more," I say. Then I reach back, snatch up the tablecloth, and hurl one end of it into the burning fire.

The cloth catches quickly, and I spin around, letting it fan out and fling sparks in every direction. Fire licks rapidly up the length of the cloth, warming my hands, but I don't dare let go. The thief whose name I don't know backs up and stumbles into Keene. I lunge toward Gannon, forcing him to back away from the flames. I reverse several steps, putting a few feet between us, with the exit right behind me.

Then I throw the fiery fabric toward Gannon with all of my might.

I don't stop to see what happens next. I spin around and make a break for the back door, throw it open, and run out into the cold.

A light snow is falling as I rush out the back alley, past a group of startled thieves who are loitering there, and dash down the street as fast as I can. The wind whips snow into my face, and I can barely see where I'm going. I tear through the streets in no particular direction, as long as it puts 218 South Astian far behind me.

When I run out of breath, I slow to a halt, skid, and collapse into the snow. I gasp for air, my teeth chattering.

I'm not going to think about the fact that I just left Beck alone with the Shadows in a room that may have been set on fire. They'll probably put it out before it spreads, and if not, I'm sure they'll get out of there fast and take Beck with them. Unless they decide to punish both of us by letting him burn alive . . .

No. I can't think about that right now. I need to focus. One step at a time. I'll go back for Beck. I'll save him. But first I need to warn Ronan.

I look up at the cloudy sky, trying to guess at the position of the sun. It's still afternoon, so Ronan won't be home from work yet. But Gannon can find him there; he gave me directions to the law office before, for God's sake. I have to tell Ronan to run.

The problem, as usual, is that I have no idea where I am. These city streets with their rows of identical brick buildings look even more identical in the snow, when any distinguishing features are buried. I know the sun is in the west, but I'm not sure which direction I need to go.

I make my way to a street corner and squint up at the sign. One of the names sounds familiar, so I pick a direction at random and make my way down it. After two blocks, I'm just as lost as I was before.

Up ahead, a carriage pulls slowly around the corner. Desperate, I flag it down. The driver pulls the horses to a stop.

"This carriage is already hired, miss," she says.

"I just need directions," I say quickly. "I'm a little lost."

She peers down at me, not unkindly. "Where are you trying to go?"

"I need Avinoch and Co.," I say. "The law office."

The driver nods. "You know what, I'm en route to pick up a client and will be passing right by there. Why don't I give you a lift?"

"Thanks, but . . . I don't have any money on me. I can't pay."

"No charge," she says cheerfully. "It's not out of my way."

Hardly daring to believe my luck, I thank her profusely and scramble into the carriage.

The going is slow given the weather, and I'm starting to think running really would have been faster. I keep my gaze fixed on the windows, looking for any sign that we're being followed by the Shadows, but the streets are mostly empty.

Just when I'm about to die of impatience, the carriage slams to a stop. "Avinoch and—" the driver starts to say, but I'm already flinging the door open and stumbling from the carriage.

I race up the slick steps of the building, past confused businesspeople carrying briefcases, and rush into the lobby. My wet boots squeak against the fancy stone floor as I cross the room, approaching the largest desk.

A man jotting something down on a slip of paper looks up at me, frowning. "How may I help you?"

"I need to see Ronan Rosco," I say. "It's urgent."

The man puts down his pen. "What is this regarding?"

"Please. It's an emergency."

The man looks me up and down. "I'm afraid Mr. Rosco is out on an errand. You'll have to wait."

"It can't wait!"

"I apologize, but Mr. Rosco isn't here. You're welcome to wait in the lobby until he returns, or leave a message with me."

I can't wait. *Beck* can't wait. "All right. I need to leave him a message," I say. "A *confidential* message."

"I understand," the man says, passing me a piece of paper, a pen, and an envelope.

I move to the far end of the desk, where the man can't see what I'm writing, and scribble quickly:

> You're in danger. Leave the office now, but don't go home. Garil Gannon and other bad people are coming for you. They know where you work and live. Stay hidden.
>
> I'm sorry. I'm going to try to make it right.
>
> Love, Alli

I fold the note up, stuff it into the envelope, and seal it. I write Ronan's name carefully on the outside, then pass the message to the secretary. "Make sure he gets this *immediately*,"

I say. "I'm not kidding. As soon as he walks in, not a second later."

"I understand," the man says again. I'm pretty sure he doesn't, but I don't argue. I run back across the lobby, out of the office, and into the snow.

Okay, next step. I need to find Rosalia. Somebody has to warn the king about the ambush the Shadows are planning at the Night Market. Someone needs to tell him about Gannon and about Beck getting captured. The king's the one who got Beck involved in this mess; surely he'll help. If not, I'll make Rosalia help me. We'll go to the market ourselves, find Beck . . .

But Rosalia and Beck were supposed to meet up to head back to the Guild right about now, and I don't know when or where. I guess the chapel is my only option. Rosalia might still be there, and if she isn't, she might show up looking for Beck.

I run up the hill and through the woods in record time, and burst into the chapel only to find it empty. The fire in the grate is out, but the embers are still burning, so she was here recently. I probably just missed her.

I run through every curse word I've ever learned as I pace the floor of the chapel. If only I could just go to the Guild for help myself. But it's high in the mountains, and I'd need a thilastri to take me. If only I'd paid more attention, let Beck tell me about Guild hideouts in the city, then maybe I could find help. Then again, I might run into Shadows instead.

I could try to go to the Night Market, but I'm not sure I can find it on my own, and even if I could, what then? Try to find Beck? Try to find the king? Try to find the coin?

I don't know what else to do except wait for Rosalia to show up. God, I am *so* not good at waiting.

I kick the nearest pew in frustration, but all it gets me is a sore foot.

The light filtering through the stained-glass windows has dimmed, and I'm considering lighting another fire to keep warm, when I finally hear a sound outside. It sounds like something moving through the snow—or someone?

I take a few steps down the aisle toward the doors, waiting. It's times like these when I really wish I'd started carrying a weapon around. Something a little more subtle than a flaming tablecloth would be a good idea.

The door slams open, and my whole body tenses. A shadowy figure stands in the doorway. It steps forward, revealing brown hair and a familiar white coat.

"Rosalia!" I say, rushing forward. "They have—"

Rosalia tries to take another step and collapses, her white coat stained with blood.

Chapter Twenty

I run to Rosalia, coughing at the dust churning in the air. "What happened? Are you okay?"

She lies flat on the ground, one hand pressed to her side. Dark red blood pools between her fingers. She opens her mouth, coughing, trying to speak.

I kneel beside her in the dust. "What is it? What's wrong? Are you okay?"

She closes her eyes. "Do I *look* okay?"

I'm so startled, I almost laugh. "On second thought, maybe I won't try to save you," I say, but I'm already unbuttoning her coat, trying to find the source of all the blood.

Rosalia hisses as I move the fabric, her face contorted in pain. "They found me," she says between gasps. "Shadows. At . . . at the Guild meeting. Cornered me right as I was getting into a carriage to leave and . . ."

I finish the sentence for her. "And stabbed you." I can see

the cut now. A deep gash in her side, oozing blood everywhere. I can't even see how long or wide it is with all the blood in the way.

If only Beck were here. He probably doesn't have enough healing magic to save her, but he could do something to help, maybe, if—

I have to push aside the burst of panic. I can't think about Beck being held by the Shadows right now, can't wonder if Gannon has hurt him or—or—

No. I need to focus. Make sure Rosalia isn't going to die first, then get help for Beck.

"Okay, well, let's stop the bleeding," I say, trying to sound like I know what I'm doing.

If Rosalia weren't gasping in pain, I'm pretty sure she'd be rolling her eyes at me. "You're a medical genius."

"*Or* I could just throw you outside in the snow and leave you there. Want to take bets about what would kill you first? I'm thinking blood loss for sure, although getting eaten by a wild animal is a definite possibility. Or freezing to death, but that's a bit slow, really . . ."

I don't have anything else on hand, so without thinking about it I take off my scarf and try to wrap it around the wound, with little success.

Back when I failed my trial and saved Ariannorah Atherton's life, I wished at the time that I knew how to make a tourniquet to stop *her* bleeding. You'd think I would've learned by now, but did I? Of course not. Here I am making the same stupid mistakes, trying to save a girl who's bleeding to death. Because I couldn't just live a normal life. Because I couldn't give up thieving. It's all my own stupid fault.

But I didn't let Ariannorah Atherton die, and I won't let Rosalia Peakes die either.

"Okay," I say, pulling the scarf as tight as possible, "on to the next issue. Let's get you in front of the fireplace instead of the doorway."

"Your brilliance knows no bounds."

"Or you can get mauled to death in the woods by wild animals. Your choice."

"I thought I was going to bleed to death first?"

"That was before my brilliant bandaging services were in effect. Now I put the odds on wild animals, then blood loss, *then* turning into a frozen ice cube. Now, if you lean on my shoulder, do you think you can walk over to the fire?"

Rosalia looks skeptical. "You're so short."

"Wild animals it is."

She grunts. "Just help me up already."

Very carefully, I manage to ease her into a half-sitting position as she wraps one arm around my shoulders, keeping her other hand pressed against her wound. "On three," I say. "One, two, three!"

I push her to her feet, and she puts almost all of her weight on me, nearly knocking me over. We stumble around for a second before I find my footing, Rosalia's hand digging into my shoulder. We make slow, agonizing progress down the aisle of the chapel, Rosalia barely dragging herself forward and trying not to cry out in agony.

We make it to the fireplace and collapse in exhaustion. A sheen of sweat dots Rosalia's forehead. When she can speak again, she says, "I don't think this scarf is working." She holds up her hand, showing me the glistening blood on her palm.

I gulp. I'm totally out of my depth here, and we both know it. But I'm going to fake confidence until we figure it out. "Okay, new plan. I'm going to go get some real bandages and first aid supplies. You just . . . wait here by the fire and try not to bleed to death."

"Rosco." Something about her voice has changed. Serious, not sarcastic. "You have to warn them. There were Shadow members at that meeting, they know what the king's planning tonight, it's going to be an ambush—"

"Yeah, I know. They said as much at the Shadows meeting."

She reaches for my arm and grips my sleeve tightly. "You have to stop them. They'll take over the Guild and kill the king, kill anyone who tries to stop them. My brother. Beck . . ." She frowns. "What happened to Beck? He wasn't at our meeting place, so I had to leave for the Guild without him."

"Yeah, about that." I tell her the whole thing, all in a rush—about Gannon and the woman named Leta, the things they said, the way they captured Beck and tried to capture me, Mead's betrayal, the way they threatened Ronan. "I came here to get your help," I finish.

Rosalia is wearing an expression I've never seen from her before. Her usual determination—the set of her jaw, the glint in her eye—is gone. She looks . . . resigned.

"Go," she says. "Go to the Night Market. Warn the king. Stop the Shadows."

"But how do I save Beck?"

"Save the king, and you save Beck."

"I don't understand."

She sighs, grimacing. "They kept him alive. That wasn't an accident. They're still planning to use him."

"Use him how?"

"My guess? Leverage. They may be trying to capture thieves who remain loyal to the king, to use them as bargaining chips."

"I thought they wanted to kill the king, not bargain with him."

"They do. But they'll have to get the rest of Kerick's men to stand down before they can get close to him. They may threaten Beck's life, as well as anyone else they've captured, to force Kerick to fight alone."

She pauses, straining for breath. "Maybe Beck will even be at the Night Market and you'll be able to free him. Maybe not. But it won't matter if you don't stop the Shadows, do you understand? If the Shadows take over the Guild, they'll kill anyone who wasn't loyal to them. Beck is now at the top of that list. If they win the Guild tonight, you lose any chance of saving him."

"Okay. I'll go get you some bandages, and then—"

"No," she interrupts. "Don't stop for anything. Just run."

"Don't be stupid. I'm not just going to leave you here on the ground to die."

"Alli—"

"You'll ruin the flooring," I say, trying not to think about what it means that she called me Alli for once. "The stains will never come out."

"Don't—"

"I'll stop the Shadows, just like you said. But it'll only take a minute to bring you a bandage or something. My brother's got supplies in his apartment. It's not far." I don't mention that I'm not sure if it's safe to go back to the apartment. Gannon probably knows where we live.

Rosalia sighs. "You've always been too stubborn for your own good."

"Reminds me of someone else I know," I say. "Someone who really ought to be using her stubbornness to fight impending death instead of arguing with me about it."

It might be my imagination, but I think she almost smiles. "I was right about you. You're too good for the Guild."

"You're not so bad yourself."

She tries to respond, but whatever she was going to say morphs into a moan of pain. She grips her side tightly.

"I'll take that as my cue to leave," I say, standing up. "Oh, er, Rosalia? How do I get to the Night Market, exactly? Mead took me there by thilastri before."

She takes a deep, painful breath before she speaks. "There's a thilastri in the stables in the Miagnar Gardens," she says. "He often takes Guild members to the Night Market. Show him the Guild pendant, and he'll take you there. His stall is painted mauve, with a gray falcon for the crest. The Miagnar Gardens are—"

"I know where they are," I say quietly. Beck and I were there, during our trial. It was the last place we went before we broke into the Atherton mansion and everything went wrong. "Okay, I'll find it. Thanks."

Rosalia exhales sharply. "Hurry. You don't have much time."

I make my way to the apartment in the dying light of dusk, trudging through freshly fallen snow. I don't have time to cover up my tracks, so I just have to hope the wind does the job for me.

I stop at every corner and peer down every street, looking for shadowy figures, anyone who might be following me, anyone who looks even slightly suspicious. But I don't see any sign of the Shadows. Hopefully they're too busy preparing for their big coup tonight to waste any time looking for me or Ronan.

Still, I'm extra cautious as I peek around the last corner, where our apartment building comes into view—

Protectors.

They're everywhere, covering the sidewalks, their red

uniforms bright against the white snow. There must be five or six of them, mostly grouped around our building. The carriages that must have brought them are parked right out front.

Saint Ailara help me. They've found out about the Guild somehow, or about the Shadows. They know everything; they've come for me—

No. That doesn't make sense. How would they . . . ?

The note. The one I left at Ronan's office. Either he got it and decided to call the protectors, or someone else intercepted it and did so themselves. Maybe they're guarding the apartment, since I said it wasn't safe . . . or maybe they're looking for me.

I duck back around the corner, hidden from view. Okay, think. How can I get into the building without them seeing me? There isn't another way in . . . except the windows. If there's an open window in the back, maybe I could crawl through; I might just fit.

I double back and go up a side street, then turn into the alley behind our building. As I suspected, no protectors back here, because there aren't any doors and the windows are small. Maybe too small even for me, but I've got to try something. I don't have much time. Scratch that—Rosalia and Beck and the king don't have much time.

I scan the back of the building, but all the first-floor windows are shut. I'm not sure if I'll find—

There. A curtain flutters in a second-story window. It's

open. But there's an obvious problem: It's on the second floor. Unless I can somehow scale the side of the building, there's no way up.

Except. There's a rickety metal fire escape wrapping around the building. It doesn't actually reach the ground over here, which, again, is why the protectors didn't even bother watching this side. But it's lower than the window and easier to reach. If I can just find a way onto the fire escape . . .

I survey the alley. It's boring and mostly clean, nothing useful. Nothing at all except a few scraps of litter and—

And a set of trash bins.

I grab a round bin, knock it onto its side, and roll it across the alley. I prop it upside down and position it as best I can beneath the fire escape. I'll just have to hope it's tall enough. *Please, Saint Ailara, please . . .*

I scramble on top of the bin and reach upward. As usual, Saint Ailara hates me. I'm too short. But I'm all out of options, so I do the only thing left. I jump.

My fingers scrape the bottom of the fire escape, but I fall back before I can get a grip, and land with a thud on the bin. My ankle rolls painfully underneath me. With my luck, it's probably sprained. Great.

I want to give up. I want to curl into a ball beside these trash bins and let the protectors find me in this stupid alley—

Allicat.

Beck's voice is in my head. All the times he called me

that. All the times he looked out for me, and trusted me to do the same for him.

I won't let the Shadows take him.

I steady myself, bend my knees, and jump.

My hands find the rusty metal bars of the fire escape and lock on. I reposition myself, tightening my hold, and reach up, grabbing a higher rung on the side. I repeat the movement with my left hand, then my right hand again. Inch by inch, I creep my way up until I'm clutching the top of the railing. With the last of my strength, I heave my body up and over, and land hard on the other side.

I made it. I'm on the fire escape.

I stand shakily, my injured ankle throbbing, and I wipe my rust-covered gloves on my pants. The fire escape creaks dangerously with my weight, as if it might give. I'll have to mention this to Ronan later; this thing is a death trap waiting to happen.

In a few quick steps, I reach the open window and peek carefully inside. Beyond the thin, mint-green curtains, I spy a cluttered kitchen that opens into a small living area, much like our apartment. No one is in sight, but there's a bag of groceries still sitting on the kitchen table. Someone is probably home.

The window is a tight fit, but I manage to lower my legs inside and slide through, narrowly avoiding banging my head. I land basically in the kitchen sink and clamber down to the floor. The mismatched teacups in the sink rattle alarmingly, and I hold my breath, but no one comes in.

I tiptoe into the living room, peering down the hallway. The bathroom door is closed, and the light is on. Not even daring to breathe, I rush across the living room, ease the front door open, and dash out into the hallway.

I make a run for the stairs. I've wasted too much time, and I need to get those bandages before—

I turn the corner in the stairwell and run smack into a protector.

The man looks down at me, and his eyes widen. "You're—"

I duck under his arm and run.

I don't dare look back, just sprint up the stairs, into the hall, and straight toward the apartment. The door is unlocked, and I practically throw myself inside, slamming it shut behind me.

A second later I realize my mistake. I didn't check to see if the apartment is empty. It isn't.

Ronan and Mari are both standing in the living room, staring at me.

Everyone starts to speak at once.

"Alli, where—"

"What's going—"

"Ronan! What are you doing here?" I glare at him. "Didn't you get my note?"

My brother looks lost for words. "Yes, I got your note. Alli—"

"Then why'd you come back here? I told you it isn't safe!"

"Isn't safe from *what*?" Ronan says.

At the same time, Mari starts, "There are six protectors watching the building, Alli. We're perfectly safe—"

"No, we are *not* perfectly safe," I say. "No offense to your protector friends, Mari, but they don't have a clue what they're dealing with. I mean, I just got into this building despite them, didn't I?"

That shuts everybody up for a second.

"I don't have time to explain," I say, starting toward the hallway. "But you need to get out of here, and you need to do it now. Get the protectors to escort you somewhere safe. There are . . . there are bad people looking for you."

"Wait," Mari says as I take another step, "you can't just—"

"No time to explain. Just trust me," I say, and I head for the bathroom.

I rummage frantically through the cabinet until I find the stash of first aid supplies. I have no idea what Rosalia needs, so I just grab everything. Maybe she'll know what to do with this stuff.

"Alli." Ronan stands in the doorway. "You need to tell us what's going on." Then he sees the stuff in my hands and the blood all over me, and his eyes widen. "Is that blood? Are you hurt?"

"Not mine," I mutter, adding a roll of bandages to my pile. "We have to go, Ronan, we all have to—"

"Not until you tell us why, Alli. What were you thinking, leaving me a message like that? Do you know how worried I've been? How worried we've *both* been? I didn't know where you were, I didn't know what was wrong, I didn't know how to find you. . . . Mari's had half the protectors in the city out looking for you and the other half here, trying to guard against some unknown threat! I don't—"

"Look, I'm sorry, okay? I'm sorry I scared you and I'm sorry I put us in danger, but none of that really matters right now."

"Of course it mat—"

"People are dying," I say loudly, talking over him. "Dying or about to die, right now, and I'm the only one who can help. I'm the only one who can stop the—the bad guys, so I need to go. You have to let me go."

Before he can respond, I push past him. He reaches for my arm, but I yank myself free, sending first aid supplies flying, and run into the living room.

Mari stands in front of the door, blocking my way.

"Stop," she says. "Explain."

"I—"

Ronan walks in and stands beside me. "The whole truth this time, Alli. Please."

I look back and forth from his face to Mari's. They're not budging.

I know I have to tell them something. I haven't been fair to them. But how do I even start to explain?

And I can't tell them everything. If I do . . . Ronan will

hate me when he learns the truth, that I'm a thief and a liar and I've been one all along. Mari was right about me from the beginning. She'll probably throw me back into prison once I confess, only this time I won't have my brother waiting for me on the other side.

My brother. If I don't tell him the truth, he'll never trust me again.

If I tell him, I'll lose him forever.

This is it. The two halves of my life have collided, and I can't keep them both anymore.

"Alli." Ronan's voice is soft. "Just tell us the truth."

So I do.

Chapter Twenty-One

I sit down on the sofa, dumping the first aid supplies in a heap beside me. Ronan moves to sit in the armchair. He leans forward, elbows on his knees, giving me his full attention. He doesn't look angry—yet.

I take a deep breath. I still haven't figured out how to tell them about the Guild without incriminating Beck.

I look at Mari, who's still standing in front of the door, her arms crossed. Her expression is impossible to read. "So here's the thing," I say, mostly to her. "There are some friends of mine who are . . . they're good people, really, who are kind of mixed up in some bad stuff, and I don't know how to tell you about them because I don't want to get them in trouble. I know being a protector is your job and that means you'd have to report them, but I really, really need you to not do that. Please."

Ronan looks at Mari, who thinks this over for a long minute. "You're right," she says. "It's part of my job to report criminal activity. I'd be obligated to report something if I knew about it."

My heart sinks. How can I be honest without getting Beck arrested?

"But," Mari continues, making my heart perk up a little, "if I didn't know a crime had happened—if I were to hear about a completely *hypothetical* situation, for example—I wouldn't have to file a report. Not without concrete evidence."

Now she tells me. "So if, say, I were to tell you a completely hypothetical story that isn't at all based on anyone I know, you'd be able to keep that entirely hypothetical story to yourself? Hypothetically?"

"Hypothetically speaking, yes," she says. "Although I would feel obligated to report it anyway if I thought someone's life was in danger. If, for example, you tell me that someone may or may not be about to walk in here and murder Ronan, I would need to report that to the protectors downstairs as a precaution to make sure he's safe. But if you tell me that someone may or may not have committed a crime in the past, well, I don't have to report my suspicions unless I have hard evidence."

I mull this over for a moment. I need to choose my next words very carefully. "Okay," I say, looking back at Ronan, "I'm going to tell you a *very* hypothetical story now. I need you to listen and not interrupt until I'm done, and then you can be mad at me if you want. Okay?"

Mari nods. Ronan just looks concerned, which makes me

feel more guilty than ever. "All right, Alli," he says, "start at the beginning."

I take a deep breath, and then I let everything out in a rush before I can think better of it. "So you may or may not have heard of certain legendary organizations for people whose activities are . . . less than legal. Organizations like, say, a group or a society or a *guild*."

Mari's eyes widen. Whatever she expected me to say, it wasn't this. Ronan takes a second longer to catch on, but he masks his surprise more quickly.

"So, *hypothetically*," I continue, "let's say there was this orphan girl in Azeland who ran away from an orphanage and ran into some protectors and got cursed. But luckily she ran into this boy—his name was possibly Berkeley or perhaps *Beck*—and he was a member of this secret illegal organization. And he told the orphan girl that if she joined this organization, then she'd have the money she needed to buy a cure and not die. Which sounded pretty great to her, because she's a fan of not dying.

"So, long story short, she goes to Ruhia to join this group, but things go really wrong during these illegal activities that were hypothetically done, and someone died. The boy was able to go back to the secret organization, but the girl got caught and went to prison awhile. Which turned out to be a good thing, because actually the girl has this long-lost brother who's really pretty great, and he let her come live with him and everything, and so all she wanted to do was just live a normal life and not do anything else illegal and not go back to the secret organization ever again. There was just one teeny tiny little problem: Beck showed up on her doorstep, and he told her that some bad people might want to kill her brother, and he needed her help to stop them."

Both Ronan and Mari are listening quietly, trying to keep their expressions masked. I can't look at them during the next part, so I stare down at the rug and tell them the rest. "So hypothetically the girl starts helping the boy in secret, and she doesn't want to tell her brother because she doesn't want to get Beck in trouble, and also she really doesn't want her brother to send her away. But then things get more dangerous than she thought. The bad people in this hypothetical organization are called Shadows, and these bad people want to do some bad things, and Beck tried to stop them and he got caught. So now he's been captured, and possibly the Shadows are going to kill him, and the girl needs to rescue him. But there are a couple of other problems.

"Problem one: Beck has another friend whose name is Rosalia. She might hypothetically be a member of this hypothetical organization, maybe, and she's really rude and annoying but also not such a bad person deep down. But one of the evil Shadow people stabbed her in the side, and she's kind of bleeding all over the place, and I think she might die, *not* hypothetically." I hold up my bloody hands for emphasis here.

"Problem two: The evil Shadow people are led by a guy who knows the girl's brother and who threatened to kill him only a few hours ago. A guy who is not hypothetically named Garil Gannon."

Ronan blinks, looking more than a little stunned. Mari glances at him in confusion.

"Gannon?" Ronan asks. "Are you *sure*?"

"Very, very sure," I say. "He mentioned you by name, Ronan. He knows where you work, and I'm not sure if he knows where this apartment is. That's why I went to the office to warn you."

Ronan just shakes his head. "I never thought . . ."

"He's . . . he's leading some very bad people. He wants to overthrow the current leader of the . . . organization and put himself in charge, and I think he'll kill anyone who gets in his way. Which kind of accidentally includes me. And he seems to have some kind of vendetta against you for some reason."

"Wait," Mari says, breaking in for the first time, "let's back up a minute. This girl who's been stabbed. Where is she?"

Rosalia's going to kill me for this later, but if I don't tell, she'll die first. "She's hiding in an abandoned chapel on the top of the hill down the street."

Mari frowns. "The little Harona chapel? That was closed ages ago. I forgot it was still standing."

"We've kind of been using it—Beck and Rosalia and me—as a hideout," I confess. "It's where I've been going, mostly, when I've been sneaking out."

Ronan and Mari look at each other. There's so much

going on in their expressions that I can't even begin to decipher it. But they know each other well enough to converse without even speaking. I wait.

"All right," Mari says, "here's what we'll do. I have first aid training, so I'll go find this girl and make sure she's okay. Ronan, Alli, you need to get out of this apartment. Go to the protectors downstairs and tell them where these Shadows are keeping the boy, and they'll—"

"No!" I say quickly. "We can't tell the protectors, Mari. They won't distinguish between the Shadows and the other thieves. They'll just arrest everybody, Beck included."

Mari presses her lips together.

"I know what you're thinking," I say quickly. "But not all of them should be arrested. Beck is just a kid who was raised in the G—the organization. His mom died, and he's all alone, and it's the only life he's ever known. He's a good person, really, who's saved my life more than once. You can't arrest him."

"I know you want to protect your friend, Alli, but—"

"If you need to arrest someone, just arrest me, okay? I knew better than to steal and get mixed up with thieves again, but I did it anyway. I lied to both of you and I snuck out and I've been hanging out with thieves. You can throw me in prison if you want. But don't punish Beck just because of how he grew up."

Mari looks unsure, so I keep going. "If you send protectors in there, you and I both know it'll get dangerous really fast. They'll be arresting people left and right, and the thieves will try to run or fight their way out, and people on both sides might die. Your protector friends aren't prepared for what they'd be walking into. But if you let me go, I can find my friend and stop the Shadows. I can tell the leader of the thieves about Gannon and his plan, and then the thieves will take care of him themselves. Nobody except the Shadows will get hurt, Mari. But you have to let me go *now*."

"I'm going with you," Ronan says immediately, standing up.

"No, I—"

"I'm not letting you walk into this by yourself. I don't want you to do this at all. But if you want to try to save your friend, I'm coming too."

Mari finally leaves her post by the door and gathers up the first aid supplies I've scattered across the sofa. "I'll tell the protectors downstairs that it was all a false alarm, and then we can leave. I'll find the girl in the chapel and see if I can help her."

"We'll meet you there after," I say. "Beck has some healing magic—his mother was a healer—and he might be able to help her after we rescue him."

Mari nods, tucking a roll of bandages into her pocket. "All right. But if you don't show up after a few hours, I'm sending the protectors after you whether you like it or not. Where will you be?"

"The Night Market," I say. Mari opens her mouth to ask,

but I hold up one hand. "No time to explain all that right now, but yes, it's real, and no, I don't know its exact location. But I know a thilastri who can take me there. That's all I can tell you."

She frowns. "Be careful."

"And, Mari? That girl you're about to help—she doesn't deserve to go to prison either. She's just been trying to help her family."

Mari sighs. "I'm not making you any promises. But I'll do what I can to save her."

I don't have time to argue the point, so that will have to be good enough. "All right, let's get going."

I turn to Ronan. "Are you sure you want to go? You could leave with the protectors and—"

Ronan reaches out and pulls me into a hug. I'm so startled, I don't know how to react, so I just sort of stand there, but it feels nice anyway.

"You don't have to do this alone, Alli," he says.

And for the first time ever, I actually believe it.

Chapter Twenty-Two

Ronan and I run through the dark, small halos of streetlights guiding our way. It would be faster to take a carriage, but there aren't many out after dusk, and it would take too long to find one. So we run, our boots sloshing through the snow on the pavement.

"So tell me," I say as we pause on a corner to catch our breath. "Who is this Gannon person, and why does he want to kill you?"

"I never would've thought . . ." He hesitates. "Gannon used to be another apprentice at Avinoch's. We were sort of competitors, since both of us were hoping for promotions someday, but we were on pretty good terms at first. He was always this friendly, unassuming guy that everybody liked. But after a while I realized there was something off about him. He would come and go at strange hours, he was often late, he never shared anything personal about himself or let anyone see where he lived.

"Then some strange things started happening. Important files disappeared. Paperwork got messed up. Pieces of evidence vanished. And almost all of it involved this big fraud case Avinoch's was handling against this prominent businessman."

"Let me guess. Gannon was the one behind it?"

Ronan nods. He glances up and down the street before we turn the corner and rush down the next block. "I never managed to prove how Gannon was connected to that businessman or why he did it, but I caught him red-handed stealing a file out of the office one night, and I told Avinoch about it myself. Gannon tried to deny it, and things got ugly. Avinoch tried to call the protectors, but Gannon fled before they arrived. That was the last we heard of him, and I honestly hadn't thought much about him since then. I knew he was corrupt, but I never thought he was violent or dangerous. I certainly never thought he'd hold a grudge against me, though I suppose I did get him fired and nearly arrested."

"Well." I leap over a puddle of slush in the sidewalk. "To say he holds a grudge is an understatement. He's serious about coming after you. He put your name on a list of people that the Shadows want to target, and one of those people is already dead. And when he saw me earlier, he threatened you."

Ronan walks faster, his mouth drawn into a tight line.

We turn the corner, and at long last a carriage pulls into view up ahead. Ronan flags it down, hands the driver an entire pouch full of jamars, and directs him to take us as fast as possible.

A few minutes later, we pull to a stop and step out into the dark. The Miagnar Gardens look much like they did the very first time I saw them last spring. Dim lanterns provide scarce light along the curved, meandering paths, and trees sway ominously in the breeze. But this time my feet crunch against snow instead of grass, and the wind in my face is sharp and cold.

I lead Ronan down the path to the stables. "He should be in here, I think." For some reason I whisper, as if there's someone around to hear us.

"Who are we looking for?" Ronan whispers back.

"A thilastri. Rosalia said his stall would be marked with . . . something gray. A bird, maybe. A gray eagle or hawk or something. And the color of the background is . . ." I pause.

Ronan doesn't say anything, but his expression is doubtful.

"She used some fancy word, okay? She couldn't just say, like, blue or whatever. She had to say like teal or puce or . . . I don't know, maroon. Something like that."

"So we're looking for a possibly maroon-colored stall with a gray bird of some kind? Maybe?" He's trying not to sound snide but isn't quite succeeding.

"Hey, the person who told me this was sort of bleeding all over me at the time, so you'll have to forgive my lapse in memory."

"Fair point." He gives me a small smile. "And who uses

a word like 'maroon' in that situation anyway?"

"*Exactly.* Like, just say 'red' like the rest of us. I'm telling you, she's insufferable."

"I see. But your friend Beck, he isn't insufferable?"

"Oh, he is sometimes," I say, hauling open one of the stable doors. "Like, do not ask him for directions unless you want him to recite an entire map to you. And never, ever let him plan out anything in advance, or you'll have to listen to him go on and on and *on* about strategy and 'the importance of preparation' and stuff. I mean, I don't think he can even walk down the street without mapping out the perfect route first. And then he makes *you* go over the stupid chart, and you're like, 'I'm just going down the street; this does not have to be a production.' You know what I mean?"

We walk inside the gloomy, darkened stable, glancing around at the nameplates on all the stalls. I'm still not totally sure what we're looking for.

"Sounds like you like him," Ronan whispers suddenly.

"Who? Beck? Don't be ridiculous. Didn't you just hear me describe how much I can't stand him?"

"Right, sure."

"And did I mention he has a habit of making me do ridiculous things like finding a thilastri in the middle of the night in order to rescue him from cutthroat thieves? *Obviously* I'm not fond of him. At all." I pretend to gaze down a row of stalls so that Ronan can't see my face.

"And that's why you never risk your life or make any

other questionable decisions while trying to save him."

"Right," I say, realizing a second too late that he was being sarcastic. "Okay, you've officially been spending way too much time with me. I'm a terrible influence on you."

Ronan actually laughs, a soft, hopeful sound in the dark. "Don't think you're the first one to embrace sarcasm. It runs in the family."

My insides flutter around, and it takes a second to figure out why. I don't think anyone's ever used that phrase—"runs in the family"—as it applies to me. I never had a family to compare myself to before. Never had any way of knowing what was and wasn't a family trait. I used to wonder about it all the time when I was little—did I have my mom's eyes or my dad's curly hair, did I have their voice or their mannerisms or their laugh, did my brother look like me, did we both like white chocolate. Then I got older and tried to stop thinking things like that because I thought I'd never know the answers.

But now I have the answers—some of them, anyway. I know my brother is smart and kind, that he smiles more than me and laughs all the time, that he's sometimes sarcastic and sometimes thinks I'm funny, that we have the same hair and eyes and accent, that he's good at making hot chocolate and bad at ice-skating and likes too much sugar in his tea.

There's so much more I could learn, so much more I haven't gotten to see yet or haven't remembered to ask. I want to know if he likes summer better than winter, like me; if he opens the windows during rainstorms to listen to the thunder, like I do; if sometimes he gets so mad that he can feel the anger rising under his skin until he can't see straight. I want to know him when he's angry and when he's sad, when he's tired or irritated or impatient or when he's really, truly happy. Those are the things families get to have—to see each other at their worst moments and their best moments and all of the moments in between. I missed out on most of Ronan's moments, and he missed out on mine.

Now, too late, I know that I don't want to miss any more. I want to know all of these things about my brother, and I want him to know me. I want us to figure out this whole complicated mess together and somehow end up a family in the end, like we were supposed to be. I want to go ice-skating every winter and drink too much hot chocolate and go to Wintersnight festivals just to see him get confetti in his cider.

But I ruined it. I ruined all of it.

It's a miracle that Ronan is still here, that he's helping me, when he should be running as far from Gannon and the Shadows as possible. But that's the kind of person my brother is. The kind who will follow me into a dangerous situation in order to save a boy he doesn't even know, just because he wants to help and watch out for me. But I'm not fooling myself into thinking that this means anything. After tonight, it will all be over, one way or another. If we survive this, I'm sure Ronan and Mari will ship me back to prison, or an orphanage if I'm lucky, and cut me out of their lives for good. And who can blame them, after everything I've done?

I learned back in the Azeland orphanage that I should never get my hopes up when it comes to adoption, that it never works out for kids like me. I let my guard down when it came to Ronan, because I wanted it to work so badly this time. But that was stupid. I can't become somebody I'm not just by wanting it. I can't be the kind of sister Ronan deserves, no matter how hard I try.

And now on top of lying to him and keeping secrets and betraying his trust, I've gone and put him in even more danger. If we survive this, I won't beg Ronan to let me stay. I'll only put him in danger again. I *am* a bad influence, for real, and I might just get him or Mari killed. I should get out of his life right away before I make things worse for him.

Assuming we survive tonight, of course.

We turn down another row of stalls, and I keep my face away from the lantern light so that Ronan can't see my expression. My eyes are all watery for some reason.

I scan the row of stalls, but I don't see one that fits Rosalia's description. They're painted all different colors—reds and yellows and greens and blues—and many of them are decorated with the noble crest of the family they belong to. My gut twists sharply as I remember the shape of the Atherton family crest, and I hope I don't have to see *that* painted on a stall. I don't want to think about whether or not the Athertons used to come here, or whether the remaining Athertons still do. Now is really not the best moment to remember that the last time I was involved with the Guild, I got somebody killed.

Tonight is not that night. It will be different this time. It has to be.

"Hey, Alli," Ronan says suddenly. "You said a gray bird, right?"

I turn around and join him in front of another large stall. The door is painted a pale purple, with a light gray bird like a falcon or a hawk in the center. "I think this might be it," I say, without much confidence. "Although I don't think that color qualifies as maroon."

Ronan tilts his head, staring at the painting. "Is it possible that the color she said was 'mauve' instead of 'maroon'?"

"A definite possibility," I say. "Is this mauve?"

Ronan nods. "I'd say it qualifies."

"Looks purple to me."

He looks a little exasperated, but he still gives me a tired smile. "Okay, let's go meet our thilastri."

Inside the stall, a single lantern flickers in an upper corner. A massive thilastri with shockingly blue feathers rests on a plush, gigantic cushion. He cracks a big yellow eye open as we walk in.

The feathers on his head bristle. "Who are you? What do you want?"

"Um, hi," I say. "I'm a . . . friend of Rosalia Peakes. You

know her, don't you? She said you'd be able to take me somewhere. A certain *marketplace*. One that I think is open at this time of *night*."

The thilastri lifts his head, staring at us with both eyes. "And why would I do something like that? I don't know you."

If Rosalia is wrong about this, I'll go back to that stupid chapel and stab her with something sharp myself. "Rosalia said you'd help. It's urgent. Really, really urgent. An emergency."

"I still don't know you."

Wait. The pendant. She said I need to show him the pendant.

I reach into my pocket and dig around until I find the Guild pendant and bring it out. The green gem shimmers in the light. Ronan's eyes widen, but he doesn't say anything.

I dangle the pendant in front of the thilastri. "Actually, I think you do know me. I think we have a lot of mutual friends. And some of those mutual friends are truly in danger right now, and I need your help to save them."

"Put that away," the thilastri grumbles, his voice so deep, it sends tremors through the floorboards. "I think you've got some bad information, girl. The market's not open for business tonight."

"This isn't ordinary business."

The thilastri stares me up and down with his big golden eye. "I don't think so. I don't know who you are or why Rosalia Peakes would give you her Guild pendant, but if she wants me to take you somewhere, she can come down here and say so herself."

"Actually, she kind of can't," I snap, "seeing as how she's been stabbed and all."

"That's her business, not mine."

"Ugh!" I throw my hands up. "I'm so tired of you rotten, stupid thieves and your stupid, selfish rules. Every thief for themselves, right? Don't get involved if it's not your business; don't trouble yourself to help somebody else. Really, it's no *wonder* the Shadows were able to corrupt members so easily. I ought to just let them have you!"

Too late, I realize I've raised my voice, and it's echoing. Rustles and murmurs sound from outside the stall.

"Alli," Ronan says quietly, "I think we'd better go."

"We can't go," I say, jabbing a finger in the thilastri's direction. "He's the only one we know who can take—"

"Alli Rosco?" The voice is another deep thilastri rumble. A familiar one.

"Ser?" I call, turning around.

I step out into the aisle, only to see several big blue heads poking over the tops of their stalls and staring at me. "Serenier? Is that you?"

"Rosco!" One of the thilastri clicks his beak, and I run into his stall with Ronan right behind me.

It really *is* him. The first thilastri I ever met, the one who took me from Azeland to the Guild with Beck.

"Rosco," he rumbles, looking first at me and then at

Ronan. Thilastri can't really frown, given that they have beaks instead of mouths, but somehow he still manages to give me that impression. "What are you doing here? What's all the commotion?"

"Beck's in trouble," I say. "I don't have time to explain. But I need to get to the Night Market. Right now."

Ser stands up quickly, shaking out his feathers. "I can take you there. What happened to Beck?"

"Nothing, if I can help it. Long story. We need to go *now.*"

"Who's this?" He eyes Ronan.

"Erm, this is my brother. Ronan. It's another *long* story. But it's okay. He's here to help."

Ser looks doubtful, but he nods. "All right. Hop on."

"Um, Alli?" Ronan whispers in my ear. "Would now be a good time to mention that I've *never* ridden a thilastri?"

"Oh, it's easy. Don't worry. It isn't scary at all," I lie.

Ser lowers his shoulders to the ground so that we can reach. I hop on, clinging tightly to his feathers, and Ronan follows my lead, sliding up behind me. We stay low as Ser trots out of his stall, through the open stable door, and out into the gardens. He unfurls his wide, wide wings, and Ronan lets out a sharp breath.

Another thing my brother and I have in common: Neither of us really seems to like heights.

"Hang on," Ser says. "I'm going to fly fast."

Oh. Great.

Ser bursts forward, takes a running leap, and launches himself into the sky. Ronan and I cling to his back for dear life, the cold wind whipping wet snowflakes into our faces. I squeeze my eyes shut as my heart thunders in my ears, faster and louder than the powerful beats of Ser's wings. I repeat Ser's advice in my head: *Hang on, hang on, hang on, hang on . . .*

Hang on, Beck. We're on our way.

Chapter Twenty-Three

When Ser finally lands, Ronan looks just as queasy as I feel. "Remind me to never, ever do that again," I say as I hop down.

Ser chuckles. "Won't you need another ride back?"

"Okay, well, after *that*, remind me to never ever do it again."

Ser folds in his wings, his feathers ruffling. "It's best I not continue with you," he says.

"Yeah. No offense, Ser, but you're kind of . . . noticeable. It would make sneaking in a bit difficult."

He nods. "I will wait for you over there, out of sight." He tilts his head toward an abandoned-looking building on the corner. "Find me when you're done."

"Okay. And—thank you, Ser." I'm pretty sure he's never been my biggest fan, ever since our first meeting, and he certainly could've turned us away like that other thilastri did.

Ser clicks his beak in what I assume is acknowledgment.

"Get Beck out," he says. He trots down the street, melding into the darkness.

Ronan still looks a little green. "What now?" he asks.

"We go this way. Um, I think." I lead Ronan through the dark streets, trying to picture Mead taking me here the first time. But the snow has all shifted around, deepening in some places and melting in others, and it's hard to figure out where I am.

Finally we pass the spot where the strange guard woman stopped me and Mead before. I hope I don't have to remember the passcode phrase or whatever, because I have no idea what it was.

But nothing happens. No one is standing guard tonight, and as we walk deeper into the Night Market, the reason becomes clear.

That thilastri was right about it not being a market night. Most of the stalls and carts have packed up already, likely preparing to move to a new location. The crowds are gone, and so are the vendors. A few tents and larger stalls remain, still needing to be packed up, but otherwise the space is mostly deserted. I have no doubt the remaining tents are enchanted to prevent intruders and thieves, though. Which presents a problem for us.

But maybe it won't matter. Maybe we'll find Beck outside somewhere—unless the Shadows find us first.

"We need to keep off the main path and out of sight," I whisper to Ronan. "There are going to be a lot of thieves here tonight, and I doubt many of them will be happy to see us."

"Good plan," Ronan whispers back.

We weave behind the tents, and I try to remember the way to the Treasury. I'm pretty sure that's where the big heist will go down—that's the main vendor who was doing business with the Shadows, the one the king would want to rob.

The problem is, I have no real idea what we're about to walk into. I don't know how the king was planning to rob the Treasury, or how the Shadows are planning to stop him. I don't know what to expect when we get there. But if it's where the king's thieves are going, it's where the Shadows are going too. Which means that's likely where Beck will be, if Rosalia was right about them trying to use him as leverage.

"What *is* this place?" Ronan whispers, gazing in wonder at the stalls and signs we pass.

"The Night Market," I say. "It's like a black market, for stolen goods and . . . illegal things."

"Illegal *magic*," Ronan says, reading a sign offering POTIONS, HEXES, AND MORE!

"That too."

We wander around awhile, trying to keep out of sight in the darkness. The bright white tents make it difficult, though, since they don't hide our shadows at all. But I'm afraid to venture too far from the main path. If I do, I'll never be able to find my way out of this place again.

Up ahead, I finally see something I recognize—the mirror. The one that shows wishes that Mead had to pull me away from. It's still standing there, alone and seemingly unguarded. At least now I know we're headed in the right direction—

Wait. The mirror.

The mirror that shows you how to get the things you wish for.

I stop so abruptly that Ronan almost crashes into me. "What is it? What's wrong?" he whispers, his eyes darting wildly along the path.

I glance around, but the woman who told me about the mirror before is nowhere to be found.

Mead warned me it was dangerous, but there's no one here to see me. And no one to stop me.

"Wait over there," I whisper to Ronan, gesturing toward a dark corner by the side of the nearest stall. "I need to look at this mirror for a second."

"The mirror?"

"It's magic. Just trust me."

Ronan looks uncertain, but he nods. "I trust you."

He hides behind the stall, and I approach the mirror.

The sign still hangs from the corner: MIRROR OF WISHES.

What do I wish for?

I could wish to save Beck. But Ronan's here, and I have to worry about him too. What if I wish to save Beck, and do whatever the mirror shows me I should do, but then something bad happens to Ronan?

The woman said that the mirror would show me consequences of the things that I wish for. But what if Ronan gets hurt during the fight with the Shadows, and it *isn't* a consequence of me saving Beck, just something that's going to happen regardless? Would the mirror still show me that? And even if it did, what good would it do? The woman said she only granted a single wish in the mirror, so I only get one try. Whatever it is that I wish for, I have to make sure it doesn't endanger Ronan while also saving Beck.

But how can I do both?

It's the same question I've been asking myself all along. How to help Beck and keep Ronan safe while still being part of Ronan's life. How to get close to Ronan without driving him away. How to be the good thief Beck thinks I am and the good sister Ronan wants me to be.

Maybe that's the problem: I've been trying to choose. But that's impossible. I can't divide up parts of myself and cast aside the ones that I don't always like. I can't pretend that I was never a thief, that I was never Beck's friend, that I don't struggle to fit into my brother's life. But despite all of that, I am still Ronan's sister. I can make different choices than I made before, but the old Alli is still part of me. Old Alli and New Alli both exist at once.

Both at once.

I know what to wish for.

I stare directly into the mirror, meeting the brown eyes of my own reflection, and whisper the words.

"I wish to save both Beck and Ronan."

The mirror's surface ripples.

Gray fog swirls across the glass, moving in every direction simultaneously. As the fog solidifies, shadowy figures emerge, like a black-and-white sketch.

I see a girl standing in front of a mirror.

The girl turns. She walks across what looks like a cobbled street and approaches a small cart that bears no sign or hint of its purpose. The shadowy girl—me—crouches down behind it. A moment later she stands, holding something in her hand. The image morphs, the background fading as the girl and the object she's holding grow larger and larger before me, until the object begins to take a shape. Some kind of square, with a small circle embedded in its center.

A circle that might be a coin.

The fog swirls again, shapes vanishing and reforming. A new scene emerges: dozens of figures, many of them fighting each other. One of them falls to the ground, then another. More figures enter the scene, and they're all swirling past so quickly, I can't really tell what's happening or who anyone's supposed to be.

Abruptly something changes. Most of the figures stop moving. One stands alone in the center—a small form who looks like the girl from the previous image. She's holding the square with the coin in it again, and she's doing—something?

Before I can figure it out, the picture is gone. The fog swirls. The shadows dance, rippling across the glass and vanishing.

A heavy sinking feeling fills my chest, like a weight is settling between my ribs, but I'm not sure what it means.

The mirror shows nothing but my own reflection once more.

"Wait," I say. "Can you show me that last bit again?"

Nothing happens.

"Oh, come on! This isn't fair. I couldn't tell what happened!"

The mirror is unmoved.

I sigh. "Well, thanks, I guess."

I step away from the mirror, toward the stall where Ronan is hiding. There's still no sign of the woman who was here before. If Mead was right about there being consequences for using the mirror, I'll just have to worry about that—and whatever this weird weighty feeling in my chest is—later.

"You can come out now," I tell Ronan's shadow.

"What happened?" he asks, looking confused. "I just saw you staring at the mirror . . . ?"

"No time to explain," I say, "but I found out something important. We need to make a quick stop."

I lead the way across the street.

A few stalls down from the mirror, the little cart where Mead stopped before still sits there, completely unassuming. I still don't know who owns this cart or what its purpose is, but I know the vendor was helping the Shadows. I knew it the day Mead stopped here to sell something for them. I just didn't realize how *much* this vendor is helping them.

The King's Coin is hidden here.

I crouch down behind the cart, scanning its shelves, but they're mostly empty. Of course the coin wouldn't just be lying around in plain sight. But how am I supposed to find it? The mirror was way too vague about that part.

"What are we looking for?" Ronan whispers, watching me scan the cart's shelves.

"A coin," I say. "Not like ordinary money. Something unusual. Probably gold or silver."

"Let me guess. It's magic?"

"Um, probably." I run my hands over the wooden surface of the shelves, but I don't feel anything unusual. There has to be a hidden compartment or something, though. Gannon wouldn't just leave it out in the open. He'd hide it carefully, someplace only he knew about, someplace—

Someplace only members of the Guild could access it.

I dig Rosalia's Guild pendant out of my pocket. In the flickering blue light from the nearest lantern, its golden surface gleams.

The pendant must be the key, but how?

"Does it fit right there?" Ronan asks.

I follow where he's pointing. In one corner of the bottom shelf, mostly masked in shadows, an indentation is carved into the wood. An indentation that might match the pendant.

I lean forward and press the pendant into the space. It fits perfectly.

"Now what?" Ronan whispers, but I know what to do.

It's just like the wall that hides the entrance to the Guild in the mountains.

I press the pendant in and give it a twist.

The whole thing swivels around with a scrape, followed by a loud click.

A little panel pops open, revealing a hidden space behind it.

It's too dark to tell what's inside. There is a very big possibility that I'm about to stick my hand into a trap.

But the mirror said the coin was here, so . . .

I take a deep breath and reach carefully inside. My fingers close around something hard and smooth and cold.

I pull the object out and examine it. It's a solid square of thin glass, like a protective casing. And embedded inside is a single coin.

It looks nothing like any coin I've ever seen. It's brightly polished silver. A thin cord is looped through a small hole at the top, like someone used to wear it as a necklace. The design is hard to see in the dark, but it features a twisting snake, not unlike the one on the Guild pendant.

And the snake is twisting around a crown.

"This is it," I say, hardly daring to breathe. "This is it!"

Ronan looks like he wants to ask a thousand questions, but he doesn't. "Okay, let's get out of here."

I tuck the Guild pendant and the glass-cased coin into the pocket of my coat; then I slide the little compartment closed and leave the cart exactly the way we found it.

Not that it makes a difference if Gannon knows we were here. I'm going to get this coin to the king, and then it won't matter. For the first time all night, I feel something like optimism. I have the coin now. The mirror was right. Maybe, just maybe, we can actually pull this off.

"Let's go get Beck," I say. Without another word, we hurry down the street and into the depths of the market.

We walk in silence for a couple of minutes without encountering anyone. We must be getting close to the Treasury—

Footsteps. Ahead, up the path. I pull Ronan aside, and we hunker behind a nearby cart.

The footsteps pass us, and I peek out. A pair of shadowy figures disappears into the darkness, heading in the same direction as the Treasury. I have no idea whether they're with the king or with the Shadows, but either way, I think it means we're running late.

"Come on," I say, "let's hurry."

We creep along for a few more minutes, keeping the figures within sight. Sure enough, they lead us straight to the Treasury. The massive white tent is still intact, apparently not packed up yet, its sign swaying gently in the breeze.

The two figures ahead of us don't even hesitate before ducking inside.

"Now what?" Ronan whispers, and I don't respond because I don't have an answer.

Save the king, and you save Beck. That's what Rosalia said. But how am I supposed to do that? I have the coin, but what do I do with it? The mirror wasn't clear enough.

If the king were to walk by, I could just hand it over to him, tell him what I know about the Shadows and their ambush, and let him take care of them, problem solved. But Saint Ailara and I both know I'm not that lucky. If the king came in person at all, he'd be in hiding somewhere. Either that, or we're really late and the Shadows have already caught him.

So what next? Storm inside the tent? Creep around and see if Beck happens to be nearby? Wait to see what happens? Maybe I could—

Another set of footsteps, stomping up the street. *Multiple* sets.

Ronan and I quickly duck behind a tent across from the Treasury, listening to what sounds like a whole group of people making their way up the path.

"Wait here," I whisper to Ronan. "I need to get closer and see who that is."

"Alli, wait—"

I'm already gone, creeping up the side of the tent and peeking around the corner. Five or six cloaked figures are headed straight for the Treasury. I can't make out any of their faces. Are they Shadows, or do they really work for Kerick? If they were sent by the king, I need to warn them. I need to—

The tent beside me shudders, the fabric waving, and a shout rips through the still night air. A shout that belongs to Ronan.

I tear back down the length of the tent, my boots pounding, and turn the corner—

Keene has one arm wrapped around Ronan in a tight hold. His other hand clenches a knife. Its silvery blade gleams at my brother's throat.

Chapter Twenty-Four

No. "Let him go!" I shout, no longer caring who hears me. Maybe the king's thieves will come help—

"Don't say one more word, Rosco," Keene warns, tapping the flat side of the blade against Ronan's chin. "Let me guess: This must be the famous brother. Oh, Gannon is going to be *so* pleased. You wouldn't believe how long he's been looking for the two of you."

"You don't have to do this, Keene," I say desperately. "We're not here because of the Shadows. We don't care about Guild business. We won't be any trouble to you. Just let us go."

He laughs. "Nice try, little Rosco, but I find that a bit hard to believe. How about we all take a trip up to the Treasury to see what Gannon has to say about it? I'm sure he'll be thrilled to see you."

Keene drags Ronan toward the path, and I have no choice but to follow. Ronan's eyes meet mine, and then flick deliberately away toward the market entrance. I know what he's telling me—run. But I won't. Whatever happens next, I won't abandon my brother.

The mirror told me I could save them both. I just have to figure out how.

Keene hauls Ronan through the open flaps of the Treasury tent, and I hurry in after them.

We're too late. The Shadows ambush has already started.

The room is in chaos. Much of the furniture has been shoved to the sides, creating a large clearing in the center of the tent. Several thieves are fighting throughout the room, moving so quickly, it's difficult to tell who's who. Gannon whips through the center of the space, wielding a pair of gleaming daggers. He faces off against a pair of thieves, but they're too far away to identify. Behind them, two women are fighting with swords, the steel blades flashing and clanking against each other. Keene drags Ronan forward, and we duck past another pair of sparring thieves as one of them throws a punch. It's Mead.

Off to the left, a body is splayed on the ground, unmoving, and I am afraid to look. I'm pretty sure someone is dead.

We weave around the edges of the space, drawing nearer to Gannon, and I get a better look at his opponents. One of them, bearing a long silver blade, is Kerick. The king of the Thieves Guild.

Keene must recognize him at the same time I do—he

stops, hesitant to move any closer. Kerick and Gannon dance around each other, blades glittering in their hands. The thief beside Kerick—one of his guards—is armed too, but Gannon barely seems to notice. His eyes are focused on the king.

Kerick raises his sword, preparing to strike—

"Stop!"

From the back of the tent, Leta emerges. She's hauling two hostages whose arms are bound behind their backs. My heart sputters.

One of them is Peakes, Rosalia's little brother.

The other is Beck.

His right eye is blackened and swollen, and a spot of dried blood stains his mouth, but otherwise he looks unharmed. Intact.

Trapped.

"If you don't want your young thieves here to die, Kerick," Leta calls, "you'll stand down."

Kerick and Leta stare at each other.

He lowers his sword but doesn't drop it. He gestures to the thief standing beside him, who backs off. One of the sword-fighting women follows their cue and steps away from her opponent. All across the room, the fighting stops.

Keene takes advantage of the silence and drags Ronan forward. "Look who I found lurking around!" he crows. "Two Roscos for the price of one!"

Keene keeps far away from the king and his knife as he moves toward Gannon, whose eyes light up at the sight of us. "Well, well, well. How nice of you to join us!" Gannon says to me. "We were so disappointed when you ran out earlier."

Then he looks at my brother, and his charming smile turns into something slick and sinister. "Ronan. It's been a long time."

"Not long enough," Ronan says, his voice quiet but unwavering.

Gannon gestures to Keene. "Tie them up in the back. We'll deal with them momentarily."

"Wait!" I shout, and every eye in the room focuses on me.

Except Leta's. She hasn't stopped staring at Kerick, and there's something strange about her expression, like she's seeing a ghost made flesh. I don't have time to wonder about it—everyone is waiting for me to speak, and I don't know yet what I'm going to say.

I open my mouth and let the words come out. "I have something you need," I say to Gannon. "Something I found in this tiny little cart in the market, across from a stall full of gemstones and a really weird mirror."

Gannon's eyes go wide, and Leta tears her gaze away from Kerick for the first time to glare at Gannon. "What does she mean, Garil?" she asks.

"You didn't," Gannon says to me, his voice dangerously low. His glare is as cold as Ruhian ice. "You're bluffing."

"Am I?" I say. "Why don't I show everyone what I found?"

Slowly, not taking my eyes off Keene and the knife at

Ronan's throat, I reach into my coat, grasp the thin square of glass, and pull it out.

A long, seemingly infinite moment passes as everyone stares at the silver coin.

Kerick is the first to react. He moves in my direction, whether to protect me or attack me I can't tell, but Leta barks, "Don't move!" He stops.

Leta gestures to Beck and Peakes. "Don't think I won't do it, Kerick."

I look back and forth between Beck and Ronan. Both of them stare back.

The lump in the pit of my stomach grows, and my gut is tangled up in knots. I have the coin. If I play this right, I can save them both.

If I mess up, they both die.

I'm not the only one staring—Kerick is looking at Leta, his expression unreadable, his eyes cold. "Is this the kind of leader you would be?" he says softly.

"I am the kind of leader who will do whatever it takes. Something I learned so well from you."

Her eyes are the same color as his.

Suddenly everything makes sense.

The story Beck told me about the King's Coin. About how Kerick and his sister killed the former king together, but Kerick won the coin and became king, while his sister was exiled from the Guild.

The sister was Leta.

She's probably been planning this all along, ever since she was exiled from the Guild. She's been biding her time, making plans, preparing for this moment. Preparing to overthrow her brother and seize his power.

But she couldn't do it alone. That's why she formed the Shadows. She couldn't get Guild members to help, not by herself, but with Garil Gannon as an inside man, she started corrupting the Guild, turning her brother's thieves against him. And this time, this time she made sure to get the coin. That's probably why it took her so long to form the Shadow Guild—she had to find the coin first. It was the one thing she needed to make her claim to the throne legitimate. The one thing she didn't have before.

The coin is the only thing standing between Leta and the throne, and it's in my hands.

Leta turns her gaze on me. "Hand it over," she says.

I take a deep breath. "Sorry, but I don't think you understand how this whole negotiation thing works. Let's see. I have something you want, you have something I want. . . . How about a trade?"

Her face twists into a snarl. "How about I kill you and take the coin myself?"

Oops. I was really hoping she wouldn't think of that. "Wait," I say. "Let's not be too hasty here. Sure, you could have one of your lackeys in the shadows over there kill me—only then *they'd* be the one holding the coin, and do you really trust them to just hand it over to you? I don't think so. And you can't send Keene to do it, since he's a little preoccupied threatening my brother. You can't do it yourself, because you've got to stand guard over those prisoners—they're the only thing keeping the king from killing you now, right? And sure, you could send Gannon over here to do it, but you won't. Because you and I both know how that whole splitting power thing worked for you last time, don't we?

"You let Gannon hide the coin to prove you trusted him, but you never really planned to give him any power. You were just using him to kill your brother, and then you were going to kill him and take the coin for yourself. And you know that if he comes over here to take it from me, he'll do the same to you."

Gannon whips around, staring at her. "Is that true?"

"Of course it isn't true," Leta snaps. "She's trying to turn us against one another." But something about the way she says it doesn't come out quite right, and Gannon frowns.

"You're lying!" he shouts.

"It isn't a lie!"

"All right, then," he says, suddenly using his calm, charming voice again. "In that case, you won't mind if I take the coin from the girl myself."

Leta's eyes narrow. "On second thought," she says quietly, "the girl is right. I do mind."

In one swift movement, she draws a dagger and plunges it into Gannon's chest.

Keene lurches away from her, dragging Ronan with him, as Garil Gannon slumps to the floor, blood pooling around the blade stuck in his heart.

Kerick jolts forward, toward Peakes and Beck, but Leta anticipates the move—she whirls around, brandishing her bloody knife, placing herself between her brother and the prisoners.

I can only stare in horror as Gannon dies on the floor.

The weight that's been in my chest ever since I looked into the mirror lifts, so suddenly that I almost gasp.

Leta doesn't even look at Gannon. "Hand over the coin, girl," she says, "or Keene will slit your brother's throat."

"I don't think you want to do that either," I say quietly, trying to keep my voice from shaking. Did *I* just kill Gannon? Did my words do that? Or did it have something to do with the mirror, and that weird weighty feeling?

"And why not?" she says, her voice deadly and low.

"Because if you kill my brother, you lose your only leverage over me. If you kill him now, there will be nothing stopping me from handing this coin over to the king. And something tells me you don't want him to have it."

More pieces click into place as I think about it, and I blurt out my next words. "The coin *does* have some kind of magic, doesn't it? Just like the legend says. That's why you took the coin from the king long before you tried to fight him tonight. Because you're afraid that if he has the coin while you fight him, you'll lose. And that's why you hid the coin away instead of bringing it here tonight to use its power yourself—you're afraid of it."

Leta's expression betrays nothing, but it doesn't have to. I'm right, and she knows it. "What do you want?" she says. The words I've been waiting to hear.

Only, now I don't know what to do with them. *What do I want?*

A shiver races down my spine. I've made a terrible mistake.

I just told her that Ronan was her only leverage, which of course was a lie. Beck is leverage too. She doesn't know that—and I can't tell her. If I ask her to free both Beck and Ronan, then she'll know the truth. And once she knows I care about them both, then all she has to do is threaten one of them and I'll have to hand over the coin. At which point she'll probably kill all three of us, not to mention the king.

Which means I cannot ask her to let Beck go.

If I ask her to let me and Ronan go, I'll be leaving Beck behind. No, worse than that—I'll be handing over the coin to Leta, who will use it to kill her brother and then probably kill Beck and anyone else loyal to the king, for good measure. It would destroy Beck, the king, and possibly the Guild itself.

If I try to save Ronan, Beck might die. If I try to save Beck, my brother might die.

Either the mirror was wrong or I messed everything up. I don't know how to save them both.

"Ticktock," Leta snaps. "Make your request, girl, before I change my mind and kill you myself."

"All right," I say, stalling for time. "I . . ."

It's like I'm standing in front of the mirror again, facing the same question. *What do you wish for?*

Beck or Ronan. Ronan or Beck.

I am torn in two.

I take a deep breath. "I . . ."

There has to be a way out. The mirror was right about the coin, so it must be right about this. I refuse to choose between them. I'll save them both. Maybe I'll save everyone. Beck and Ronan and Peakes and Kerick and Mead and myself and . . .

Kerick.

Rosalia's voice echoes in my head: *Save the king, and you save Beck.*

Save the king. Save *the king.*

To hand Leta the coin is to kill the king. So I can't do that. But I can't hand it to Kerick, or Keene might kill Ronan. I can't hand it off to anyone. I have to—

The idea flashes through my head, and I don't stop to think. I hold the coin out, like I'm offering it to Leta, but I'm bringing it closer to Kerick, too. Both of them follow my movements, their eyes glued to the coin.

I drop it.

The glass smashes against the ground, splintering into a thousand jagged pieces. Before anyone else can react, I reach down and snatch up the small circle of silver.

Warmth sinks into my palm, and a jolt surges through my

veins like a bolt of lightning. For a second my surroundings vanish completely, and nothing exists but me and the power, bursting through me like a wave.

I look down at the coin, which glows in my palm. Its surface seems suddenly reflective, my own face staring back at me, and the image morphs into something different, stretching and growing and playing out in front of me—

It's as if I'm looking at my reflection in the wishing mirror, only this time I don't get to choose what I wish for. The coin shows me an image of myself, looking eerie and beautiful, with a Guild pendant looped around my neck and hundreds of gold coins heaped at my feet. Silvery strands of magic swirl and twist around me, issuing from the single silver coin in the palm of my hand. I am wealthy, I am magical, I am powerful, I can do whatever I want—

The image in the coin morphs again, showing Beck, laughing, his brown eyes warm—

It could be mine; it could all be mine. The power sings with promise in my veins. All mine, forever. Whatever I wanted, I could make happen. The coin would help me, it would give me all the power I needed, it will make this vision come true. Everything I've ever wished for, everything I've ever wanted—

Except Ronan.

The thought rips through the haze of the images, a black hole bursting through a shower of silver and shadow. This ancient power will promise me anything, everything—

except that. This power is hungry and dark, and if I choose it, I lose Ronan forever.

I suck in a deep breath and squeeze my eyes shut, forcing the images away.

I don't want it. I don't want it. I don't want it.

I may be a thief, but I am also Ronan Rosco's sister, and I won't give that up for anything. I won't choose between Beck and Ronan, and I won't choose between halves of myself.

I push the power away, imagine it surging back through my veins and into the coin. The heat is scalding, scorching, as it floods back into my arm, my hand, my fingers. The coin grows hotter and hotter, a burning silver sun in the palm of my hand, but I can't let it go. I can't—

I open my eyes, and the world comes rushing back.

A cloud of heat and silver sparks has enveloped me, separating me from everyone, but it's fading now. The coin is fading too, growing dim and cool in my palm. I wrap my fingers around it, gripping it tight.

I think Kerick knows what just happened—he looks confused and hopeful all at once—but no one else does. No one else knows what I saw, what I was promised. No one else has touched the coin and experienced its power. And they don't know that I just gave it up.

Just in case, I reach down and scoop up a piece of broken glass—the nearest available weapon. "Keene," I say calmly, "I would suggest you drop that knife and let my brother go now. Otherwise, I might have to use the power in this coin to set you on fire."

"She's bluffing," Leta snaps.

"Am I?" I look at Leta. "You know the power this coin holds. You've seen that happen to Kerick, haven't you? You saw what happened when he touched it the first time. How it gave him his power. And I bet you've seen what he can do with it." I narrow my eyes and try to look as threatening as possible. "Tell all of your Shadows to stand down."

For a single second, Leta says nothing. Then she looks at Keene. "Do as she says."

And just like that, Keene steps away from my brother. Ronan crosses the room quickly, and stands beside me. "Are you okay?" he whispers, so low that the others can't hear.

I give him a nod. "Trust me one more time," I whisper back.

Leta turns, and I follow her gaze. Several of the Shadows who'd been flanking her have melted away. They saw it all—how she killed Gannon, how I grabbed the coin—and decided to run. But I can't worry about that right now.

I clear my throat, bringing Leta's attention back to me. "Free the prisoners," I say, pointing to Peakes and Beck.

Leta doesn't untie them, but she backs off. Both Peakes and Beck scramble forward, moving toward me and Kerick.

Suddenly Keene lunges toward Beck, his knife gleaming—

Ronan snatches the broken shard of glass from my hand and leaps in front of Beck, blocking Keene's path.

I doubt Ronan has any idea how to use that piece of glass as a weapon, but Keene doesn't know that. He backs off, slinking toward Leta, and Ronan bends down to slice through the ropes binding Beck's hands. As soon as the ropes fall off, Beck whips out his own knife and helps Peakes.

Once both Beck and Peakes are free, I turn to Kerick. "I think this belongs to you."

I hand him the coin.

A flash of silver sparks explodes from Kerick's hand, and Beck pulls me back as the shower of magic envelopes the king. It lasts only a moment, and then a shimmering, twisting tornado of gray smoke bursts from the silver haze and lurches toward Leta, Keene, and the remaining Shadows. The thick smoke swirls around the room, the heat of the magic simmering against my skin, and a bright white light bursts from the king. I blink, and when I open my eyes, Leta and the Shadows are gone.

The king stands before us, looking the same as he ever did, the coin clenched tightly in his fist. Ronan, Beck, Peakes, and the king's guards are the only ones left beside me. Gannon's body lies alone on the floor. I sneak a glance at the other corpse, the one that I was too afraid to look at before. It's Ivo, the bodyguard from the Shadows meetings.

Mead is nowhere to be seen, but he wasn't standing with Leta and the other Shadows when they vanished. He must have slunk away at some point when no one was looking. Typical.

"Alli Rosco," the king says calmly, meeting my eyes. "This is a surprise."

"Er . . . you're welcome," I say. "Well, it looks like you've got everything under control now, so we'll just be going—"

"Wait." He glances from me to Beck to Ronan to Peakes. "I'm afraid I can't allow you to leave just yet."

Peakes looks panicked. "I'm sorry, sir," he blurts. "I—I didn't realize what the Shadows were planning, sir, or I never would have—as soon as I realized, I tried to stop them—"

The king shakes his head, and Peakes falls instantly silent.

This is it. The part where the king offers us an amazing reward in thanks for our service, like Beck thought he would.

Except the king doesn't look like he's about to hand out a generous reward. At all. He frowns, his eyebrows drawing together, his gaze fixed mostly on Beck. Like someone about to deliver bad news.

"Unfortunately," he continues, "I can't allow too much information about what happened tonight to circulate in the Guild. There may still be those who wish to remove me from power, and too much knowledge about these events could enable them to do so. For that reason, I cannot allow either of you"—here he looks at Beck and Peakes—"to return to the Guild."

For a second, his words don't make any sense.

He's throwing Beck and Peakes out of the Guild.

Peakes's mouth drops open, and Beck flinches as if from a physical blow. For a moment, they both stand silently, seeming unable to comprehend it. But I understand.

I always thought it was strange, that Kerick would pick Beck for this assignment when there are so many older, more experienced thieves to choose from. I thought it was because it was so risky and Beck was expendable. I was half right.

Kerick is secretive about the coin for a reason. He can't have other thieves in the Guild knowing how much power the coin holds, how easy it might be to overthrow him if they obtain it. So he had to have known all along that he would do this, that no one can be allowed to know what Beck knows about the coin.

One way or the other, the king never intended for Beck to return to the Guild.

Beck unfreezes all at once, having finally understood. "I'll take memory potion," he says quickly. "You can wipe my memory of the coin and what it does."

Kerick considers this for only a second before shaking his head. "Memory potions are often unreliable, and altering such specific memories would be difficult. One doesn't maintain his power as king by taking chances. My sister just reminded me of that."

"I won't tell anyone," Beck says. "You know I won't."

Kerick regards him with an unreadable expression. "I know you've always been loyal, and I regret that this is necessary. But I believe tonight's events prove that it *is* necessary, to keep something like this from happening again."

Between the lines of what he's actually saying, there are

other words. If Beck ever decided to turn against Kerick someday, he'd have enough knowledge of the coin's power to pose a real threat, if he could get other thieves to join him. Forcing Beck out of the Guild and cutting him off from its members lessens that risk.

Kerick holds out his hand. Peakes is reluctant but resigned; after betraying Kerick by joining the Shadows, he's probably lucky that this is his only punishment, and he knows it. He reaches into his pocket, withdraws his Guild pendant, and passes it to Kerick.

Beck draws his own pendant from his pocket slowly. It flashes in the light, reminding me of the first time I ever caught a glimpse of it, that night in Azeland when Beck told me I was cursed.

Beck runs his thumb along the edge of the pendant one last time and drops it into Kerick's waiting hand.

The king turns suddenly to me. "Rosco. I should probably require both you and your brother to drink a potion and remove all memory of the Guild's existence. But, as I said, such potions are not always reliable, and given your seeming . . . *tendency* to get into trouble, I'm not convinced that you wouldn't simply rediscover the Guild eventually. At any rate, I am grateful for what you did tonight. So, as a show of thanks, I will allow you and your brother to leave with your memories intact, on the condition that neither of you speak of the Guild to anyone or become involved with the Guild in any way, ever again."

This is the so-called reward. We can leave. And that's it.

It's totally unfair, but given what Kerick just did to Beck, I'm not going to complain.

"Thank you, sir," I say quickly. "We won't tell anyone anything. Promise."

Kerick nods. "Very well."

The king glances around the room, surveying the damaged Treasury and the bodies on the ground. For a second, I'm tempted to ask him what his magic did to Leta and the other Shadows, but then again, I'm not sure I want to know.

"Okay, then. We'll just be going," I say, nudging Ronan toward the exit. The king doesn't respond—he stares at the empty spot where his sister disappeared. Beck just stands there, still looking shattered, so I grab his arm and tow him through the opening after Ronan, Peakes scurrying along after us. We close the tent flap, leaving the king alone with what I think might be grief.

The second we're outside, Ronan wraps his arms around me and hugs me tight. "Oh my God, Alli, oh my God—"

"I'm okay," I say. "We're all okay. Now let's get out of here."

I look at Beck. "What happened? Did they hurt you?"

Beck points to his blackened eye. "This is the worst of it, I think." It takes a tremendous amount of effort, but he manages a small smile. "That was so cool, Alli."

"What, me?"

"No, the *other* person who just saved all of our lives."

I grin. "Oh, Beck, this is my brother, Ronan, by the way. Ronan, this is my friend Beck Reigler."

Beck gives me a confused look, so I elaborate. "I kind of had to tell him about the Guild and everything in order to come down here and save your life."

Beck doesn't appear thrilled at this news, but Ronan offers his hand, and the two of them shake.

It would almost be a heartwarming moment, but it's quickly interrupted by Peakes. "Where's my sister?" he asks. "Has anybody seen her? She disappeared from the guildhall."

"Oh, yeah, about that." I take a deep breath. "She was stabbed by one of the Shadows. She's hiding out in an abandoned chapel right now. Ronan's girlfriend went there with some first aid supplies to help her."

"I have to go see her!" Peakes says. "Will you take me there?"

"Yes, of course," I say, "but there's something you should know. Ronan's girlfriend is . . . a protector."

"What?" Peakes yelps.

"Calm down. I explained everything, and I think she just wanted to help. I don't think she would hurt Rosalia. But I don't know how she'll react to seeing you. She might decide to arrest you." I look at Beck when I say that last part. "So if you don't want to come until she's gone, I understand."

Peakes shakes his head. "I need to see Rosalia. I have to make sure she's okay."

Beck nods in agreement. "I should come too. Maybe my healing magic can help her."

"All right. But don't say I didn't warn you."

We hurry through the deserted market, the white tents looming like ghosts in the darkness. When we pass the place where the mirror sits, I stop.

The woman is back.

She sits directly in front of the mirror, her legs crossed, her eyes closed. She looks exactly like she did the last time I saw her. Even her clothes are the same.

"Wait here," I say to the others. "I need to ask her something."

I leave the path and walk toward the woman before anyone can object.

She doesn't open her eyes, but I know she sees me. "Hey," I say.

No response.

"I know you can see me."

"Only one wish per customer," she says without opening her eyes.

"I don't want another wish. I want you to explain what happened back there."

"Many things have happened, in this world and in others."

I sigh. "Yeah, whatever. You know what I mean. What was with that weird weight thingy? Did you put some kind of spell on me?"

"I did nothing of the sort." She folds her palms in her lap, still refusing to open her eyes. "You did it yourself."

"You mean when I used the mirror?"

"Mm." She smiles in that creepy way she did the first time I spoke to her. "I did warn you there would be consequences."

"So that weight thing was the consequence? Why did it disappear?"

"That magic was the debt you owed. It vanished when the debt was paid."

"You mean when Gannon died."

She doesn't answer, but her smile widens.

"So that was the consequence of making my wish? That you killed Gannon?"

"I did nothing. You did."

"It wasn't *my* magic."

"It was your wish."

I cross my arms over my chest, glaring at her. I'm pretty sure she can tell, even with her eyes closed. "I don't get it. What does Gannon dying have to do with my wish?"

Her teeth flash in the dark as she speaks, still smiling. "The mirror takes what the mirror is owed. Your wish saved a life. The magic is simply restoring the balance. Resetting the scales. Taking its due."

"So because I saved someone, someone else had to die?"

She just smiles.

"But why was it Gannon? I mean, don't get me wrong, I'm not exactly upset about that particular choice. I just don't get it."

"The choice was yours."

"Um, no. I'm pretty sure the mirror didn't consult me before making this decision." I'm also getting really tired of her pointless, cryptic statements.

"But was it not your actions, your words, that preceded his death? Was it not you who put it into motion?"

"Well . . ."

"The choice was yours," she says again.

I sigh. "Whatever. This whole conversation is worthless." I turn, intending to walk away, and see Beck and Ronan, both watching me like they're just seconds away from intervening. Which reminds me.

I turn back around. "Wait a minute. I wished to save *two* people. Both Beck and Ronan. Shouldn't there have been two deaths, then? If this is all about restoring balance?"

"Without your wish, only one would have died tonight. You simply swapped one life for another."

"Which one?"

"Some things," she says, "are not for us to know."

"But you do know. You just won't tell me."

She smiles.

"Oh, whatever." I turn my back on her and stomp away.

Beck and Ronan rush up to me as I approach, with Peakes hanging back behind them. "What happened?" Beck asks.

"What was that about?" Ronan says.

"Don't worry about it," I say. "Let's get out of here."

Chapter Twenty-Five

We find Ser right where he said he'd be, behind the abandoned building. He grumbles a little about the two extra passengers, but he's thrilled to see Beck.

Both Beck and Peakes seem too stunned by their exile from the Guild to mention it just yet, so we don't talk about it. Instead we regale Ser with the tale of my heroics as we fly back to the Miagnar Gardens.

Or rather, Peakes and Beck regale him. Ronan and I are too busy holding on for dear life and keeping our eyes closed. But I don't need to jump in anyway—Beck and Peakes do a pretty decent job of making me sound all brave and daring, dashing in with the coin to save the day. By the time they're through, it sounds like I threatened all of the Shadows and harnessed the coin's power to defeat them myself. I don't feel the need to correct them.

Ser takes us as far as the gardens, and we walk the rest of the way toward the chapel, the four of us tearing a path through the woods.

"I can't believe you found this," Ronan says, staring up at the chapel. "I didn't know it was even here."

"Yeah, well, it could use some remodeling," I say. "Makes for a pretty substandard hideout."

We rush inside, Peakes leading the way, and find Rosalia in front of a roaring fire, bundled in a pile of blankets. Mari sits in a nearby pew, watching over her.

Mari leaps to her feet. "Oh, thank God." She pulls Ronan into a hug and kisses him, which is super gross but also kind of sweet, I guess.

Then, to my surprise, she pulls me in for a hug too. "I was so worried," she says.

Peakes and Beck stand pretty much as far away from Mari as possible in the small space, lurking by the door. "Is Rosalia okay?" Peakes asks.

I disentangle myself from Mari's hug and explain, "This is Peakes, Rosalia's little brother. And this is my friend Beck that I was telling you about. He's a healer, sort of."

Mari smiles at both of them. "I think Rosalia's going to be fine. It was a nasty wound, but the bleeding has stopped and there aren't any signs of infection so far. Still, she will need to be very careful as it heals."

"Let me take a look," Beck says. "Maybe I can help."

He and Peakes tentatively step forward, and I roll my

eyes. "Just get over here," I say. "She doesn't bite."

Beck and Peakes pass Mari quickly without really looking at her, and crouch down beside Rosalia. Beck unwraps the blankets to examine her wound while Peakes holds her hand. Rosalia glares weakly as Beck's hands glow blue with healing magic, and the glow engulfs her for a moment before flaring out.

"I can't do much," Beck says sheepishly, "but that should help a little."

"Good enough," she says, which is as close to a thank-you as Rosalia will ever utter. Then she glances at me. "Rosco."

"Yes, Rosalia?"

"I'm really glad you're alive, because I'm going to have to kill you."

I laugh. "Glad to see you're feeling better."

Ronan pulls Mari aside, and the two of them start speaking in hushed tones. I'm afraid to find out what they're saying. Maybe Ronan's just filling her in on what happened at the market . . . or maybe they're making plans to call Mari's protector friends and arrest all of us.

Beck and I step away from Rosalia, giving Peakes and his sister some privacy.

"So," I say, "that happened."

"Yeah," Beck says quietly.

"What are you going to do now?"

Beck's mouth twists. "I don't know."

"And Peakes?"

He shrugs. "Peakes'll be fine. Their family's already hiding somewhere outside the guildhall, so there's no reason he can't join them. His dad and Rosalia will look after him."

He doesn't add what we're both thinking: Beck doesn't have any family to look after him.

Still, Beck makes an effort to pretend like nothing's wrong, like he hasn't just lost his entire world. The corners of his mouth twitch in that achingly familiar way. "Thanks, Allicat. For everything."

"Yeah, well." I wave my hand like it was nothing.

"Sorry I was wrong about the king's reward. I really thought . . ."

I take a deep breath. "It's okay. The truth is, I never really wanted to join the Guild again. I was just trying to save Ronan. I really want to stay with him, and not go back to being a thief. Not that it matters now, after . . . all this. He won't let me stay regardless."

Beck nods. "I guess we're both on our own, huh?"

"I guess so." He looks so sad that I can't stand it. "It's probably better for you this way. The Guild's no good, Beck. You know that."

He doesn't say anything, but he doesn't argue either. "I . . . I guess we'll find out."

I look down, not wanting to ask the question that's been building in my head, but I need to get it out anyway. "Do you think I did the right thing? Giving the king the coin?"

Beck frowns. "Of course. What do you mean?"

"I mean, is the king really all that different from Leta, in the end?"

"Of course he's different. Alli, you saw what Leta did to Gannon. And . . . and Kerick tried to save me and Peakes. When Leta had us tied up, Kerick could've just let her kill us. That's what most members of the Guild would've done. But he risked everything, just to try and save us. And as much as I hate it, I understand why he had to make me leave."

"I guess." I still can't help feeling like I chose between two bad options, and I wish I didn't have to. I felt the power of the coin, how strong it was, and it seems wrong to have handed it over to Kerick. But I don't know what else I could have done.

I guess I'll just have to live with it, like I'll have to live with the other things I did tonight. With the way Gannon looked as he was dying: cold and small and alone.

"I guess I just don't feel much like a hero right now," I say.

"You saved a lot of people tonight, Allicat. Me, Peakes, Kerick, your brother, and loads of other Guild members too. The Shadows were going to cut down anyone who tried to stop them. People were already dying when you got there."

"Did . . . Did any of the king's thieves die?" I say, barely daring to ask.

"A few. When they were ambushed outside the tent, before you got there. Not anyone you knew, but . . ." He swallows hard. "They shouldn't have had to die like that."

I nod, not knowing what else to say.

"Alli," Ronan calls, "would you come over here for a second?"

I gulp. "Well, this is it."

"Good luck," Beck says.

I cross the room and approach Ronan and Mari.

Ronan takes a deep breath. "I'm going to need you to explain everything that's happened tonight," he says. "We are in no way done talking about this."

"Understood," I say quickly.

"But Mari and I agree that you've been through enough just now, so it can wait until tomorrow."

"Right, so . . . how soon do I have to pack?"

He casts a confused glance at Mari. "Pack?"

"You know, for prison or an apprenticeship or wherever it is you're sending me."

He still looks confused. "I'm not sending you anywhere."

"But . . ." Now it's my turn to be confused. "But I lied to you and I stole things and I put all of us in danger and—"

"And we're going to talk about all of those things," Ronan says. "I can't say that I'm not disappointed by some of your choices. You're basically grounded for the rest of your life."

"But you mean I can still live with you?"

"Of course." Ronan smiles. "You're family, Alli. I want you to stay, no matter what."

I glance at Mari. "And you're fine with this? You're fine with not arresting me even though I broke the law?"

Mari pretends to look confused. "I don't know anything

about anyone breaking the law," she says. "Except in purely hypothetical scenarios."

"But I thought . . ." I turn back to Ronan. "I thought you were going to send me away when I turned thirteen, with all that talk about apprenticeships and tutoring and—"

"Oh, no, of course not," Ronan says quickly. "I didn't mean you have to leave right away. I just wanted you to be prepared for a career someday, that's all. You're welcome to stay with me as long as you want."

Before I can think better of it, I throw my arms around my brother and hug him tight. "I want to stay."

We hug for a long moment, but then I have to pull away because I'm getting all teary-eyed and mushy.

"Alli," Mari says quietly, "what are your friends planning to do?"

"Well, assuming you're not going to arrest them . . . Peakes and Beck can't go back to the Gu—hypothetical organization. The king just kicked them out. Rosalia can probably go back, though, and I think she will. Rosalia and her brother, their whole family's in it, their dad and everything, so they'll be with their family."

"And Beck?" Ronan asks quietly.

"He's an orphan. His mom died a few years ago. But he grew up there, and it's the only thing he knows. He doesn't have anywhere to go."

Mari and Ronan exchange glances and have an entire conversation without speaking.

Mari calls, "Beck, can you come over here, please?"

Beck walks slowly toward us, giving me a questioning look. I shrug, equally confused.

He stops beside me, and Mari addresses him. "It's come to my attention that you're leaving the Thieves Guild. Is that right?"

Beck looks a little panicked, but he nods. There's no point in denying it now.

"Alli has explained to us that you grew up there and don't have anywhere else to go. So I'd like to make you an offer," Mari continues. "I know there's no love lost between you and the protectors, and I can certainly understand why. But some of us are doing good work and trying to make a difference. And we could really use the help of someone with your experience and knowledge of criminal organizations."

Beck opens his mouth, about to protest, but Mari holds up one hand, silencing him. "I'm not asking you to betray your friends," she continues. "Or to share anything you're not comfortable sharing. This isn't an interrogation, and you're not under arrest. What I'm asking for is help in stopping murderers and violent criminals, in saving innocent lives. You probably have information that would really make a difference. Think of it like an apprenticeship with the protectors. You teach us, and we'll teach you."

Beck still looks uncertain. "I'm not sure that I could help."

"How about a trial run, then? We just give it a try and see how it goes. You'll be free to leave at any time."

Slowly Beck nods.

"But where will he live?" I say. "I don't think this chapel is a great long-term plan."

"True," Mari says. She smiles at Beck. "I live next door to Alli and Ronan, and I have a spare bedroom. How about you stay with me for now? Again, just on a trial basis, and we'll see how things go."

Both Beck and I stare at her, shocked. "You mean he can come live with you?" I say when I find my voice.

Beck is stunned into silence for a moment. "I . . . I don't have any papers," he says finally. "I was born in the Guild. Legally I don't exist."

"I know," Mari says. "But if you can provide the protectors with as much valuable information as I suspect you can, I think we'd be willing to pull some strings and have the papers drawn up." She pauses. "I want to be clear, though—this will mean no thieving, no rule breaking. If you're going to live with me, you'll have to be on the straight and narrow from now on."

"Oh, he's fine with that," I say quickly, giving Beck's shoulder a nudge. "Beck is *very* good at following rules."

Beck still isn't saying anything, so I give him another nudge. "Say yes, Beck!"

He still doesn't speak, and my heart sinks. He's going to say no.

"All right," Beck says. "I . . . Thank you."

"Yes!" I grin. "Beck, we're going to be *neighbors*!"

"Er, on second thought," Beck jokes, but he's smiling too.

"This is going to be amazing," I say. "Maybe I can get an apprenticeship somewhere too, and—" I stop as a terrible new thought occurs to me. "But what if the Guild finds out that you're working with the protectors? Do you think they'll find out? Will they come after you?"

"I don't know," Beck says. "It's a risk. But as long as I'm careful, as long as I don't say anything that would be too damaging to the Guild, I think Kerick might let it go. He wouldn't want me to start talking about the you-know-what, after all."

I grin. "Yeah, if the king has any complaints, just remind him again how I totally saved his life because I'm *awesome*."

Beck pretends to sigh. "There's going to be no living with you now, is there?"

"Too late!" I say. "You're stuck with us."

Ronan yawns. "I don't know about you, but I'm starving," he says. "Who wants to go eat dinner?"

"Yes, food! Take me to the food," I say.

Beck grins at me. "I can definitely see the family resemblance."

I give him a harder nudge in the shoulder this time. "Mari, is it too late to take back your offer?" I joke.

"Too late," Beck teases. In a normal tone, he adds, "Let me get my stuff from the loft."

As he walks away, Ronan gives Mari a confused look. "There's a loft?"

Mari can't answer, because at that moment I throw my arms around her and give her a hug too. "Thank you," I say. "Thank you, thank you, thank you." She can pretend that she made this offer just to get information for the protectors, but she isn't fooling anyone.

We invite Peakes to dinner too, but he says he's going to go see his family and have them come pick up Rosalia. Mari gives Peakes instructions for changing Rosalia's bandages and stuff while Beck packs up his things, and then the four of us leave the little chapel behind, walking through the woods together.

When we emerge from the trees, a light snow is falling. Ronan wraps one arm around me, and I let him. Beck stands on my other side, with Mari beside him. Our long shadows blend into one.

Together the four of us walk home.

Acknowledgments

I am tremendously grateful to the many people who helped bring this book to life:

To my editor, Alyson Heller, who knew exactly how to shape my early drafts and make Alli's story shine; to Tricia Lin, for her editorial insight; to Eric Deschamps, who created the gorgeous cover art; and to the entire team at Aladdin for all their hard work.

To my agent, Victoria Doherty Munro, whose wisdom and guidance aided me every step of the way.

To Alexandrina Brant, Rachel Done, and Allison Pauli, who critiqued this book in its early stages and provided much-needed feedback.

To Kate Brauning, Bethany Robison, and all the members of Team Brauning, from whom I learn so much every day.

To the librarians, booksellers, and educators who have so graciously supported me and my books.

To all of the friends and fellow writers who cheered me on along the way.

To my extended family, for their support and encouragement.

And to Mom, Dad, and Katie, my most enthusiastic champions. I love you.

Alexandra Ott holds a BA in English from the University of Tulsa. She lives in Oklahoma with her tiny canine overlord. Visit her online at alexandraott.com and on Twitter @Alexandra_Ott.